VENGEANCE

A Jon Steadman Thriller

Nellie Neeman

ISBN: 978-1-7351505-7-4 (Paperback)
ISBN: 978-1-7351505-6-7 (E-Book)

Author Photo: Elan Sachs
Library of Congress Control Number:
Printed in the United States of America

For my boys.
143, always.

THE PAST

T he moment of impact played out in slow motion. Horns blared. Tires screeched, as if terrified of what was barreling their way.

It was early afternoon, an otherwise beautiful day in Southern California. Clear blue skies. A rare reprieve from the ubiquitous smog. Nothing to blame for what was to come. He had scheduled a deposition downtown and was running late. His wife wasn't feeling well, her coughing keeping them both up all night. She'd asked him to drop off their son at a friend's house for a play date. He agreed despite the time crunch. And despite having enjoyed three or four drinks before getting in the car. Later he couldn't remember if it had been three *or* four. Not that it mattered now. But if he had to guess, it was the fourth that prevented him from strapping in his son. He knew he was compromised. Admitted to it countless times during gut-wrenching accounts in the AA meetings that were to follow.

He was driving southbound on the 5 when the Honda Odyssey broadsided his compact Toyota, the minivan materializing on the wrong side of the road. He'd later learn that it was *he* who was on the wrong side, veering across the lone stretch of freeway with no median.

Every millisecond would be seared into his brain for life. The fierce power of impact, the shriek of tearing metal warping into unintended shapes, the wild spin blurring the cars desperate to get out of the way. And finally, the flip of his vehicle, coming to a sliding stop on a patch of dried grass. Witnesses would later report finding a broken Game Boy twenty feet from the wreck. Others noted the smaller car hadn't slowed before impact.

Somehow, the driver never lost consciousness. The same couldn't be said for his son.

THE PRESENT

CHAPTER 1

Monteverde, Costa Rica

J on Steadman flew through the cloud, his gloved hands gripping the cable above him. Forcing himself to keep his eyes open, he soared past the mist, taking in the leafy treetops far below. Thick layers of lichen and algae blanketed the ropy trunks, the wild density of verdant foliage both wonderous and frightening.

If he were to unhook his harness, he'd plummet hundreds of feet before hitting the tropical forest floor. Jon knew there were worse ways to go.

He didn't have a death wish. It was one of several self-discoveries he'd made in therapy. No, he wanted to live . . . to the fullest possible extent. Even when living proved unbearable.

The zipline took him at speeds nearing forty miles per hour across the length of four football fields. The feeling was true exhilaration.

Pura Vida. Pure life. Simple, happy, calm. He'd heard the greeting many times since arriving in the Central American country, seen it on t-shirts and street art. It was an admirable sentiment, though one he didn't expect to ever perfect.

The smooth, melodious calls of the Resplendent Quetzal echoed through the forest. Its vibrantly hued plumage deemed it one of the most beautiful creatures in the world. Along with a rainbow of bromeliads, the forest was a wonderland of brilliant colors.

Jon slowed as he approached the landing. A man approximately ten years his senior—late thirties at most—was waiting to assist him. "Thanks, Jorge."

"You got the hang of that muy rápido." The man's accent was thick, but his English adequately conversational.

They climbed down the ladder and removed their harnesses and helmets. Jon combed his fingers through his thick, collar-length hair, and out of his face. "What's next on the agenda?" he asked.

His research had paid off in spades with Jorge, a jack of all trades. A CIA contact Jon had met in Rome hooked him up with Jorge, who had done some work for them in Caracas and other turbulent hotspots in the region. Jorge referred to himself as a locksmith and illusionist. In other words, a thief and pickpocket. Turned out he had a variety of other valuable skills. Among them, creating one's own zipline. If Jon had more time, he'd learn Spanish from the man as well. He was an outstanding teacher.

A year ago, Jon would have never considered making such a trip, let alone spending his week off from work aligning with a glorified con man, but he'd seen the value of mastering unique talents from his past partner. *Carrie.* He was driven to achieve what she had, or at least get close.

Jorge said, "We're done for today. Tomorrow we practice sleight of hand."

"What time?

"I will get you before dawn."

Jon was about to ask why so early but thought better of it. "I'm leaving tomorrow."

"Si, vamanos. Get some rest. If your practice fails, you won't be leaving tomorrow. You'll be the guest of the San Jose police department."

***

New York City

Laughter woke Jon from a rare restful sleep. He opened his eyes, touched his tingling lips, mentally grasping at the fleeting wisps of the dream, hoping they'd linger a little longer. It was her again. Ashleigh dancing joyfully, her sequined lavender dress billowing around her like an early morning fog. She'd kissed him. Overflowing joy enveloped him and he'd laughed. Waking himself up.

He was momentarily disoriented before realizing he was back home. He'd learned a great deal in Costa Rica. The last exercise—pickpocketing early morning commuters—had gone smoothly enough. When he'd proven his competence, he made sure Jorge returned the marks' wallets to their rightful places.

Jon pushed aside the comforter, sensing the threat of a familiar melancholy. He snuck a glance at his bedside table. The Klonopin his shrink had prescribed sat there, teasing him. He was careful only to take it when desperate. Another dream of his dead fiancée no longer qualified.

It was seven-fifteen a.m. He'd left the a/c on full blast. The room was freezing. Just how he liked it. The Lower East Side studio came with a sky-high rent, but utilities were included. He got out of bed, dropped to the floor forcing out fifty push-ups, hoping the physical activity would stave off the sadness. Too bad there was no time for a run before work. Despite his bum leg, he'd worked himself up to a seven-minute mile. Maybe he'd run along the FDR after work if it wasn't too hot. He took a quick shower, making a mental note to call the landlord about the poor water pressure. He dressed in a pressed white shirt, black suit, and tie, still unaccustomed to the confining attire. So far, he'd managed to avoid cutting his hair to a more appropriate professional length, despite the HR lady mentioning it twice.

For a while, it was unclear if he'd stay in New York. He'd been offered an enticing position—liaison between the FBI and

Israel's counterpart, the Shin Bet. Yosef Kahn, the director of the Mossad, had made the recommendation. The meeting with the deputy head of the Shin Bet had gone better than expected. Jon's boss, Doug Matthews, heard the woman liked Jon's style, which Matthews found absurd. Apparently, Israelis viewed Jon's chutzpa as an asset.

It was an attractive job offer. Several trips a year to Israel with a generous expense account split between the countries. An apartment in Tel Aviv. But in the end, he'd decided against it. His therapist told him to write it out, pros on one side, cons on the other. Turned out there was only one item on the cons side of the ledger—the deciding factor, the tipping point.

Jon looked at the paper, now attached to his fridge by an octopus-shaped magnet, the one he'd bought at the Brooklyn Aquarium. On it, he'd written, *Randy*. The boy would be turning five soon. His mother, Carrie, had been Jon's partner and one of the most talented people he'd ever met, her skills stretching from sleight of hand to hacking and lock picking. Languages and self-defense. He'd made a point to study those skills, even if they were not part of FBI training. Even though Carrie was dead.

She'd left Randy an orphan—like himself. Since then, Jon had developed a burgeoning sense of duty. The boy's father was a deadbeat, visiting only twice since his ex-wife's sudden death. Randy's grandparents were devoted but getting older. Jon would step in, happily.

Carrie had given her life in the line of duty, saving another's on her way out of this world. Her name was now engraved on the wall at CIA headquarters in Langley, Virginia. Along with the other operatives who had paid the ultimate price. One day when Randy would be older Jon would take him to see it.

Jon looked at the microwave's digital clock, grabbed his jacket and a granola bar on his way out, and walked the zigzag mile to Federal Plaza.

***

"You owe me," Ed Hernandez said, his in-your-face attitude losing nothing through the phone.

Jon didn't have the patience for this. His leg was aching something bad. The walk to work was blustery. A storm was coming. The run would have to wait. He peered out the seventeenth story window at the clouds rolling in over the East River.

"Nice try, Ed, but I think we're more than even once you add your Pulitzer to the tally. If anything, I'd say you owe me."

"Ornery, are you? Fine. Touché. You never were one to toe the line," Ed replied. "I can't argue that the story you gave me was by far the best of my career. Still, don't forget, I went out on a professional limb for you with the LAPD. Could have cost me everything," Ed said, referring to their past ordeal together. "So, let's call it even. How about we start a new agreement?"

Jon was dubious. "What sort of agreement?"

"I've got what could be a blow-your-mind story. I just need a solid, trustworthy connection inside the FBI."

Jon eyed his boss through the glass of his office. Special Agent Douglas Matthews was pacing while shouting into the phone. "Listen, Ed. I just got this job. I'm not going to jeopardize it."

"No one's asking you to. Just an occasional verification of facts that I can't get on my own. My resources are good, but they go only so far."

"So, where's the agreement part? What's in it for me?" Jon asked.

"Now there's the negotiator I know, back in business," Ed said.

"He's never left, just has more to lose now."

Ed chuckled. "Understood. I'll be in New York on Tuesday. We can discuss it face-to-face."

Jon knew there was no point in pushing the issue further over the phone.

"Fine," he said. "First Avenue Deli at seven p.m. And don't be late."

"Done. Thanks for hearing me out, kid."

Jon hung up wondering what he was getting himself into.

***

Bronx Zoo
New York City

Randy put his hand up to the glass, his eyes as big as saucers. The gorilla on the other side sat mere feet away, slowly chewing on a bamboo stick, indifferent to the latest observer. Jon took a photo with his phone and sent it to the boy's grandmother. "That's one big momma."

Randy's mouth twitched into a shy smile. "Momma?"

"Yup, that's a girl gorilla."

Randy looked unsure.

"I know, she's not pretty. But I guess to her family, she is."

"My momma likes gawillas, too." His *r*'s were still turning to *w*'s. In Jon's estimation, it was too cute to correct. He was just glad the boy was speaking. He had spent months in silence. Randy had had his share of challenges, even before his mother died.

"Your momma was a smart lady."

No smile. "And pwetty." Randy began waving his hands furiously.

Jon spoke softly, bringing the boy closer to him. "Yes, and pretty." Jon ruffled the boys thick, dark locks. "You know buddy, you look a lot like her."

Randy's melancholy momentarily seemed to lift. His hands fell to his side allowing Jon to take hold of one. "You ready to go home?"

"No! We need to see the tigers."

"Ooh the tigers! Nah, we can see those on TV. They're too scary for me."

Randy looked like he was about to argue the point, then smiled. "You're funny, Jonny."

"Come on, let's go check out those tigers. Then ice cream."

The boy cheered.

By the time Jon brought Randy back to his grandparents' home—a ten-minute drive from the Bronx Zoo—the boy couldn't keep his eyes open.

Esther Santiago met him at the door, quietly told Randy to wash his hands and take a nap, then turned to Jon. "Gracias, Jon. Looks like he had fun."

"No need to thank me. We both had a great time. How about I come see him again in a few weeks?"

Carrie's mom stood on her tiptoes and gave him a peck. "You're a good boy. Carrie would be so proud of both of you."

Ten minutes later, Jon left, heading to the elevator, a bag of homemade empanadas in hand. It dawned on him that he had both tears in his eyes and a smile on his face.

CHAPTER 2

New York City

Ed Hernandez hadn't changed a bit. Still slovenly, uncouth, and oddly likeable.

The deli, a mainstay of old New York cuisine, was not the sort of place Jon frequented. Red pleather booths, scuffed dark wood tables, worn tile, and autographed photos of decades-gone celebrities. Places such as these were only still in business because of their outstanding high-fat menus.

Jon took a seat opposite the reporter, scrutinizing Ed's plate. He summoned the waitress, ordering the same.

The woman didn't bother writing it down. "Pastrami on rye with a side of slaw. Coming right up."

"And a black coffee, please."

Jon turned to Ed. "So, what's this all about?"

"Fine, no chitchat. I'm good with that. Just let me say I'm sorry about your partner."

Jon softened to Ed's caring words. "Yeah, thanks. Look, I don't mean to come across as abrupt, but I put a lot into this new job, and I don't want to blow it while I'm still a relative rookie."

"Understood. I have no interest in you losing your job. If anything, I'd be thrilled if you stayed with the FBI forever. Nothing like having friends in high places."

The waitress placed a white ceramic coffee mug, matching saucer, and creamer on the table. Gingerly, Jon took a sip, squinting above the rim of his cup. "Let's hear it."

"About three months ago I took on an intern at *The Times*. Now that I'm a big shot they gave me an assistant to do a lot of my grunt work. Name's Luanne Parker. She just graduated with a journalism degree from Berkeley and for some crazy reason didn't get any job offers. Could be the writing on the wall with the inevitable demise of hard print papers. Anyway, she's an outstanding writer, was working well below her capabilities. I'm not stupid, so I gave her more responsibility, told her to find her own story leads. Rather have both our names on a standout piece than nothing. Mutually beneficial you could say. Hey, you listening?"

Jon was eyeing the people coming and going. Though he wasn't always conscious of his behavior, his paranoia was ever present. "Every word."

"Good, well anyway, I put her out there and boy did she deliver."

Jon raised a brow. "How so?"

"She'd been following some conspiracy stories on social media about compromised DNA samples. People posting all sorts of crazy stories about fetuses being genetically modified and crap like that. Stuff sci-fi movies are made from."

"If it's all BS, then what's the story?"

Ed took a large bite of his sandwich, making Jon wait till he finished chewing. "Turns out several related posts were more credible, had real details about shady confidentiality practices of genetic testing. Company names, lab facilities, and the like. She figured what the hell, she'd look into it. Looks like she may have hit pay dirt."

Jon's sandwich arrived, the pastrami spilling out the sides. He slathered it with mustard and took a bite. *Heaven!*

"She found hard evidence?" Jon asked, his mouth nearly full.

"Not exactly."

"Then what?"

"She started making calls. Spoke to some big company

reps, that sort of thing. That's when the warning emails started coming in. At first, she assumed they were from a concerned party trying to keep her from stirring up trouble. Then they became more threatening. Telling her to back off, not go forward with her investigation if she wanted to keep all her limbs, that sort of thing."

"Can I see the messages?" Jon asked.

"Luanne has them."

"Quite honestly, anyone will tell you that isn't much to go on."

"My gut is telling me there's a big story here."

"What could I possibly do with all this?"

Ed leaned forward, his gut squeezing against the table's edge. "Are you kidding? Don't you realize you're now a full-fledged member of the Federal Bureau of Investigations? That's nothing to sneeze at. You have access to information most journalists can only dream about."

Jon knew it was true even at his low level on the totem pole. He still couldn't believe he'd wiggled his way in the door. "Why not just get the FBI on the case legitimately? Wouldn't that make more sense?"

"What case? There is no case yet. You just said so yourself. What I need is to dig deeper. Find out if there's a real conspiracy here. Who sent the threats and why."

"You could start by tracing the sender's IP address."

"We're working on it."

"I hear where you're going with this. You think if someone's willing to issue threats, they've got something big to hide."

Ed took a bite of his pickle. "Here's hoping."

"Okay, What's in it for me?"

"If there really is something here, and I can smell it, you'll be the one to break it on the Fed's side. Of course, Lu and I will do it from the media end. But you'll look like a hero, taking down the bad guys yet again, only this time from inside the FBI. You're sure to climb the ladder."

Jon liked the sound of that. He wasn't a patient guy and would love nothing more than to skip the line by breaking a big case to get ahead faster. Until recently he would have figured out how to help Ed by bending the rules without actually breaking them. Not anymore.

"Sorry, Ed. I can't risk jeopardizing my dream job. Matthews warned me if I ever went rogue again, he'd kick me out on my ass. I won't give him a reason to do it."

Ed pursed his lips, shook his head slowly. "Can't say I'm not disappointed. Maybe it was a long shot now that you've entered the inner sanctum. If you change your mind and you want to speak to Luanne, let me know."

Jon stood. "Not happening. Sorry. Just meeting you here could get me in hot water." He downed what was left of his coffee. "Thanks for dinner. Best sandwich I've had in years." He stood, headed to the exit, and turned. "It was good to see you again, Ed. Let's hope I won't live to regret it."

***

"Jonny, that you?" Eunice Steadman said into the phone.

"Hi, Granny."

"What's the matter?" Her tone quickly changing to worried.

"Nothing. I'm fine."

"Don't nothing me, sweetheart. I can hear it in your voice."

Jon exhaled. "Things are heating up at work."

"Sorry to hear it. But if anyone can get things on track, it's you."

"Thanks for the vote of confidence."

"Are you enjoying the new job overall?"

"It's great."

Once again, Granny, his only blood relative, managed to turn his mood around. "So, how are your surfing lessons going?" he asked.

His grandmother laughed aloud. "I'm way too old for the water. But if by surfing you mean on the internet, you'll be happy to know I've graduated to wireless. No more dial-up."

"Better late than never."

"Right. Now when I read the news, I can do it from anywhere. I'm catching up on the royal engagement now. The wedding is set for next month. They are such a lovely couple. But enough about that. When are you coming for a visit? I'm not getting any younger."

"Are you guilt tripping your favorite grandson?"

"Busted."

Jon could envision his grandmother's devious smile.

"How's Melanie?" Eunice asked. Melanie worked as a biochemist in Northern California.

"We're in loose touch. We're both so busy, but last I heard, she's doing well. Already lining up for a promotion."

"Good for her."

"Yeah, but with her in San Francisco and me here . . ." Jon trailed off.

"I know, honey. If it's meant to be, it will. But I don't want you lonely. Go out, meet people. Make new friends."

The old refrain. "Granny, I'm okay, I've come a long way since I came out of hibernation."

"And no one is prouder of you than I am. Say, what about those dating sites? The one where you swipe right or left. It's fun."

"Granny?"

"Yes, dear."

"How do you know that?"

"Umm . . . well."

"No way!"

She giggled. "It's fun," she repeated.

Jon couldn't help but laugh along with her. "Just be sure to be home by midnight."

"Midnight? I'm usually home by six."

After a few more laughs, Jon asked, "How's your hand?"

Granny had been through an awful ordeal, lucky to survive. Abandoned in freezing temperatures, she'd recovered but lost two fingers.

"Just fine. Stop worrying. The ladies are going to the mall shortly and then to see a movie."

"Sounds fun. Have a great time. I'll call soon."

"Looking forward to it already. Love you, sweetheart."

"Love you too."

He hung up, thankful his grandmother was always there.

CHAPTER 3

Masada, Israel

Gabe Lewis stood atop the mesa, looking out on the expanse of the Judean desert far below, shades of ecru dotted with patches of incongruous green. Perfectly lined rows of date palms—the result of cutting-edge agricultural technology—stood like sentinels along the tiny country's eastern border. Just beyond, the still, sulfuric waters of the Dead Sea separated Israel from Jordan. He raised his water bottle to his forehead, hoping for a cool reprieve, but it was useless. His fiancée, Dr. Terry Lavi, had warned him, yet he couldn't have imagined how brutal the heat would be.

They'd risen before dawn, taking the snake path up to the top rather than wait until the cable car opened. Terry had slathered him in sunscreen, insisting they each bear the added weight of several bottles of water. He wore Nike shorts, a UNT tank top and a Cowboys ballcap. Terry set the pace and twice he'd asked her to slow down. Her petite frame belied her strength. She was in peak condition, her regular krav maga practice resulting in a toned physique.

A strong hot wind blew across the sandy ground. If not for the intense heat, he'd stay for the early tour. What he had learned online was remarkable. Only thirty miles south of bustling Jerusalem, the landscape seemed other-worldly, as if driving south on Highway 90 had ushered them through a time portal, dropping them into the distant past.

Gabe approached Terry standing beside one of many archeological digs. The rock formation surrounded a squared depression in the ground, remarkably well-preserved given it was dug in 66 CE. The fortress itself had been breached by the Romans, leaving the inhabiting Jews to choose between servitude or death. The community decided as one. To die.

Terry said, "This was the mikvah, the ritual bath. It's incredible that in the face of an existential threat, they maintained the sacred tradition. One that carries on still today." Her accent turned the *r*'s guttural. She paused, looking Gabe over. "Have you been drinking enough?"

"Yes, doctor. But I'm ready to get back to the hotel. This temperature is beyond what my delicate system can process."

Terry went to her fiancé. "I'm impressed how you managed the hike up here. With no complaining."

"Aw shucks." He took her in his arms. "Ani ohev otach" *I love you.*

She kissed him. "I'm so glad you're learning the important words."

***

Gabe and Terry descended by cable car, returning to their hotel in nearby Ein Bokek. There, they showered and fell into the deep, restorative sleep that follows exertive exercise. The first time the phone buzzed, neither one stirred.

"Honey?" Terry heard Gabe mumble.

She kept her eyes closed.

"Terry?"

"Mmm?"

"Your phone."

Terry opened one eye, turning to see her phone creeping across the nightstand as it buzzed. Unknown number. She sat up, let out a loud yawn, and answered the call.

"Hello?"

"Efoh at?" *Where are you?*

"Good morning to you, too, Yosef."

Yosef Kahn was the director of the Mossad, and Terry's erstwhile employer. He had recruited her for a mission that had taken her from Israel to D.C. and Rome. A dangerous operation, but one she was proud of. She'd lost a new friend, but her relationship with Jon had solidified in the process. She could only guess why Kahn was calling her now months later.

"I'm by the Dead Sea. Everything all right?"

"You need to come in."

Terry bristled. She didn't do well with people telling her what to do. Even if it was a man as powerful as Kahn. "What's happening?"

"You know better than to ask that over the phone."

Terry looked over at Gabe who was now fully awake, watching her. "But I'm on vac—"

Gabe shook his head vigorously, gave a thumbs up.

Terry sighed. "Okay, when and where?"

Kahn told her and ended the call.

Terry asked Gabe, "Are you sure? We're having such a lovely time. We still have two more nights here."

"I know, sweetheart, but if that's the Yosef I think it is, we have to go back. An ally like that will only help advance your work. He's one of the most influential people in this country."

Terry knew he was right. Kahn had already made it possible for her lab to acquire major funding, allowing her to purchase the best equipment available, accelerating her work in predictive genetics.

Gabe got out of the bed, dressed, and began packing. "Let's grab a quick lunch and hit the road. The bus to Jerusalem comes every two hours. If we hurry, we can make the next one." He looked up from his duffle. Terry wasn't budging. "Something wrong?"

Terry opened her arms wide. Gabe let the t-shirt he was holding fall to the floor, and hopped back into the bed, covering Terry's face in kisses. "Message received."

"What about the bus?" Terry asked through her giggles.

Gabe stopped what he was doing, looked her in eye and with a perfectly straight face said, "What bus?"

CHAPTER 4

Los Angeles

E d parked his beloved Camaro convertible in the garage, farther than usual from the gym's entrance. *I'll get a few more steps in,* he thought as he took a giant bite out of his jelly donut, polishing it off. *Probably not a great idea to walk inside a gym with a powdery pastry in hand.*

Diabetes, the gray cloud following the Hernandez clan through the generations, had claimed his Grandma Fortuna, her name betraying her as she died at fifty-eight. His sister was in and out of the hospital with gangrene. And now him. At forty-four, he was bordering on obese, high risk for type 2 diabetes. The doctor had scared him enough to join the gym and pay for a personal trainer. Said if he didn't shape up, he'd never make it to fifty. Clara, his long-time flame had been nagging him for years. *Well, here I am.* He flicked a crumb off his shirt, grabbed his gym bag from the back seat and got out of the car, clicking it locked.

He considered his trip to New York, his mind taking him to his talk with Steadman. The kid was going places. Unless of course he got in his own way. His cocky manner had a tendency to get on people's wrong side. But he had stellar instincts, even if he still was wet behind the ears.

Ed made for the garage elevators. A well-built young man wearing a scuffed ball cap was heading his way, clicking his Benz open. *Gym rat. Weightlifter. Show off.*

As the man walked by, he grabbed Ed from behind, shoving him against a concrete pillar and sticking a long-needled syringe in his face.

"Don't make a peep Ed or you're dead," the man whispered an inch from his ear. "Ha, good rhyme. Actually, you'll be dead in five years anyway. I'm just speeding the process up some."

Ed nearly wet himself. "W-why? Why are you doing this?" he stuttered.

"You've been sticking your nose into other people's business."

Just then two middle-aged ladies came by, chatting and laughing, oblivious to Ed's plight. One said, "You see Cheryl in that ridiculous leotard? Does she think we're reliving the eighties?"

The attacker lowered the weapon, even with Ed's abdomen, positioning himself so it appeared as if they were having an intense conversation.

My only chance to walk away from this, Ed thought.

Ed screamed, kicked as hard as he could and pulled away.

No use. The man had him in a vise grip.

The women turned quickly in their direction, saw the commotion and screamed in unison. The man raised the syringe, plunging the needle deep into Ed's carotid artery, its contents flowing directly into Ed's bloodstream. He convulsed, his body shaking uncontrollably then crumpling to the ground with the full weight of his hefty girth.

***

FBI Headquarters
New York City

Jon gripped the phone listening to Luanne Parker, Ed's assistant. He couldn't believe what he was hearing. *Ed in a coma?*

How could that be? He just saw him on Tuesday and he was fine.

"You there, Jon?"

"Sorry, Luanne. I'm processing."

"Yeah, I know how you feel. I was supposed to meet with him this morning. He's never late. Always first at his desk unless he's meeting a source or on assignment."

Jon noted Luanne sounded stricken but professional.

"Do you know his prognosis?"

"From what I hear, it's not good. He's in critical condition, unresponsive. You know Ed. He's not in the best of shape. That's why he was at the gym in the first place. His doctor put the fear of God in him."

"What happened?"

Luanne provided all the details she had, calmly and coherently. A true reporter even when it was personal.

"And the perpetrator?"

"Got away. Two witnesses saw the whole thing. They said Ed was being held at knifepoint, screamed and tried to get away and the man stabbed him. Turns out it wasn't a knife, but a syringe. Whatever was in it took him down fast, they said. Then the a-hole got in his car and raced away."

"Any camera footage?" Jon asked.

"No idea. The police are still working it. I can tell you which officer called to tell me what was happening. Ed had me as one of his emergency contacts. Who knew? I guess he doesn't have a lot of people checking up on him."

The guilt hit Jon like a sledgehammer. "If I'd just helped him when he asked . . ."

"What are you talking about?"

"He asked me to follow some story leads, and I declined. Didn't want to take any chances with my new job."

"Come on, Jon. No one saw this coming."

"I should have. Give me the officer's number."

She did.

His job at the FBI had been really good while it lasted.

CHAPTER 5

New York City

J on walked past City Hall and through the adjacent park carpeted in an autumnal spectrum of color, his feet crunching on scattered mounds of fallen leaves. Toting his lunch, he made the ten-minute walk from his office to the Brooklyn Bridge. It was a perfect fall day. Nippy with puffy clouds. He found a free bench and took a seat, taking his time savoring his egg dumpling soup he'd had delivered from The Noodle Bar. He pulled out his phone and called the LAPD.

The officer who worked Ed's case had directed Jon's call to the captain of the precinct. The conversation was getting off to a poor start.

"Why are the Feds getting involved in this? Something you're not telling me?" The captain sounded close to losing his patience with Jon's evasiveness. "Ed was a friend of mine, Agent Steadman. I'd appreciate a candid explanation for your involvement." A pause. Then, "Wait a second. Steadman. I know that name. Aren't you the guy who got caught up in the UN debacle, the one Ed wrote about in *The Times*?"

"Yeah, that's me," Jon said.

A change in tone. "I take my proverbial hat off to you. You're one brave dude."

"Thanks." Jon was not interested in reliving that time.

"So, what's the story here?" the captain asked, his tone friendlier.

"I honestly don't know if there is one. All I can tell you is that Ed asked me for help days before he was attacked. He knew something bad was coming his way."

"Help with what?"

"Digging up info for a potentially big story."

"You know better than most that a guy like Ed can make friends and enemies with any story. Investigative journalists are in the business of unearthing dirt. Often it's dirt the bad guys don't want moved around," the captain said.

"And yet he managed to keep out of this kind of trouble for years. My spidey senses are telling me this time he poked a hornet's nest."

"Spidey senses, huh? How old are you exactly?"

Jon coughed, deepened his voice. "Not the point here, captain. I just want to get all the data and go from there."

"Even if there was something sinister going on, the guy bolted, no trace of him. The area cameras were tampered with. We got no feed whatsoever."

"Just more proof it was premeditated."

"No one is disputing that. Let me ask you something. If this wasn't Ed, would you be wasting your time on this? This doesn't rise to the federal level."

Jon remained silent.

"Your superiors know what you're up to?" the captain asked.

In for a penny, in for a pound. "I was given this job because I have a nose for smelling out trouble that others don't. But to answer your questions, I'm doing this for Ed. I let him down and I won't do that again. As much as I love my new job —the one where my boss has no idea that I'm speaking to you— I joined the Bureau to help people." His voice rising, he added, "I won't let this job change me. If anything changes, it'll be the job."

"Whoa, take it easy. Yep, confirmed. You're a young one. Bright eyed and idealistic to a fault. You're in it for the right reasons, I'll give you that. I'll help you as much as I can. But let's be clear, if I get a call from your boss, I won't cover for you. You'll be on your own with that."

Jon let out his held breath. "Understood. And thanks." He sat up straight, readied his personal computer. "Now what else can you tell me?"

***

The captain was dead on. Virtually nothing to follow up on. The assailant left no DNA and had the presence of mind to take the syringe with him. The one new piece of information that stumped him was what was in the syringe. The doctors couldn't find any poison or drug that could explain Ed's physical reaction. He had not suffered a heart attack from the stress or fear but went into debilitating shock. The witnesses had no usable information other than the assailant's height and build, which Jon knew was frequently unreliable testimony.

The only thing he could think to do was speak to Ed's doctors. If they would even talk to him. It would require feigning FBI involvement. He needed to figure that one out. *How did I get into this mess?*

***

"What do you mean you're too busy?" Jon said with frustration. "We need to work on this."

Luanne loudly yawned. "I wish I could but with the royal wedding only weeks away, the newsroom is in a panic. I've been reassigned to working on it full time."

Jon persisted. "What about Ed? I thought you wanted to find his assailant."

"Of course I do! But I don't make the rules here."

Though he was giving Luanne a hard time, Jon knew how she felt. "What if you do what your boss is asking of you but use your time off to help with your previous investigation?"

"I doubt he'll see it that way. Journalism isn't a nine to five job."

"Then don't tell him. Put in your hours on the wedding and help me in the evenings and weekends."

"And when do I sleep exactly?"

"Sleep is overrated."

When she didn't laugh, Jon said, "Come on, Luanne. Think of Ed." Deciding to lay it on thicker with a dose of guilt, he added, "He's lying in the hospital in a coma. He needs us."

Luanne sighed. "You're right. I know you're right. I'm just overwhelmed. Went from no work to way too much of it."

"So, you'll do it?"

He could visualize her shoulders slacking. "Of course I will. If it weren't for Ed, I'd still be looking for employment. You'll need to come here. I can't get away now. There's just no way."

"Understood. I'll be there tomorrow morning and we can collaborate. Please have all your research ready and I'll bring mine."

"Will do. Meet me at the Westwood Library on Glendon Avenue."

They agreed on noon.

Jon felt a little bad pushing so hard, but there was no choice. They needed to find Ed's attacker and bring him to justice. Ed would have done the same for them. Only now he had to take his own advice and put in the hours for his day job before Matthews caught on to his extracurricular activities.

***

Jerusalem, Israel

A soft breeze carried the intoxicating fragrance of roses in full bloom as Terry walked beside Yosef Kahn. The Wohl Rose Park was a five-minute walk from the Knesset, where Kahn kept an office for when he was in town. His permanent office was elsewhere, but Terry understood she would never be privy to its location.

Given the magnificent weather, Kahn suggested taking a walk in the park, nineteen acres displaying over four hundred varieties of roses, many of them gifts from other countries. Two bodyguards wearing headsets and beige short sleeve Guayaberas were steps behind them creating a protective barrier. The boxy shirts were well suited to conceal their Berettas.

Terry regarded the fit, fifty-something-year-old ex-commander strolling by her side. Theirs was a nebulous relationship. When she'd first met the man, she'd been in awe. Stalwart and indomitable, his reputation was larger than life. While much of that sentiment remained, her view of him had evolved into something more balanced. He was a brilliant strategist, each act and word thought out well in advance. Aware his ethos was to protect and defend his homeland, Terry tolerated his penchant for manipulation.

Yosef pointed to a climbing vine of large pale pink blooms, its berry-like fruit a striking red. "Ahh, the Rosa canina. Isn't it beautiful?"

Terry wasn't expecting a class in horticulture, but admittedly the flower was exquisite. She leaned in to fully capture its scent.

Yosef continued. "It's also called the 'Dog Rose.' In the days of the Temple, roses were used as an additive to the incense mixture, which was burned twice a day."

"Truly fascinating." She meant it, allowing a moment to pass in what felt like comfortable camaraderie. Then, "Why am I here?"

"As you know I was hoping your colleague and friend, Agent Steadman, would take the role of liaison between the Shin Bet and the American FBI." The Shin Bet was Israel's internal security service. "I've been notified that he declined the offer."

"And you want me to convince him to reconsider." It was not a question.

Kahn offered a toothless grin. "B'diyuk." *Exactly.* "That objective is secondary, as a favor, so to speak, to my colleague at the Shin Bet."

"What is my primary function?"

"To attend the World Symposium in biogenetics."

Terry furrowed her brow, certain he was easing her into something. "I presented at the San Diego conference a few years ago."

"I'm well aware. However, you won't be presenting this time."

Yosef took a seat on a stone bench across from the Japanese section of the garden. The bodyguards halted nearby, their eyes in constant motion. Yosef looked up at Terry. "Please join me."

Terry sat.

Yosef spoke softly. "There are a handful of elite and highly secretive individuals who illegally trade in digital data. Essentially, they are brokers, buying and selling spyware, classified government documents, valuable scientific records, and such."

"Brokers?"

"Think of them as the equivalent of black market arms dealers but for high-demand intelligence, rather than weaponry."

Terry was dumbfounded.

"In recent weeks, there has been an unprecedented uptick in aggressive cyberattack attempts here in Israel. Both in government and laboratory systems."

Terry blanched. "Are you saying someone is trying to steal my work?" As the words escaped her lips, she realized how self-absorbed she sounded given the bigger picture.

Undeterred, Yosef nodded solemnly. "We are facing a different sort of enemy. One who wishes to undermine our country's security by mining our computer networks for sensitive data . . . yours included. Fortunately, we have some of the world's best programmers, experts in defensive countermeasures. They have managed to stave off these attacks. For now."

A mother pushing a baby carriage walked nearby. From where she sat, Terry could hear the infant's suckling noises. She watched as one of the bodyguards steered the woman away. "If these so-called terrorists succeed, the ramifications are far beyond losing my lab's professional accolades. Much of the research would be dangerous in the wrong hands."

"You and I are among a limited few who understand that." Yosef was referring to the last mission that had brought them together. A scientific breakthrough that nearly ended in a global disaster. "It's precisely why they *are* terrorists. Perhaps not in the conventional sense but no less lethal."

"These brokers purchase classified intelligence and sell it?"

"Correct. To our competitors . . . and enemies."

Terry felt a growing sense of dread. Even if Yosef was holding back as he was apt to do, the possibility of her work being stolen was unthinkable. "How can I help?"

"We've gained valuable intel that one of these power brokers will attend the symposium. We have not yet succeeded in identifying the individual in question. This person is savvy, knows the way around computer systems to remain undetected. We must assume the purpose is to negotiate dealings with hackers and buyers."

"What will my role be?"

"To trace the source of the attacks by identifying the broker. You will attend the symposium under the guise of networking with others in your field as a representative of your country. Your true objective however will be to weed out the culprit, make a positive ID and report back."

Terry thought of Gabe. "How long will I be away?"

"I can't predict the precise timing, but I estimate a week."

Terry breathed a sigh of relief. A week was doable.

Yosef said, "The symposium begins in one week from today. Before you leave, meet with Shira to review some tactical plans." Shira had been Terry's handler on the last mission. Terry knew the "plans" would include a rigorous refresher in the finer points of shooting and hand-to-hand combat. "Shira will provide you with what we already know about the broker and how to elicit contact. Let's see who we reel in."

Terry felt a now-familiar prickle. "So, I'm bait."

"Is that an issue for you, doctor?"

Before she could reply in the negative, he went on. "This is a highly sensitive matter. You've been chosen not only for your scientific expertise, but because of your basic nature."

Terry wanted to ask him to elaborate when he cut her off again. "You are scheduled to arrive in New York a day in advance of the symposium. It will give you a chance to meet with Agent Steadman."

This was the part of the bargain she was least comfortable with. As much as she detested being manipulated, she knew Jon well. He hated it even more.

CHAPTER 6

Los Angeles

J on pulled into the lot of the Westwood Library, a nondescript building just off Wilshire. Los Angeles continued to perplex him—a strange demographic mess of self-absorbed wannabes and middle-income families just trying to get by. It remained his least favorite city, mostly for the unrelenting traffic. It was a wonder more people didn't die of road rage. The only upside he could think of was getting to wear his cowboy boots. No one looked at him funny like they did in New York.

Last time he was here it was to meet Ed on his turf. He thought back to the first time he'd met the reporter. Not what he'd expected to find of an eventual Pulitzer winning writer. Yet another lesson in not judging a pro by his potbelly.

The library's interior was contemporary and well-maintained. People were sprinkled about, hovering over books and laptops, many even further closed off from the world around them with noise-cancelling headphones.

A slender young woman, tomboyish with maroon-tinged jet black hair and a killer smile traced in black lipstick, stood to face him. Piercings with no studs, the hint of ink on her wrist mostly covered by her black and red boatneck sweater. Looked like she was outgrowing a fairly recent Goth phase. She was holding a large portfolio.

"Jon?"

He nodded. "The one and only."

"Nice to meet you in person." Her open demeanor took him off guard. New York City must be rubbing off on him.

"Same. Good thing you introduced yourself. You don't resemble your *Times* photo in the slightest."

"I get that all the time. I've never come out good in pictures."

Jon doubted that.

"There's a small meeting room upstairs where we'll have privacy and can speak above a whisper. It's where I go to concentrate on my research without interruption."

"Lead the way."

They took the stairs up to the second level and situated themselves in one of the rooms.

Jon asked, "How are you liking LA? More or less than NorCal?"

Luanne looked up at Jon quizzically. "You've done your homework."

"Always."

"Hmm, good to know. Can't say I've made a firm impression yet. I'm not here long enough. But at first glance, it's too congested. The air too smoggy, and if I didn't need this job, I'd never have left NorCal. I'd be spending my days hiking in the Sierras."

"Sounds like a pretty solid impression to me." Jon took out his computer and logged in on his secure hotspot, watching as she extracted sheets of paper with feminine handwriting. "I see you're a fan of old-fashioned longhand."

"Mmhmm. I'm told I'm an anachronism. There's something about the feel of paper and pen I just don't get when typing."

He looked at the volume of papers. "To each his own."

"How about we start with my update?" she said.

Jon raised a brow. "What update?"

"After our last conversation, I called Ed's doctor. I wanted to go see him, but visitors aren't allowed in the ICU.

Since he had me as his contact, the doctor was willing to speak."

"What did you learn?" Jon asked, relieved she solved the problem for him.

"He said they've determined that the syringe was filled with sucrose."

Jon was perplexed. "I'm not following. Isn't that sugar?"

"Yep."

"How does that make sense?"

"I didn't get it either, but apparently Ed is diabetic. I told the doctor Ed liked his pastries, but he said the amount of sucrose administered by the attacker was way above a donut or anything Ed's body could tolerate. It put him into an immediate state of shock."

Jon was stunned. "But that would mean . . ."

"That his attacker knew he is diabetic. But what's crazy is the blood results had only just come in. The doctor never even had a chance to tell him."

"So, the attacker somehow had access to Ed's medical information even before he did."

Luanne said, "Seems that way. Needless to say, I asked the doctor about that. He of course was very disturbed by the suggestion. Got defensive. Claimed their records, while electronic, are highly secure, using the most advanced software."

"Oh, come on, everyone knows for every security platform there's a hacker that can bypass it."

"That may be true, but then answer this—why would someone go to the trouble of hacking Ed's medical records? Even if they had the capability, it seems a lot of trouble and risk when he could have just administered a poison. It's not like the guy was trying to kill him and make it look like an accident. He attacked him out in the open."

Jon pondered the problem. "I see what you mean. It does seem over the top. There has to be an explanation."

She paused, deep in thought. Then said, "Maybe it's as simple as sugar being a whole lot easier to get one's hands on than a poison."

"True. But still, how did the guy know Ed is a diabetic?"

"I haven't the foggiest idea," Luanne said.

"What about the project you were working on that Ed mentioned to me?" Jon asked.

"You mean the social media DNA conspiracy theory? He told you about that?"

"Yeah, he said you may be on to something."

Luanne was quiet a moment. "With everything going on, I let it go for now. This royal wedding has taken over my life."

"Seriously, who cares about some entitled figureheads living a continent away?" Jon typed something into his computer.

"Are you kidding? It's the biggest story of the year. People are obsessed with anything royal. Especially an American commoner marrying a British prince. I'm just lucky they're not sending me over there."

"Sorry, I tuned out there for a second. Focusing on the DNA thing. What's the Facebook page you found it on?"

Annoyed by the slight, she told it to him, and looked over his shoulder while he searched.

She pointed to the screen. "There, that's it."

"Wait, it says these comments were from Ed@Times."

"Yeah, I used Ed's account. It was already set up and I figured people would be more open with him than some lowly intern."

"Hmm, okay. Looks like you put out a lot of feelers with your comments."

"I did, but I didn't have a chance to follow up with any of those posts. Like I said, I got caught up with the royals."

Jon scrolled through a string of comments. "Okay, I'll go over it tonight."

"What are you looking for?'

"If any of these so-called conspiracy theories rings legitimate. Maybe there's some connection to Ed's attacker."

"That seems a stretch," Luanne said.

"For now we have nothing more to go on. So that's where we'll have to start."

"I'm working till six-thirty and then can help you out." Luanne stood, gathered her papers. "I need to get back to the office."

"Great. I'm staying at the Versailles. We can work there."

Holding her portfolio, Luanne opened the door. "Fine. Just do me a favor and have takeout ready to eat."

"Deal."

CHAPTER 7

Jerusalem

T erry spent several days working with Shira in the afternoon and reuniting with Gabe in the evening. Their
flight to New York was leaving in the morning and
they'd agreed to a romantic dinner at the Mamilla Hotel's rooftop restaurant.

Gabe was waiting for her at the apartment, as excited as
a child with a new toy.

The twelfth-floor city center unit was on loan from the
government. With sweeping views of the Old City, the smart
apartment had been designed to sense the needs of its occupants. Terry had stayed there before and was once again navi-
gating a love-hate relationship with the technology.

Gabe said, "You won't believe this, but I spilled a glass of
Merlot and a moment later a robo-mop came by to clean it up.
And let's not forget the shower. Oh. My. God."

Terry laughed, happy her fiancé was enjoying the perks
of her side gig. At least that's how she referred to it. If the situation had been reversed, she would not have liked being kept in
the dark about her partner's vocation. To his credit, Gabe never
pressed her on what Yosef Kahn wanted her to do.

Gabe said, "Are you sure you don't mind that I won't be
in New York with you? If we're heading back to the States, I
really need to see my parents in Austin."

"Of course, motek. I'll miss you, but this way we will both meet our obligations and hopefully have time for fun when we're done."

Terry quickly changed into a blue shift dress and black pumps, and together they walked to the Mamilla Hotel, situated a short distance from Jaffa Gate. The sun had just set, leaving a kaleidoscope of color in its wake. The hotel's rooftop was elegantly appointed. Overflowing pots of fragrant gardenias separated the glass top tables and plush lime green sofas.

They dined on mushroom risotto and roasted sweetbreads with an artichoke confit. The meal ended with a heavenly chocolate fondant topped with chamomile honey ice cream.

Gabe wiped his mouth with the cloth napkin, exhaled. "I'll never eat again."

"Don't tell your mother that."

"Speaking of my mother, she asked when the wedding is. So . . . when's our wedding?"

Terry laughed. "What do you think about next summer?"

Gabe made a face. "That's way too long from now. How about the spring?"

"Hmm, the spring *is* beautiful here."

Gabe's brow shot up. "Oh. You want to get married here in Israel?"

"I just assumed . . ."

"No, that's fine. As long as my family and friends can get out here. Looks like we have some decisions to make. No rush. We've got nothing but time." Gabe extended his palm in invitation.

Terry took her beloved's hand in hers, thoughts of her upcoming mission filling her mind. *I hope to heaven you're right.*

***

Los Angeles

"Where the hell are you, Steadman?" Matthews shouted into the phone. He was his usual convivial self.

Here we go. "Actually, I'm in Los Angeles."

"What?! What are you doing out there?"

"Family emergency."

"What family? You don't have any family in California. You only have a grandmother and she's in Florida."

Rookie mistake, Jonny, he scolded himself.

"That's true, sir." He hated calling him *sir*, but it came with the job now. Doug insisted on it. If the others heard Jon referring to his boss as Doug, Matthews, or a-hole, for that matter, it would undermine his authority. One thing Matthews would never tolerate.

Jon said, "With so little family, some close friends have become family and I needed to come out here for a few days."

"And didn't bother telling me or anyone else for that matter."

"Sorry sir, everything happened so fast."

"Are you up to something Steadman?" Matthews asked.

"No sir. What could I possibly be up to?"

"With you, it could be any number of harebrained things. Get your ass back here by the end of the week or you won't have a job to come back to."

***

The knock on the door came to the beat of Shave and a Haircut, Two Bits.

Jon opened the door allowing Luanne inside. She'd changed her clothes and was now wearing jeans ripped at the knees, funky glasses, toting a leather messenger bag. Her hair was wet and curly.

"Didn't bother dressing up then, huh?" Jon asked.

She shrugged. "Is this a date?"

"No."

"Then who cares? I'm clean and ready to work." She put the bag down on the table next to the bed. "Smells like dinner time to me."

"There's miso soup and sushi. Help yourself."

"Don't mind if I do." She took a set of chopsticks and not bothering to sit, scarfed down one of the sushi rolls.

"Hungry?"

"Always."

He watched her finish a bowl of soup and then pull a bag of cookies from her bag.

Munching, she said, "Remember to always end on a sweet."

She took a water bottle from the minibar and drank it without coming up for air.

"That'll be four dollars," Jon said.

"Your treat."

"How generous of me."

She sat down in the chair beside the room desk, pulled out her laptop. "Got a girlfriend?"

"You always so blunt?"

"We're in a hotel room together eating spectacular Japanese cuisine. It's a fair question."

She had a point. "The answer is, not really."

"Not really, huh? Sounds magical," Luanne said.

"Just forget it."

"Okay, sorry. Tell me. I'm curious now."

"Great girl, great guy, poor timing."

"I'm assuming you're the great guy."

"That's right." He gave her a toothy grin.

She laughed. "Humility is not in your top ten qualities." Then adds, "I noticed you walk funny. What's that about?"

"Subtlety is not in your top ten qualities. Never ending

43

questions."

"I'm a reporter for God's sake. What did you expect?" Luanne retorted.

Sitting on the bed, Jon opened his laptop. "Let's get started on the first conspiracy theory."

Luanne got her game face on, ready to work, fully aware that he never answered her question.

***

Two hours and four mini vodkas later, they were on data overload.

Jon, now leaning against the headboard with his Mac propped up, said, "Jeez, I need a break. Who knew there were so many paranoid people out there?"

Luanne lay prone across the bed, propped on her forearms. She lifted her glasses, rubbed at her eyes. "I know. But don't you think there's an odd pattern forming?"

"Maybe. I see it too. The few sane-sounding posts seem to have a common theme."

"So now what?"

Jon pulled a plastic yellow ball out of his backpack and threw it at her, hitting her in the shoulder.

"Hey, what the hell is this?"

"It's a stress ball. Squish it and it will calm you down."

Luanne snatched the ball, tossed it back to Jon. "If I were any calmer, I'd be comatose."

Jon laughed. "You have a point." He stood, stretching. "Let's go for a walk around the block. Get our blood flowing."

Luanne groaned. "Can't I just stay here and fall into a blissful sleep?"

"Not yet. We still have too much work to do before I have to get back to New York."

"Ball buster."

Jon offered his hand, which she took. Jon pulled her off the bed. "Up and out."

"Aye aye sir," Luanne saluted.

They grabbed their jackets and headed out the door.

***

Jon and Luanne's walk around the block turned into a stop at the corner all-night cafe. Copious amounts of caffeine and sugar insured a night of no sleep. Jon learned a great deal about his collaborator in that time, finding himself surprisingly entertained. She had a certain openness, no airs about her. She'd been a track star in high school, clearly evident in her athletic build. A connoisseur of coffee. Or in her words, a coffee snob. It took her a full minute to order the brew sitting before her. He also learned she'd been on the frontlines of legalizing cannabis in California. Perhaps explaining her ever-present hunger.

When they got back to his room, Jon said, "We still have a few posts left. How about we divide and conquer?"

"Fine, I'll take the next three and you read the final three."

They both got back to it.

"Here, take a look at this," Luanne said pointing at the screen.

Jon bent over her shoulder to look at the post. Her hair smelled of fresh strawberries.

He read to himself.

After fifteen years as a research assistant at a top hi-tech firm, where everyone loved her, my wife was let go and replaced by a woman ten years older(!) than her. Her health insurance just lapsed, but thankfully my coverage kicked in. Just in the nick of time 'cuz yesterday she was diagnosed with stage 2 breast cancer and will need long-term expensive treatment. It's like the company knew what was coming and canned her. If I wasn't scared of being sued, I'd splatter their names all over the internet.

Jon checked the time on his laptop. It was nearly two a.m. His battery was almost dead. He looked over at Luanne, seated on his bed, her shirt scrunched up revealing her pale, toned stomach. Jon shook his head trying to clear his thoughts from the path they were leading him down. Thoughts of Mel came rushing in.

He moved his eyes back to his screen. "You tired?"

Engrossed in whatever she was reading, she mumbled, "That would be a yes."

They both yawned in unison.

"You can stay over if you want," Jon offered.

She lifted a brow.

"I don't mean it like that. It's too late to drive home and we'll want to get back to this in the morning."

She sat up eyeing him, assessing, "Great. I'm cool if you are."

He got up to move a pillow to the floor.

She angled to take the pillow from him. "You're not sleeping there. I have no problem sharing the bed if you don't."

Without another word she slipped the shirt over her head, pulled off her pants, standing there for a moment in her purple lace underthings, then got under the covers, turning away from him. "Thanks."

When Jon finally closed his mouth, he managed to say, "You're welcome."

Despite the fury of carnal thoughts running through his mind, Jon eventually fell asleep and dreamt of Ashleigh, his one-time fiancée, dressed in a purple lace wedding gown. She looked happy and kept coming closer for a kiss, but somehow their lips never seemed to meet.

CHAPTER 8

Los Angeles

Peter Cromwell held his head in his hands. *How are we going to get out of this?* Last quarter's numbers were abysmal. If they didn't meet their expected sales for the upcoming quarter, the company wouldn't recover. He didn't know what he would say at next week's board meeting. As CEO of last year's Forbes *Most Promising Online Startup*, the buck stopped with him. The IPO had been a huge success but then began to plateau. Now he feared it would tank. They called it overly aggressive growth.

He couldn't put his finger on the cause. Had they expanded their workforce too fast? He'd been in more dire financial situations before but never with so much riding on his success or failure. He'd crunched the numbers countless times. Pamela, his CFO, made recommendations but none were to his liking. He expected her any minute.

Susan, his secretary, appeared at the door. "Pamela is here for your ten o'clock."

"Thanks. Show her in."

Pamela was a prim woman of brilliant mind and poor social graces.

"Good morning, Pamela. I hope you've brought me good news."

"We've been through this before, Peter," she said abruptly. "Unless you're willing to make real cuts we risk losing all our past gains and then some."

"I know, I know. I just can't find any place to slash."

"No matter what, it will be hard, but you need to think long term. I still think benefits are the place to go."

"If we do that we'll lose our best talent. You said to think long term. If we don't have top people, the business will tank anyway. How about that hiring freeze?"

"Still in effect. It's helped marginally, but it's not enough. What about reducing or eliminating our compensation packages?" Pamela asked.

"Same problem as slashing benefits. We should be focusing on increasing streams of revenue."

Pamela shook her head. "That's all well and good but as you know, new initiatives take time to impact the bottom line. By then the point will be moot." She placed a folder on his desk. "I've prepared this report for you to review. You'll need to pick one or more of the listed areas to cut, and I mean significantly, if we are going to stay afloat. I suggest you change your mindset, or everyone will be out of a job this time next year."

Without further comment, Pamela stood, straightened her suit jacket, and retreated from the office, leaving Peter once again holding his head in his hands.

***

For your eyes only. The email was sent to his personal address, one only his close friends and family knew and were careful not to divulge. Peter opened the mail and was stunned to see his company's prospectus. The one that had not yet been sent to the board members, and certainly not to the public.

He looked closer at the sender. Sherman@cavalry.org. The prospectus of course was meant to capture his immediate attention. He read on.

Dear Mr. Cromwell,

While we have never met in person, I am a huge fan of your business acumen. You've managed to turn several startups into

huge successes. It has come to my attention that you are now strug-
gling far more than your previous ventures. This is where I come in
—the cavalry, so to speak. I have taken it upon myself to review
your prospectus and have found a solution that will not only keep
your fledgling business afloat but solvent for at least the next
twelve months while you develop and launch your new marketing
strategies. As you can assess by the contents of this correspondence,
our methods are not conventional. However, I can guarantee suc-
cess and offer a full refund if you are not perfectly satisfied with
the results.

If you wish to learn more, please contact me at this email.
Wishing you a successful afternoon.

William Sherman

The name was vaguely familiar. His search engine told
him why. William Sherman was a notable general during the
Civil War serving valiantly in the U.S. cavalry.

***

Peter knew better than to speak to anyone about the email.
Pamela included. He needed first to see what the man was suggesting and if it was above board. He wasn't foolish enough to
allow a scam artist to con him even at his most vulnerable. *Es-*
pecially at his most vulnerable. He had to be careful. Hundreds
of jobs were on the line. Including his own.

Using a secure network, Peter replied to the email requesting a face-to-face meeting to learn more, while also expressing his discontent with the sender for gaining access to
his company's confidential documents. He would need to get
his IT guys up here for an explanation.

Within seconds he received a reply. Sherman was not
available for in-person consultations. All agreements would be
done virtually or not at all. *Shady business.*

Under any other circumstances, Peter would have never
given the email the time of day other than to track down the IP
and threaten a lawsuit for privacy infringement. But he was in

no position to do that. He needed a quick fix at this point, and he would be remiss if he didn't at least find out what this person had to say.

What can you offer? he typed.

Sherman sent a link to a chat software allowing them to communicate more efficiently. For all Peter knew, Sherman was a sixteen-year-old girl living in Minneapolis.

Hello, Mr. Cromwell, I'm pleased you're choosing to move forward.

Why don't you tell me your strategy and we can go from there?

Of course, but before we proceed, I will need to insist on you signing a non-disclosure agreement.

An NDA? For what purpose?

As one businessman to another you undoubtedly understand my need to protect my information from potential poachers. You'll see it is a standard agreement. No ruses. If you choose to decline our services, there's no concern on either of our parts.

Peter looked it over and satisfied, signed it, fully aware of the irony.

Very good. Please download a video I have designed for prospective clients. It will explain the main premise and if you are interested, we can go from there.

A video popped up on his screen and he clicked play. It was exceedingly professional, produced with state-of-the-art animation and graphics. Clearly the man was well-funded. A notion corroborated by claims of helping over thirty mid-level businesses around the world with financial solvency.

As the seven-minute presentation played, Peter began to realize what was involved and his pulse quickened. *This can't be right.*

Is this for real? he typed.

Most certainly. Our methods have salvaged billions for our clients allowing them to get back on their feet and thrive.

Peter's insides were in turmoil.

What's your fee? Peter couldn't help but think he was

making a deal with the devil.

Sherman told him, taking Peter aback.

It may sound high, but that's it, no hidden fees. All technical and processing costs are included and I will only make money if you are successful. So only I bear the risk.

Maybe the financial risk, but your methods are clearly questionable. What of those risks?

Mr. Cromwell, I know you to be a most astute businessman. Are there any worthwhile ventures that don't harbor risk?

Silence.

Please feel free to contact me with your decision at your earliest convenience. I hope we can do business.

Peter logged out of the chatroom, wondering who else was privy to what they were writing. Risk. So much risk. But the reward was now in arm's reach, something he couldn't have fathomed an hour ago.

By the time he left for lunch, his decision had been made.

***

The moment Peter signed into the chatroom hidden spyware infiltrated his system. All his outgoing emails, chats and video conferences linked to his accounts would be monitored for keywords alerting Sherman to any breaches of confidence. All clients faced the same scrutiny. It was an insurance policy.

Sherman sat behind the cluttered desk, musing over the intricacies of human nature. Several prospective clients had grappled with moral ambiguity. A wide majority found a way past their personal conundrums and proceeded without incident. No one had yet broken the NDA. Self-preservation always won out. Having the signature of leaders of industry on what many would view as a morally reprehensible endeavor was insurance enough to keep them quiet.

***

Peter was awestruck by the length and detail of the spreadsheet Sherman sent him. Every one of his six hundred and twenty employees was listed, along with a basic description of their current role, age, and vital stats. The last column provided a number from one to five that corresponded to a key code. Anyone with a four or five was highlighted in red. Peter read the key. One was a healthy employee with no detrimental genetic markers. As the numbers increased, the likelihood of impending illness increased significantly. A number five corresponded with an eighty-five percent chance of catastrophic illness within the next twenty-four months requiring a minimum of 200k in annual medical expenses. All those designated with a red five were to be offered early retirement or fired within the next two weeks. All fours were given a month to clear out. Threes would be monitored closely for signs of increased medical visits and reassessed in six months. Peter was relieved to see both he and Pamela were twos. *What had he gotten himself into?*

He could see how easy it was to forget that each line item was a human being with a family and an impending medical scare. It was daunting to think he was given this power to see behind the scenes at his employees' most personal data before they knew it themselves. A man of no morals could easily develop a god complex.

Peter did not think of himself as one of those people. If anything, he'd been accused more than once of being a bleeding heart to the detriment of his projects. The moral quandary played over in his head. If he didn't follow through with Sherman's strategy, everyone would be out of a job, not only the number fours and fives. He had a responsibility to those employees as well.

***

Wall Street Journal

Peter Cromwell, CEO of OBooks, the up-and-coming online book-store has announced what he is calling a "changing of the guard." Nearly 20% of OBooks' workforce has been overhauled, usually a sure sign of financial distress, something the company leadership emphatically denies. CFO Pamela Jackson said, "We're working to energize the future of our business. Generous compensation packages have been offered to the outgoing employees." Laid-off workers disagree, as many are scrambling to find affordable health insurance before the company ceases their coverage.

Insiders are expressing widespread confusion as top performers are being let go. "It makes no sense. They're purging some of our best employees," said one anonymous source. Board members are reportedly supporting the drastic measures, expressing trust in Cromwell, a man known for salvaging sinking businesses. Along with a temporary hiring freeze, some forecasters expect a sharp upturn in productivity and revenue. Only time will tell.

CHAPTER 9

FBI Headquarters
New York City

I'm a zombie, Jon thought as he looked at his reflection in the men's room mirror. Blood-shot eyes, gray pallor. He hadn't slept in nearly two days with the exception of a few interrupted hours on the flight back to New York. At least he and Lu—the name she asked him to call her—had made some progress.

He splashed water on his face and stood up to see a pissed off Matthews looking back at him in the mirror. Since their last case together, the two men had reached a truce of mutual respect, but of late, Matthews appeared agitated and short-tempered.

"So," his boss drawled dramatically, dusting off his Texas twang. "How's your family in LA?"

"Improving. Thanks for your concern."

Matthews blew out a breath, not holding it in any longer. "I got you this job because of your past outstanding performance but you've been riding that wave for long enough, Steadman. You need to prove yourself worthy of this job. There are countless qualified people itching to take your place."

"Listen, Doug." *Screw the 'sir.'* "We both know I earned the spot here. So why don't you take it down a notch? I'll do my job well, just cut it with the weekly threats."

Matthews looked like he wanted to deck him. Seething,

he gritted his teeth. "This morning, there have been three new terrorist threats. Get on that and let me know what you come up with by the end of the day. And if you disappear on me again, I won't give a second thought to kicking you out on your ass. Do you understand me?"

Jon wiped his face off with a paper towel, balled it and threw it overhand into the bin. "Yes, sir," he said as he walked out the door.

***

Los Angeles

Luanne stared at her meticulous handwritten notes. *What ties all the layoffs together?* It was like one of those riddles she loved as a child. *There's something here. I'm just not seeing it.*

So far, none of her calls to the relevant companies were answered. She received two emails from PR reps patronizing her and was waiting for a call back from a company called OBooks. Her intention was to start off amicably, but if necessary, was prepared to drop words like "class action lawsuit."

Within the last week, she had compiled a list of nine people in LA who had eerily similar stories about being fired shortly before a diagnosis. She had arranged for all of them to meet at the lounge of the Hotel Valencia at seven p.m.

By seven-fifteen all the participants were there, several with their significant others. Everyone found seats by the reserved rectangular table in the hotel restaurant's party room. The atmosphere was warm and inviting. Luanne opened a tab at the bar and told the bartender to let the alcohol flow. It would serve a valuable purpose—create a less formal, more relaxed vibe and get people talking. She hoped she wouldn't be spending her entire paycheck on alcohol alone. The investment proved to be worth it. By the second round, her guests were comfortable, making friends with one another and swapping stories. Luanne stood at the head of the table and asked everyone to quiet down.

"I've convened you all here today to see if what we have is not merely a few conspiracy theories, but an actual story that *The Times* can stand behind. If we can find a connection among all your accounts, we can run the piece."

"Even without proof?" called out a woman in her mid-fifties.

"We're not a court of law. Of course we'll need to be careful about naming names as no one wants to get sued. All we will do is report the facts, which we will verify. Who was let go and when, and when each of you was subsequently diagnosed. Then we let the readers make up their minds."

Everyone nodded in agreement.

Luanne turned to the woman who'd spoken up. "Mrs. McAdams, would you like to begin?"

She was a rotund red-faced woman who clearly had imbibed more than enough before arriving here. "All right. I was a lab technician at a well-known pharmaceutical facility for nearly thirty years. Last month I was given notice. They told me that new techs were coming in and were much more affordable with fresher ideas. I was stunned and hurt. I've kept up with my field and trained countless other techs over the years. My employee rating was an A plus. I later found out from a colleague that a forty-year-old had taken my place. Not a new graduate. Bunch of liars." She sniffled. "I still can't believe I don't have a job to go to every morning."

"I'm sorry Mrs. McAdams, it must have been quite a shock."

The woman took a long drink from her glass.

"Can you tell us about the diagnosis?"

"As if things weren't bad enough, I get a call from my doctor. I had a checkup maybe six weeks ago. My blood test came back with some issue, and they sent me for an MRI. Turns out they found a growth on my liver." She could see several people eyeing her drink. Annoyed, she added, "I know, liver disease is a direct result of drinking. Well, I sure as hell am not going to stop now. That's for sure."

Luanne asked, "Are you covered by insurance?"

"That's the biggest hit of all. The severance package was quite generous, but my insurance already stopped. The payout won't cover even a month of treatment. I'm applying to Medicaid and praying for the best."

"Terrible. Let's hope all this," Luanne gestured to the group, "will lead to proper restitution. Thank you for sharing. Ms. Goldstein, your turn."

Susan Goldstein was a zaftig woman in her late twenties with a utilitarian haircut and neat clothes. She spoke in a low voice.

"Hi, everyone. I worked for the last four years as the executive secretary at OBooks."

"What is that?" asked the man sitting next to her.

"Pretty much what it sounds like. They're a virtual book publisher and seller. Basically, they publish independent authors online."

"I don't have the best education in the world—an associate's degree from a community college. But I was good at my job. They told me so regularly and even gave me a raise a few months ago without my asking. Peter—that's my boss—was great. He offered to give me extra time off when my father fell ill. Without counting it towards my sick days. Nice guy. But then last week, he called me into his office. The CFO was there. Peter told me as gently as one can in this sort of situation that they had to let a lot of people go because they were faced with dire financial circumstances. He was very apologetic. Looked sincerely distraught. I felt like I had to make *him* feel better. Anyway, they gave me a good severance and I've been looking for another job."

"What about a diagnosis?" Luanne asked.

"Actually, I haven't had one."

"Oh, so why did you respond to our post?"

Everyone turned to look at her.

She proceeded to explain that breast cancer was very

prevalent in her family history and she was planning to have a preventative double mastectomy within the next year. She hadn't told anyone but found it strange that her insurance would be cut off before she could have the procedure. She was scrambling now to find a new job and would probably need to defer the surgery.

***

It took nearly an hour to listen to everyone's tales. One thing became crystal clear. They had all been fired without justifiable cause and apart from Susan, each had been diagnosed shortly thereafter. Most didn't have a spouse with family coverage.

Ms. Goldstein raised her hand. "We all work for different companies in completely different fields. How can our cases be related?"

Luanne said, "That is the million-dollar question, isn't it? Honestly, I don't know yet, but I am committed to figuring it out."

The group lingered until an alcoholic-infused melancholy blanketed the room. The first few people stood to leave.

A middle-aged man with graying stubble approached Luanne, extending his hand. "Simon Davidson, good to meet you in person. Thanks for doing this. I don't know if anything will come of it, but it feels good to know someone is seeking justice. God bless." He gave her a warm handshake.

All Luanne could think was this man had better get a lung transplant soon or he won't be around to see what happens.

***

John F. Kennedy Airport
New York

Terry escorted Gabe to his gate.

When the passengers began boarding, Gabe pulled Terry close, whispering in her ear. "Parting is such sweet sorrow, my love."

"Quoting Shakespeare? How very romantic."

"I'll miss you."

"I love you."

"That too."

They kissed deeply, and Terry, once a fully independent woman, wondered how she would manage an entire week without her guy.

***

The cab ride into Manhattan took over an hour thanks to construction on the Long Island Expressway. By the time she checked in to her room, Terry was exhausted. She desperately needed sleep but napping now would wreak havoc on her circadian rhythm. Best to stay awake until the evening. She knew one way to ensure that. She dug her phone out of her purse and called Jon.

"You're in New York?" Jon asked. He sounded excited.

"I just arrived."

"Welcome to the Big Apple. What brings you to town?"

"A conference." She left it at that. Yosef had made it clear that unless Jon signed on as liaison, not to share the true purpose of her visit.

"Is Gabe with you?"

Terry unpacked her bag, placing her cosmetics case in

the bathroom. "He went on to Austin to see his parents."

"Oh, too bad. I mean I love his folks, but it would've been great to see him."

"How about a consolation prize? Maybe you and I could meet for dinner?"

"Sure!" He suggested a couple of places and they settled on an artisanal burger place on the Upper West Side. "See you soon. And Terry?"

"Hmm?"

"I'm really glad you're here."

Terry swallowed down a lump of guilt. "Me too."

***

"Something on your mind?" Jon asked, concerned. They'd spent an hour catching up over burgers and curly fries, but the vibe felt off.

Terry fidgeted in her chair, causing the table to shake. "Why do you ask?"

"You haven't made eye contact with me all evening. Everything okay with Gabe?"

"Everything's amazing. It's just . . ."

A scrawny waiter barely out of his teens stopped by with the check, handing it to Jon. Terry reached for it. "I'm paying."

"All right. Thanks for the treat." Jon waited for her to hand over a credit card. When the waiter stepped away, Jon said, "Will you tell me what's going on?"

"Yosef Kahn asked me to persuade you to reconsider the job offer with the Shin Bet." Terry's words came out in one breath.

Jon leaned back. "Is that all? You had me seriously worried."

Terry looked Jon in the eye. "I don't like playing people."

"I appreciate that . . . and you haven't."

Terry sighed. "I'm sure Yosef intended for me to lure

you in. I just can't do it."

Jon patted her hand. "Don't worry. There's really nothing you could have said to change my mind. I'm otherwise committed."

"You mean to your New York office?"

"Nah, Matthews would have been on board. He'd do anything to get me out of his hair. Sending me across the globe would be like an early X-mas present for him."

Terry laughed. "Then what commitment are you talking about?" A pause. "Oh, a woman!"

Jon shook his head. "No. Definitely, no. My love life is currently a hot mess."

"Then what?"

"It's Carrie's little boy, Randy."

Terry raised a brow. "What about him?"

Now it was Jon's turn to break eye contact. "He needs a role model, you know?"

Terry's face softened. "I thought he has a father."

"He's never around. And, well, Randy and I like hanging out together."

"That's wonderful, Jon. You have a good neshama." She must have noted his perplexed expression. "A good soul," she translated.

Jon shrugged.

"Do you have a photo of him?" Terry said.

Jon pulled out his phone, began scrolling, a broad grin on his face. "I thought you'd never ask."

CHAPTER 10

Manhattan Psychotherapy Associates
Lower Manhattan

"Have a seat. How has your week been so far?"

Jon sat in his favorite chair, the one that leaned back like his grandfather's recliner had. He relaxed and faced the therapist, a fashionable woman in her late sixties. An iPad rested in her lap. "My boss just chewed me out in the bathroom. So pretty much status quo."

"Your relationship with Special Agent Matthews is one of the more unique ones I've come across."

Jon shrugged. "I guess."

"I was actually referring to your mental health."

"No freak attacks, if that's what you're asking."

"That's good to hear. Have you been doing your exercises?"

"When I have the time. I especially like the one where I have to put a war movie on in the background just to desensitize to gunfire. Makes for a fun evening."

The therapist ignored the sarcasm. "You've come a long way Jon, but you know that there are still things that can trigger your PTSD and if you're not tuned in, it can take a heavy toll on you."

Jon didn't reply.

"Any more dreams of Ashleigh?"

"I had another one this week. She was happy but we

couldn't get together."

The therapist typed something into her iPad. "Sounds to me like your subconscious is letting you heal. No more waking up in a cold sweat or reliving what you went through."

"Then, I'm progressing."

"Baby steps, Jon. The combination of regular therapy and your PRN meds is working well. I know patience isn't your strong suit, but trust me when I say slow and steady wins this race. And will keep you on active duty."

"We had shooting practice a few days ago and I kept it together. Like a normal guy would."

"Well done. Any news from Melanie?"

An image of his on-again, off-again girlfriend ran through Jon's mind. Her long, wavy hair, blue eyes. Thoughts of her, once joyful, were now laced with stress. They'd met in university after a particularly challenging time in Jon's life. Since she'd moved out west, their relationship had settled in the gray zone.

"We're still in loose touch. We spoke a few days ago. It's getting harder. Every time we speak I feel further away from her and I'm fairly certain the feeling is mutual."

"Long distance can be hard to keep up. Especially with two very busy people."

Jon looked out the window, seeing nothing in particular. "I wasn't the best boyfriend."

"We've discussed that. And what have you concluded?"

"She loved me anyway."

"And?"

"And . . . self-flagellation doesn't help, self-improvement does."

The therapist smiled. "That's right."

"So you'll tell Matthews I don't need to come here anymore?"

She laughed. "Is that what you really want?"

He pursed his lips. "Nah. I'm good with this."

"Good, then I'll see you same time next week. Your

homework will be to do one thing just for fun."

He left the therapist's office thinking, *How hard could that be?*

***

Austin, Texas

Congressman Richard Taylor ascended the dais. His red and blue tie boasted a perfect Windsor knot, the lapel of his pressed navy suit sporting a tiny Old Glory pin, its real-life counterpart positioned behind him.

He looked out at the sea of faces, his supporters and constituents filling the room. Reporters up front, his family on both sides flanking him. Beside him was his wife of thirty-two years, Mary. Her persona strong, yet feminine. She put out her hand and he took it. They had begun this journey together and would see it to its unexpected end. Here. Now.

Noting the number of cameras, he was glad he had hired a makeup artist to camouflage the pallor that came with days of fatigue and worry.

As the frontrunner for the soon-to-be vacant governorship, Richard had made these appearances more times than he could count. He was favored to win in a landslide, moving the populous state back to its previous party's capable hands. He approached the lectern and raised the microphone to match his tall stature, took his glasses from his breast pocket, and put them on. He took a sip of water from the glass sitting beside his prepared statement.

"Ladies and gentlemen, honorable citizens of this great state. Thank you for coming on such last-minute notice for today's press conference." He spotted Beverly, his long-suffering campaign manager, in the front row, offering a silent message of concern and support.

"Six days ago, I received an unidentifiable email. Its contents have shaken me to my core and uprooted the stability of my family members."

Murmurs could be heard around the room. Reporters grasping recorders angling for a better position.

"The insinuation was that it was being sent from our opposition. While it was tempting to fall into that trap, I have been given emphatic assurances that it is not the case. I choose to believe them." He waited for the shouts to die down to continue.

"The message consisted of a detailed medical profile. It took me a moment to realize it was actually mine. One I had never seen before. You can imagine my concern over privacy and theft, but I read on, only to discover a list of predispositions. They included among other lesser concerns, the high likelihood of my developing rapid onset Alzheimer's within the next year."

Murmurs turned to shocked outbursts. Someone yelled, "It's a hoax! They're trying to derail us!"

The congressman waited once again for the crowd to settle down. "Needless to say, I've followed up with my personal physician. I've undergone exhaustive testing. And as it turns out the profile is accurate."

People were now on their feet shouting, a television cameraman scrambled to get a closer shot of the congressman's face.

"Given these unforeseen circumstances I have no choice but to step out of the race for governor of the great state of Texas."

***

Salt Lake City

Franklin Oakley watched the news with amazement. His strategy had worked brilliantly. The congressman was stepping down, leaving the door wide open for his opponent to waltz straight into the governor's office. It was too late in the race for another member of Taylor's party to step forward and have a chance at victory.

His timing had been impeccable. The close-up of Richard Taylor's face revealed a person of determination and power. Yet, Franklin, a young man living miles away had not only brought him down but changed the course of a free election. He marveled at his handiwork, eager to see what else he could accomplish.

Franklin's gaze shifted to the muted television propped up on his dresser. The news ribbon at the bottom of the screen highlighted yet another inane report about the upcoming royal nuptials. *Did he dare?*

He crossed the room and took another slice of cold pizza from the open box on his chipped wooden nightstand. He needed a mental break. His appointment wasn't for another couple of hours, but he called the shuttle service to pick him up early just to feel the fresh air on his face. He turned back to his work console, shut down all the screens, shuffled awkwardly into his jacket and left his room, locking it behind him.

"Mom, I'm leaving," he called out.

No response. He hadn't expected one.

He let himself out, glad for the sunshine and waited on the porch for his ride.

***

Memorial Sloan Kettering Cancer Center
New York City

Doug quietly walked into the room. He no longer noticed the ever-present beeping. He placed a vase of daffodils on the nightstand, next to his photo. He never liked that picture, but Erica always said he looked just like when they first met. He was about to sit down when she stirred, opened her eyes and looked at him.

"Hi," she said softly.

VENGEANCE

"Sorry I woke you."

"These days I'd rather be awake."

"Brought you some flowers."

"They're beautiful. How was your day?"

It was hard to talk about the mundane, but it seemed to give Erica a sense of normalcy.

"Steadman's still a pain in the ass."

She laughed softly. "You know why the two of you are always butting heads, right?"

He shook his head.

"Because you're so much alike. He's basically a younger version of you, Doug. Don't you see it?"

"Most certainly not. He's arrogant, stubborn and thinks he knows everything better than everyone else. And he's insubordinate."

She laughed again, put a hand on her husband's arm.

"Did I just describe myself?" Doug asked.

Erica said, "He's also brilliant, thinks outside of the box and is fiercely loyal."

"I'm not sure if I've been insulted or complimented."

"A little of both, sweetheart. If you two can get past your own pride, you would make a great team. An epic FBI duo."

Now it was Doug's turn to laugh.

He puffed up her pillow, straightened her turban. "Can I get you anything?"

"Your being here is enough. I know how hard it is to get away."

"There's nowhere else I'd rather be."

Erica smiled, closed her eyes.

Doug watched as her breath became even and his wife fell back asleep.

67

CHAPTER 11

Los Angeles

L uanne's thoughts were interrupted by an alert on her work phone. She read the AP report in shock. *So much for giving the firings my undivided attention.*

For the next two minutes her phone notifications didn't let up. Among them was a text from her boss. *ROYAL WEDDING CANCELED! All hands on deck!*

***

New York City

"Jon, you won't believe what I just heard from my colleague about the royal breakup." Luanne spoke rapidly into the phone.

"I have no time for that now."

"It's relevant! Just hear me out, okay?"

Jon looked at his watch. "I can give you five minutes then I have to get back to work."

"You're an asshole, you know that?"

"So I've heard."

"Glad to be part of the majority opinion. Anyway, according to a confidential source, about two weeks ago, the queen requested that the bride-to-be take a blood test."

"Isn't that standard procedure?" Jon asked, pulling up the *LA Times* on his screen. The headline read, "A Royal Jilt."

"Apparently not. In any case the results came in the day before the breakup."

"You think the blood test revealed some sort of infection?"

"Unlikely they would create such a media hoopla for a run-of-the-mill treatable infection."

"Then what?"

"What if the blood was sent out for genetic testing? They could have checked for serious diseases or a predisposition."

"Don't they already do that to check for Tay-Sachs carriers?"

"Sure, some U.S. states require it. But federal law protects against analyzing without the express permission of the donor."

"Maybe UK laws are more lenient."

"Actually, they are way more protective of individual rights. I checked. I'm talking about something much more comprehensive. Huge strides are being made in DNA coding. What if someone in the royal family was given access to the bride-to-be's DNA without her knowledge or compliance? And what if they determined she was a carrier of some genetic disease? If they had access to that kind of information . . ."

Jon interrupted. "That's a lot of 'what-ifs.' But assuming those unlikely circumstances, it would stand to reason they would do what they could to protect the bloodline."

"Exactly."

"Okay, I'll bite. Why would someone set out to intentionally break up the wedding?"

"Maybe for attention, glory, whatever. Maybe an old lover who missed out on being a princess. Who knows? But I'll tell you this—from a newspaper point of view, a royal breakup is bigger and better news than a wedding. That whole train wreck phenomenon. The public can't look away. Together for years, lowly commoner bagging the third in line to the throne, primed for a life of the queen's service, and then within weeks of her wedding she's tossed. There's a big story there and no stone will go unturned as far as our editor is concerned."

"You do realize we sound an awful lot like those conspiracy theorists we saw posting online."

"Maybe they're not theories, Jon. Maybe it's exactly what happened to the laid-off workers."

"Whoa. Hold your horses. We need actual facts, Luanne."

"You can use your FBI credentials for that."

"That would mean me telling Matthews what I've been up to," Jon said.

"Okay, then how about this? My colleague has the source—someone inside the palace. He won't speak on the record but maybe he can shed some light on what's going on."

"Good place to start. Keep me posted."

Jon hung up, certain they were disturbing a hornet's nest.

CHAPTER 12

Los Angeles

*T*he *Times* newsroom was in a frenzy, the atmosphere electric. Luanne loved it. The excitement of a breaking news story, meeting impossible deadlines. It's what drew her to journalism in the first place. Now she had a potentially credible—and invaluable—source on the line.

The Brit's diction was crisp and precise, despite his whispered tones. Rather than ask the man to speak up, she quickly moved to an unoccupied office and shut the door, taking a seat behind the desk.

Luanne pictured a balding man in his forties dressed in a black uniform with official ribbons and gold buttons. Of course, who really knew how the British chauffeur dressed when off duty.

"I'm not accustomed to speaking with anyone other than your associate, Ms. Robinson," he said, his voice shaky.

"I understand and greatly appreciate your willingness to talk with me today," Luanne said.

"I only agreed to do so because she reassured me that you are an honorable young lady and will keep my identity under lock and key."

"You have my word."

"Very well. What would you like to know?"

Luanne looked at her hand-written notes. She'd prioritized her list in case he decided to end the call prematurely.

"Can you confirm that the queen requested her son's fiancée undergo a comprehensive blood test prior to the wedding?"

"Yes, I can. All new members of the royal house are required to undergo a blood test. I drove Caroline to the doctor's office myself."

"Have you seen the results?"

"No, ma'am, but that was months ago, and all appeared to be fine. In my estimation the breakup had nothing whatsoever to do with that blood test."

"I'm sorry, I'm confused. I thought that's what led to the breakup."

"From what I've heard, what led to the breakup came only a week later. Someone offered the queen more extensive results. Based on DNA analysis. Apparently, that's when the trouble started."

"So the fiancée agreed to further testing, beyond what is normally done?"

"She claims she did not. It would appear someone gained access to her blood sample, extracted the DNA and proceeded to test it further."

Luanne was stunned. *How could something like that happen?* "What are you basing your theory on?"

"It's not my theory. I have been close friends with Her Majesty's personal secretary since grade school. All correspondence passes over his desk before it reaches the queen. He told me once Her Majesty reviewed the information, she had no choice but to act upon it."

"Well, I'm glad to hear she didn't seek it out. So, what did the DNA reveal?"

"I did not see the report with my own eyes. Please be aware of that. However, my friend did. He said, according to the results, the fiancée had a very high probability of passing along a chromosomal abnormality to her offspring."

"And that could not be tolerated?"

"Absolutely not. While it is not openly discussed, most royal families throughout Europe and Asia have an increased incidence of deformity and syndromes. For generations, the same families—cousins, essentially—married into each other. The babies born with those issues were quietly sent away or left to die."

Luanne was appalled. "But in this day and age, technology can identify those possibilities and early term abortions can be done."

"True, but keep in mind, we are also living in the information age. It would not go over well if the princess was reported to be pregnant and never give birth. An abortion is a highly religious topic and the royal house is ostensibly still under conservative Protestant constraints. It would be a media nightmare. One with which the queen cannot afford to be associated."

"Yet Caroline's test results were never released to the media."

"Discretion is the better part of valor."

"Not in my business," Luanne said.

"Then perhaps you should consider a change of profession."

"Maybe someday, but for now I'm hoping to make a living off of journalism's high road."

The man laughed heartily. "Quite noble of you."

Luanne did not laugh in kind. "I have to ask, but with all due respect, why are you speaking with me?"

"I agonized over this. But in the end, I cannot remain silent. It's such an awful shame. Caroline is a special young lady, full of spirit and grace. She would have added a new vibrancy to the royal house. The public knows that and loves her. And might I say, she really loves the prince, it wasn't just for show. Her unceremonious dismissal is a disgrace to the throne. The queen's subjects have a right to know."

Luanne was impressed with the man's response. "Thank you for your candor."

"Will you print the story?"

"I'll speak with my editor, and he will be the one to determine that. You are one step beyond a direct source and that can be tricky. However, if we do run it, I'll leave out your name and any hints of who my source was."

"Very well, then. I have done my duty and leave the matter in your capable hands."

***

New York City

Jon sat at his office desk, looking at his to-do list. *Do something fun.* His therapy homework. *Fun.* His mind went blank. Gabe and Mel were far away, Terry at a conference. His other good friends were back in Dallas and Granny was in Florida. How was he supposed to have fun by himself?

Even Luanne was on the other side of the country. *Guess I'll be late with this homework.*

His thoughts turned to Matthews. Jon found himself between a rock and a hard place. Nowhere to go. He would have to throw himself at the mercy of the court. Namely the Matthews court. It didn't help that lately Doug had been even more cantankerous than usual. Or that Jon would have to admit that he'd been lying to his boss all along. Let the chips fall where they may. *I need to see this through. For Ed. For Ashleigh. For all those who couldn't fight for themselves.*

Jon could see Doug through the glass door to his office, his regular disheveled self, yelling at someone on the phone. Maybe it wasn't the best time. But lately, the man was like this *all* the time. Jon watched Doug slam down the phone, girded himself and knocked on his boss's door.

Doug gestured for him to come in. "What do you want Steadman? Got something on those threats?"

"Still working on it. Got a minute? We need to talk."

Doug saw the seriousness in Jon's face. "Close the door and have a seat. What's going on? Something up with your family in LA?"

That's as good a segue as any.

"Actually, I need to come clean about that."

Doug lifted a brow. "So, I was right. You *are* up to something."

"I wouldn't exactly put it that way. It's not like I was going out there to surf or anything."

"Then how would *you* put it?"

Doug put his legs up on his desk, shoving some papers aside, and gave Jon a 'can't wait to hear this one' look.

"Remember Ed Hernandez?"

"The reporter?"

"Yeah, he helped us a lot with the college killings investigation, if you recall."

"What I recall is he bent the rules, almost as bad as you did."

Jon had enough. "Jeez Doug, what is going on with you? You're on edge all the time. Cut me some slack, will you?"

"Personal stuff. None of your concern. Go on."

"Sorry to hear it."

"Go on," Doug reiterated.

"Ed called me a few weeks ago asking if I could help on a potentially big story. Something about companies illegally accessing employee DNA data."

"Did you tell him that wasn't your job?"

"I did, as a matter of fact."

"But . . ."

Jon let out a lungful of air. "But then he got assaulted going to the gym. A guy stabbed him with a syringe full of sucrose, sugar essentially. Put him into a severe diabetic shock. He's in intensive care now in critical condition."

Doug put his feet back down, leaned towards Jon. "That's some story. Let me guess. You decided you needed to investigate, do what he asked of you, because now you assume it's related to his attack."

Jon nodded.

"Why didn't you just tell me this from the get-go?"

"Because you've been such an asshole lately," Jon blurted out. "I know it's not my job and I don't want to jeopardize this position. But I'm here to tell you that I need to go back to LA. Ed's associate, Luanne Parker, has uncovered some real evidence and she needs my help. I'm going. And I'd like to use my FBI creds to help Ed and whoever else is caught up in this."

"You still haven't figured out the hierarchy that comes with a real job. You're supposed to ask, not tell."

Suddenly hopeful, Jon said, "Can I have a leave of absence to help Luanne find Ed's attacker?"

"No."

Jon stood, defiant. "Then I'll be handing in my resignation."

"Sit down."

Jon's face was angry. He didn't sit.

"I said, sit down, Jon." Doug's tone was firm and controlled.

Jon sat.

"As much as I detest your insubordination—and something tells me that's not likely to change any time soon—it sounds like you may have a real federal case here. Send me what you have and I'll review it. If it falls into our jurisdiction, I'll allow you to work on it until the end of the month, as an FBI employee. Not as a rogue one or a civilian. Understood?"

Jon's demeanor changed instantly. "Yes! That's all I need. Thanks Dou—sir. I'll send you my notes right away."

***

Shortly before five, Jon received an email from Doug.

I read through your and Ms. Parker's notes. There's enough compelling evidence to warrant a preliminary federal investigation. For now, I'll put another agent on the terror threats.

Attached is the manual for preliminary investigations. Read it.

You'll see info about the expense account. Use it wisely.

When conducting FBI research or communication, only use the secure interface. You have until the end of the month. If you are not back at your desk by then, you're out. Next time, and I know there will be a next time, tell me what's going on from the beginning.

Jon had a clear sightline to his boss's office. Doug was looking right at him, then nodded. The look on his face was one Jon hadn't seen in months. Determined, supportive. Agreeable.

CHAPTER 13

Los Angeles International Airport

J on left a message on Melanie's phone.

"Hey Mel. I'm in sunny California. Gonna be here for the next couple of weeks. Any chance we can get together? I'd love to see you."

Then he deplaned his flight from New York.

***

Luanne was waiting for Jon at arrivals. She wore all black, a studded leather choker around her neck. And a new hair color. *Fire red.* She gave him a big smile.

"I see your boots are back. Not the typical Fed look of black suit, shades, and wingtips," Luanne said.

"Not my style."

He wheeled his suitcase to her habanero orange retro Beetle convertible, stuck it in the back seat. Other than her hair, it seemed to be the only thing she owned with color. And it was *some* color.

Luanne let the top down, donned her sunglasses and got behind the wheel. "I can't believe your boss gave you the go-ahead. The FBI resources will make a huge difference." She slowly pulled away from the curb.

"They already have," Jon said.

"What do you mean?"

"I called the princess-wannabe. We're meeting her tomorrow afternoon. I got us both flights to San Francisco."

Luanne hit the brakes, turned to him. "What?"

"Whoa, take it easy. I told her I'm with the FBI New York office and need to speak with her." Jon took a measure of pride at impressing Luanne with his clout.

"Did she question why?"

"I'm sure she gathered it relates to her breakup. She sounded overwhelmed and resigned. Said we could meet her at her Glen Park home. She was hoping we could help make some sense of the whole thing."

"I'm going to need to prepare my notes. Organize my questions."

"Relax, Lu. We know what we need to ask her. If we come across as too scripted, she won't open up to us. We need to go in chill."

She pulled into traffic. "Chill, okay, I can do chill."

***

The corporate office of Farmstand Industries, a produce packaging facility, was located in southeast Los Angeles. Jon chose it as their first stop, at random. According to Luanne's thorough notes, they had laid off sixty-two people in the last few weeks. One of her meeting participants, Simon Davidson—the lung guy—had been among them.

The lobby attendant directed them to the eighteenth floor. The elevator doors opened to a drab anteroom. Old paneling and flooring. The woman behind the desk looked up.

"Can I help you?" she asked.

Jon took out his FBI ID tag.

"FBI? What's this about?" she asked, alarmed.

"We're here to speak with the CEO."

She appeared nervous. "Do you have an appointment? He's a very busy man."

"No," said Luanne. "We've tried to reach him several times to no avail. Please let him know we're here."

The receptionist picked up the phone. "Sir, there are two people here from the FBI." A pause. "Yessir, that's what I said." Another pause. "I don't know, sir. They want to speak with you."

They could hear the raised tones through the phone.

"I tried, sir," she whispered, her eyes welling.

Moments later a balding man in his mid-fifties, wearing jeans and a sweater vest, came barreling down the hallway. "What's this all about?" he demanded.

Luanne responded. "Mr. Livingston, I work for *The Times*. I've tried to reach you without any reply."

He peered at the receptionist: "You said two people from the FBI."

The woman froze.

The man looked askance at Jon and Luanne. "What kind of game is this? I received nothing from the FBI."

Jon knew it was a lie. The man was likely hoping the problem would go away if he ignored them. Jon showed him his credentials. "Ms. Parker is working with me. We've stepped up the investigation."

"What investigation?"

The receptionist's head was bobbing back and forth between the parties.

Jon said, "Would you like to continue having this conversation in the hallway?"

"I would prefer not to be speaking to you at all. As a matter of fact I'll call my attorney now."

"What for? What are you scared of?" asked Luanne.

"Nothing! But it's basic common sense. He's in-house. I'll get him here in ten minutes. Have a seat out here."

Thirty minutes later a bespectacled, emaciated man in his late thirties came through the door.

The receptionist said, "Marvin, Mr. Livingston is waiting for you in his office." She turned to Jon and Luanne. "You will be sent in shortly."

The man scurried off to the back office.

They heard a door slam behind him.

Another ten minutes dragged by until they were escorted to the back. Livingston was seated behind his desk. "Okay Agent Steadman. I called your office. You're legit. As are you Ms. Parker. Now what is all this about?"

Jon decided not to mince words. The man had wasted enough of his time already. "We have reason to suspect that your company is infringing on the privacy of your employees, grossly violating HIPAA laws."

Livingston turned to his attorney. "I have no idea what they are referring to."

Jon ignored him. "Your company has been using employee medical DNA to determine who should, in your assessment, be kept on the payroll and then firing the rest."

Livingston looked at them stoically. "That's absurd."

Marvin glared at his boss, silencing him.

"Sixty-two of your employees were unceremoniously fired without the traditional two weeks of notice. A meager severance and gone. Some of those people have been with the company since its inception," Luanne said.

"That's business," he spread his hands. "Nothing unusual. We had to make cuts."

"Then explain how two thirds of the people you let go are facing serious maladies. Quite the coincidence, wouldn't you say?"

Livingston was about to respond when Marvin interjected. "I'm sorry but I must advise my client to discontinue this conversation. Mr. Livingston has been more than accommodating, speaking with a member of the press present."

Jon fumed. "Accommodating? He hasn't said anything useful . . . Marvin."

The attorney's cheeks turned red. "If you have further questions, please send us a subpoena and we can go from there."

The wall was erected.

"So that's it? No explanation?" Jon said.

"That's it, Agent Steadman." Marvin said. "There's a proper procedure, and this isn't it."

Jon wanted to wring the lawyer's scrawny neck. All this waiting for nothing.

He and Luanne stood. "Be warned Mr. Livingston. You and your company are now on my radar, and once I lock on, I don't let up. They call me The Pitbull."

As Jon and Luanne took the elevator down, she couldn't contain her laughter. "They call me The Pitbull?"

Jon's face reddened. *Well, they did.*

***

The next two companies they showed up at yielded similar results. They were belligerent and refused to speak with them without a court order.

"So much for my FBI creds," Jon said, as they got back in the car.

Luanne seemed to sense his frustration. "If it weren't for your creds we wouldn't even be getting in the door." She looked at her notes. "Next up is OBooks. Big cuts but sent off the furloughed employees in style. I emailed them again early this morning. Just got a response from their community outreach department. Whatever that is. Said we can stop by any time before three."

Forty minutes later, they pulled up to a modern glass three-story building.

A young, stylish woman approached them as they emerged from the car. "Ms. Parker?"

"Yes, how did you know?" Luanne asked.

"I've been eyeing the front door waiting for you. Yours are the only new faces here. Peter asked that I show you around."

"We're here to meet your boss, not waste time," Jon said. He had enough of the run around.

The greeter said, "He'll be happy to meet you. He's finishing up a meeting, so he thought this would be a good use of the time rather than sitting around with a magazine."

Luanne whispered to him, "Come on, Jon, it will be informative."

As soon as they entered the building, they were hit with a wave of cold air. Luanne wrapped her arms around herself. "Why is it so cold in here?"

"Research shows colder air boosts productivity. Sorry, I should have warned you about that in my email."

The facility had a distinct vibe. It was divided into two sides. The west wing of the building was devoted to technology and designed with open spaces. There was no one over the age of thirty and most were dressed in casual attire. They appeared to be working in teams. One group was tossing around a ball while they brainstormed and coded on their laptops.

The east side of the building was for marketing and finance. Older employees, cubicles. Each species in its own domain.

"What exactly does OBooks do?" Luanne asked the greeter.

"We are an online book retailer, primarily showcasing works by independent authors. Think of us as a mini Amazon publishing outfit."

"No hard copy books?"

"That's right. Everything is electronic."

Luanne shook her head. "No offense but there's nothing like cozying up under the covers holding a real book in your hands."

Jon said, "You really are an anachronism."

"Maybe a reincarnation of some old spinster who loved to smoke weed, read, and write letters to her lovers."

Jon smiled. "Sure, or that."

The greeter looked at her phone. "We can head to Peter's office now. He's ready to meet you."

***

Luanne's first impression of Peter Cromwell was that he was gorgeous. Fit better on the cover of GQ than stuck behind a glass desk. He was tall, maybe 6'3", dressed in distressed, skinny jeans and a cashmere sweater that zipped at the neck, just snug enough to show off his biceps. He stood to greet them.

"Hi, I'm Peter. Please come in." The office was enormous and modern, with one wall of floor-to-ceiling glass, though not offering the most attractive of views. Awards for top California entrepreneur adorned the walls. Jon and Luanne took seats on the pale blue sofa.

Their tour guide quietly stepped out.

"Can I offer you some coffee? I just got this Nespresso machine and I'm addicted." Jon declined but Luanne got up to check out the espresso selections.

"May I help myself?" she asked.

"Absolutely."

While the men sat in awkward silence, Luanne busied herself with the choices and made the froth. She took a seat beside Jon and sipped from her cup. "Divine."

Jon said, "May we get started now?"

"How can I help you?" Peter asked.

Jon explained why they were there. Gave the same opening speech he'd given to the others. Only this time the response was significantly more collaborative.

"Let me pull up my most recent roster from human resources. Okay, here we are. Yes, you're correct. Within the last few weeks, we've had to let go some good employees. It wasn't just about productivity, but our bottom line."

He looked up at them. "It may appear that our choices were haphazard in who we let go, but they were not. Many factors were taken into consideration. Their current pay grade, job redundancy, among other variables. It's actually a complex formula. As anyone here will tell you it was very hard for me on a personal level to implement these cuts. But there was no choice. When I came on board here, I was expected to turn around a distressed startup. Since then we've had some highly profitable months, but it seems we've overextended ourselves. Grew our workforce faster than we should have. I take full responsibility for that. Ultimately, if we hadn't made the cuts, within a year, everyone would have been out of a job. It's one of the toughest decisions I've had to make since I started here."

Luanne said, "And yet unlike other companies in your situation, you provided excellent severance packages."

"My CFO was livid about that, but I couldn't in good conscience do anything else. Many of them have families. They'll need a way to get back on their feet without worrying about paying their mortgage."

Luanne nodded in agreement.

"Can you explain why so many of those you fired began showing signs of severe illnesses?"

Luanne was taken aback by Jon's bluntness. It was more her style.

Peter frowned. "That's awful."

"You know nothing about that?"

"How could I? What do you think happened?"

"There have been too many similar situations with other companies. Has anyone approached you to review your employees' medical data?"

"Of course not. I don't even have access to that. Wouldn't that be available only to the individual and their physician?"

"That's how it should be. In any event, someone is using that information and deciding who to fire based on if they're an expected financial burden to the company."

Luanne added, "Either to save on hefty insurance costs the company would need to bear, or for loss of productivity when the employee is out for sick leave."

Peter appeared riveted. "That's quite a theory. Do you

have any practical evidence?"

"We have many people who have recently come forward with critical medical conditions after being dismissed."

"It must be a horrible coincidence. Again, I don't have access to their medical records."

The conversation appeared to come to a halt. There was nowhere left to go with it.

Jon stood first. "Thank you for your time. Here's my card in case you think of anything that can help the investigation."

Luanne followed suit. "And here's mine. That's my personal cell, if you need to reach me." She smiled brilliantly. She caught Jon's eye. He was glaring at her, seemingly annoyed.

Peter walked them to the door. "Sorry I couldn't be of more help."

Back in the car, Jon appeared more relaxed. "Initial impressions?"

Luanne said, "My spidey senses tell me he's telling the truth."

"Spidey senses?" Jon looked at Luanne, brow raised.

"Yeah, it means my intuition."

"Yeah, I know what it means."

A pause. Then, they broke out in laughter. Whatever seemed to be bugging Jon had passed.

***

Peter closed the door behind them, his heart beating through his chest. He needed a stiff drink. He took a glass from the dry bar and poured himself two fingers of Wild Turkey, swallowing it in one shot like bad medicine. He couldn't tell if Agent Steadman was feeling him out or really had something, closing in on him. Like the old television detective, Columbo.

He poured himself a second drink, this time nursing it. He needed to think clearly, calm himself down. Maybe he should talk to someone he trusted for guidance. Explain everything. He hadn't sought out the damning DNA reports.

No, they were offered to him. He wanted to save the business, save jobs. He just didn't know who to call. He was single, never married. Had a few friends but no one who he could turn to with something like this. He needed someone understanding. Someone savvy. He sat there pensively, his heart rate approaching normal range. And then an idea came to him.

CHAPTER 14

San Francisco

T he house was a spectacular example of old California glamour. Some would call it gauche or ostentatious, but Jon thought it elegant, a sign of a long gone gilded era. The marble exterior boasted grand windows, several chimneys, and magnificent landscaping.

A red Porsche Roadster was parked at the center of the grand curved driveway. Luanne pulled the Beetle up behind it. She and Jon stepped out.

The front door opened.

Caroline Atwood was a stunning redhead. She wore a forties blue and white polka dot dress belted at the waist, and Chinese satin shoes. "Ooh I love your Beetle! It's so retro."

Luanne was momentarily starstruck. "Thanks, it's my parents' car, but I have one just like it at home. I bought mine from an aging baby boomer and spent much of my savings making it road worthy."

"Maybe we can go for a spin?"

Jon interjected. "Perhaps another time. We're on somewhat of a time crunch."

The woman sobered up. "Of course. I apologize. I'm still in the mode of letting just about anything distract me from my reality. But come on in."

"Thanks."

They walked inside the vestibule.

"Nice house," Jon said.

"Thanks, but honestly, this isn't really my taste. The queen wanted us to have a regal home. She agreed to let me keep it. Sort of a consolation prize, I guess. I plan to sell it and buy a modern villa in the hills. Regroup. Start over. Not the easiest thing with my mess in every paper across the world."

Photos of her and the prince were everywhere. Yachting, golfing, and smiling beside a towering, decorated tree.

She led them to a beautifully designed living room. Light fabrics, wainscoting, airy. "Have a seat."

The sofa emitted an overpowering smell of deodorizer. Jon took note of the ashtray on the side table nearest the woman, a joint lying in it. *This stuff's everywhere.*

He handed her his credentials.

She looked at them briefly. "Agent Steadman, you seem young to have such an important job."

"I'm older than I look," he lied.

Luanne handed over her Times badge. "I'm a recent hire. And I *am* as young as I look," she smiled.

Caroline laughed. "So what would you like to know?"

Jon began. "Our sources tell us that prior to your breakup—"

Luanne interjected, "For which we are so sorry. It must be very hard."

"Thank you. It is. But this too shall pass. I'll be all right. Stiff upper lip, as they say." She reached for the ashtray, then reconsidered, putting her hand back in her lap.

Jon thought her stoic demeanor was incongruous with the circumstances, and likely attributable to what was perched on the ashtray. He continued. "Yes, we are very sorry. But what we learned is that you were dismissed, if I can call it that, shortly after your blood test results were analyzed."

Caroline froze. "How do you know that? That was never made public."

"I'm sorry, but I'm not at liberty to say."

Luanne added, "Whatever you share with us will remain off the record."

Caroline said, "Fine. I'll confirm that."

"Can you also confirm that your tests were further analyzed for DNA, namely predisposition for certain illnesses or abnormalities that could emerge down the line?"

Caroline looked stunned. "Is nothing private anymore? You know, as much as I miss Harold and will always love him, I won't miss the intrusion into my private life. None of this is anyone's business, not the queen's or yours. I was never asked, and certainly didn't agree to further testing. Frankly, I would have been just fine not knowing any of those details, same as anyone else walking around. Now I'm being penalized for something I have no control over and that may never even become an issue at all." This time she reached for the joint and took a deep toke.

"It's legal here," she said.

Luanne, said, "You don't need to explain it. As far as I'm concerned, there should be no restrictions on cannabis whatsoever."

Caroline smiled. "You're my kind of gal. Maybe we can hang out some time. We could ride around in your Beetle. Unless you're squeamish about having your face in the paper."

"Sure, sounds like fun. We can take turns with the Porsche."

Jon needed to move things along. "Ladies, we need to figure some things out."

"Of course. My apologies," Caroline said, taking another drag. She passed the joint to Luanne who took a draw as well. Jon waved the smoke away and refused the offer for himself.

"May I know why the FBI is interested in this?" Caroline asked.

Jon said, "We've recently come across a slew of recent layoffs in the LA area. Companies are pink-slipping qualified employees shortly before those people are diagnosed with serious illnesses. We're trying to determine if there's a connection—perhaps someone out there accessing people's DNA and using it against them."

"That's insane. Do you think that's what happened to me?"

Jon said, "From what we hear, your blood test landed in unauthorized hands, someone who sent the less-than-optimal results to the queen."

"If it's any consolation, we understand that she cares for you and was happy to have you in the family." Luanne embellished a bit on what Caroline's ex-chauffeur had told her.

Caroline sat more erect, crossed her ankles. "That's of little comfort. What if it was Harold who had the defective genes? What would she have done then? Prohibited us from having children? It's absurd."

They had no answer.

"Who would do such a thing? Mess with people's lives like that?" Caroline asked.

Jon said, "That's what we're trying to find out. Can you think of anyone who would want to break off your engagement?"

"I imagine there were countless people. When you're in the public eye, weirdos come out of the woodwork. But I can't think of anyone who would go to such lengths to derail my life. In the cases you mentioned, it sounds like the companies were responsible. Have you spoken with them?"

Luanne said, "We're working on it."

Caroline said, "I can't see how corporate greed would be related to my situation."

Neither could Jon.

Caroline pulled out her cellphone. "I'm starving. I'll call for takeout. Either of you want anything?"

Jon stood. "No thanks. We'll be on our way."

Caroline escorted her guests to the Beetle.

"If we have any more questions, can we contact you?" Jon asked.

"Sure. Anytime."

Luanne unlocked the car. "When things calm down I'll

call to take that joyride."

Caroline brightened. "I'll look forward to it. Good luck, you two."

Luanne got behind the wheel, Jon taking the seat beside her. She looked back at the stately mansion, the sun gleaming off the gilded windows. "I can't help but think how lucky I am."

***

The drive took them past the colorful houses of Sausalito, perched on a hill overlooking the Golden Gate Bridge. The sun was beginning to set, the bridge's namesake hue at its peak. "What did you think of Caroline?" Jon asked Luanne.

"I feel bad for her. It must get lonely in that big house all alone. But she seems to be a strong woman. She'll land on her feet."

"Not if she stays high like that."

"Especially if she stays high," Luanne replied.

"Whatever."

"That woman has been through the worst media nightmare out there. Cut her some slack."

Weren't those the words he'd used on Doug?

"Fine. Point taken," Jon said. "Any updates on Ed's condition?"

"Last I heard he's in critical but stable condition. Still unconscious." A pause. "Now what?"

"Now we go through the rest of the companies your group worked for and we track down who's in charge of dismissals."

"At this point it's our word against theirs. We have no evidence," Luanne said.

"True, but I've learned that the threat of a media circus that casts aspersions on someone's business is taken very seriously."

"They'll threaten to sue us for slander."

"Let them. The Feds are behind us. Hopefully that will

scare some of them into talking."

Luanne looked skeptical. "Where do you want to begin?"

Melanie had still not returned his call. "How about at dinner?"

"Pizza?"

"No, let's go out nicely. We've been working hard and deserve a special treat."

"You rich or something?" Luanne asked.

"Not even a little bit. But I do have an expense account."

"Even better."

"And," Jon added, "I was told recently that I need to have some fun."

"Fun, huh?"

"Yeah, have any problem with that?"

"Nope, no problem with fun. But fun requires a wardrobe change. After I drop you off, I'll head to my parents' house. I can pick you up on the way to the restaurant."

"Great. Wear something nice."

"Is this a date or something?" she laughed mockingly.

"No."

Jon watched as she exited the car.

Maybe.

***

Mr. Sherman,

I recently had two visitors to my office. Ms. Luanne Parker from the LA Times and Agent Jon Steadman with the FBI. They wanted to know if our company has stolen employees' medical data. As you can imagine I am terribly concerned given your assurances of the confidentiality of our agreement. I expect you will address this issue with great haste.

Peter Cromwell

Mr. Cromwell,

Your email is very disturbing. I am dedicated to providing the best and most confidential service in order to maximize your profitability. The impact of a breach in our operational security could be devastating to both me and my clientele. I apologize for these unfortunate circumstances and will initiate immediate and aggressive measures to correct the situation, and prevent any future scrutiny into our dealings. In addition, I will reduce my rate as a show of good faith.

William Sherman

As Peter logged out, he realized he'd made an egregious error. He felt a sense of foreboding, fearful of the aggressive measures Mr. Sherman intended to take.

CHAPTER 15

San Francisco

Jon looked at Luanne seated next to him at the elegant bar. She was striking, in her unique way, strangely fitting alongside the photos of old movie stars, writers and poets lining the walls around them.

The concierge at his hotel pulled some strings, reserving them a table at Le Marais. He hoped Doug wouldn't look too closely at his expenses. He spotted several wines he was certain hit the four-figure mark.

"How can you afford this place?" Luanne asked.

"Like I said, expense account. I won't do it again, at least not on this trip. But we're talking business and need to eat, so why not here?"

She shrugged. "Works for me."

"Mr. and Mrs. Steadman, your table is ready for you. Please follow me."

The maître d' held the chair for Luanne and handed each a menu. "I'll send over our sommelier now. Enjoy your meal."

"So, Mrs. Steadman, what's your fancy?" No prices were listed on the menu. He knew full well what that meant.

She laughed. "He certainly jumped to conclusions."

Jon's phone rang. *Melanie.* "Please excuse me, I need to take this."

He stood and walked near the washroom.

"Hey, Mel. How are you?"

"Good. You're in LA?" He was struck by her southern lilt, aware he'd once been accustomed to it.

"Actually, I'm in San Francisco now but only for a few more hours."

Melanie let out a half-hearted chuckle. "Would you believe if I told you I'm in New York? I just arrived. I was hoping to get together with you here."

"You have to be kidding me. Why didn't you tell me?"

"I thought I was being spontaneous. It's almost like someone's trying to keep us apart." A pause. "Why are you in California?"

"Work."

"Same here. Doug already put you on a new assignment? That's impressive."

"It's sort of a unique situation. I can't say much but it all started with Ed."

"Ed Hernandez?"

"Yeah, he was assaulted."

He heard Melanie gasp. Her father and Ed had been friends for years. "Is he okay?" Melanie asked, concerned.

"Right now it doesn't look good. I'm trying to find out who did this to him."

"Please keep me updated as best you can."

"I will."

"What's all the noise in the background?" Melanie asked.

"People talking, I guess. I'm in a restaurant."

"Which one?"

"Le Marais."

"Fancy. Got a raise?"

"Not exactly," Jon replied.

"Expense account?"

"Yeah."

Melanie let out her sweet laugh. "Doug's going to kill you."

"What else is new?"

Luanne walked by. "Excuse me, Jon, can I get by? I need the bathroom."

"Who was that?"

"Luanne Parker. Ed's assistant. She's helping me work on the case. Just a friend."

"Oh."

Jon asked, "Can you come to LA for a few days on your way back? It's been too long since we had face time."

"I know. I'll be back home tomorrow night. Can you stay a little longer in San Francisco?"

"No. I need to get back to LA."

He heard Mel's exhale. "Too bad. I don't see how I can do it on such short notice. I wish I'd known earlier. I could have asked for some time off."

"Can't you pull off even a short weekend?"

"Sorry, Jon. I'm just overloaded. I'm sure you understand."

Unfortunately, he did. He wouldn't have been able to take a whole weekend off from this anyway.

Jon conceded. "Yeah, I do."

"Let's try again with a little more lead time."

"I'll do my best."

"Miss you," Melanie whispered.

"Me too."

As he hung up he realized maybe he didn't miss her as much as he should.

**

Dinner conversation had started out about Ed but soon turned to their personal lives.

"You never answered me about your limp," Luanne ventured.

Jon cut into the sugar-sprinkled souffle, chocolate oozing out. "Right."

"That's why I Googled you."

Jon rolled his eyes. "I suppose that's what journalists do."

"Just as you did to me."

"Touché." He leaned forward. "I'm on the edge of my seat. What did you learn?"

"You never Googled yourself?"

"No. I probably don't want to see what comes up."

"Based on what I read, I now have a whole new respect for you and deeper insight into your psyche."

Amused, Jon said, "Really now. Do tell."

"Well, for one, you're a survivor. In the literal sense."

Jon didn't respond.

Luanne's smile vanished. "Sorry about your fiancée." The words were kind but no looks of pity. He was grateful for that.

Jon looked away. "Thanks."

"Did you get the limp from the explosion?"

"Yep." He was uncomfortable with the line of questioning, but his therapist would want him to trudge through it. Put it on the table rather than under the rug.

"You helped solve a major case, saved many lives."

"Yep."

"That all—yep?"

"Not sure what you want me to say."

"You can elaborate."

"Fine. Ashleigh, my fiancée, died in the attack. I broke some bones, left me with this limp. Upside is I'll always be able to predict an oncoming storm."

Luanne appeared puzzled by Jon's flippancy.

He went on, looking at her now. "That first case you referred to is how I met my boss, Doug Matthews. Total asshole but also a cool guy who opened doors for me, though I'll never admit that last part to his face."

"Do you miss Texas?"

Jon knew she was steering into less challenging waters.

She had good instincts.

"Sometimes. It's friendlier there. I'm originally from Boston. My personality is probably a better fit for the Northeast." He broke eye contact again, ran a hand through his hair.

"A little bit 'o cowboy, little bit 'o Fed."

"That would be me."

"Where are your family and friends?"

"Is this an interrogation?"

She made a face. "Forget it."

"My grandmother is my only family. She raised me. Lives in Florida now. My friends are spread out all over the place." He decided it was time to turn the tables. "What about you? What's your story?"

"Way more boring than yours. Only child, doted on. Republican parents. I rebelled, and here I am. A left-leaning journalist who's dedicated to getting Prop 64 passed around the country."

"I gather that's the marijuana thing," Jon said.

"Correct."

Jon decided to leave that topic on the table.

When the bill arrived, only a few tables were still occupied. Jon did his best to put on his game face when handing the business credit card to a passing waiter, noting it totaled close to half a week's pay. He couldn't argue that you got what you paid for. Everything they had ordered was outstanding. The flavors distinct and well-paired with the wine they had selected.

"Ready to hit the ground running tomorrow?" he asked.

"Actually, I was hoping to get in a good hike and camp out overnight. My folks are out of town, so I think I'll raid their garage and grab my camping gear. I'll drive down to LA in the morning."

"You serious? By yourself?"

"Not unless you want to join me."

He'd already considered staying in town to overlap with Melanie for one night. But something told him to hold off.

They'd both be exhausted, and he didn't want their reunion to be rushed and tiring. That was his story, and he was sticking to it. "I think I'll pass on that. Camping is not my thing. How about we meet back in LA tomorrow night?"

"Sure. I'll cancel my return flight. I think I'll get a rental and drive down. I love the PCH. Takes you straight down the beautiful coast. If I get on the road early, I should make it to LA by one tomorrow afternoon. Be at the next company headquarters at two."

"An hour to get downtown?"

"That's LA, Agent Steadman."

"Thank you very much, Mrs. Steadman."

Jon accepted back the credit card, relieved it hadn't been rejected. Spending the evening washing dishes was not his idea of fun.

***

Salt Lake City

Franklin had learned long ago how to control his anger. He would internalize and redirect it where it belonged. Toward those who had wronged him. His business was developing into a lucrative and impactful enterprise.

Who did that FBI agent and Hernandez's reporter friend think they were to interfere in his important work? He was making monumental changes in the world. From behind the scenes. He felt like the wizard in the Oz movie. But unlike the film character, he was anything but a fraud. He was a computer genius. A talented and creative hacker. A trailblazer.

Until he came along, no one thought to use DNA to their advantage. To exploit its inherent power. Not only had he conceived of it, he'd implemented it. And was making a killing. In the future he would recommend firing more level threes into the mix of fives and fours so the immediate diagnoses after firings wouldn't raise a red flag.

The man he contracted with to handle Hernandez would do the next job too. Franklin had dug deep in the dark web to find him, searching for the right people to handle his dirty work, the work he himself was incapable of doing.

Soon he would be out of this hovel. Get his own upscale smart home with a dedicated computer room filled with top-of-the-line equipment. And a trusted aide to assist him. At the rate he was going, before long he would have more than enough money for all that. But he had to be careful not to invite suspicion. Throwing around that kind of money would draw unwanted attention. From his mother, among others. He felt no inclination to give her any of his earnings. She was a mess. Anything he'd give her would be squandered on cigarettes and big screen televisions.

He was slowly building a plan of execution but for now he would sit tight, satisfied in running the world from his humble bedroom. There was no way he was going to allow some rookie Fed and half-wit reporter to ruin all his plans. Going after the agent would be risky but the reporter was a whole other story.

CHAPTER 16

Sonoma Mountains, California

Luanne waited patiently for the first rays of daybreak to shatter the night sky. She drew in a lungful of crisp mountain air, a sense of gratitude filling her. She exhaled, her breath creating a foggy, evaporating cloud. It was her favorite time of day, though she was rarely awake for it. She pondered her streak of good luck. Her dream job had brought her here, to these mountains surrounding the valley below. And on someone else's dime, no less. If the theory surrounding the royal breakup proved true and if Caroline would agree to go on the record with an exclusive, Luanne would soon have the story of her career.

She watched as the sun broke, mesmerized by the simple but awesome beauty of something that happened every day. To the west was the Pacific, gleaming in the early morning light; the vineyards of Sonoma Valley dotting the eastern slopes below. She stood, grabbed her pack, bear bell and flashlight and reversed course. The trail, still dark, was damp with morning dew, but she'd come prepared for a full-on rain shower that never arrived, her hiking sandals offering solid traction. It was time to head back to civilization, shower, eat some breakfast and get on the road back to Los Angeles. Thirty minutes to the parking lot, an hour at her parents', then six plus hours on the PCH. She'd be back in the newsroom before the end of the workday. Not that journalists kept a nine-to-five lifestyle, but she didn't want to risk missing her new boss—the interim assistant editor of the *LA Times*. It was time to finally share what she was working on.

A tingly feeling ran up her spine, as she sensed a presence nearby. No sounds but the wind between the pines. She shook her bear bell just in case. She wasn't overly concerned. She was a seasoned hiker and camper and had crossed paths with enough bears to know what to do. She had made sure to keep all food wrapped, its scent undetectable. A mountain lion though was a different story. She'd heard of a woman who'd been attacked and escaped with her life when another hiker scared the beast away. The likelihood though was slim given cougars' tendency to stay away from humans. But she was prepared even for that.

That's when she heard the distinct sound of a gun being cocked. No sound like it. She'd grown up around guns. But hunting was prohibited in these mountains. It was California law.

"Hello, I'm out here!" she called out. "Hunting's not allowed in this park. And I don't want to be your unintended target."

A muscular hunter dressed in fatigues, a John Deere cap low on his brow, rifle at his side, emerged from the trees not fifteen feet from where she stood. Her pulse quickened.

She said, "You're out early. Guess you didn't know the wildlife here is protected."

"The wildlife may be, but you're not, Ms. Parker. You are very much an intended target. Just like Hernandez was."

She was stunned by the stranger's reply, her heart racing. "Who are you? What do you want?"

Instead of answering, he raised his weapon, his gaze soulless. A smirk crossed his lips. "Run."

Instinctively Luanne reached a hand out to stop him, then bolted. She ran, desperately trying to stay on her feet on the slick ground.

What the hell? Who is this guy? How does he know my name?

"That's it! It makes the hunt all the more exciting."

She looked around, panicked, trying to make herself a moving target. *Please God don't let me fall.* She left the trail behind, hoping for camouflage. She tossed her flashlight, aware it would only draw attention to her location and heard the crack of the rifle when the flashlight hit the ground.

A bolt of electricity ran through her leg as she slammed against a jagged rock. Her vision blurring with the pain, she kept running, dragging her wounded leg behind her, falling backward into the tangled roots.

And remembered.

Her dad's Remington handgun. In the unlikely case of a cougar attack. She pulled it from her pack, then lay still looking up at the foliage above her. She watched in horror as the hunter approached her, his prey. With eerie calm, he took aim, preparing for the kill. He never got his chance.

Luanne shot him right between the eyes.

CHAPTER 17

Los Angeles

J on entered his hotel room and sat at the desk, placing the muffin and coffee he'd bought at the corner café beside him. He checked the time on the hotel room's alarm clock. Quick math told him it was noon in New York. He dialed Terry's cell, then pulled up a list of questions he'd prepared on his laptop. "Hey, Terry. Are you still in New York?"

"Yes. At the conference I told you about. What's up?"

"I'm working a case and have a few questions I'm hoping you can answer for me."

"Sure. Good timing. We're on a lunch break."

Jon saw another call was coming in from an unfamiliar number. He declined it. Looking at his list, he read the first question. "Is it possible to get a good DNA sample from blood?"

"Yes, but blood doesn't last as long as saliva. The bigger challenge would be analysis. It requires sophisticated equipment, know-how, and time. The more detail you are looking for, the more time it will take."

"How long are we talking?"

"Anywhere from one to sixteen weeks."

"Hmm."

Terry asked, "Do you want to tell me what this is all about?"

Another call from the same number with a 707 area code. No voicemail. "I wish, but I can't." He knew if anyone understood it was Terry.

"Anything else I can help with?"

"A few more questions, please. Do genealogy labs have the right to test for diseases?"

"That's a grey area. Most people don't realize that according to company privacy policies, they actually take ownership of your DNA forever."

"Scary thought."

"Most definitely. Who takes the time to read the terms and conditions prior to accepting them? We just assume it will be a fair contract. That is not always the case."

"I don't get why someone would choose to have genetic testing in the first place. It just seems like DNA testing is opening a can of worms."

"For many, there are great benefits. Like confirming a diagnosis or determining if they are carriers of a genetic disorder. People with a family history of a genetic abnormality —such as sickle cell anemia or cystic fibrosis—may choose to have genetic testing before having children."

"Do the test results show which diseases a person could get?"

"Predictive testing is still evolving, becoming more advanced every year. At this point testing can detect the risk of developing certain diseases."

Jon didn't think he'd ever want to know that sort of thing. *Ignorance is bliss.*

Terry continued. "Like anything else, there are pros and cons. I use genetic mapping as a means of helping patients who are predisposed to certain illnesses and treat them prophylactically. It has the potential to save or extend countless lives."

Jon said, "With all that risk of privacy invasion, the cons seem to outweigh the pros."

"It's complicated. Many people agree that genetic testing makes sense for disorders that are preventable or treatable. But it's a murkier area for diseases with no available preventative measures. For now, much of it is up to personal morality."

His phone rang yet again. "I need to run now. Can I call you later if I have more questions?"

"Sure. I'll be at a work function later, but if I miss you, I'll call back."

"Thanks, Terry. You're a treasure." He hung up.

Jon accepted the call, then pulled up an email from Matthews. "Steadman."

"Hey Jon, got a minute?" Luanne's voice sounded funny over the line.

"Not really. My boss is asking for a status report. I need to get it to him asap or I'll never hear the end of it."

"Interesting. So, anyway, I'm at the police station in Sonoma." She said it like it was a common occurrence.

"Say what? Wait, are you smoking something?"

"You bet your ass, I am. I was almost killed! Stepped outside the station to smoke and call you."

She had his attention. He closed his eyes. "It was you calling me?"

"Uh, yeah, like three times."

"Rewind please."

"I was hiking my favorite trail and some guy with a rifle came out of nowhere, aiming it at me."

A weird sensation came over him. "Jeez. Are you alright?"

"Just peachy."

Jon thought sarcasm was as good a cover for fear as any. "How'd you get away?"

"I shot him right between the eyes." Her quivering voice no longer masking the terror.

"What!"

Now she began to sob. Gut-wrenching sobs. He waited as she calmed down, blew her nose.

"Yeah. I've never been so thankful for my years of target practice."

"Is he dead?"

"As a doornail."

"Listen Lu, you need to get your head on straight about this. Do you have anyone that can pick you up? Don't your parents live up there?"

"I told you they're out of town, and I think this would kill them anyway. I'm planning to come back to LA after I'm done here. It's going to be a very long night."

"What about a friend?"

"This may come as a surprise, but I don't have a lot of those."

"That's a long drive to make alone after such an ordeal." *Not to mention when you're high.*

"Then I'll stay at my parents' house."

"You really shouldn't be alone now." He felt like the responsible adult. "I have an idea."

"Stupendous," she slurred.

"Just hear me out. I've got a friend that recently moved to San Francisco. Her name's Melanie. She'll give you a bed for the night."

No immediate answer. He assumed she took another draw on her joint.

Then, "Okay."

"Great! I'll call her now. Wait there."

The call to Melanie was cordial and awkward but they worked out all the necessary arrangements. "Thanks. You're a good egg."

"Sure, no problem. I'll call her now with my address. Bye now."

"Bye Mel."

No love you's. From either of them.

***

San Francisco

Melanie stood aside as Luanne entered her condo. "I really appreciate this," Luanne said, putting down her backpack. "Fortunately, one of the officers brought back my stuff from the mountain." She looked around. "Nice digs."

"Thanks." Melanie took in the sight of her unexpected houseguest. Close to her own age—mid-twenties—with an unnaturally red, bluntly cut 'do. She was dressed in filthy hiking gear, smelling like a pot farm. And really pretty if you took a closer look.

"I could use a shower."

"Be my guest. Second door on the right. I'll have a cup of tea waiting for you."

"You're a saint."

Twenty minutes later, Luanne came out wearing clean leggings and a 49ers sweatshirt. She sat across from Melanie at the kitchen table, selected chamomile from the tea box.

"Can you tell me what happened?" Melanie asked.

Luanne did.

Mel said, "You're lucky to be alive."

"Luck and a steady hand."

Melanie was amazed by Luanne's seemingly relaxed attitude. "You work with Ed Hernandez?"

"More like *for* him. I guess you heard of him. He's an amazing journalist."

"He and my dad are great friends. I've known him my whole life."

"What a small world. He's not doing great. So sorry."

"Thanks. You know, he helped Jon out a lot on an important investigation."

A pause. "Oh, so you're the girl."

"What do you mean?"

"Jon mentioned a girl in his life. Implied it was complicated and dropped the subject."

Melanie remained silent.

"Sorry, was I not supposed to say that?"

"No, it's fine."

Luanne looked around uncomfortably.

"So, found yourself in a pickle this morning, huh?" Melanie asked.

"I guess you could say that. You're not from around here, are you?"

"You can tell? I've been trying to tone down my accent." She laughed. "I have certain southern proclivities, and all," she said with a long drawl.

"Makes sense. What brought you cross country?"

"An amazing job offer," Melanie said.

"Now *that* I can relate to. What do you do?"

"I'm a biochemical engineer. I work for a pharmaceutical company analyzing medicinal compounds."

"Lost me again."

Melanie smiled. This odd woman was spunky, cool, and self-deprecating. "Sounds loftier
than it actually is."

"But you love it."

Melanie smiled. "I do. My work ultimately helps people. How about you?"

"I went to Berkeley, spent a hundred grand on a journalism degree and couldn't get a job."

"How's that possible?"

"Well for one thing, true unbiased journalism is becoming a thing of the past and secondly, I guess I don't have the look. And I was a crazed activist on campus. Must've earned myself a reputation."

"Have you thought about changing your image to get a job?"

Luanne chipped at her black nail polish. "That's not how I roll."

Mel thought this woman sounded oddly like Jon. Pig-headed to their own detriment. Yet they both had jobs they loved. As far as she could tell, that's where the similarities ended. "Then, how did you land at *The Times*?"

"I got in as an intern, unpaid of course. But Ed saw something he liked and hired me as a full time employee. He carries a lot of clout there."

"You're headed back there tomorrow?"

Luanne nodded. "I would've driven tonight but Jon was worried it wouldn't be a good idea."

Jon was worried. Melanie frowned.

"Well, I'm sure he's right. Let me know if you need anything. I'll be up for another hour or so."

Melanie watched as Luanne headed for the guest bedroom, wondering if *she* should start worrying.

CHAPTER 18

Los Angeles

"Y ou ever kill anyone?" Luanne asked.

Jon was sitting on the lanai of Luanne's studio apartment, a matchbox space, cramped and messy. It reminded him of his place back in New York. He took a sip of his Budweiser.

"Well, have you?" she pushed.

"I try not to talk about it."

"Sounds healthy."

Silence

She continued. "It's the worst feeling ever. Even when it's in self-defense. Taking someone else's life, their future. The guy who attacked me will never have a chance to mend his ways."

"Maybe he never would have. Maybe he would have spent the rest of his days terrorizing people."

Luanne looked away. "Well, now we'll never know."

"Listen Lu. I know all about guilt tripping. It's not worth the ride."

"I don't think it's guilt I'm feeling. More like regret. Had I not gone out there . . ."

"The guy was seeking you out. It wouldn't have mattered where you were. Thankfully, in this case you were armed."

She thought about that for a moment. "I guess that's

true. And I wouldn't want to face that guy unarmed."

"Exactly."

"Thanks, Jon. There's more to you than meets the eye."

He winked. "And don't forget the silver lining."

She raised her brow questioningly.

"We now know we're onto something. You said the guy mentioned Ed. He was targeted. By a man who knew his medical condition."

"All that's true, but so far the guy's a dead end. By the time I left San Francisco he was still a John Doe. The police said they'll keep me posted."

"I spoke with the homicide detective. He was pretty forthcoming." He handed her a two-page printout. "Read this. While you were in transit I went to the local FBI office, requested the San Francisco FBI office update the database with the perp's prints and the DNA the M.E. gathered. It'll be quicker and more comprehensive than going through the PD."

Luanne started perusing the pages. A mug shot was included in the file. She didn't look at it. "He had a rap sheet a mile long but nothing that ties him to any of the companies."

"But now we have a name. Carlos Chavez. Born in Mexico City thirty-six years ago. Crossed the border with his brother at fourteen. Never left. His brother had ties to MS-13, one of the worst gangs in the world. Notorious for torturing their opposition."

Luanne thought of how he waited for her to run, like a rabbit he could stalk and hunt down. She shuddered.

"So, what now?" she asked.

"We need to get his bank statements. See if he was paid for the hits on you and Ed and by whom."

"I guess they taught you something in FBI school."

"A thing or two. But most of this is my own brilliance."

She gave him a playful pinch on the cheek.

"Ow," Jon said, feigning pain.

"Sorry." She leaned over and kissed the spot. "All better," she said, then went back to reading.

Jon touched his cheek. It was on fire. Temptation was pulling at him to upgrade the playful kiss to a real one. While he was deliberating, Luanne's phone rang.

Luanne said, "Hey, Caroline. How are you holding up?" She put the call on speaker.

"Day by day. Thanks for asking. Just wanted to see if you were up for taking a drive."

"Oh, sorry. I'm back in LA."

"I may be down there in a few weeks. For the time being, I'd prefer to remain in seclusion while the paparazzi is still fixated on the story."

"Understood."

"I'm also calling because with all the time on my hands now, I've been watching a lot of C-SPAN. It's the one channel I don't have to worry about seeing footage of me and Harold. I just watched Congressman Taylor's press conference. "Did you see it?"

"No. What happened?" Luanne decided not to mention her attack in the Sonoma mountains. No point in further upsetting the woman.

"He stepped down. Pulled out of the gubernatorial race."

Jon met Luanne's gaze, raised a brow.

Luanne said, "That's unexpected. It looked like he would ace the primary."

"It was really strange."

"How so?"

"It's probably better if you watch it yourself without my biasing your opinion. See if you hear what I did."

"Wait a second, I'm turning on the television."

Every news channel was covering it. The anchorman was recapping, saying the congressman was stepping down in the eleventh hour after discovering he had early onset Alzheimer's.

Luanne channel surfed till she found a replay of Taylor's speech. She watched the Texas congressman approach the microphone. And listened.

Luanne told Caroline she would call her right back and ended the call. To Jon, she said, "It has to be connected. Someone out there derailed the prince's wedding *and* the congressman's gubernatorial bid."

Jon knew they'd reached the point of a true conspiracy. "I think you're right. The question now is, who's next?"

CHAPTER 19

San Antonio, Texas

J on slid in beside Luanne who was seated behind the wheel of a black Dodge Durango. Luanne had arrived an hour before him and used the time to rent the truck. The layoffs story had taken on a life of its own. Now that the would-be wedding date was behind them, *The Times* newsroom was finally beginning to slow down to its normal frenzied state. New divorce rumors were leaking out of Hollywood for an A-list couple and attentions would soon turn there. Luanne's editor told her she could go back to whatever she'd been working on before. Little did he know she had never stopped. The time was ripe to investigate the shocking upset in the gubernatorial race.

"Welcome to the Lone Star State," she said in an affected drawl.

"Thanks, Lu. I lived in Dallas for several years. Feels like coming home."

Luanne handed him two tickets.

He looked at them. "A rodeo?"

"Didn't you tell me you're supposed to have fun?"

"Yeah. But . . ."

"But what? We're in cowboy country. What could be more fun than Texas barbecue and rodeo?"

Jon laughed. "I see your point. But you do realize that's not why we're here."

Luanne rolled her eyes. "Oh, really? I thought this was a vacation. You're only meeting with the congressman in the morning. Why waste the day?"

***

An hour later, Luanne walked through the door connecting their hotel rooms. She was dressed like a cowgirl in a sequined and tasseled mid-thigh dress, her flaming locks incongruous with the look. She twirled.

"I dug this out of the back of my closet before leaving LA. Wore it two years ago for Halloween."

"Sexy. You've been planning this."

"As soon as I learned we were coming out here," she said.

"You're something else."

"I'll take that as a compliment."

"You should. That's how I meant it." Jon felt the heat rise in the room.

Luanne didn't seem perturbed by the blatant flirting but didn't take it any further. She said, "If we don't leave now, we won't make it in time."

Jon said, "I'm in no rush."

"No way. We have to go." She grabbed his hand and pulled him to the door. "C'mon cowboy. We can enjoy some horseplay later."

***

Bulverde, Texas

Jon and Luanne walked under the wooden ranch gate, a giant icon of a cowboy, arm flailing in the air as he struggled to hang on to the bucking bronco, hung above their heads. The smell of barbecue wafted through the cool air. Country music emanated from a shelter with a sign that read, "Hootenanny

Sundays."

After finger-licking ribs and local brew, an older man with a long gray ponytail and braided leather bolo tie, took to the stage. He began playing his guitar, fast, belting *"Mama Don't Allow."*

Men in Stetsons, boasting belts with elaborate metal buckles, escorted their denim-clad and fringed ladies onto the dance floor. Children mimicked the adults. Jon felt at home. He extended a hand to Luanne, inviting her to dance. The moment they got onto the dance floor, the musician announced a square dance. Rather than leap off the dance floor, Luanne appeared to jump for joy. She was an anomaly.

They laughed like kids in their attempts to follow the leader's calls for "do-si-do" and "swing your partner." It didn't matter neither of them knew what they were doing. They were having a blast.

***

Salt Lake City

When Franklin saw who was calling, he turned on his humidifier. The monstrosity was ridiculously loud, but he'd quickly learned it served a dual purpose in masking his voice, in case his mother was eavesdropping. She never showed any interest in his dealings. Probably thought he was playing video games all day. But he couldn't risk it. The walls were paper thin.

"Got an update?" he asked.

"I'm on them." The man's pitch bordered on the feminine. He didn't sound like the type of guy Franklin knew him to be. Dangerous.

"Them?"

"Steadman's with that reporter. The weird chick. The one whose picture you sent me."

"Luanne Parker. She's like a weed. Keeps popping up." He didn't mention she was responsible for getting rid of his last hired help. "Where are they?"

"At a rodeo, forty-five minutes outside San Antonio."

"What? What are they doing there?"

"Right now they're square dancing."

"You've got to be kidding me. Well, that beats him poking his nose into my business. But if they're near San Antonio, they're headed for the congressman."

"What do you want me to do?"

"Give them a scare. And keep me posted if they head to Taylor. I'll need you to prevent their arrival."

"Define prevent."

"Broad definition. I'll leave it to your judgement."

"Fine by me, boss."

Franklin hung up, smiling at his new title.

***

When the dance ended, Jon and Luanne took their plates of pecan pie to the grandstand and found their seats. Kids dressed as miniature cowboys and cowgirls hung on to the corral bars waving American flags, staring agape as a rodeo clown with spurs on his boots, frolicked inside the arena taunting an angry steer.

The crowd was hollering and laughing, having a good, old-fashioned Texas time.

They watched in fascination as performers wrestled bulls, and competed in team roping, bronco riding and barrel racing. Jon realized for the first time in a long while that he was having fun. Once again, his shrink was right.

When the show was over, Luanne said, "Did you bring a change of clothes like I told you?"

"Yep."

"Let's go change out of these costumes. We've got one more activity on today's agenda."

This time Jon didn't question it. "Bring it on!"

CHAPTER 20

Bulverde, Texas

J on mounted the ATV, straddling the seat. Luanne got on behind him.

"Sure you don't want to drive?" Jon asked.

"Yeah, I've done this before. Go for it." Luanne's nose and mouth were covered with a black bandana, muffling her voice. Both donned helmets and goggles protecting them from the upcoming onslaught of flying dust.

Luanne couldn't help but laugh. Jon was certainly multi-faceted. She sensed he was more in his element here than sitting in his New York FBI office. He was smart, complex, quick on his feet. Also, sexy and a bit of a jerk. But she liked him.

Jon revved the engine and she took the cue, wrapping her arms around his waist. He drove toward the off-road circuit. They had the ATV for the next hour and could go wherever they wanted as long as they brought the vehicle back on time. Luanne could already tell Jon was going to take it to the max. Boys will be boys. Well, she could play just as hard. Always had. A tomboy throughout her early childhood, she grew up literally climbing the walls. In her house, on the playground. "Fearless Lu" is what they'd called her. Regretfully, she'd lost some of that wildness.

Jon took the first hill getting his bearings. At the top they had a view of the rugged expanse, the ground dry and rocky. Luanne could see several dirt bikes in the distance, their wide threaded tires jumping and swerving, like Evel Knievel of the seventies, the stuntman her dad had once told her about. The noise was near-deafening and she wondered why they weren't given ear protection like at a shooting range.

Within five minutes, Jon had the hang of it and was speeding along, the dry grass shivering in their wake, stirring up clouds of dust.

Luanne shouted, "Having fun?"

Jon turned his head a bit and yelled back. "This is amazing!"

She felt a jolt of joy that she was the one to introduce him to what could become a favorite pastime. *Get a grip.* Her last relationship had spanned a two-year period. Leading nowhere. Mostly because he had no drive. Her thoughts were broken by the powerful sounds of a dirt bike descending the hill ahead of them. The rider wore a black helmet, the visor making it impossible to see his face. It took a moment for her to realize he was heading straight for them.

"Jon!" she shouted, bracing herself for a head on collision.

"Hold on!" Jon shouted.

In an instant, Jon shoved the handlebars, careening to the left, swerving out of the biker's path, missing the collision by a hair. They had come so close Luanne could have reached out and touched the fringes on the biker's jacket. She turned to see the guy brake hard, his booted leg hitting the ground . . . and rev up again.

"He's coming back!"

Dead ahead was a hill, its steep rise preventing her from seeing what lie on the other side. Instead of slowing, Jon sped up. She had a vise grip on his waist as they went airborne, landing on the back wheels, then coming down hard, their bodies bouncing forward. It felt like her spine had compressed like an accordion. Miraculously, they were both still in the saddle. The maneuver had allowed Jon to make a U-turn, face his adversary. He wasted no time. Luanne sensed his strategy. It was the only thing that made sense—try to take the guy down while he was airborne.

Jon slowed as if timing his attack. The moment the biker crested the hill, Jon went for him, cutting off his descent. The biker's instinct to turn his handlebars was futile without ground beneath his wheels. At the last moment, Jon sped out of the way. Luanne watched in horror as in mid-air, the bike—its wheels still spinning fast—went one way—the man another, his body rolling to a stop at the bottom of the hill. He wasn't moving.

Jon braked abruptly. "Stay here!"

Luanne watched him pull out a pistol from a holster under his jacket. He held it outward as he approached the motionless biker. He shouted, "FBI! Don't move, asshole!"

Jon took a step at a time, finally hovering over the man, remaining out of reach of the man's splayed arm, ready to shoot if need be. No movement. He kicked the guy's leg, hard. Still nothing. "You can come here, Lu. Hold the gun on him."

She did as he asked and watched as Jon kneeled beside their pursuer and lifted the man's visor. His eyes were closed. She felt the bile rise, pushed it down. "Is he dead?"

Jon lifted the man's sleeve, took his pulse. "He's alive. Call 911. He look familiar to you?"

"No, I've never seen him before."

Luanne got her phone out of her pocket and dialed.

***

Jon and Luanne spent the rest of the day dealing with the local authorities, updating Matthews and identifying the guy —a thug for hire with a rap sheet a mile long. They had yet to determine who he worked for.

Back at the hotel, Luanne collapsed on the bed. Her back was killing her. A medic at the scene had checked her, and despite his coaxing, she declined going to the hospital. He said she would be sore for a few days, but it was likely nothing was broken.

"Someone's dead set on stopping our investigation," she said to Jon who was now lying beside her. He looked the same as she felt. Sore, drained.

"Sorry you had to go through that, Lu."

She had a hard time keeping her eyes open. "So much for a fun time, huh?" she mumbled.

He turned his body toward her. "Until that nut came after us, it was an amazing time. That hasn't changed. I appreciate the effort. I totally understand if you want to go home. Just say the word."

"No chance. I've got a huge story. I'm staying with this."

He kissed her on the nose. "All right. Get some rest, cowgirl."

If Jon had said anything more, she didn't hear it. She was already asleep.

***

The next morning, Luanne agreed that Jon should speak to the congressman alone. He probably wouldn't want a reporter tagging along and she needed to rest her back for a few hours. Maybe find a place to buy some weed. Texas was known as one of the most restrictive states even for medicinal cannabis. She'd go to the closest college campus. She'd find some there.

CHAPTER 21

San Antonio, Texas

C ongressman Taylor was sitting at the breakfast table holding a cup of coffee in one hand and a folded *Journal* in the other when the doorbell rang.

"I'll get it," his wife, Mary, called out.

"Who's stopping by so early?"

"Don't you remember that federal agent who called? Said he wanted to talk about your decision to pull out of the race."

"Of course. Sorry."

"No problem, honey. I'll be right back."

She opened the front door to what her mother would have called a strapping young man. Rugged with dark, longish hair. He was wearing cowboy boots.

"Good morning, ma'am. I'm Agent Jon Steadman with the FBI New York office."

"Please come in." She led him into the foyer. "I'll admit when you emailed us I wasn't expecting a southern gentleman."

Jon smiled. "I'm a hybrid. Born and bred in New England, educated in the South."

"Had me fooled. Which school?"

Moved around a bit but graduated from UNT."

"Then as far as I'm concerned, you're a local."

"Thank you, ma'am."

"No more now with the *ma'am*. Call me Mary."

She led him into the kitchen.

Jon took a look at the congressman, straight posture, greying at the temples. A pile of morning papers surrounded him. A lab mix was curled at his feet. CNN was muted on the television behind him. When he saw Jon, he started to stand.

"Don't get up, sir."

Taylor sat back down, gesturing to the chair beside him. "Have a seat, young man."

Jon sat. Mary quietly placed a cup of steaming coffee in front of him, dropping two sugar cubes into the brew, and left the room.

"Must be important that you flew out here to meet me," Richard Taylor said.

"Yes sir, I believe it is."

"If my memory serves me, and lately that's a crap shoot, you work for Doug Matthews."

"That's right."

"He assigned security detail for me a while back when he was working out of Dallas. Ball buster that one."

"Yes, sir. "

The congressman laughed.

Jon cut to the chase. "I watched your speech. I'm sorry for your diagnosis."

"Thank you, son."

"You referred to an anonymous letter that provided your medical prognosis."

"That's right. As far as I know the FBI was working on locating the sender. As you can imagine no one wants a U.S. representative's email being hacked, no matter which side of the aisle one supports. So far no luck."

"Do you know the name of the agent leading that effort?

"Um, Steve Reynolds . . . no, Stan . . . you know I'm not really sure."

Jon saw Taylor's frustration as he struggled to come up with the name.

"No problem. I'll find out and check in with them."

"All right. So what would you like to know?"

"First of all, do you have a copy of the original email?"

"Yes, I printed one out for you." He handed it to Jon.

Jon glanced at it. "Thanks. If necessary, I may need to access your email account."

"No problem. Just let Rowan know. That's my aide. He'll only be with me till the end of the month. I'm quickly being put out to pasture."

"I'm sure there's lots of things you've been wanting to do but didn't have the time. Now you can do them."

"You're right. I need to look at the brighter side. I'll knock things off the old bucket list. For as long as I can. I hear there are medications now for what I have. Slows the progression. Especially for early onset forms."

"That's good news."

They sat quietly for a moment.

Jon said, "Sir, can you think of anyone who would have it in for you? A political foe would be a good place to start."

"I've spent a great deal of time thinking about that. My supporters are convinced it originated from our opposition. But I'm not convinced."

Jon wasn't ready to rule out that theory.

Taylor stirred his coffee, went on. "What people don't realize is even those of us in political circles who fight one another on the government playing field often get along in real life. Many of my so-called opponents are personal friends. And while I'm well aware that in politics it's no holds barred, I simply cannot think of anyone who would stoop to this level. And logistically, I can't fathom how they got my DNA. I haven't had my blood drawn in two years. Too busy."

"It wouldn't necessarily have to be a blood test. Someone could have taken anything from a drinking glass to your hairbrush. It's really quite simple if you know what you're doing."

"Maybe it's a deranged supporter of my opposing candidate. Someone who just couldn't stomach me being the governor."

"It's possible, but there's another major factor here."

"What?"

"The same thing was done to Caroline Atwood."

The congressman squinted in thought. "Name is familiar."

"The woman who was to marry into the royal family."

"What are you saying? Someone accessed her DNA?"

Jon nodded. "Same as you. Only in that case, her results were sent to the queen, unsolicited."

"Unbelievable. How devastating for Miss Atwood."

"She's a strong woman. But yes, it has taken a real toll on her. At this point, we need to anticipate others will be targeted. We just don't know the motive. There have also been many people coming forward with stories of being fired, then soon after finding out they're sick. We believe the same people who targeted you are helping companies by exploiting their employees' DNA."

Taylor drummed his fingers on the table. "Criminal minds never fail to amaze me. With each technological advance there grows a new type of scofflaw."

"Human nature. Good versus evil. It will always be that way."

"I hope for a better future than that."

A woman in a white coat came in to the kitchen accompanied by Mary.

Richard smiled. "Hello, Denise."

"Congressman."

"Please. I've asked you to call me Richard."

"I'm still trying," she laughed.

"Jon, this is Denise, my speech therapist. She's working with me on holding on to whatever memories I have. Things like word retrieval and retention."

He watched as the woman took out an iPad and some worksheets. It was his cue to hit the road.

"Well, I'll leave you to it then. Thanks for your help," Jon said.

Jon put his untouched mug in the sink.

Richard said, "I would have to step down anyway."

"Excuse me?"

"While the invasion of privacy is horrible, the truth is, it kept a deteriorating mind out of office."

Jon nodded, and shook the man's hand.

Mary escorted Jon to the front door. She said, "It's good to be home on a regular basis now. Austin is a sweet city but we much prefer it here in San Antonio. The river, the history."

Jon had never been good at small talk. "He's a remarkable man."

She looked at him, her eyes tired and sad. "Yes, he is. And I want him to be remembered that way. He deserves that." She said goodbye, painting a smile on her face, and walked back inside.

Jon stepped onto the sidewalk, momentarily pausing in front of the congressman's stately Spanish Revival home, its red-tile roof atop an asymmetrical façade. It was a house fitting for a man who had served his country well, a man of honor. A family man. Jon felt a familiar and fierce passion. He would not allow Richard Taylor to be thought of as a victim. Whoever was behind these invasions, these virtual attacks, would be stopped. But first the Pitbull needed to pick up the scent.

***

New York City

The symposium was held on the third and fourth floors of the Grand Hyatt on 42nd Street, next door to Grand Central Station. Known for its world-renowned lecturers, the conference attracted scientists from all over the world. Terry entered the cavernous, high-ceilinged lobby, her heels clacking on the marble floor. She wove through a throng of lanyard-wearing attendees in search of their next class, made a beeline to conference hall A and took a seat in the back to the right of the double doors. She was ten minutes early, positioned to observe all who entered.

When Shira had explained what she had done, Terry was more than uncomfortable. She was distressed. Following Yosef's instructions, posts had been crafted and strategically placed on the dark web, ostensibly coming from Terry's personal device. The message, directed at info traders, alluded to her interest in selling her lab's latest advances, claiming she had been unsuccessful obtaining necessary grants. It stated that she planned to attend the World Symposium. In essence, Shira had turned Terry into bait, setting the stage.

Terry's role was to make herself easily approachable. Where she'd positioned herself, anyone entering the room would easily see her. As people began drifting inside, she scrutinized the influx of attendees. Not one made eye contact. When the lecture finished, Terry timed her exit to walk out after everyone had left. Except for a woman in her late twenties who lingered, staring at her laptop. Seated alone in the corner, she was easy to miss. Rail thin, limp hair, she was the quintessential wallflower. Terry was about to offer a smile when the woman stood and walked past her without saying a word. *Strange girl.* But no cyberterrorist. Terry knew it wouldn't be so easy. Clearly the broker was taking extra precautions, unlikely to show without establishing a secure environment. Terry would have another opportunity to draw out the broker later at the after-hours cocktail party.

Terry looked at her watch. Her rendezvous was set to start in a few minutes. If she didn't get moving, she would show up late.

***

Terry tried to keep up with the flow of speed-walking commuters pouring out of Grand Central Station. She turned left at the corner and walked a block south on Park Avenue, arriving at Blue Bottle Coffee. She ordered a skinny latte to go and stepped back outside. Seven minutes later she was walking past the New York Public Library, its entrance flanked by the iconic pair of stone lions. As a teenager, she'd been in awe of the ornate ceiling murals. Today there was no time to go inside. She entered Bryant Park, situated behind the library. She took a seat in view of two elderly gentleman engrossed in a game of chess. Focused on their match, they paid her no mind. She enjoyed the milieu, until Shira took a seat beside her, her hair up in a tight ponytail, Snickers bar in hand. "Shalom, doctor."

Terry knew Shira well enough to cut to the chase. There would be no small talk, only a status update.

"Jon was emphatic. He doesn't want the liaison job."

Shira said nothing, so Terry continued. "No one approached me." She hesitated, then told her handler about the young woman in the lecture hall.

"Never be fooled by appearances." Shira spoke in her characteristically abrupt manner.

Terry knew her handler was right. And yet. "You think it's possible someone like that is responsible for the hacking attempts on my lab's system?"

Shira took a bite of her candy bar, chewing slowly. "Possible? Without question. It's best you keep that fact in mind if you are going to succeed in this operation."

Terry didn't appreciate the rebuke but let it go.

One of the elderly chess players called out, "Check mate!" He raised his hands in victory.

Terry asked, "Why aren't the Americans dealing with this?"

"I imagine they are. But we look out for ourselves, doctor. The Americans are our friends and will remain such, but when it comes to security, we take care of our own business."

"Why do I have the feeling I'm being kept in the dark about some of this?"

Shira shrugged. "We all are. Think of yourself as a violin playing in a concerto. One of many musicians."

"I suppose Yosef is the conductor."

"Correct. Focus on what you do best and let Yosef manage the bigger picture."

Terry didn't like it. As a self-professed control freak, ceding it to others was a challenge.

Shira said, "Make sure you arrive on time to the cocktail party, hope the broker shows. If not, we'll make other arrangements."

Terry hoped that wouldn't be necessary. All she wanted was to get the whole thing over with and make her way back into Gabe's loving arms.

***

The Monarch Lounge was located on the top floor of a thirty-two-story building on the West Side. The space was classic Manhattan. Upscale, understated, tastefully appointed. And outrageously expensive. Terry was familiar with the borough's sentiment. *I'm better than you, but I'll do my best not to shove it in your face.*

Terry helped herself to a flute of champagne from a passing waiter and took in the scene. Tonight was surely not the crowd typically seen at the venue. Several people stood around awkwardly sipping daiquiris and screwdrivers. Scientists were not known for their social skills. She sat alone at a two-person table, no one venturing to approach her.

How will I ever find this broker?

Several people were milling about. One woman appeared nerdier than the rest. She was dressed in a modest grey frock. Her glasses were out of date. With poor posture, she seemed to blend into the background. Yet something about her was familiar. It took a moment, but Terry realized. The same woman had been in several of the sessions she had attended earlier in the day. *Is she following me?*

Terry reached for her purse digging for her phone so that she could photograph the woman and send the picture to Shira. As she did so, a waiter cleared Terry's empty glass, momentarily obscuring her view.

"Dr. Lavi, it's a pleasure to see you here. I'm a huge fan."

Terry looked up. Standing there was a thin woman, five feet at most, sporting a neatly styled head of short silver hair, intelligent blue eyes smiling down at her. She was dressed elegantly in a fitted black knee-length dress, its low neckline showcasing her crepey decolletage. A fashionable grandma. Terry was impressed. Unlike many women in her age group, the woman wasn't covering up. She appeared at ease in the surroundings, tapping her foot to Sinatra's *Fly Me to the Moon* playing on the overhead speakers. The woman exuded confidence.

Terry looked past the woman, relieved to see the nerdy girl was still lingering in the corner, peering at her phone, and gestured to the unoccupied chair. "How nice. Won't you please join me?"

The woman sat. Up close, her petite frame made her seem as fragile as the wine glass grasped in her manicured hand.

Terry said, "Have we met?"

"Sadly, no. But your work in predictive genetics is well-known. I read several of your journal articles." She offered her hand. Terry took it. "I'm Charlotte Colbert."

"What a lovely name. Is it French?"

"It is. Though it goes back a few generations."

"You're American, then?"

The woman nodded. The nerd was now on the opposite side of the room, a finger in one ear, speaking into the phone. She turned, made brief eye contact with Terry and quickly turned away.

Terry asked Charlotte, "What sort of work do you do?"

"I suppose you could say I'm a jack of all trades. Though my primary job is headhunter."

The woman chuckled at Terry's aghast expression. "It's just a funny name for recruiter. I look for the best talent in the science fields and hook them up with compatible companies."

"Fascinating."

"I enjoy it. As a matter of fact, I would love to discuss options for you."

Terry smiled, held up a hand. "I'm very happy at my job."

"Israel is certainly at the forefront of scientific research, but there are outstanding facilities here in the U.S. with significantly greater salaries than you could ever earn in your current role. Not to mention grant opportunities."

"Thank you, but I'm perfectly content in my Haifa lab."

"Of course. I understand." Charlotte stood, offering a business card. "Please reach out to me if you change your mind. If you'll excuse me, there are a few people here I'd like to meet."

Terry said, "It was nice meeting you."

Charlotte Colbert offered a polite smile and walked away. Terry scanned the room. The nerdy girl was gone.

Terry rushed out to the elevator just as the door closed. If it weren't so many flights to the ground level, she'd have run down the stairs. But not in heels. It seemed to take forever till the elevator returned. She punched in the lobby and minutes later was running out the building. The woman was on the opposite side of 12th Avenue, her hand in the air, hailing a cab. Terry saw one waiting at the red light, its numerals lit up, indicating it was available. She only had seconds. Swiftly, she raised her phone, zoomed in on the woman and took a burst of photos. Moments later the cab blocked her view. As it rolled away, Terry saw the girl. She was looking directly at her.

133

CHAPTER 22

Austin, Texas

Jon met up with Luanne at The Two-Step, a live music bar. They both needed a reprieve. He loved Austin, a magnet for country music's best talent, often performing for a pittance. He considered calling Gabe to meet up but decided it would be better when Luanne wasn't around and they could have a real guy talk. Right now, Luanne needed a friend. She'd had no success finding a joint and seemed uncharacteristically stressed out. She jumped on his suggestion to take in the music scene before catching their flights back to LA. It also gave him the chance to bring her up to speed on his meeting with the congressman.

The place was a local hangout, with a well-stocked bar, several chipped wooden tables and a tiny stage. Four musicians were playing some of the best music Jon had heard in a while. Within minutes, Luanne appeared relaxed, sipping a Heineken. Between sets, Jon excused himself and stepped outside to the outdoor patio to make a call.

The phone rang several times before Terry answered. "Hi, Jon. Give me a second. I just got out of the shower."

Jon could hear Israeli pop music playing in the background. It made him smile.

When she came back on the line, he asked, "Got another question."

"Go ahead."

The music started up from inside the bar. Jon moved to the far end of the patio, put a finger in his open ear. "Once my DNA is out there in a database, are precautions taken to protect it from theft?"

Terry said, "Labs take confidentiality seriously or they would go out of business very quickly. That said, once someone's personal information is out there, it's impossible to know who will access it."

Precisely.

Someone exited the bar, the band's tunes pouring out.

"Where are you . . . or shouldn't I ask?"

"I'm in Austin," Jon said.

"With Gabe?" Jon heard the excitement in her voice. It was sweet.

"Nope. With a colleague." He left it at that.

"If we're done, I'll go get something to eat. They're serving a dish I've never had before. The chef said I'll be his hamster. Wish me luck."

"Guinea pig."

"Huh?"

"Never mind." Jon hung up laughing out loud. It felt real good.

***

Austin-Bergstrom International Airport

"Steve or Stan Reynolds." Jon gave the names to Craig back in the New York office while he waited at the gate for his flight to LAX. Luanne had left ahead of him.

"Which is it?"

"I'm not sure. Just look for both." Jon didn't mention the congressman's defective memory. He could hear Craig typing. He asked, "How's the slave driver?"

"He's out again today."

Jon snorted. "For a guy who's always on my ass for not

following protocol, he's been AWOL a lot."

"Lay off him," Craig said.

"Huh? Since when are you Matthews's big defender?"

Craig lowered his voice. "Since his wife's been diagnosed with stage four cancer."

Jon was stunned into silence.

"You there?" Craig asked.

"I had no idea. He didn't say a thing."

"You surprised? He's not one to look for sympathy."

"Then who's running the ship over there?"

"He is. Back and forth to Sloan Kettering. Every day."

It explained a lot. Doug's recent agitation, low tolerance threshold. Ripping him apart in the men's room.

Craig interrupted his thoughts. "I got a Stanislaw Reynolds based out of the D.C. office. Here's his number."

Jon wrote it down. The flight agent called for passengers to begin boarding. "Thanks. Hey, listen, send Matthews my best."

"Do it yourself, Steadman."

Craig hung up.

Jon was making friends quickly at his new job.

***

Los Angeles

Pamela walked in to Peter's office without knocking. It wasn't the first time she'd done it. He seemed to tolerate her occasional intrusions, understanding her lack of social proclivities. But she wasn't prepared for what she saw.

He looked terrible. His shirt was wrinkled, his hair looked like it hadn't been washed in days and his eyes, drained of all energy. It looked like he'd aged ten years since she'd seen him last.

"Peter?"

He looked up. "Pamela. How can I help you?"

"Are you feeling all right?"

"Why?"

"You don't look so good. Maybe you should take the day off, get some rest. And a shower."

"I have work to do. All I need is a good night's sleep."

"Anything you want to get off your chest?"

He looked up. As if he were bursting to say something. Dying to.

He just shook his head.

Pamela said, "All right then. I just wanted to bring you this week's numbers. They're terrific. First time in months. Looks like the measures you've taken are working." She waved a report emphasizing her point. "We expect significant savings in employee expenses. If we can keep things steady, we'll be in good shape by next quarter. Congratulations."

Peter didn't reply.

Pamela said, "Aren't you happy with this news?"

"Just leave the paperwork on my desk and I'll review it."

She pushed further, uncharacteristically trying to cheer him up. "The board will be thrilled. Once again it will be Peter to the rescue. You'll be a hero, and rightfully so."

Peter looked like he was about to be sick.

"You know what Pamela? I think I'll take your advice." He grabbed his briefcase and his jacket and headed to the door, leaving her staring at his back. She turned to his desk. He had left the prospectus behind.

***

Peter was certain William Sherman could hack his phone. He didn't dare email or call anyone about this. It wasn't just the NDA. That he could deal with. Even jail time. What he'd done was reprehensible. He tried to rationalize it but his subconscious wouldn't allow it. When he'd heard that one of his best employees—one he had just fired—had been hospitalized and now had no insurance, he decided to break the agreement he'd made with Sherman. Sherman didn't seem the run of the mill hacker. Peter was scared for his safety.

For all he knew his house and clothes were bugged. When had he become so paranoid? He couldn't continue like this. The guilt was too much. Instead of driving east toward his house, he turned westward. Toward *The Times* building.

***

Salt Lake City

Franklin was scanning his sample results, looking for the next big target. He was amazed at how many people put their DNA out there for all the world to see. These genealogy sites' privacy claims were all BS. Once someone sent their sample willingly, the genie was out of the bottle. No way to put it back in. For a hacker, it was data mining on steroids.

Who would have thought he would make it this far? When he was fired from ItsRelative.com he was sure his life would take a downturn that he would never dig himself out of. But he'd learned to compensate.

Franklin took a deep breath, and another cookie from the chipped plate beside him.

Truth was he missed the job. It was good money, he could work remotely part of the time, and he made his first real friend.

Wang was an outstanding computer engineer. He'd gone to Stanford, one of the country's most prestigious universities, but never made Franklin, a graduate of Brigham Young, feel inferior. If anything, he claimed Franklin was the better programmer. They both admitted to hacking now and then just to prove they could. Sometimes they challenged each other on who could hack into a system faster, keeping them up into the wee hours until one of them succeeded.

When Franklin got canned after throwing a hot cup of coffee at a colleague, Wang came to his defense. Tried to convince the higher-ups that it wasn't a big deal. The woman wasn't even hurt, but they said that was it. While Franklin was incredibly talented, their work environment and safety was priority. They sent him off with two weeks' pay. His insurance ran out a month later. There was no choice but to sign up for government assistance. Embarrassing. He'd always looked down at those people who couldn't find a way to support themselves. Even the disabled. There was always a way. It took him a while, but he found *his* way.

Wang stayed in touch calling regularly and saying how disgusted he was with how things were handled. Said it reminded him of his younger years in Beijing. Where no one was ever given the benefit of the doubt. He said if it were him, he'd fight back, use their system against them.

That was the seed of their idea. Wang would access the samples on their way from testing to being discarded and salvage what he could. Franklin would be in charge of exploiting the resulting data without detection.

Their first victim was Franklin's ex-boss. All employees were offered free genealogical testing and nearly everyone had done it. Support for the company's mission. Wang took the boss's sample to his analyst, a woman he ironically knew from his church, who worked for an independent lab focusing on predictive genetics. As long as she got paid, she asked no questions. Turned out his boss had a genome linked to Spina Bifida.

It took them time to figure out what to do with the results but then the answer presented itself when the man became engaged. Franklin sent the results to his fiancée. One week later the engagement was off. No one knew what happened except for Franklin and Wang. The experiment had proven successful and a segue to what would become a thriving enterprise.

Since then they'd learned that they didn't have to stay confined to ItsRelative.com's samples. They could hack into any of the medical DNA sites that had already done all the work, and just pass along the data either for a fee, or as blackmail. Or as he was currently doing, to change the course of history. He hadn't shared everything with Wang, knowing he would frown upon some of his choices. Sometimes it's better to leave people in the dark. Even your only friend.

He loved that no one would ever suspect him, a pathetic ne'er-do-well, living in his mother's house. It made him feel powerful, something he never had felt before in his miserable life. And he would do anything to protect that power. Anything.

CHAPTER 23

New York City

Shira sat behind the metal desk on the seventh floor of the Israeli consulate. Concrete barriers ran along the exterior of an otherwise nondescript building. Sheets of rain pounded the windowpane, a myriad of droplets obscuring the view of what she deemed a perpetually gray city.

Shira uploaded the photo Terry had sent her of the woman at the cocktail party. A "Plain Jane" as the Americans would say. Unfashionable, awkward, forgettable. Desirable attributes for someone keen on maintaining a low profile. Terry had dubbed the woman, "Netta," short for the Hebrew slang for Netta Zar, a wallflower. Shira ran the picture through AnyVision, Israel's biometrics software, cross-referencing it with IFRS, Interpol's facial recognition system.

As she waited for the software to run its course, she considered how far Terry had come since their previous joint operation. The geneticist was more confident in the field, less jittery. Her self-defense skills were improving nicely. Still, in Shira's opinion, Terry wasn't the optimal asset. Yosef touted her scientific expertise, but Shira saw it differently. Terry had too much to lose. That fact alone could be easily exploited by potential adversaries. Unlike herself, Terry enjoyed close family bonds and was engaged to be married. Her fiancé, Gabe Lewis was an operational liability. Though he'd recently learned of his Jewish roots, Gabe was an American whose patriotic duty rested with his country of birth. As such, he was being kept in the dark when it came to Terry's clandestine work for the Israeli government. Until Yosef cleared Gabe, determining how much he could know, Gabe would remain on Shira's radar.

When the program stopped running, Shira was dismayed to find no hits. Netta was clearly keeping an impressively low profile. Or had managed to hack into some of the most secure websites in the world, wiping her profile from their databases.

Shira sat back in the chair, closed her eyes, allowing the sound of the falling rain to focus her. As Terry's handler, she needed to think what the next step would be.

***

Los Angeles

Peter pulled into *The Times* parking lot. He sat in his car for a few minutes convincing himself to go ahead. He left his phone behind and walked inside. He asked the lobby attendant to tell Luanne he was waiting in the lobby.

The man looked askance at Peter's appearance. "Your name?"

"Peter Cromwell."

He waited while the guard called. "She says to come right up."

"Please ask her to meet me down here."

The guard looked wary but did so. "She'll be down in a minute."

Peter paced the floor until he heard the elevator ring open.

"Mr. Cromwell, what a pleasant surprise."

"Sorry I didn't call first. I couldn't."

She wasn't sure what that meant, assumed he'd get around to it. Clearly, he was under stress.

Peter eyed the guard. "Can we speak in my car?"

"Sure. Should I bring my recorder?"

"Please don't."

He led her to his silver Mercedes sportscar and opened the passenger door for her.

Luanne noticed it smelled like it had just come off the showroom floor. "Nice wheels."

"Thanks."

"So what's up?" she asked.

He looked at his phone. It was off and so was the GPS. He knew he was acting paranoid. But better paranoid than dead.

"I'm not sure how to begin," Peter said.

"Take your time."

"I lied to you and more importantly, to a federal officer," he blurted.

Luanne was taken aback by the bold confession. "Do you want to call a lawyer?"

"It won't matter. I need to say what I'm going to say. What you do with that information is up to you."

Luanne let him speak until he was done. She was speechless. It was almost the same story the congressman had told Jon.

Peter said, "My conscience won't let me rest. Some of those people were excellent employees. They deserved so much better than what I did to them."

"Yes, they did. And restitution can be made."

He sat quietly, then said, "It will put the company out of business."

"Maybe you can start over again once the dust settles."

Peter shook his head. "My reputation will be demolished. I'll be through."

Luanne felt bad for him. She appreciated that he came forward even though it was too late for so many. But she felt even worse for people like Mrs. McAdams and Susan Goldstein.

"Why didn't you simply downsize?"

"It got to a point where we needed more drastic measures." A pause. Then, "I am so very sorry for naming you and Agent Steadman in my correspondence to William Sherman. I fear he may interfere with your investigation."

"Too late for that. My boss and I were both accosted since we began looking into this. So you can stop worrying about that. It was going to happen anyway."

Peter's face turned white. "If I'd thought he was capable of violence, I never would have agreed."

"There's no reason for him to suspect you're breaking your terms. But watch your back anyway. These people have a lot to lose."

"I've been vigilant."

"Good. Your coming forward is a huge break for us. It will give the Feds a place to start. They'll need your emails and chatroom access to trace the guy."

"Or gal."

"Right."

Peter asked, "Will you tell Agent Steadman?"

"Yes, Peter. He needs to know. I'll explain that you came to me on your own volition. Hopefully it will help diminish the consequences."

"Whatever happens, there's a huge weight off my shoulders." He let out a sigh.

Luanne got out of the car and watched Peter Cromwell, the CEO of OBooks drive away.

***

Salt Lake City

Franklin knew something was wrong the minute he saw Wang's number come up on the caller ID. He never called before midnight.

"Wang?"

"Sorry I'm calling now but I didn't know what else to do."

"Don't say anymore. Meet me at Boosters."

"Okay, on my way."

Franklin shut down all his equipment, called for his ride, getting himself as fast as he could out the door.

***

Boosters was a next-generation arcade. A huge space with laser tag, retro pinball machines, virtual games, and fast food. Franklin hated the noise but knew Wang loved the place, and it served the purpose of drowning out their voices.

Wang met him next to the flight simulator. He was dressed for work. Button-down oxford, pleated chinos, and loafers. His spiky hair was gelled. They fist-bumped.

Wang said, "We have a problem. Not something we can't solve, but a big problem."

"Okay. What?"

"You know how I installed an audio bug in each of our clients' phones?"

"Yeah, great idea by the way. Works even when the phone's off. Real state of the art tech."

Wang grinned. "Thanks. It still needs work." He chewed on his lower lip. "Anyhow, that guy Cromwell, the one we sold the whole employee list to?"

"Yeah, all those names took tons of time in the lab."

"He's bailing."

Franklin peered at his friend. "What do you mean *bailing*? He signed the NDA and paid us. We saved his company a ton of money."

"I got alerted when he left his office hours early and shut off his phone. I just listened to his chat with a reporter."

Franklin had never told Wang that he'd hired someone to take care of *The Times* reporter and her boss. There was no point. Wang wouldn't like knowing the methods he took to protect their business.

"Oh yeah? What did he tell her?"

145

"He spilled the beans. She's planning to go to the Feds to trace our emails and chatroom."

Franklin felt a prickle of fear. The woman was still alive, and he couldn't risk another attempt so early. Especially since he didn't have another brute lined up. He needed to think.

"This is really bad. They could expose our entire operation."

Wang said, "Smartest thing to do is go quiet for a while. Lay low until they give up. I'd guess a month or two max."

"No way. Who knows how long they'll stick on us? And we have contracts with other clients. We can't just shut it all down."

"If we stay active, the Feds will trace us eventually."

"I'll take care of it."

Wang raised a brow. "What does that mean?"

"Better if you don't know. Let me handle it."

"I don't know, man. I say we just shut down."

"Trust me. Just for the next few days. They won't be able to trace us that quickly anyway. If they're still on our tail, we'll shut down."

Wang looked wary. "Ok, Frank, I trust you. Always have, always will."

They fist bumped again and went to play some Skee-Ball.

CHAPTER 24

New York City

Doug got back to his office after four. He had hit traffic coming downtown from the hospital. He looked at his desk piled high with new reports. It would be a long night. He didn't know how much longer he could keep up this schedule. His boss suggested he take time off, but he'd refused. There was too much to do. And lately Erica was asleep most of the time.

He still couldn't grasp how drastically their lives had changed in such a short time. The cancer came out of nowhere. One day she was at the courthouse giving a closing argument and the next in the emergency room with debilitating pain. They admitted her right away and diagnosed her by the end of the day. If the oncologist's prognosis was right, she had three months max.

Everything felt different. He wasn't used to sleeping alone. He didn't know how he would live without her.

Craig knocked on his door. "Sir, got a minute?"

"What's up?"

"Steadman called with an update. He's back in LA from Texas."

"What the hell was he doing down there?"

"Following a lead. Looks like he's onto something. I can get him on the phone for you. Let him explain it."

Doug rubbed at his eyes. He was spread too thin. The

last thing he needed right now was to deal with Steadman.

"Just tell him to email me an update tomorrow. Dismissed. Close the door behind you."

***

Los Angeles

Jon was famished. After landing, he texted Luanne and they agreed to meet at the sushi place on Pico and debrief.

"Are you a sushi nut or something?" Luanne asked him.

"Since moving to New York, I've developed a real taste for it. Just look at this sweetheart roll."

"Okaaay. Maybe we can find a seafood anonymous meeting for you to join."

"Yeah yeah. So what's been happening here?"

She brought him up to speed on Peter Cromwell's confession.

"He also got an email from an unidentified hacker?"

"Yeah, who offered him access to medical DNA of his entire workforce."

"That's crazy," Jon said.

"What's crazy is he accepted. Trying to save the floundering business. He figured better to sacrifice some jobs than all of them."

"And that could only be done by invading his employees' privacy rights?"

"He felt he had no other option. But the guilt was eating away at him. He admitted to telling the hacker that you and I are investigating. He was told they would take care of any breaches. Bottom line he is scared now for our safety and his own."

"What an idiot. What did he think would happen?"

Luanne broke eye contact. "I kind of feel sorry for him."

"Well, I don't. Not one iota. He preyed on peoples' weaknesses to make a buck."

She had no answer to that.

Jon said, "I'll get local agents. They'll need access to his office, confiscate everything, get into his computers and trace them. See what they can find."

"He'll cooperate."

Ignoring Luanne's misguided empathy, Jon said, "You bet he will. If he knows what's good for him."

***

Salt Lake City

Franklin aka William Sherman had embedded Wang's spyware into Peter's system as insurance for cases like this. The app was genius. It would erase all his messages even from the hard drive. Any correspondence would be eliminated, never to be retrieved. Though Wang's spyware app was still in the beta phase, they'd used it successfully with their clients. Peter Cromwell's computer system was the most recent one they'd surreptitiously commandeered. And now wiped clean.

The app's design was still clunky, making the work painstaking but necessary. Once betrayed, Franklin was no longer playing the role of savior or cavalry. He was on the offense. And he wouldn't lose.

He didn't think of himself as a violent person. But he needed to make an example of Peter. Other potential clients must see there were consequences to breaking a contract.

He spent the next hour studying Cromwell. When he was satisfied, he turned his attention elsewhere, playing the latest Call of Duty video game. At one a.m., not tired enough to sleep, he decided to check one more thing. Wang's phone.

Franklin logged into his friend's apps. He didn't use a backdoor. Wang would quickly be alerted to that. And it wasn't necessary. Franklin used Wang's actual password. Several months ago, the friends had met for drinks at a local dive bar. Wang, a self-described lightweight had enjoyed one too many, leaving his phone behind when he rushed to the bathroom. It was an opportunity Franklin couldn't pass up. While sounds of hurling emanated from the men's room, Franklin ran password cracker software on Wang's phone. By the time Wang returned, Franklin had broken the code. It was more about the challenge than lack of trust, and Franklin seldom checked his friend's phone activity.

Franklin scrolled through Wang's recent emails and froze. Two days ago, he'd received a message via a VPN. The virtual private network allowed access to the dark web and prevented Wang's real IP from being tracked, a tactic all hackers employed. Franklin stared at the sender's name on the screen. The message had come from one of the world's most infamous black market traders of classified information. The White Knight. They were discussing terms of sale for Wang's spyware app. Further developed, the software would demand many millions.

Franklin read the email thread three times, unable to shake the growing sense of betrayal. Some might say he was a hypocrite. After all, he had kept secrets from Wang. If he was being fair, his secret could spark harsher ramifications for them both. And yet, discovering that Wang was negotiating a deal with a big-time broker behind his back was painful. Perhaps Wang would still tell him what he was up to. Maybe he was waiting until the deal was sealed as a surprise. Or maybe there was more to Wang than he'd realized.

Franklin would need to compartmentalize. He'd handle Wang later if needed. For now, he had Peter Cromwell to deal with.

***

Los Angeles

Peter knew the young Fed, Agent Steadman, was coming today. He was more relieved than scared of the punishment that would be meted out. He would need to call an emergency board meeting and warn them. And hand in his resignation. He felt bad for Pamela. She would be the one left to pick up the pieces. He had created a mess and now she would have to try and clean it up.

He stopped at his favorite coffee shop as he always did to pick up his drink for the drive in to the office. It was one of the few cafes that was completely peanut-free. A new guy worked behind the counter.

"Iced chocolate with low fat milk and light on the whip please."

He paid for the drink and walked to the door, taking a long draw through the straw.

He never made it to his car.

***

Jon arrived at OBooks with two other LA agents hauling cardboard boxes to confiscate Peter's computers. Curious stares all around. The worried-looking greeter told him Peter had not yet arrived. Jon would be livid if the man decided to back down now. He'd go after him with force.

Ten minutes later, a prim woman whom everyone called Pamela came running into the lobby.

"I'm Pamela, the CFO. I'm not sure what all of this is about, but I was told to cooperate with you. However, I just got a call from UCLA Medical Center. Peter was just brought in. He's unconscious."

Jon asked, "Did they tell you what happened?"

"He had a severe allergy attack. Closed his throat off."

Jon ran to the door telling the other agents to stay put.

By the time he arrived at the ER, Peter Cromwell was dead.

CHAPTER 25

Los Angeles

"**N**othing?? You've got nothing?" Jon was shouting at the lead field officer in charge of Cromwell's computer.

"That's what I'm telling you, Steadman. It's all gone."

"You mean to tell me there is no one in all of the LA tech office that can outsmart some random hacker? There's got to be a way to retrieve that data."

"If there was, they would have found it. Let it go. We'll keep on it but don't expect anything."

His one lead just hit a dead end. He had only ten days left to break the case.

***

Salt Lake City

"Oh God. What did you do?" Wang looked like he'd have a heart attack. He and Frank were back at Boosters, but the camaraderie was gone.

"Calm down. We had no choice. He was going to expose us."

Wang lowered his voice. "Cromwell's sudden death is all over the news. You killed him."

A young boy materialized beside them, his eyes wide,

clearly having overheard what Wang said.

Frank turned to the kid. "My buddy here is talking about a soldier in Battlefield One," he said, referring to the popular video game.

"How'd he do it?"

"With the mighty flame thrower."

The boy's eyes grew large. "Way to go. That one's hard."

Franklin gave the kid some prize tickets and he ran gleefully to his mother.

Franklin stared at Wang. "Take it down a notch. The man had an allergic reaction."

"You *knew* that. You got someone to serve him peanuts so he'd go into anaphylactic shock."

Franklin remained silent.

Wang was pale and sweaty. "I can't go along with this. We need to stop."

"You can't back out now. We have six other active clients. Let's finish those jobs, and then we can close up shop. You'll sell your app and never have to work again. If we're careful, we'll have enough money to last us the rest of our lives."

A tear slid down Wang's cheek.

Franklin said, "Look, you've already submitted all the samples for our current clients. All that's left is my job. I'll send them the data and get payment. Then we can both be done."

That seemed to calm Wang. "Okay. We can never speak of this again."

"Agreed. I'm sorry I upset you."

Wang looked away, said a quiet goodbye, and left his friend behind.

***

The truth was Franklin had no intention of closing his growing business. At least not until he got his full and final retribution on one more target. He had been tracking the man for years, well before he was fired from his job at ItsRelative.com.

He had bided his time, waiting for a ripe opportunity to take his revenge. He had the means to do so.

A hit man wasn't sufficient for this job. Neither was a dose of something deadly. No, those methods would only destroy the target. Franklin needed to destroy all he held dear. His family.

Sitting at his bedroom desk, Franklin pulled up the DNA results again. When the lab tech sent them over, he had to read it three times till he believed it. It was a jackpot.

The man had an illegitimate child no one knew about. Including his wife. The child was eighteen years old. A girl. The man had been married for twenty. Perhaps a need to learn her lineage had compelled her to submit to a DNA ancestry test. Finding her had not been a real challenge anyway. Franklin had submitted his own DNA when he took the job at ItsRelative.com.

His and the girl's DNA were a near perfect match.

***

Los Angeles

Jon knew it was only a matter of time before Doug would comment on his lack of progress. He was back at square one with Peter Cromwell's case. He'd skipped the memorial service but heard from Luanne that it was sparsely attended. For years, Cromwell had been a well-respected man until the final few months when he went down in a scandal. An unfortunate state of affairs. She did mention that Pamela, the once-stoic CFO, was sobbing uncontrollably. Maybe she had unrequited love for her boss.

With no reliable evidence from Cromwell or Caroline Atwood, Jon felt like the investigation was taking one step forward and two steps back. In Caroline's case, there was no obtainable paper trail. It had been sent directly to the queen's secretary. It would take an act of Congress to get his hands on it.

Jon spoke with Stan Reynolds to swap information. The man had conducted a thorough probe into the congressman's emails. The hacker must have a private server as no ISP was locatable. But there was a flicker of hope. One payment of two grand had been made to Chavez a week before Luanne's assault in the mountains. If a second one was supposed to be made following the success of the attack, it never was. After all, the man had a bullet in his head and wouldn't need the money. The issuing bank was based in Utah. That surprised him, given that all the victims currently resided in California. He would check it out.

***

New York City

The season's first snowfall was always a romantic time for Doug and Erica. On their first 'morning after' Erica had woken up in Doug's bed, opened the shades. "Snow!" she'd exclaimed with sheer delight.

Overnight, the world had turned into a winter wonderland.

They had gone outside and made snow angels.

From then forward, they managed to be together for each first snowfall and make love fireside.

As he looked out the hospital window, Doug knew they had shared their final winter together. Erica had opened her eyes only once since yesterday. They were giving her stronger medications for the pain. The cancer was raging inside her, more aggressive than they first believed. He knew her wishes were to not offer any lifesaving efforts. He prayed he wouldn't have to face that. He sat in the chair beside her, took her hand and fell into a fitful sleep.

His eyes shot wide open in response to a loud sustained alarm. Two nurses ran into the room, firmly telling him to leave. He was shaken to his core but abided them. On his way out the door, a doctor ran past him. He turned to look at his wife. The woman who stood by him the last fifteen years. As the door was shut behind him, he heard a sound he would never forget. The piercing sound of the heart monitor flatlining.

***

Salt Lake City

Wang returned to his apartment, drained, scared and confused. He thought he knew Franklin. Thought his brilliant friend had been mistreated. Thought they were alike, always on the hunt for a new challenge, even if it was occasionally outside the lines of legal practice. Most prolific programmers had dabbled in hacking at some point. It was a thrill. So what if he and Franklin did it a bit more than most? The business started out as a means of seeking justice, using people's own identity, no false accusations.

Even though Franklin had his own motives, Wang was glad to help. Granted, things shifted when he'd followed Franklin's lead to upgrade their efforts to a money-making enterprise. If they made a good living in the process, where was the harm? It was the American way.

Expanding to "social enhancement," as Franklin referred to it, was more of a leap, but there too, Wang allowed Franklin to talk him into it. He'd convinced him that keeping the royal house pure and the U.S. Congress available to the able-minded, were worthy objectives.

Never had he considered that Franklin was becoming obsessed. That he had only this left in his life that mattered. That he was capable of murder. Thank heavens he hadn't told Franklin about the negotiations with the White Knight. The guy had morphed into someone else. Someone dangerous.

Wang, while single, had a loving family. Parents who put him through the best schools and gave him every opportunity to succeed. It would kill them to know how deep he'd gotten into this.

He wasn't sure how he would extricate himself without getting on Franklin's dark side. But he desperately needed to try.

CHAPTER 26

New York City

Something was wrong. It was the last day of the symposium. Terry sat alone at a large round table, people milling about exchanging contact information. She had done everything possible to make herself available, and yet "Netta" hadn't made a move since taking off in the cab after the cocktail party. A bundle of nerves, Terry couldn't help but feel like she was running out of time. Would Yosef keep her tied up with the mission until something shook loose?

Terry took a deep breath, regrouping. *I never agreed to be perpetually on call. I can stop whenever I want to.* She took solace in that realization, mentally kicking herself for being so compliant until now. She was doing her job as best she could. If she lost her chance at drawing out the broker, it wasn't for a lack of trying. Still, the stakes were dangerously high and the pressure was more than she was comfortable with. Her failure could result in a devastating theft of her country's intellectual property. Perhaps Yosef had made the wrong choice with her.

Terry was about to make her way around the room when Charlotte Colbert sat down beside her. "How are you, dear? You seem . . . lost."

Terry offered a genuine smile. "I have a lot on my mind. Thanks for caring."

Charlotte opened her handbag and unwrapped a napkin revealing two chocolate chip cookies. "I stole these from the tearoom earlier. Would you like one?"

Terry laughed. "Sure, why not?"

Charlotte took a dainty bite. "You remind me of my granddaughter. She's younger than you but has the same petite figure and lovely blond hair."

A mob of convention attendees entered the room. A panel discussion must have ended.

"If I may be so forward, do you have a significant other? You're beautiful, highly accomplished. I've been known to dabble in matchmaking."

Terry scanned the room, studying the faces.

"You seem distracted," Charlotte said.

"I'm sorry. What did you say?"

"A significant other. Do you have one?"

Terry looked the woman in the eye. Charlotte dabbed at her mouth with the napkin. Two middle-aged men took seats at the far end of the table, chatting among themselves.

Terry said, "Actually, I'm engaged to be married." She turned her attention back to the doorway.

"How delightful. He's a lucky man. Is he here with you?"

"I wish. He's visiting his parents in Austin. If I can get away for a few days, I hope to go meet them."

Terry looked around, stunned at the sight of Netta outside the room walking quickly down the hallway. Terry jumped to her feet. "It was lovely speaking with you, Charlotte, but there's someone I need to catch up with."

Charlotte frowned slightly. "May I give you my card? I'd love to stay in touch."

Terry didn't hear her. She had already grabbed her bag and was running for the door.

***

Terry collapsed onto one of the lobby's leather chairs. She'd lost Netta. Again. She was sure she'd seen her, but by the time Terry made it out to the hallway, the woman was gone, swallowed up by the throngs of participants being let out of the final lectures of the symposium.

Terry was messaging Shira, requesting another meeting, when her phone rang. Her mood changed instantly. "Gabe?"

"Hi, honey. How's the conference going?"

"Disappointing."

"Oh, sorry to hear that." No follow-up questions. The guy was a saint. He knew she was on assignment for Yosef Kahn, but he somehow managed to keep his curiosity at bay. "Isn't today the last day?"

"It is."

"When can I see you?" he asked.

Terry's heart sang, grateful Gabe missed being together as much as she did. "Actually, I'm working on that. I'll get back to you later."

"If you need incentive, my parents are offering us their vacation home this weekend. If you like it, maybe we can get married there."

But I want to get married in Israel. "That's generous."

"Are you okay? You sound funny."

"I'm fine. Now that I hear your voice. If I finish up here, the weekend sounds great. Please thank your parents for me."

"Will do. Love you, Dr. Lavi. Hang in there."

"Love you, too." Terry hung up glad to have a possible reprieve from her current mission.

It was time to get out of New York, even for a little while.

***

Los Angeles

Theodore Davis turned over the non-descript mailer, inspecting it. No return address. It looked like junk mail but in a nicer envelope. And his name was hand-written, not the typical impersonal print. He added it to the mail pile to look at later.

His wife Nicole had asked him to drive their daughter to Little League practice. He didn't mind. Was glad to do it. He wanted to coach the team but for that, the time demands were too great. His growing business wasn't a nine-to-five venture. After years with Big Law, he'd gone out on his own, several of his big-money clients choosing to follow him. For the practice to thrive he needed to give it the TLC it deserved, even on the weekends. His wife was supportive of his good work ethic and looked forward to the fruits of his labor—remodeled kitchen and new flooring. But she also knew he'd regret it if he missed seeing their daughter grow up, and she was right. Their daughter, Lizzy, was a natural athlete. She could out-pitch any boy on the team.

"Come on Lizzy, let's go."

"Ready Daddy!" He delighted in his nine-year-old's exuberance, watching as she ran to the door in her red and white uniform, mitt in hand.

Nicole came to the door to see them off. "Have fun, honey. Break a leg."

"What?" Lizzy looked mortified.

Theodore and Nicole both laughed. Nicole said, "It means good luck."

"That's a weird way of saying it."

"I suppose it is." Nicole kissed her daughter on the head. "See you later."

"Bye, Mommy."

Theo said, "Me too." And Nicole kissed her husband as well.

***

Hours later, Theo and Lizzy came home. He heard his wife in the kitchen, then watched her walk toward him, donning a chocolate-stained apron, a bowl of cookie dough in her hands.

"Theo? How'd the game go?" Nicole asked.

"They lost but no tears so all in all it was a win."

Lizzy came in trailing after her father. "We had them, but then Jason hit a homer and we couldn't catch up."

"Sorry, sweetheart. Better luck next time."

"Yeah, next time we'll cream 'em."

"Lunch is ready. Go wash up."

Lizzy dropped her mitt on the floor and ran upstairs.

Theodore bent to pick up his daughter's mitt, tossing it in the front closet, then followed his wife to the kitchen. "Nic, I need to get some work done."

"No problem. I won't bother you until dinner." She handed him a plate with mini sandwiches, crust off.

He gave her a quick peck on the cheek, went into his office and closed the door. He took a seat behind his desk, moving a Lego castle to the floor and turned on his computer. He needed to attend to the last few emails that had come in.

An hour into his work, he needed a break and took to his mail pile.

***

Los Angeles

Luanne was reviewing her notes along with those Jon was able to share with her. Among them was his call with Dr. Terry Lavi, a premier geneticist in Israel who had helped the FBI on a recent high-profile case.

Something nagged at her. Then she saw it. Dr. Lavi had made a point that a hacker capable of obtaining such detailed genetic data would have needed both know-how and sophisticated equipment. How could random people access the equipment necessary to analyze DNA? It occurred to her that it must be a relatively small percentage of the population that had such skill and an even smaller one with access to the required equipment. In her estimation, it would need to be someone entrenched in that world, who had easy access. Perhaps a scientist, someone like Dr. Lavi. Or perhaps academics or lab techs. People who worked in places like Ancestry.com. Luanne felt like she was on to something. And needed to brainstorm. Two heads were always better than one. Even when the other head belonged to the cocky Agent Steadman.

***

Jon called Utah Bank and Trust. They would not provide any information about the transfer of funds without a warrant. He'd known that was likely, but it was worth the try. Having never obtained a warrant, Jon was unsure about the proper protocol. He called Doug. No one answered. He didn't know what that meant. The man was always available by phone. He left a message.

In the end, Matthews's assistant returned his call. A no-nonsense woman in her sixties. She explained the procedure was to call a local judge and obtain the paperwork. She would need a copy for their records.

"When will Agent Matthews be available to speak?"

"He'll be out of the office for the next several days."

Jon got a pang. "All okay?"

"It's personal. Have a good day, Agent." She hung up

Jon looked at the phone. He called Craig. "Any word on Matthews's wife?"

Craig instinctively lowered his voice. "She died this morning."

Jon felt his stomach drop. "Oh, no."

"Yeah, the service is tomorrow afternoon."

Jon asked for the details.

He spent the next hour narrowing down which judge to call and found one in Salt Lake City. Then, he booked a flight back to New York. On his own dime.

CHAPTER 27

Los Angeles

Theodore couldn't believe his eyes when he'd pulled out the three photos. He stood quickly and locked his office door. With trembling hands he studied the images. They were closeups of a smiling girl of mixed race in a pink scarf and mittens, seated on a park swing, feet dangling. Her father standing behind her.

His heart racing, he looked at the envelope again, hoping for some indication of the sender. There was none. Inside, remained a single sheet of paper. It was a printout of sorts. The type was small with lots of numbers. He put on his reading glasses, trying to decipher it. Only when he reached the bottom of the page did he really understand. DNA match: 100%. Paternity confirmed.

It had been fourteen years since he'd seen Abigail in person. The time had flown by. He felt a sadness come over him. So many emotions but mostly sadness. He missed his eldest daughter terribly. She was the spitting image of her mother, dark, flawless skin, fine features. She had a wicked sense of humor. Cheery disposition. The only resemblance to him was in her eyes. Blue just like his. Abigail and her mother, Janelle, had moved to Santa Fe when she was still little. Janelle had taken up art and had found some success there. Theodore sent money from a private account every month. And sent birthday cards every year, the last one for her eighteenth. He knew she was doing well in school, showing an interest in law, just like him.

From what he could gather, Abigail took a DNA test, possibly looking for details about her lineage, or to find unknown relatives. It made perfect sense for someone who had grown up without family. Janelle's family had disowned her once she'd become pregnant with a white man's baby, something her activist father would never tolerate.

The thing was he had never submitted to a paternity test or ancestry site. Yet, someone had obtained his DNA. But how? *Why?*

Abigail was a secret he had managed to keep for eighteen years. A short-lived torrid affair. He'd already been divorced from his first wife and remarried to Nicole. Janelle was a beauty, kind and generous. And forbidden fruit. Her father, a leader of the short-lived resurrected Black Panthers. Theodore had defended the man after a particularly violent protest. And met Janelle in the process. The man had been passionate in his beliefs, though Theodore thought he was living in the past. It was time—in his outsider opinion—for the movement to look to the future.

Theo and Nicole had been married for two years at the time and had hit a rough patch. Mostly due to his tedious work schedule. She was newly married and wanted her husband around. Time with Janelle's father allowed for close proximity to both father and daughter. Which led to Abigail. He learned of the pregnancy after she had already moved in with her grandparents in Detroit. He never questioned the paternity. Along with Janelle, they agreed never to tell Nicole. While they would always cherish their time together, their lives were too different and there was no love between them. Regardless of his actions, Theodore loved his wife. They had worked on their marriage and once on solid footing, decided to try for a child. Lizzy was a very wanted baby.

It wasn't lost on Theodore that there was no blackmail letter. It was both a relief and a concern. It meant he had no control. Nothing he could do to stop the sender from forwarding all this to his wife. The stalker was putting him in a position to keep lying to her until dropping the bomb and exposing it all. *Whoever's behind this wants me to dig a bigger hole for myself.* Theo took photos of the envelope's contents, then ran them through the shredder, obsessing over it. *What did the person want? Who would want to destroy my hard-earned life?*

***

New York City

Jon stood in the back of the chapel, holding a bouquet of yellow roses and lavender stems. Only a few family members were present. He could identify them by who was visibly distraught. Scanning the crowd, he saw a mix of federal agents and lawyers. Though all were dressed conservatively, the distinction was clear by their demeanor. The Feds kept to themselves while the lawyers worked the room. Some seemed to know each other, likely having worked cases together. Could be how Doug had met Erica.

The pallbearers had just set down the casket. He watched as his boss made his way to the podium, positioning his written speech before him, doing his utmost to maintain his composure, though unsuccessfully. He looked up at the crowd, spotting Jon dead ahead at the back of the room. He raised his brow in surprise and offered a nearly imperceptible nod.

As Jon listened to the eulogy, he was taken with how much the man had loved his wife. They had been what Doug called a perfect match. Simpatico, complementary. It dredged up thoughts of Jon's own lost love. As he watched Doug step down, he felt the anxiety rising, the sweat building on his brow and turned to leave. He needed air. He stepped outside, trying to recall the exercise his therapist told him would reduce the intensity of an oncoming attack. He closed his eyes, took in a long slow breath, held it and let it out to the count of four. On his third cycle, he felt a hand on his shoulder. He turned and faced Doug Matthews. They looked at each other, two faces distorted in pain, and before he could think, he brought his boss into a tight bear hug. No words were said. He felt the older man's body shake, and then with his head down, Doug broke away and walked back inside the chapel.

CHAPTER 28

New York City

The funeral, the lavender, the interaction with Doug. It was too much. The breathing exercises worked until Jon got back home. Still, he was glad he'd never refilled his anxiety meds. In recent weeks, he'd managed to wean himself off them and was determined not to go back. He knew about their destructive capabilities.

Entering his empty apartment, the weight of having no one there waiting for him settled heavily on him. Thoughts of Ashleigh resurfaced with a vengeance. It was more than four years since his fiancée's death. Since he failed to save her. Leaving him with a limp and a lifetime of guilt. He was overcome with sadness and a desperate need to find photos of her. When he'd started dating Melanie in graduate school, he put them away. Having them out had felt inappropriate. He searched for the box in the back of his closet. Since the breakup, they'd remained hidden. But now he knew seeing Ashleigh's face would be a lifeline.

Frustrated at shuffling through the boxed mess of junk and random papers, Jon spilled the contents out onto the floor, vilifying himself for not taking better care of them. He knew he had pictures from school and from the day he proposed. Instead, his hand hit upon the invitation to Ashleigh's memorial in Austin. Seated on the floor, his back against the sofa legs, Jon looked at it, wide-eyed. His life would have taken a vastly different trajectory if she was still here. He missed her to the bottom of his soul. He let out a deep sob, tears streaming down his cheeks.

Jon dug out an old stash of whiskey from the back of a kitchen cabinet. He'd intended to get rid of the bottle but never had the chance. His shrink would have a field day with that one. He made a feeble attempt at recalling her prescribed mental exercises, then took a long pull straight from the bottle. He knew where it would lead. He'd been there before. But now, as he sat among the paper-strewn floor, he simply didn't care.

***

Pounding in his head, pounding on the door. "Jon, you in there?"

Jon couldn't feel a thing. Exactly what he'd hoped for. It took great effort even to get his eyelids open. When he did, he groaned deeply, not so much from physical pain but from knowing he fell off the wagon. *Dammit.*

More pounding.

"Whoever you are, go away!"

"It's Doug."

No.

"Open the goddamn door!"

Jon heard the mania in his boss's voice and stumbled to the door.

Doug stood there, disheveled, a mess. His stubbly face was red with anger. Or was it anguish? For a moment, they merely stared at each other.

He has no one. Just like me, Jon mused. *What a pair.*

Doug pushed past him and into the apartment, sniffing Jon's clothing as he did so. "Nice." Then, "That reporter, Luanne Parker, called me. Said you rang her up in the middle of the night in a drunken stupor, babbling about Ashleigh in a purple dress. She thought you had a heart attack when you stopped in the middle of a sentence . . . Goddamn it. My wife's funeral was yesterday. Can't a man get a moment's peace?" He said it without conviction. A beat. Then softer, "Come on, Jon, let's get you cleaned up."

***

Los Angeles

Two days later, Jon sat in the lobby of his hotel, nursing a beer, its frothy foam dripping down the side of his ice-cold glass. He was waiting for Luanne. She said she needed to talk some things out about the case. He also had an update to share. The coast-to-coast flights were becoming more manageable. He'd slept fitfully for half the flight, caught up on some work, and read Luanne's most recent article—a take on Americans' obsession with royalty. She made no mention of the breakup. Or what led to it. The piece was impressive. Luanne was an excellent writer, offering the reader just enough compelling information to keep them reading until the end, leaving them feeling informed but not overwhelmed.

Jon drained his beer and watched as Luanne walked through the entrance. Today her hair was streaked purple. A line of studs trailed up her left ear. He questioned if the current state of print journalism was why she hadn't found a job right out of college. One look at her conjured up visions of a rule-breaking satanic worshipper. He laughed at the thought. She was one of the more level-headed people he'd met. As pop psych went, he guessed she was using her outward appearance as a defense, to keep unwanted attention at bay.

"How're you doing?" she asked, taking a seat on the leather chair across from him.

"Sorry about the drunken phone calls."

"Sorry I called your boss. I didn't know who else to contact. I was worried you'd hurt yourself."

Jon studied his empty glass.

"Wanna talk about it?" she asked.

"Not especially." The whole episode was embarrassing. To Doug's credit, after brewing a pot of high-octane coffee, he'd left Jon's apartment, didn't mention the episode again. Said nothing when Jon went back to LA. Seems there was a new truce in place.

"How was the funeral?" Luanne asked.

Jon shifted in his chair. "As one would expect."

"Good of you to go."

"He's my boss."

"And apparently a friend, if you flew cross country to be there."

Jon shrugged. His relationship with Matthews was way too complicated to decode. Changing the subject, he said, "An email came in this morning. The payments in Chavez's account were sent from a shell company in the Bahamas. Our techs will need to go backwards and figure out who established the company. Retracing the financial steps is like following a windy path of breadcrumbs where many of them have been eaten. It's a tedious and sometimes fruitless process."

A waitress walked by, and Luanne raised a hand, summoning her. "Please bring me a screwdriver, straight up. On Mr. Steadman's tab."

Jon looked at her.

"Business expense, right?"

"Whatever." He faced the waitress, lifting his glass. "And another one of these, please."

When the waitress left, Luanne said, "I was reviewing your notes. Your professor friend in Israel said something that got me thinking. We need to figure out which people have both the skill set *and* equipment to pull off the OBooks scandal."

Jon thought a moment. "That's good. I should have come up with that angle."

"We're not competing."

He let that go. "I suppose academics, lab workers, that sort of thing."

"Think your FBI magic can look into people who are in

those fields and cross-reference with criminal records?"

"Possibly, if the person had his or her fingerprints taken —like someone who'd been arrested or who works for the government. Otherwise, it's unlikely we would have them in the database. Besides, we'd need to drastically narrow down the pool. I'm only profiling and could be way off, but taking your thinking a step further, we're probably looking for someone who works for a lab located in the West. We could start by isolating DNA testing labs. How many could there be?"

Luanne looked on her iPad. "Twenty-eight to be exact according to Google. Now what?"

"We get our guys to compile lists of employees who have direct access to submitted samples."

"Sounds excruciatingly time consuming."

"I'll call my office and see what's involved."

***

New York City

It was three a.m. when Doug woke with a start, thinking it was all an awful nightmare, only to realize in the early seconds of wakefulness that none of it had been a dream. The space beside him in bed was empty. Erica's nightshirt was still in the bed among the sheets. He pressed it to his face, drinking in the remains of her scent. He was alone now.

Knowing he'd never fall back asleep, Doug got up, used the facilities and moved to his home office. He poured himself a scotch and went over his accumulating emails. There was one from his assistant, offering an update on Jon's investigation in Los Angeles. Steadman had surprised him, showing up at the funeral. And again when he found him passed out afterward. Maybe there was more to him than he realized. Just like Erica had said.

He read the case status report, realizing Jon may be in over his head. Warrants, probes. Doug felt a rare pang of guilt throwing Jon into the game without real guidance. With Erica's hospitalization, Doug had not been available. But Jon did have the resources of the FBI behind him, if only he knew how to properly use them.

He looked at the clock. It was twelve-thirty in LA. *What the hell.* He dialed.

"Sir?" Jon answered on the first ring, sounding fully awake.

"Just saw your update on the DNA case. Looks like you could use some help."

Thankfully, and he guessed purposefully, Jon didn't ask how he was managing. "The LA field office and Luanne are helping."

Doug said, "You'll need more."

"Okay. Who do you have in mind?"

Doug set his empty tumbler down on the wood desk, leaving a damp ring. "Me."

***

Los Angeles

It had been pure serendipity. Theo rarely brought in the mail since Nicole typically got to it first. But he had been running around with Lizzy that day, and the envelope was waiting in their box when they got home. Since then, he made sure to be first to the mailbox.

Now, another mailer had arrived, exactly like the last one. But this time it was addressed to Nicole. Theo freaked. *What is this crazy person doing?* Grabbing it, he took it to his office and locked the door. He opened the envelope. Inside, he found only the pictures of Abigail, no DNA printout. Just enough of a tease to stoke Nic's curiosity about who the girl was.

CHAPTER 29

Metropolitan Museum of Art
New York City

Terry sat beside Shira on an isolated wooden bench in the middle of the second-floor gallery, enjoying an unobstructed view of Renoir's *By the Seashore*. The painted woman was seated in her wicker chair staring back at them with hooded eyes.

Keeping her head facing forward, Shira said, "There's no way you can leave now. You're in the middle of a mission. A few days off can result in an egregious attack on our classified systems."

"I'm not the right person for the job."

"I agree, but it's too late. You signed up for this —"

"For a few days, not indefinitely," Terry interrupted, irritated by the quick affirmation of her inadequacy.

"Your personal life is of little concern at the moment."

Familiar with Shira's poor social skills, Terry tried to maintain her composure. "This is not only about Gabe. I still have a very demanding job at my lab. There is only so long I can allow others to handle my workload."

An elderly couple holding hands entered the gallery, stopping in front of *In the Meadow*. It was one of Terry's favorites. A poster of the oil painting still hung on the wall of her childhood bedroom, a gift from her grandmother who claimed the blond girl in the white dress reminded her of Terry.

Shira said, "I'm sorry that our country's security issues are not occurring at a more convenient time for you."

Terry felt her face heat up. It took all her restraint to wait until the couple walked away. When they did, she turned to face Shira's still profile. Terry's volume crept up several notches. "I think we've already established that guilt tripping me will only backfire!"

A stout female guard standing along the far wall stared at the women, lifting a finger to her lips. Terry stood up and without another word, strode to the exhibit's exit. She flew down the grand marble staircase, whisking past the rotunda's information desk and out the front door.

Shira caught up with her atop the museum's iconic steps where tourists and New Yorkers sat eating their lunch. She spoke just above a whisper, her tone void of emotion. "You have a decision to make, doctor. If you choose to bail out now, it will delay us, but we will find someone else. I can say without question that you will no longer be called upon to assist in government matters. This is not a guilt trip. It is basic logic. We need operatives who can see a mission through to its end. I will need a decision by the morning." With that, Shira descended to the sidewalk of Fifth Avenue and disappeared from sight.

Terry felt her ire abate. She caught a glimpse of her reflection in the museum's large glass door. Her face was drawn, conflicted. Once again, she found herself torn between love and duty.

***

FBI Field Office
Los Angeles

Doug Matthews sat across from Jon in one of the smaller conference rooms. The smell of burnt coffee permeated the space. "Profiling is a quasi-science, but one that is used regularly in our field. Not especially PC, but it works."

Jon sized up his boss. He appeared thinner, gaunt. Defeated. He knew Doug had come to LA more so to get his mind off his wife's death than to help with the case. But that was fine. He had been in Doug's shoes and knew the drill. Distraction was nearly as good a healer as time. If losing himself in work would numb the pain, all the power to him.

Doug looked down at Jon's report and continued. "Seems Ms. Parker got started on profiling. Let's see if we can further narrow the field. Who would fit the bill of this sort of perp?"

"How do you mean?"

"Let's start with age."

"I'd say probably someone on the younger side."

Doug nodded. "Yes, likely. And backed by stats. Write that down."

Jon took a red marker, stood, and wrote it on the white board bolted to the wall.

Doug asked, "Ethnicity? Gender?"

Jon shrugged. "Could be anything."

"We're talking likelihoods, not facts. Take an educated guess."

"From what I've read, statistically, hackers tend to be white males."

"Correct."

Jon added that to his written list.

"Marital status?"

"Almost always single," Jon ventured.

"Now I'll add in my experience with hackers. Usually unemployed, living with another family member who financially supports them, social pariahs, exceptional IQ."

"If they're so smart, why are they unemployed?"

Doug put down the report, looked at Jon. "There's IQ and EQ. Those with emotional or social ineptitude are less likely to hold down a job for extended periods."

Jon thought about that. "That would eliminate professors. Especially if they are tenured."

"Good."

Jon enjoyed the rare praise.

"So, that leaves us with who?" Doug asked.

"More transient but knowledgeable workers."

"Right. Think lab techs, computer geeks, those sorts."

Jon jotted down all the traits. It was a long, impressive list.

Doug pointed to the board. "That's where we start."

**

New York City

Terry tossed and turned, unable to sleep. As much as she hated to admit it, the decision was an easy one. For better or worse, she was a pragmatist. Her country needed her service, and she loved her country. She loved Gabe as well, but if she missed the weekend with him, there would be no ramifications. She couldn't say the same for taking a few days away from the mission. Even if she was severely burnt out.

Despite their temperamental differences, Shira was right. If Terry wanted to keep her unique role with the Mossad, she would need to stick with the mission to the end. She wasn't ready to permanently walk away from her special status with the intelligence agency. She'd been handed a unique opportunity to make a difference and knew it was an honor and a privilege. Decision made, she called Shira. It was nearly one a.m. If she woke Shira, so be it.

Her handler picked up on the first ring. "What's your decision?"

Terry no longer expected a proper phone greeting. She had long ago assumed Shira was on the spectrum, the subtleties of social interaction lost on her.

"I'm staying."

"Tov." *Good.* "Check your email for further instructions."

Terry heard a click. The conversation was over.

***

Los Angeles

The next morning, Jon and Matthews were back in the same seats. With the Fed techs having more manageable parameters to work with, they'd sent over a short list of nine names. Jon was hopeful to finally get a lead.

"None of these are perfect matches. Let's start at the top."

The two men worked through the list, pointing things out along the way.

Jon said, "Seventy-nine percent match with Jason Wang. Thirty-two, works for ItsRelative.com, an online genealogy company in a place called Lehi. Been there for six years."

"Pretty stable career. That's why the lower relevancy score." Matthews read from his copy. "Computer programmer. No record. Went to Stanford. Seems he dabbled in hacking while there, almost got suspended but was given a pass for first offense. Without malice."

Jon pulled out the paperwork on the next name. Then stopped. "Hey, wait a second. Where's Lehi?" He pulled out his iPhone and checked. "No way."

"What?"

Jon ecstatically drum-rolled the table. "Sir, I think we got him."

***

The next few hours were spent pulling up everything they could find on Jason Wang. Lehi was in North-central Utah, the same area the payments to Chavez were sent from. It was too much of a coincidence.

Wang was the only child of Chinese immigrants who resided in Los Angeles County. After he had excelled in high school, his parents scraped and sacrificed to send him to one of the best schools in the country.

A warrant allowed for access to his credit cards. They showed he flew home once a month to visit his parents for the weekend. Helped them with expenses. No girlfriend but was well-liked at work. Hadn't missed a day on the job since he started. Till now.

Jon didn't think Wang matched the profile they came up with and said so.

Matthews said, "I agree. Something feels off. But we need to check it out. Determine if the Utah connection is nothing more than a strange coincidence."

"You don't believe in coincidences."

"Correct."

"Then, what's the strategy?"

"We contact the company and tell them there's been a breach in confidentiality. Then we lie in wait. See who bails."

"Why not target him directly?"

"Never a good idea in these sorts of situations. He would clam up, claim he had nothing to do with it. Without proof, it's a false accusation and a black mark for the Feds. This isn't a police state. He needs to mess up for us to go after him."

With that, Matthews wrote a strongly worded letter without pointing fingers, addressed to the CEO of ItsRelative. Vague but suggestive. He sent it overnight delivery. Signed on New York FBI letterhead. A letter like that would get their full attention.

***

Salt Lake City

Franklin checked the Facebook page, something he did nearly every day. He was a voyeur, wanting to know everything about the man's life. He knew he should stop, but he couldn't help himself. For years he cyberstalked the man. Well, now he could finally exact his revenge.

***

Los Angeles

Theo's mind was spinning, unable to focus on anything. He understood whoever sent him the letter was toying with him, watching him squirm. Technically, it wasn't blackmail if they weren't asking for anything. He briefly considered telling Nicole everything but shelved the idea. He knew his wife. Infidelity, even years old, would not be tolerated. Let alone a child she never knew of. She would view it as the ultimate betrayal. Their marriage would be over. He'd have to fight to see Lizzy. He couldn't bear having no relationship with another one of his children. It was time he did something about it.

***

Luanne was keeping vigilant. She never left home without her Sig now. The coldness of the metal at her back was comforting. Stepping into the hospital lobby, the smell of antiseptic stung her nostrils. She looked around, grateful there was no metal detector. The doctor had called saying it may be helpful for Ed to have visitors. She knew his girlfriend had stopped by but no one else.

Ed had no family other than an ailing sister. Luanne approached the information desk, asked the attendant for Ed's room and was guided to the third floor ICU. Despite her arrival during visiting hours, the corridor was deathly quiet, save for the ubiquitous sounds of beeping machinery. She supposed most patients were not conscious in this ward.

Luanne passed the nurses' station and made her way to room 302. A large window offered a view of the interior from the hallway. Ed lay in bed, gaunt, hooked up to various monitors, an IV stand beside his bed. She'd never seen him so thin. If he was awake, she knew he'd joke about what it took to lose a few pounds. Quietly, she opened the door and stepped inside, unsure what she was supposed to do.

She sat down, noting the flowers she'd sent were arranged at the bedside. Ed stirred, flickered his eyes open and looked at her. For a moment his face remained blank, then a slight expansion of his eyes and a look of recognition. The tube in his throat prevented him from speaking. He blinked and raised a hand a few inches in greeting.

Luanne smiled. "Hi, Ed. Funny meeting you here." *What the hell am I saying?* Humor had always been a defense mechanism. Even back in school when kids made fun of her 'look.'

Gearing for a one-way conversation, she began. "The guy who attacked you is dead. I shot him when he came after me." This seemed to agitate Ed more than appease him.

"I'm fine, see?" She stood, twirling, then sat back down, Ed watching her closely throughout. "Put my dad's gun to good use. Whoever is behind this wants us to stop investigating the layoffs. I've made a lot of headway but still haven't found who's behind it. Actually, the case has grown exponentially. I won't get into the details now, but Jon Steadman is the one that got the ball rolling and has the FBI behind him. We're not pulling any punches."

With the mention of Jon's name, Ed seemed to calm.

He believes in him, Luanne thought.

"There's more, but I'll let you rest. Just get better fast so I can have my mentor and friend back soon. Okay?"

Ed gave a small smile, nodded, and closed his eyes.

***

Lehi, Utah

Wang arrived at his cubicle at 7:45. He liked coming in early, before everyone, when the floor was still quiet. It was his most productive time. He also intended to catch up on some work he'd neglected. Over the last several days he'd lost his focus.

He looked at the photo pinned to the board on his divider wall. It was of him with his mother on his graduation day. His father had taken it, making faces to get them to laugh. His father's usual stoic demeanor was superseded by the joy of having their son graduate from Stanford. That was a great day. Since then, he'd designed a sophisticated ten-year-plan comprised of goal markers he'd set for himself. So far, he was on schedule—tech-based job with a promising company, check. Enviable starting salary and benefits, check. He'd even met his deadline for the beta stage of his surveillance app. He wondered what would happen if his parents learned of his involvement with Franklin. It had begun with good intentions. He'd befriended the shy programmer, a co-worker for two years. They had gaming in common, and Wang grew to feel protective of him. Other employees either ignored or just tolerated him. It amazed Wang how few people were comfortable with someone like Franklin. He never really understood it but as always, he took up the cause of the underdog. When Franklin was put on probation for using expletives to describe his department manager on social media for all to see, Wang was the first to defend him, saying he'd been under a great deal of stress with family problems.

Franklin had believed he couldn't get fired. Turned out he was wrong. He went too far when he threw his coffee at a co-worker. She had made an insensitive comment she later attributed to hormones. She'd been pregnant at the time, and the company could be liable. They fired Franklin the next day. Wang kept up with his friend, checking on him periodically and playing games online nearly every evening. When Franklin told him his idea of selling DNA data, he was skeptical . . . but intrigued. Franklin was, if nothing else, persuasive, even charismatic when he wanted to be. When they'd made a killing on their first client—more than three months' salary in two weeks—Wang was sold. He used the windfall to buy his parents a new car, insinuating he'd saved the money. By the second sale, he had a list of things he would spend the new-found money on.

Seated at his desk, Wang took a sip of his ginger-peach green tea and opened his email. A company-wide memo sent only minutes earlier informed all personnel of a virtual live meeting with the CEO later that morning. For a moment, he wondered if Franklin had surreptitiously taken on his old employer as a client. Was his own job in jeopardy? He realized he was being paranoid but couldn't shake his unease.

As workers started piling in, he heard the worried whispers as they opened their own email inboxes. "This can't be good," he heard one woman say. "They never do these virtual meetings unless they're announcing something big. And big is almost always bad."

Ten minutes prior to the presentation, Wang and his coworkers shuffled into the assembly room. The floor manager set up the screen and audio. At the top of the hour, the face of the company's CEO filled the screen, a highly fit man in his late fifties.

"Thank you all for attending. It's been quite a morning." His demeanor was frustrated and resolute.

Wang's shoulders slouched. Any hopes of good news were dashed.

"Yesterday I received a certified letter from the New York office of the FBI. They are planning to open an investigation into our company for privacy law infringement. While I don't yet have details, they believe at least one employee—and possibly more—is selling our DNA results to outside parties for profit."

Wang thought he'd pass out.

The people in the room looked around, as if the CEO was Hercule Poirot. *Who was the culprit?*

"Needless to say, this is an egregious breach of confidentiality and of our company's creed. Consequences are severe.

Immediate dismissal and federal charges. That being said, they've agreed to give us a week to weed out these employees. During that time they will keep the matter under wraps. It is in all of our best interest to keep a lid on this until either the culprit presents himself or the FBI makes it public. We are appealing to those who have done this. You have an opportunity to redeem yourselves. Perhaps not from prosecution, but from some of the havoc you've caused. Coming forward quietly will allow for this company to remain in good standing with our customers. We will of course need to overhaul our privacy software and determine a more secure method of human access to the samples.

"If the person or persons responsible for this crime come forward within the week, I will personally request leniency of punishment, though to be honest, I have only so much clout. This sort of breach has the capacity to ruin our business and the livelihood of hundreds of employees. We don't take this lightly."

Wang felt beads of sweat bleeding through his button-down. He couldn't catch his breath. He needed to get out of there but didn't want to bring attention to himself. He closed his eyes. *Calm down. Think.* There was no benefit to coming forward. The punishment would be jail time no matter what.

He had to contact Franklin. But what if the Feds were tapping their phones already?

He had no choice but to wait until the end of the workday, then see Franklin in person. He thought of his bright future. His app would make millions and allow his parents to retire. His ten-year plan couldn't be derailed.

CHAPTER 30

Los Angeles

"Jon, I need a favor." Terry's voice sounded strained, stressed.

"Sure, what's up?" Jon said, driving to the hotel from the field office.

A pause. "Let me rephrase that. *Israel* needs a favor."

"Oh, you're back in the field."

"It will need to remain classified," Terry said, avoiding a direct reply.

"Whoa. If you mean that I can't share it with Matthews, then no. It would be the fastest way to getting fired . . . if I'm not charged first with treason."

"I'd never ask you to withhold information. We'll both need to get clearance for this from our bosses."

"What makes you think Yosef Kahn is going to be okay with talking shop with the FBI on sensitive matters?"

Terry had already considered that. "Because he's been trying to get you to act as liaison."

"With the Shin Bet, not the Mossad.

"Wouldn't this be a version of that very objective?"

"I'll speak to Matthews."

"Thanks, Jon."

"You're welcome. Terry?"

"Hmm?"

"Be careful. My best friend is counting on you being

around for a very long time."

***

Jon wasn't good at playing the waiting game. He left a message for Doug to call him, but needed something to keep his mind occupied until something or someone shook loose in the investigation. He looked inside the hotel room's mini-bar. Nothing but a miniature Budweiser.

He grabbed his phone, punched in the number. "Hey, Mel."

"Hey." She sounded distracted. "How are you?"

"Just thinking about you."

"That's nice. You still in LA?"

That's nice?

"Yeah, there's a temporary lull in the case. Thought I'd see what you're up to."

He could hear her typing in the background. "You busy?"

"Just finishing up some work." She continued typing. "Job's great. My apartment is awesome. I'm actually going to a building party tonight. That's why I'm doing some work now so I won't have it weighing on me at the party."

"What's a building party?"

"Pretty much what it sounds like. Most of the occupants are young and single."

Jon felt a pang of jealousy. He had no right. They'd agreed to see other people. But it was still hard. His feelings were confusing. He loved her, but maybe the distance *didn't* make the heart grow fonder. Maybe the old adage was a crock. If he was honest with himself, the intensity of his feelings wasn't what it once was.

She asked, "Any chance you can come for a couple of days?"

"I wish I could Mel, but I need to be around in case something breaks."

Mel was quiet for a moment. The typing stopped. Then," Jonathan . . ."

Jonathan?

He girded himself for what was inevitably coming next. "I've been doing a lot of thinking . . ."

***

San Francisco

Melanie hung up the phone. It was one of the hardest things she could remember doing. Breaking it off completely with Jon. Again. They'd been through so much together. But the on-and-off was too much. For both of them. She still loved him, but the last few months felt like purgatory . . . neither one of them able or willing to make the sacrifice of relocating for the other. What did that mean in the grand scale of things? Besides, Jon had issues. She knew everyone did, herself included, but Jon was on another plane. An orphan with no siblings, brought up by his grandmother, the survivor of a campus massacre, losing his fiancée. *His fiancée.* Sometimes it felt like the ghost of Ashleigh Lewis would always be there in the background. There were good reasons for his emotional problems. And yes, he'd made significant strides, but maybe the old expression was true. There are people who come into your life for a reason, a season, or a lifetime.

The Meatloaf lyrics came to mind. *Two out of three ain't bad.*

***

Los Angeles

It felt like a punch in the gut. Pain, deep down. Heartache. Loss. He knew these feelings well. Better than most. Yet, those experiences had taught him the pain would dull with time. He would be okay. There were so many things worse than a broken heart.

Lying on the bed, his phone still on the blanket beside him, he forced down the impulse to throw it against the wall. Despite the tsunami of emotions, he realized he hadn't had an anxiety attack since Erica's funeral.

Mel was right. Their lives were not converging, the feelings between them growing increasingly complicated. He was happy for her, but truth be told, he wasn't ready for her to move on. He'd hash it out with the therapist at their upcoming meeting. It was good to unload to an objective party. But for now, he needed a distraction. Badly.

He didn't think, just grabbed his jacket and keys and headed out the door.

***

Luanne was surprised to hear the buzzer on her intercom. It was nine p.m. People didn't just show up unannounced in Los Angeles. "Who's there?"

"It's me." The voice was masked by the sounds of passing traffic.

"Jon?"

"Yeah."

"Sheesh. Why didn't you call first?"

She was in sweats, her hair held back in a headband. She needed a shower.

"Can I come up?"

"I'm in the middle of something. Meet me at O'Tooles on the corner in thirty."

"Fine. I can wait thirty."

"How good of you." And smiled to herself.

She hurriedly took a shower, changed into something more feminine than usual, sprayed her favorite scent, and before opening the door, took a deep breath. She stared at herself in the hallway mirror. "He has a girlfriend. You're not a boyfriend stealer." *This is not a date.*

The guy was a bit of an a-hole *and* a heartthrob, but she recognized an emotional softie when she saw one. It takes one to know one.

***

Theo was tired of waiting for the bomb to drop. He had stayed up the whole night agonizing about who could have it in for him. Nic had woken up twice from his tossing and turning. "You okay?"

"Yeah, just an upset stomach."

"Can I get you anything?"

"No thanks. Go back to sleep. I love you, Nic."

"Love you too, babe. Feel better." She instantly fell back asleep.

At approximately four-fifteen in the morning he had reached a conclusion. He would hire a private investigator. See who was stalking him and his older daughter, Abigail. He knew just the man for the job.

CHAPTER 31

Los Angeles

Bernard "Bernie" Patton, P.I.'s office smelled like stale tobacco. The man himself was straight out of central casting. Balding, with a well-developed beer belly, the glimmer of a once-fit cop was still present. An ancient mutt crawled onto the office couch and curled up next to Theo.

This is the best, most savvy investigator in LA? Theo thought. He had made some quiet inquiries and the man's name kept coming up. For a reason he could no longer recall, he'd held off on contacting the man. Till now.

The investigator said, "Let me get this straight. You want to find out who sent you something by snail mail, but it's not technically blackmail. Is that right?"

"Yes."

"Okay, why don't you just start from the top."

The mutt laid his head in Theo's lap. "Many years ago, I had an affair. I'm not proud of it and there's no point in my offering justifications. It was wrong. But the product of that infidelity was a daughter. Her name is Abigail and she lives in Santa Fe with her mother. My wife knows nothing about her, and I want to keep it that way. We have a nine-year old daughter, and it would hurt them tremendously."

"Do you offer financial support to the illegitimate child?"

Theo bristled at the P.I.'s callous description. "Her name

is Abigail. And yes, I send regular payments from a private account and will continue to do so until she turns twenty-one."

Bernie took notes. "I'll need to check if that account had been hacked. Go on," Bernie said.

Without thinking Theo petted the old hound. "Two days ago, I received an envelope. No return address. Enclosed were several photos of Abigail."

"Do you have those pictures with you?"

Theo passed his phone to Bernie. "I got rid of the originals but took pictures with my phone. I have no idea where they acquired these shots."

"Either it's someone you know, or they were taken off the internet. Was there a letter attached?"

"No, I wish there was. But there was a printout that shows a DNA link between me and my daughter. It's almost like I'm just being given a heads-up rather than a chance to stop them."

Bernie took a few minutes to peruse the document. "I agree. Have you thought about who has a bone to pick with you —perhaps, someone with a vendetta? Enough to want to ruin your happy home?"

Theo reached into his briefcase. "I've made a short list." He handed it to Bernie.

"When was the last time you saw Abigail?"

"In person, fourteen years ago."

"Any chance it's her or her mother doing this?"

Theo vehemently shook his head. "None. They enjoyed my visits when Abigail was little but are happy with the status quo. They've both made that clear. Janelle is independent and in a long-term relationship, a guy they both care for. I would just be a complication."

"I'll need to check it out anyway." He looked at the list. "Tell me about these three names."

"The first is the managing partner of my old firm. When I went out on my own, several high-rolling clients followed me. The company lost big bucks on those accounts. They threatened to sue but I'd never signed a non-compete, so they had no leg to stand on. They could've dragged me through the mud anyway, but from what I heard they chose not to. It wouldn't be good business practice to sue your old employees. Won't be surprised if they were behind this, though. Getting revenge under the radar."

"When was that?"

"Last summer."

Bernie made a note. "And the next two?"

"Next one is my first wife. I just put it there as a precaution. She got what she wanted in the divorce. She's an alcoholic. No way she could be this organized."

Theo explained the last suspect on his list. He was Theo's one-time best friend, Ryan Cook. "We grew up together. Ryan and I met Nicole at the same time twenty years ago. He asked Nic out and they dated a few times. When Nic and I got together weeks later, Ryan accused me of stealing her away. It couldn't be further from the truth. Nic had come on to *me*. Initially, I turned her down out of respect for my buddy, but she said she was going to break up with Ryan. Said the chemistry wasn't there. My big mistake was not telling Ryan. I didn't want to hurt him or have him assume exactly what he ended up thinking. He was devastated. He lost his girlfriend and best friend in one shot. Maybe he's been harboring a grudge all these years."

The dog was now snoring softly on Theo's lap.

"I'll start with your former friend. Heat of passion. Then move to your ex-wife and co-worker."

Theo nodded, carefully moved the sleeping dog to the seat behind him, leaving the investigator to do his job.

***

When Luanne walked into O'Tooles, she spotted Jon seated in the back. He looked older somehow in the dim lighting. And painfully handsome.

She sidled up next to him. "What are you doing out here? Get lost?"

"No."

"You have an update on the case you want to share?"

"No."

"This twenty-one questions?"

"No." Then, "I just wanted to see you."

Luanne's heart lurched. She hadn't wanted to admit it to herself, but she'd been thinking of Jon nonstop since their platonic sleepover. She'd replayed it in her mind a hundred times, only a much steamier version. "Okay . . ."

Jon waved down a waiter. "Want a drink?"

"I'm not a boyfriend stealer," she blurted out.

He was quiet. Then turned to the approaching waiter. "Give me Johnnie Walker straight up."

When the man left, she said. "Okay, spill it. What happened?"

"Mel and I broke up. This time for good."

"Yikes. Sorry. Wanna talk about it?"

"There's not much to say. She said it felt like purgatory. And I couldn't disagree."

Luanne fiddled with her earring. "I'm not into rebounds."

"How is this a rebound? We already know each other. We slept together." He smirked.

"Cute. But seriously, I have a policy not to get caught up in rebounds especially those fresh off the presses. You could change your mind and be back with her in a week and then where would I be?"

"This didn't happen overnight, Lu. She and I haven't been together for months. We just called it, that's all."

Lu thought about it. She liked Melanie. "How about this? We keep things status quo while you go through your grieving process and if you're still into me in two months, we'll take it up a notch."

"Two months?"

Luanne looked Jon in the eye. "Deal or no deal?"

Three hours later, Jon lay in the tangled, sweat-soaked sheets of Luanne's bed, the smell of alcohol on his breath, her naked leg draped over his, her eyes at half-mast and a joint in her mouth.

***

New York City

Terry ended the call with Yosef, surprised that the conversation went as smoothly as it did. If he was aware of her personal conflicts, he didn't let on. Gabe had made things easy, taking her request to postpone the weekend at his family's vacation home in stride.

Yosef agreed to work with the FBI if Jon was among the players. Now all that was needed was an okay from Special Agent Doug Matthews. She could only hope Jon's tenuous relationship with his boss was at a low simmer.

***

Los Angeles

There was something about Davis that rubbed Bernie the wrong way. The kind of guy that always had an angle, never considering the results of his actions. He could imagine Davis had made some enemies along the way. If he had to guess, the list Davis gave him was missing a few names. Still, Bernie would start with what he was given. Then check out the man himself.

There were several Ryan Cooks on social media. Three whose profile indicated LA as their hometown. One that was in Davis's age range. Of course the Ryan Bernie was looking for could be off the social media grid, but it was a place to start. He sent a screenshot to Davis who confirmed it was the right guy.

Digging deeper, Bernie found an announcement in the paper from six years prior. A wedding announcement. Facebook showed the man's travel photos, smiling shots with an attractive blond who bore a mild resemblance to the photo he'd previously found of Nicole Davis. The most recent post was the couple's video of their baby gender reveal. Bernie was convinced Cook had moved on, past his resentment of Davis stealing his girl.

Next up was the ex-wife. He Googled her name, coming up dry. No Francine Corbett Davis there or on social media. Odd. He'd need to look further. While he was logged in, he checked the final name on the list. Davis's old boss. Deborah Frost, owner and managing partner of Frost, Keating & Goldin, a mid-size law firm specializing in personal injury.

Bernie searched for the woman on LinkedIn. A bookish woman in her early sixties, she had built up her father's firm to twice its original size. He made a note to check if she or the other partners had ever been accused of libel or slander. By the looks of her, a strategic personal attack on Davis seemed unlikely. But Bernie knew all too well that looks were deceiving.

CHAPTER 32

Los Angeles

J on gave Luanne credit. Instead of knocking herself for not sticking to her guns, she was going with the flow. Definitely not Type A. He liked her. Her humor and her lack of inhibition. She was smart and did her own thing. Didn't seem to care what anyone else thought. He imagined her meeting Granny and smiled to himself. That would be some interaction.

"What are you smiling about?"

"Just thinking. Last few hours were outstanding."

"Outstanding, huh?" Luanne asked.

"Yeah, you have a better description?"

"Mind blowing. Life altering. Testosterone confirming."

"Wow. No self-esteem issues, I gather."

"Not anymore." She took another toke. Offered it to him.

Jon said, "I'll pass. I'm inhaling enough without actually putting it in my mouth."

"That's why you're so relaxed."

"If you say so." They both started giggling.

"You laugh like a girl," Luanne said.

"You smoke like a guy."

Both giggled again.

Jon turned serious. "Lu, I'm not a wham, bam, thank you ma'am sorta guy. No one-night stands."

"Glad to hear it. I still think you should take some downtime between bed partners."

"I haven't been with Mel in months."

"Yeah, you already said that. But your head has."

"How about a topic change?" He grinned, "Wanna grab something to eat? I'm famished."

"That's the weed. I'd rather stay in bed where it's warm and cozy."

"Okay, I'll bring something in then. What do you want?"

"Well, if you're going anyway . . ." She proceeded to list fifteen things she was craving.

"You must be joking."

"Not even a little."

"That should take me an hour to check everything off," Jon said.

"Try to do it faster."

"Why?"

"Because once I'm full, I'll want to go for another round."

Jon's eyes widened. "Really?"

"Really."

He jumped out of bed, speed dressed and said, "I'll be back in fifteen."

When Jon returned Luanne was in the same position, in bed, hair tousled. Thankfully, the joint was gone.

"I come bearing food for an army." He handed her the packages, which she carefully set down beside her.

"Ooh. Thanks, Jon. Breakfast in bed?"

"Sure." He hopped in, opened the box of glazed donuts, took a bite.

"It's weird, Doug coming out here and all. Maybe I'll check up on him."

Luanne wiped ketchup off her face. Took another french fry. "Sounds like you guys have a really weird relationship."

Jon shrugged.

They ate in silence until Jon's phone rang. He looked at the display. "Speaking of the devil."

Luanne listened to Jon's side of the conversation. He hung up.

"We have a break in the case. He wants me to meet him downtown at the field office." Jon put the donut box on the bedside table. He stood up, brushing powdered sugar off his pants.

"What about round two?" Luanne asked.

"I wish. But I need to go. Raincheck?"

"Definitely. Hey, what do you think about my joining you? If your boss will okay it. I have all my notes right here. Maybe I could help."

Jon thought a moment. "Good idea. Get dressed and let's go."

"What about asking your boss?"

"I've learned it's better to apologize after the fact than ask in advance."

Luanne gave him a look. "Terrific. I'll be sure to keep that in mind."

***

FBI Field Office
Los Angeles

Matthews was waiting in the lobby when Jon entered, accompanied by a young woman dressed in black, down to the ripped jeans. She sported a skull nose ring, and her jet black hair was tinged with an unnatural shade of maroon. "Who's this?"

Jon said, "Luanne Parker . . . sir."

Matthews shook the young woman's hand, wondering how kids these days ever got past the interview process. They had no concept of proper attire or appearance. He looked back and forth between the two young people and picked up a vibe. It wasn't just professional. "You're the one who called me?"

"Yes, sir. Sorry about that . . . and about your wife."

Matthews nodded solemnly.

Jon said, "I thought given Luanne's involvement in the case, she may be of help."

Matthews gave Jon a withering glance. "Next time ask me first."

"I apologize." He looked at Luanne, who smiled.

Matthews said, "Everything is off the record. Understood?"

Luanne nodded.

Matthews led them to an empty office and shut the door.

"So, what's the update?" Jon asked.

"We got a call from the CEO of ItsRelative.com. Two people have asked for sick leave since he made the announcement." He put their names up on the board.

Jason Wang

Carly Weiss

Matthews said, "We'll watch them both. We should have an answer by day's end if either is really sick."

Luanne said, "People take sick days for other reasons."

Matthews looked at Jon. "Yes, I know very well."

Luanne picked up a pen from the table and began chewing on it. "What good is it even if you find these people playing hooky? Doesn't mean they're the culprits."

"True, but the opposite is also true. If they are up to no good, we may get 'em."

***

Bernie pulled out the list Davis gave him and went to work on the co-worker and ex-wife. Using an online background-checking service, he found nothing remotely incriminating about Deborah Frost or her law partners but managed to track down the ex.

Francine Davis, now forty-one, had remarried shortly

after the split from Theo, and followed her new husband to his hometown of Salt Lake City. The marriage lasted four years, but she'd remained in Utah and kept his name. She now went by Francine Oakley. She had two license suspensions for DUI. No jail time. One dependent. A self-described part-time care-giver, she had held a string of low-paying jobs.

Bernie spent the next hour mining for info . . . on his client. Over the course of thirty years of investigating, he'd learned to begin his digging with the ones who hired him. Fre-quently, there was more to the story than they chose to dis-close. On the surface, Theodore Davis had a boring life. Good job, married, small child. On the surface.

Bernie was ready to call it a night, pick up in the morn-ing where he left off. He was starving, glad to have a deep-dish pizza in the fridge. He'd bought it several days ago, so he'd bet-ter eat it soon. His last email of the day went to his IT guy—one of the best in the business—even if he occasionally operated outside the fuzzy lines of legality. Bernie had come to trust him.

He typed, asking for Davis's credit history, past legal battles or arrests. He gave what he knew about the separate child support bank account. If there was any dirt on Davis, he'd prefer to know before diving head first into the case.

Bernie shut down his computer and went to eat his cold pizza.

CHAPTER 33

Santa Fe, New Mexico

Abigail Saunders didn't want to tell her mom about her creepy feeling. Not because their relationship was strained, but because it was so strong. Her mother would only worry. Maybe even call the police. When it came to her only child, Abby knew her mother tended to overreact. Besides, it was only a feeling. Like something primal from a previous era, telling her she was being watched, followed.

It was probably just Grant, her boyfriend from junior year. Her friend Sarah told her he never got over the breakup, saying he'd never dated someone so beautiful. Light brown complexion, azure eyes. But why wouldn't he just come up to her and talk? *He's weird. That's why you broke up with him in the first place.*

The problem was her gut was telling her it wasn't Grant. He might be weird, but he wasn't a stalker.

The first time was nearly a week ago. Her last class of the day had been canceled, and they were given permission to leave school earlier than usual. Rather than wait for the bus, she decided to walk home. It was only half a mile in broad daylight. She must have turned around ten times between school and home, sensing eyes on her. Relief came when she walked through the door to hear her mom's predictable, "Hi, honey. How was school?" So relieved, in fact, she decided the whole episode was a figment of her overactive imagination.

But now, two days later, as she walked down Canyon Road toward her mother's art boutique, the feeling returned. She picked up her pace, considering maybe that instinct was actually there to protect her. She walked through the shop to the back, entered the studio, and found her mother working at the pottery wheel, her hands covered in clay. "Mom, there's something I need to tell you."

***

Los Angeles

Theo sat on his poolside lounge chair, his laptop propped up on his legs, Lizzy's plastic raft at his feet. It was a spectacular December day, the sky a robin's egg blue, not a hint of smog. Who said you needed four seasons?

Nic was running errands, giving him the opportunity to work outside without interruption. The stress of recent days was getting to him. He needed fresh air, a change of scenery.

Theo powered up his laptop and instantly noted an email from someone named William Sherman. It was marked urgent. A tingle in the back of his brain. He knew American history. After all, he'd named all his kids after important American icons. Sherman was an alias. He opened the email.

Mr. Davis,

By now both you and your wife will have received my mailing. You may be wondering why no demands have been made. That is because I have none. My objectives are solely for my knowledge which I have no intention of divulging at this time. Suffice it to say you have earned these actions I am taking. Your deceit and immorality need to be addressed. There's nothing you can do to stop me. Accept your fate as you have played with the fate of others.

At the bottom, was a thumbnail of a photo. Fear filled Theo as he clicked on the image of his daughter Abigail.

The sight of his eldest daughter was distressing. Mostly because this time it was a current photo. She was walking along what appeared to be the artist colony road in Santa Fe. He'd been there once. The picture was taken with a long-range lens. Abby was wearing a colorful sweater, carrying her knapsack on her back. Someone was following his kid. Whoever this was had crossed a line. It occurred to him, that surely the sender could have found Nic's email and sent the same to her. The guy—if it even was a guy—was playing with him. Like a cat with a mouse before killing it.

Theo heard the school bus come to a stop in front of the house. A minute later, the door opened. "Daddy!" he heard.

"Out here, sweetheart."

If the picture was meant to scare him, it succeeded.

***

When Theo clicked on the photo, Wang's virus snuck inside. Theo's location, audio and video were now accessible to Franklin. The computer's camera light would never turn on. Franklin was amazed how naïve people could be, thinking they still had any measure of privacy.

Franklin studied the man's face. It was an odd feeling. He allowed himself a moment of joy at seeing the man's distress, his lips parted in stunned disbelief. The view behind him was of a kidney-shaped pool, colorful landscaping. Opulent. It made him angry. The malware pinpointed the man's precise location.

***

Santa Fe

Janelle heard her phone buzz. She quickly washed the paint off her hands, put in her earbuds and answered the call. Her hands free, she gathered her paintbrushes, bringing them to the slop sink. "Hey, Theo. Been a long time. How are you?"

"Okay. How's Abby?"

None of the usual small talk. "You okay? Your voice sounds funny."

"Just wondering if anything strange has been going on."

Jan knew Theo long enough to be on alert. She stopped what she was doing. "What's going on?"

"Please answer me."

Jan sighed. "All right. About a week ago, Abby thought someone was following her. She was pretty shaken up, so I called the local police and filed a report. Since then, Mike's been escorting her to and from school every day."

"Why didn't you tell me?"

"Come on, Theo, we aren't exactly in regular touch."

He was quiet.

"Sorry. Listen, if there had been something definitive, I would have called. You know that, right?"

"Yeah, okay. Say hi for me."

Sensing he was about to hang up, she said, "Wait, what made you call to ask?"

A pause. Then, "I've been getting some strange mail. Just wanted to make sure everyone I care about is okay."

Jan got one of her dark feelings. Since moving to Santa Fe, she'd come to trust them. "What are you not telling me?"

"Same rule . . . if it's something big, I'll let you know. Just glad everyone's all right. Need anything?"

"No. We're good. But, Theo—"

"Yes?"

"I'll keep you to your word."

***

Los Angeles

Theo got off the phone, horrified that someone had been stalking his kid, taking her pictures to send to him. If whoever it was could get so close, would they hurt her?

The email had accomplished something more than exploiting his fears. Tired of being a victim with no recourse, Theo resolved that no matter what happened, he would find this sicko and destroy him once and for all. He picked up the phone and called the P.I.

***

Bernie was shaving when his phone buzzed.

"Patton!" No hello. "You gotta find this guy. Now." Davis explained the situation. He sounded edgy, angry, and scared. "I need you to go out to Santa Fe. Make sure my daughter's safe. The guy could still be there. You could track him."

"It'll cost you."

"I don't care."

"Fine, I'll call you as soon as I have something."

Bernie was about to hang up when over the line he heard a door open, a young girl chattering away happily.

"Please, Bernie." Theo changed his tone, using the PI's first name. "I don't want to lose my family," he whispered. "I can't go through that again."

"Understood. Keep your phone accessible. Now, go make your wife and kid happy, and let me do my job."

***

As Theo disconnected the line, he had a flash of inspiration. A family vacation. It was long overdue. Nic wouldn't question it. Lizzy was starting winter break. Their last trip was over a year ago. Now was the perfect time. It would surely make his family happy. And he could go off the grid, giving Patton a chance to find the miscreant before the next damning mail arrived.

***

Bernie's phone dinged with an incoming email. It read, "Thought this would be of interest."

Sure enough, his IT guy got access to the private account. Bernie scrolled through the lengthy list of transactions. Regular payments to a Janelle Saunders. Child support for Abigail. He expected the records to go back eighteen years. They went further. A separate group of monthly payments had stopped nearly ten years ago. As was often the case with his clients, Davis was hiding something.

Bernie let out a loud yawn. He needed a nap. Only one thing left to do. Before he closed his laptop, he booked a ticket to Santa Fe.

CHAPTER 34

Santa Fe

B ernie drove slowly down Canyon Road looking for the address. The town was different and . . . special. Surrounded by the Sangre de Cristo mountain range, the vibe felt mystical. Mom n' Pop shops extended for several blocks. What was a dying retail breed in most of the country, here they appeared to thrive, lending the city its distinct, artsy flavor. Galleries displayed an eclectic variety of Native American crafts, pottery, and handmade jewelry.

Bernie got out of the car and crossed Canyon Road. The air was nippy, the sky a perfect blue. Unaccustomed to the cold climate, he was glad he'd brought along a hat and gloves.

Vortex Arts was housed in a small adobe building fronted by large pots of bright purple and pink petunias. Deep-red dried jalapeños strung in clusters hung from the shop's eaves. Bernie entered the shop, causing a tiny bell to chime above the doorway.

A woman in a flowery dress, hair uncut for several years, no makeup, in her mid-sixties was studying a small glass dish. Behind a rough-hewn wooden chest-high table stood a stunning black woman, staring intently at the computer screen in front of her. *Janelle, Abigail's mother.*

Janelle said, "Sure Layla, I can get you a dozen of those in time for your daughter's wedding. They'll make the perfect bridesmaid gift."

Layla's joy seemed out of proportion with the pronouncement. Perhaps her mood was enhanced by an ingestible similar to those Bernie saw displayed by the register. The woman paid, then rounded the desk, hugged Janelle, and left.

"Welcome, I'll be right with you," Janelle said.

"Take your time."

Bernie walked around the quaint shop. A door at the back led to a tiny studio. All sorts of art materials were neatly arranged, a pottery wheel in the middle of the space. "Did you make all these things yourself?"

"Most of them, but not all. The jewelry bowls Layla ordered are from a Hopi Indian artisan I buy from. Are you looking for anything special?"

"Not really. I suppose I'd like to go home with something authentically New Mexican."

"Everything I sell was made here in the Land of Enchantment. Where is home if I may ask?"

"Los Angeles. But now that I'm here, I may reconsider that." He smiled warmly.

She laughed. "I know how you feel. I moved here years ago. No desire to be anywhere else."

The door opened, and a teenage girl with mild acne on her forehead walked in. She was a lighter shade than her mother and nearly as lovely. He'd timed his visit right.

"Hi honey, how was your day?"

"Fine."

"The math exam go okay?"

"Yeah."

"You hungry?"

"Yeah."

Bernie vaguely recalled his own monosyllabic adolescent phase. Seemed like it lasted forever.

Janelle eyed her daughter, who picked up on the nonverbal cue. She faced Bernie, "Hi. Can I help you find something?"

Bernie said, "Sure." He made a show of looking back and

forth between the two ladies. "Are you sisters?"

Abby laughed. "That's my mom!"

Jan also laughed. "I had her pretty young." Then, "What brings you to Santa Fe?"

Bernie studied a ceramic figurine. "Work. I'm a private investigator."

Abby perked up. "Wow, a P.I. So cool."

"It's not as glamourous as it sounds. But I get some interesting jobs sometimes. As a matter of fact I'm in town working a stalking case."

The words had their intended effect. Both women suddenly became quiet.

Then, Janelle said, "Abby, go clean the easels please."

"Mom! I want to stay."

"Now." She said in a soft but firm tone.

To her credit, Abby didn't argue further.

Janelle said, "I don't mean to be nosy, but can you tell me a bit about your case?"

"Well, there isn't much to tell at this point. My client is worried about his daughter. Seems someone's been following her around."

"She okay?"

"Yeah, so far. But the local PD said several other complaints have come in with the same M.O."

"I haven't heard that."

Bernie shrugged. "Can't speak for the PD but maybe they have a lead and don't want to scare the guy off."

She nodded slowly. Lowering her voice she said, "My daughter," she gestured with her head to the back room, "had the same thing happen to her."

"Oh?"

"We filed one of the complaints."

"Go figure. Can you tell me exactly what happened? It may help me find the guy."

Janelle shared everything Abby had told her.

When she was done, Bernie said, "If it helps any, usually

these things don't turn into anything serious. But if it were my kid, I'd take extra precautions."

"Extra precautions?"

"On rare occasion, these stalkers—usually men by the way—get so obsessed they turn aggressive. Keep a closer eye on her. I realize teenagers don't like to be monitored, but better safe than sorry, you know?"

Jan bit her lip, nodded. "Good advice." Pointing to the figurine that had caught Bernie's eye, she said, "Why don't you take that? On the house."

"Really? Thanks."

"I hope you find the guy."

"It's a matter of time, but I will." Bernie meant it.

Five minutes after he left the shop, he phoned Theo. "She's fine . . . yeah, I saw her with my own two eyes . . . I scared the mom enough to keep a closer eye on her.

He hung up wondering how an a-hole like Theodore Davis managed to snag two incredible women. He considered his next step in the case. Ryan Cook and Deborah Frost were dead ends. That left the ex-wife. In Salt Lake City. He pulled up flight information on his phone. No direct flights. He'd drive down to Albuquerque and catch a non-stop from there.

***

Squaw Valley, California

Theo closed his eyes, letting the steam from the hot tub do its work. It was the most relaxed he'd felt in a very long time. Getting away with Nic and Lizzy was a smart move for multiple reasons. Connecting with his wife, creating memories with his daughter. And leaving his problems behind. Or trying, at least.

The lake area was known for spotty reception, a consideration for where to go. He and Nic had agreed to go unplugged to allow for optimal family time. It served his purposes as well. He knew he would have to face them soon enough but if

210

he could offer Bernie more time to find his blackmailer while keeping his wife far from the mail, why not?

He opened his eyes, taking in the imposing pine trees surrounding the property, the snow-covered ski mountain in the distance, its snake-like slopes lit with tiny lights to accommodate the night skiers. They had stayed before at the private condo west of Lake Tahoe. It was a year-round destination with horseback riding and boating in the summer and perfect powder conditions in the winter. If his business stayed the course, perhaps one day he would buy the place.

Nic scooted over beside him and filled two glasses with the sparkling grape juice they'd brought. He always thought it amazing that she never drank alcohol in his presence. Not even at weddings. She stayed dry in solidarity with him. He was a lucky man.

Lizzy was sleeping soundly inside their chalet. The night was filled with stars, the smell of the burning balsam wood in the nearby firepit. For a few moments he forgot about the damning letters. His phone within arm's reach, solely in case Lizzy needed them. He took a sip of his sparkling grape juice and placed the glass at the edge of the hot tub, the chill on his exposed skin invigorating. Nic followed suit. He drew his wife to him, kissed her, tasting the sweetness on her lips. "Do you know how much I love you?" Theo asked, his voice gruff.

Nic must have sensed the intensity in his voice. He could feel her body respond. With her breath on his lips, she said, "Why don't you show me?"

And he did.

***

Salt Lake City

Franklin burned with fury listening to the man. The reception was poor, limiting the video. When the breathing became rapid, he turned off the speaker. The man didn't have a care in the world. His letters were being ignored. He wanted to scream, throw things, pitch all his monitors, keyboards. But it would only alert his mother. This couldn't stand. He needed to do something to make the man pay attention. And pay his dues. His therapist said he was ready. He knew he was. Only fear stood in his way. And he now found the impetus to overcome it.

CHAPTER 35

"**T**his meeting," Matthews began, his tone formal, "is for the express purpose of working together with our allies."

Shira was typing furiously, keeping her eyes on her screen. "In other words, Israel will owe you."

Terry raised her hand like a crossing guard. She didn't need a fight to break out before she could even begin. Something or someone had delayed the meeting with the FBI. Given that Yosef was on board, she had to assume it was Matthews. "Agent Matthews, you'll soon learn what we have to say will help your nation as well. You may end up owing *us*."

Terry spotted a rare smile on Shira's lips.

Matthews held his tongue, but his eyes spoke of skepticism.

"Israel's secure networks are under attack. We believe it's the work of sophisticated hackers mining for classified information they can sell to interested buyers. It's highly likely similar efforts are being made here in the U.S. as well as other countries around the world."

Terry saw Matthews nod at a middle-aged man sitting in the corner who stood up and quickly walked out. She continued. "These hackers are typically young people skilled in their field, designers of sophisticated malware and spyware, but unable to find the buyers on their own. For that they need a broker, someone who'll trade or outright sell for money or bitcoin. There are only a few, how do you say, high rollers?"

"Here, these crimes are known as misappropriation. It means stealing intellectual property and trade secrets. These matters typically fall under the auspices of the DOJ. If the crime is committed for the benefit of any foreign government, convictions are made under the Economic Espionage Act resulting in up to fifteen years in prison and half a million dollars in fines. Do you have reason to believe the situation has reached that level?"

Terry said, "As of several days ago, we learned the hacking software used to attack our systems will be sold."

"To whom?"

Terry paused looking at Shira, who hesitated. Terry wondered what was running through her handler's mind. Finally, Shira said, "North Korea."

Jon's face paled.

"The hackers are working day and night to perfect the app so it can be ready for sale by midnight of the thirtieth."

"That's in two weeks!"

Shira said, "Now you understand what's at stake. If the sale goes through, Pyongyang will gain access to classified intel anywhere in the world."

It was as if the air had been sucked out of the room. For several moments no one spoke.

Jon broke the silence. "How do we find the broker?"

"The suspect is here in New York, goes by the nickname, the White Knight. But we have had no luck making an ID. If we locate this person, we can prevent the sale from going through long enough to confiscate and disarm the virus."

Matthews spoke up. "How can we help?"

Shira turned her screen to face the others. "This is our prime suspect. I've run her face through Israel's and Interpol's most advanced facial recognition software but got no hits. To help, you can use whatever technology you have available to identify her."

"Please email it to Agent Steadman."

Shira did so.

Jon jumped up from his chair, grabbed his laptop and headed for the door. "I'm on it."

***

Salt Lake City

From five thousand feet, Bernie thought Salt Lake City looked like the surface of the moon. Stark with no vegetation, snow-peaked mountains in the distance. The lake itself appeared otherworldly, its shores barren. The airport was busier than expected, a hub for connecting flights. Weaving his way through the hordes of travelers, it occurred to him that he'd spent more time traveling in the last week than in nearly a year. He liked it.

Bernie rented a car, setting the heater to full blast. The drive to his destination took him past the city's pale granite capitol building, its majestic dome and Corinthian columns reminiscent of the ones in Sacramento, his home state's capital. He turned right at Temple Square, continuing southwest to the Poplar Grove neighborhood. The address turned out to be a small, neglected home with an overgrown front yard. A ramp led up to the front door. For a stroller or wheelchair, he didn't know, though there were no telltale signs of a young child. No toys strewn about, no swing set. Perhaps it accommodated an elderly parent. He parked several houses away.

To think Theo, who lived the high life, had an ex-wife residing in this dump was bizarre. Clearly, their paths had drastically diverged since the divorce. Still, looking at the run-down house, he couldn't help but wonder if he was faced with the makings of a wild goose chase. He took a few photos and waited.

At six p.m., a beat-up Ford pulled into the driveway, and a woman who looked to be in her fifties emerged. She was balancing two weighty McDonalds bags and a 7-Eleven Big Gulp, trying to keep them from falling as she approached the front door. Bernie snapped a few pictures capturing her face, then zoomed in on the shots. It was her. She'd aged poorly.

Francine Oakley. Bernie had checked her record. She had two DUIs but was released on her own recognizance after having her license suspended. She was required to do community service and enter AA. She must have met the requirements and reactivated her license, explaining her driving home. He wondered about that. Unless laws in Utah were way laxer, that wasn't typical. Why did they let her off? Maybe her wheelchair-bound ward relied on her for caregiving. Bernie watched as the woman closed the door behind her.

***

Bernie spent the next day tailing Theo's ex. For someone who repeatedly fell off the wagon, she was a hard worker. Her day began as a floor attendant for a big-box hardware store ten miles from her house. At three-thirty, she made the drive to a McDonalds, where she swapped aprons for her job as a manager. She had two jobs, neither of them big money makers. He figured after taxes she made around 50k. Once he realized she was heading home, he made sure to get back to her house before she did and check the mailbox.

Seven minutes later, he was parked at the corner, watching Francine once again pull into her driveway, fast food in hand, looking drained. As far as he could tell she had no significant other. Certainly not one that lived with her. The mailbox had revealed a pile of junk mail, several collections notices and a letter from an insurance company addressed to Mr. Franklin Oakley. That one he took.

***

FBI Field Office
New York City

Terry was tapping away on her laptop when the conference room door opened and someone walked in. Expecting Jon who'd called to reconvene, Terry glanced towards the doorway, doing a double take. Her jaw dropped. Standing there with likely the same expression Terry had on her face, was a young woman in her mid-twenties. Dressed in a fashionable professional black pantsuit, her black hair brushed against the shoulders. No glasses.

Netta.

The woman sat down across from her. "Doctor Lavi, I'm Shelby Emerson. Terribly sorry for the confusion."

Terry was speechless, giving Jon an opportunity to explain. "Shelby recently transferred here to the Cybercrime division from the DC office which is why I've never seen her around here before."

Terry studied the woman. She had the same body as the wallflower at the cocktail party but with a completely different way about her. She was fashionable, poised.

Netta aka Shelby said, "This must be beyond frustrating. It is for me as well. I suspected *you* were the White Knight."

Terry found her voice. "All this time I've been trying to lure the wrong person. An FBI agent, no less."

"Don't beat yourself up. Clearly your handler thought the same." Shelby's gaze shifted to Shira who appeared to take no offense.

After Shelby explained her role, she excused herself and left, Matthews following behind her.

Terry's shoulders slouched. She felt defeated. With only Shira and Jon left in the room, she spoke openly. "I can't start from scratch. I haven't seen Gabe in a couple of weeks. We're trying to plan a wedding and I'm stuck roaming around New York spinning my wheels. We've just wasted all this time on the wrong mark. We're no further along than when I arrived."

"Not exactly," Jon said.

"What do you mean?"

The same middle-aged man from yesterday entered, quietly taking a seat in the corner.

Jon said, "There's a common denominator with my current case that we need to figure out. Our countries have been so focused on not showing our hands, we've been oblivious to the fact that we're likely looking for the same people. It's time we fully collaborate to stop whoever is behind the cyberattacks before it's too late."

The man in the corner stood up, addressed Jon, his voice icy. "Agent Matthews wants to see you."

"I'm in the middle—"

"Now."

Jon peered at the man. The moment after he walked out the door the man addressed Terry and Shira. "Thank you for coming. We'll be in touch."

***

Matthews walked into his office, Jon a step behind him.

"Godammit, Steadman, you spoke out of turn. Get your kumbaya mentality under control."

"What are you talking about? Terry and Shira just gave us exceptional intel. There could very well be a connection to my case."

"We need to verify that. Until we do, we keep our secrets. Even if they choose to share theirs. Understood?"

Jon felt his face redden. *Will this stupid bureaucracy ever end?* "Didn't you tell me your superiors gave the green light to speak openly with the Israelis if they provide quality leads?"

Matthews's eyes flared, his jaw jutted.

Jon knew he should get out of there before his boss blew

up, yet again. But he couldn't get his legs to move or his mouth to remain closed. "This is diplomacy? The whole point was to work together." With his hand on the doorknob, Jon added, "Next time, *sir*, don't send your spy, just freakin' talk to me."

***

Shira slammed the door shut. It was rare for her to lose control of her emotions. She'd managed to contain herself in public, but now back in the consulate office, she wanted desperately to punch a hole in the wall. *What had possessed Yosef to agree to a meeting with the Americans?* The talks were completely one-sided, Terry offering what they'd learned. For free. No bartering, no give and take. They left the room with nothing other than a dead end thanks to Shelby, the FBI agent. To top it off, Terry had one foot out the door. Enough was enough. Terry wasn't cut out for the mission. She picked up her phone and told Yosef exactly how she felt. Two days later, Terry was back in her Haifa lab.

CHAPTER 36

Salt Lake City

Wang knew Franklin didn't like him coming unannounced. Or at all for that matter. Actually, he'd been emphatic about it in recent months. *I'll meet you whenever, just don't come to my house.* He assumed it was because of his mother and the condition of their house. Wang knew Franklin's mother had problems and was anything but a skilled housekeeper. He didn't care but Franklin did, so he never pushed the matter. Today he had no choice. He was scared to call or text him in case someone was watching. He knew it was paranoid but better safe than sorry. Franklin would just have to understand. He pulled up to the house. It was in awful shape. Peeling paint, gutters askew, missing shingles. With all the money Franklin had made he hoped one day they would upgrade.

He got out of the car, climbed the steps and rang the doorbell.

***

Bernie got several clear closeups of the Asian man at Francine Oakley's door. He would find out who he is. He couldn't get a good look at who opened the door for him. In his side mirror, he noticed a black sedan pull up a few cars behind him and park, but no one got out. What's that about? Did Francine spot him, call the police? He put the car in drive and made a U-turn, slowly passing the parked car and looked at the driver. The man-made full-on eye contact with him. He had the same perplexed look on his face that he did. Bernie kept driving away. He knew a Fed car when he saw one. Unmarked. He would need to play this right or he'd be in hot water. He could either leave now and try to figure out what was going on or stick around and take his chances. He pulled over and called Davis, who answered on the first ring.

"Any reason why the Feds would be scouting out your ex's house?"

"What are you talking about?"

"Someone showed up while I was doing recon outside your ex's house. Shortly after an Asian guy came over to the house. I'm texting you a picture."

Moments later, Theo said, "Never seen him before. Who is he?"

"Still working on that."

"This can't be good. What the hell did Francine get involved with now?"

"Good question. As soon as I have something I'll let you know."

***

When Franklin heard the doorbell ring, he did what he always did. Wait for his mother to answer it. When the bell rang again, he knew she was down for the count, most likely in the drunken sleep of the dead. He checked the cameras. No point in pausing his work and going all the way to the door for a stupid salesman or proselytizer. Let them think no one was home.

He was surprised to see Wang's mug on the screen. He switched to the wide lens option allowing him a look beyond Wang's head. He was checking for that car. The one that had been there all day. Yes, it was still there. Earlier, he'd seen the bald guy get out and stretch his legs. Not only that, a second unfamiliar car was parked a few spots behind it. Everyone who lived on the block knew their neighbors' cars, and visitors parked in the driveways. Strange cars stood out because strangers didn't come by unless it was to sell something, check the utility meters or encourage voter registration.

He had sincerely hoped things wouldn't go this far. But Wang literally brought trouble to his door. Unacceptable.

Franklin shut the camera feed, made his way to the door and let his friend inside.

***

Wang's conversation with Franklin helped calm his growing sense of paranoia. He was glad his friend didn't appear annoyed at him for showing up at his door and left with Franklin's reassurances that he'd shut things down. They'd gone over every detail of the past few months, Wang finally convinced there was no way anyone could finger either of them. With any luck the whole thing would blow over when the Feds' leads ran dry.

Driving back to his place, Wang couldn't shake that something was off. Things were strained between him and Franklin now that Wang knew what had happened to Cromwell, the CEO of OBooks. By the time he pulled into his parking spot, he was questioning if the friendship would weather the storm.

He needed some chill time. Instead of requesting a leave of absence, which could have raised a red flag, he'd called in sick. Franklin had encouraged him to "just act normal." Wang didn't know about normal, but he would resume his routine, be back at his desk in the morning. Tonight, he'd play a video game and go to bed early.

Wang entered his apartment, flicked on the lights, heading to the kitchen for a glass of milk. It always helped calm him. When he was a little boy afraid of the dark, his mother would come into his room with a tall glass of milk. He smiled at the thought.

"Happy?"

Wang nearly jumped out of his skin. A man was sitting in his gamer chair. Holding his controller. A lean man, built like a runner.

"Who the hell are you? What are you doing in my apartment?"

The man turned on the screen, the loud game music filling the apartment. He then took hold of the AV cables and yanked them as if they were rubber bands. They snapped instantly. Wang made a beeline to the door. The man bolted up to standing, blocking his path. He was lightning fast, the sinewy muscles of his forearms bulging.

Wang felt his body tremble as he stepped backward. "What do you want?"

"It's not about what I want."

A deep sense of dread came over Wang. "Did Franklin send you?"

The man shrugged.

"B-but he's my friend. I didn't tell a soul." He watched as the thug fondled the cable.

"You brought the Feds to his door, Wang."

Wang let out a shriek. But his screams were drowned out by the gunfire of Cyberpunk 2077.

CHAPTER 37

Salt Lake City

H e'd been sitting in his car watching the house for hours at a time. He wondered what Oakley did all day but breaking and entering were not in Bernie's repertoire. He was aware that people would start noticing him. But at least he wasn't alone. The Fed car had made an appearance early, then left. He'd taken a short drive to In-N-Out Burger and was unwrapping his meal when his phone rang. It was his IT guy.

"I found something on Davis. Scraped it from his old police file."

"Let's hear it."

"I did this on my own. Not part of the package."

"Stop nickel and diming me. I'll go to someone else."

"Fine. Have a nice life."

"Wait!"

"What?"

"How much?"

The man told him.

Seething, Bernie agreed to the terms. "So, what did you find?"

"I just emailed you the results. Have a look for yourself."

Bernie hung up without a proper goodbye and opened his email. It was a police report. At first he didn't understand what he was seeing. *Oh, shit.*

Bernie bit into his burger, mulling over the new info, when an Access-A-Ride van pulled up. He was expecting to see an elderly wheelchair-bound person exit the vehicle. Instead, it was a painfully thin young man, with patchy facial hair, moving up the house ramp in a motorized chair. The man punched in a code in a pad by the door and let himself in. Bernie lowered his window, focused his camera, and snapped a few pictures. Before the door shut, he heard the man yell, "Ma, I'm home. What's for dinner?"

Ma?

This must be Franklin Oakley, Francine's disabled son.

***

Bernie was about to call Theo and ask if he knew that his ex had a child, when a Fed car pulled up behind him. He watched in his side mirror as the man got out of his car and make a beeline for Bernie's vehicle. He tapped on the window. Bernie buzzed it down. The man stuck an FBI ID billfold in his face. Bernie scanned the badge. "Agent Loomins," he read. "So, now you wanna talk?"

"Consider it a courtesy. That man that came the other day, the Asian dude. He's been found dead."

"What the hell? What happened?"

"I'll give you that information when you spill who you're working for."

"Deal. Hop in and let's talk."

***

"Let me get this straight. You were hired by some guy who cheated on his wife and had a kid out of wedlock, and someone is threatening him with that information, with DNA stats."

"That's about the long and short of it. Your turn."

Bernie listened rapt as Agent Loomins shared what he was working on.

He was shocked to learn about Wang's extracurricular activities. Stealing DNA? What the hell was this world coming to? The FBI was trailing him, hoping to confirm or deny his involvement. They'd been following him for over a week. When he hadn't come out for his daily jog, the agent thought Wang might have picked up his tail. Instead Loomins found him hanging from the ceiling fan of his unlocked apartment, a suicide note left on the floor beneath him. In it, he fessed up to running the scam and not being able to live with the shame to his parents if he were caught.

The agent handed him a card. "Here's the name of the guy running the investigation."

Special Agent Jonathan Steadman.

"Steadman's in LA now. Maybe you can help each other out."

"Thanks," Bernie said, though dubious. More likely than not it would be a one-way conversation. The Feds were notorious for keeping things close to the vest. "You're leaving town?"

"Not a chance. I need to follow up with the local police on the deceased."

"Good luck with that. "

With nothing left to add, the man got out and Bernie drove away.

***

Manhattan Beach, California

Jon was finishing a run along the narrow walkway between the beachside cottages and the sand, dog walkers and joggers passing him by. He came to a stop and checked his smart watch, gratified to see he was going farther without excruciating leg pain. Still, he knew he'd pay the consequences for the next several hours as his leg reminded him what it had been through years ago. The awful surgeries to fix the shattered bones.

Jon used the bottom of his shirt to wipe the sweat from

his forehead and faced the ocean. Maybe he'd stick around for sunset. It was sure to be a spectacular sight. His thoughts turned to Terry. She was back in Israel. Without Gabe. He stayed in Austin to spend more time with his family and go back to work for his uncle. He hoped his friends would successfully manage the separation. Better than he had with Melanie.

Something happened after the meeting in New York that Terry left the country so quickly. Likely a result of Matthews's stubbornness in holding back intel from the Israelis. With only days to go until the spyware sale, they had no new leads on the White Knight. He heard his phone ring in his earbuds and tapped one to answer. "Steadman."

"Hi. My name's Bernie Patton. Agent Loomins gave me your card."

"You're the private eye."

"Guilty."

Jon said, "I was expecting your call. Loomins told me your connection to my case."

"Yeah. I may have some new info for you."

With Matthews to answer to, this was terrific news. "What've you got?"

"I'm glad to help out, but I'd like to close the case with my client. I'd appreciate if you'd keep me in the loop with the case. Maybe we could share info."

Jon wasn't in the mood to barter for intel, but he knew he would if he had to. "I can't make any promises. It's federal territory. But if I can help you, I will. I'll call you back from my office."

Jon hung up, excited to have finally caught a break. He did some stretches, watching the sun creep closer to the horizon over the Pacific. Today he'd miss the sunset.

***

FBI Field Office
Los Angeles

Jon was trying not to be too obvious as he studied his boss. Matthews had lost even more weight. His cheeks were sunken and pale. They sat across the table from one another, empty takeout cartons of egg foo young and a phone between them. Bernie Patton was on speaker. The P.I. had given them a tangible reason to think there was more to the case. He'd sent his case notes and photos he'd taken outside the Oakley house.

Jon said, "It's too convenient that Wang was found dead, leaving behind a typed suicide note. Granted the guy was a computer geek, but really?"

Each had a copy of the suicide note. It read,

My name is Jason Wang. I am a computer tech at ItsRelative. Over recent months I've sold stolen DNA records. My actions resulted in many people losing their jobs and lives. I veered far astray.

The Feds are on to me. My biggest regret is that my parents will learn what I've done. My arrest would destroy them. I can't bear the shame.

Forgive me.

Jon said, "Wang didn't have any reason to go after Davis."

Doug said, "Unless his ex was paying Wang to mess with his new wife and kid. Maybe that's why Wang went to the house. To discuss it or for payment."

Patton said, "She wasn't home when Wang showed up."

Jon said, "Maybe he didn't know that. I have a different theory."

Matthews drummed his fingers on the table. "Let's hear it."

"Franklin was working with Wang. He's the one sending the threats."

Patton said, "He's got no criminal history."

Jon pursed his lips. "We don't know anything about him."

Patton said, "I have some info. Franklin Oakley used to work for that company, that's where he met Wang."

Jon said, "So, he also may have had access to DNA analysis methods. He knows the business. Wang was coming to talk to *him*, not the mother. Maybe to warn him of the impending investigation."

Matthews said, "And they're running all this from his house?"

Jon said, "Maybe, I don't know. But Wang probably had a way to access the data and pass it along to Oakley. Then they sell it or blackmail people with it."

Matthews asked, "What's the motive?"

Neither Jon nor Patton responded.

Jon sighed. "Without motive, we have nothing."

Matthews said, "Correct. We don't have enough to get a search warrant of the Oakley house."

Patton said, "Combine forces and nail the guy. You get your scammer and I make my client happy."

Jon lifted a brow.

It was as if Patton saw Jon's skepticism. "Okay, maybe not happy, but informed. Davis had fair warning."

"What do you mean?"

"I told him to be prepared for anything. Things he may want to leave buried could be dug up."

Jon got the sense Patton was holding out, but it was Matthews who chimed in. "What else do we need to know, Mr. Patton?"

"Good enough. As you already know, my client, Theodore Davis, hired me to track down whoever's responsible for sending him what appears to be blackmail correspondence. He's also concerned for his child who we believe is being stalked by the same person. It led me to his ex-wife where I met Loomins. I just received a call from one of my . . . colleagues, with info on my client."

"You always background check the people who pay you?"

"I've learned it's prudent to do so."

Jon respected that approach. "I take it you found something on Davis."

"If you send me your email, I'll forward you what I've got. My resources are somewhat limited so maybe you'll find out more. Anyhow, my focus is on finding the blackmailer, not digging up my own client's skeletons. I'd appreciate if you keep my name separate from whatever you find on Davis. You can see how that could be bad for business."

"Understood. And thanks. If I can help your case, I'll be in touch."

Jon hung up, logged into his laptop, and navigated to his email. He found the one from Patton. It was a screen shot of a police report from twenty years ago. He forwarded it to Matthews, who read from his own device. He needed to get back to work. The email could lead nowhere, but it was all he had.

A man by the name of Theodore Davis had caused a motor vehicle car accident while under the influence. Two passengers were taken to local area hospitals with serious injuries. A minor was reported dead at the scene. No name was given due to the age of the deceased. Davis was disbarred, serving three years in prison on a manslaughter charge. He then went through a five-year process of getting his law license reinstated.

Maybe the earlier unexplained payments made from Davis's private account that Patton mentioned were court-ordered restitution to the family of the dead kid, paid in installments. Made sense Davis hadn't brought it up. It was a long time ago and he'd paid his dues. Not to mention traumatic. Jon wasn't ready to judge the man too harshly. After all, if anyone knew about trauma, it was him.

***

Los Angeles Times Headquarters

Jon sat on the orange plastic chair beside Luanne's desk. An identical desk faced hers. Though far messier, it was unoccupied. A rectangular nameplate sat close to the edge. *Ed Hernandez.* Last he'd heard there was no update on the journalist's condition. It was a reminder of how he got involved in the case in the first place. To find . . . and punish Ed's attacker.

The newsroom was a hectic place, even more so than any police station Jon had visited. The vibe felt more like the time he'd visited the New York Stock Exchange. Loud, urgent. Jon knew Luanne was better suited to find any writeups about a twenty-year-old car accident. Through her job at *The Times*, she'd have easy access to the old papers.

Luanne looked up from her computer. "Believe it or not, we still haven't finished uploading all the old microfiche," she said, referring to the clunky decades-old device once used to catalogue the newspaper's articles. "We'll need to go down to the records room."

They took the elevator to the lower level and entered a library-like space with wide desks topped with the old machines.

Jon said, "I haven't seen these since I was a kid."

"Know how to use them?"

"Nope."

Luanne led Jon to a row of cabinets, took a few moments to find the dates they needed and pulled open a drawer. She found what she was looking for and brought it over to one of the machines, placing the film inside. She manipulated the dials till she arrived at the date written on the police report.

Jon said, "Take it slow here. It's probably a small article."

Five minutes later, Luanne pointed to the screen. "Here it is."

Jon read aloud, "Theodore Davis, a Beverly Hills resident, faces DUI charges after he crossed a median into oncoming traffic causing a deadly pile-up. The accident occurred at eight thirty-two this morning on the Golden State Freeway. Nineteen-year-old college student, Marcus Burnett, was unable to avoid what bystanders described as a high-speed head-on collision. The Jaws of Life were needed to extract five passengers, including a minor, who were taken to local area hospitals with life-threatening injuries. At least one fatality of a child was reported at the scene."

Luanne and Jon let that sink in. Then she said, "Awful."

"Looks like the P.I.'s instincts to check out his client were on point."

"Do you think—"

Jon nodded, solemnly. "Yeah, Lu. Makes sense why Davis never mentioned he had a kid. The fatality was his own child."

Luanne put her head in her hands. When she looked up, her eyes were wet. "It's so sad."

"This accident has to be connected somehow."

Luanne said, "You think this is a lead to the hacker and Ed's attacker?"

"My gut is telling me it is. Someone's been harboring a great deal of hate toward Davis, prepared to destroy him. I need to follow this lead."

"How? Will you confront him?"

Jon shook his head. "The man is holding out. I need to find another angle."

Luanne looked at the screen. "You're going to track down the other guy mentioned in the article." It wasn't a question.

"Bingo. Let's find out whatever happened to Marcus Burnett."

CHAPTER 38

Barcelona, Spain

Jon walked along La Rambla, the famed boulevard in the heart of Barcelona. Colorful kiosks sold t-shirts and tchotchkes. Sweater-clad shoppers were out enjoying the mild weather typical of Barcelona's early winter, oblivious to the colorful Joan Miró mosaic they were traipsing upon. Bernie had located Marcus Burnett's workplace—a café on the Carrer Marlet, a narrow stone road in the city's old Jewish quarter known as "El Call." Jon strolled leisurely, taking in the quaint city's vibe, following signs to the *Synagoga Major de Barcelona*. A plaque affixed to the synagogue's outer wall explained it was one of the oldest in Europe. No longer in use, the women's section was now part of the next-door restaurant. He walked a few steps further to an ancient arched doorway and stepped into the eatery. The place was tiny with ancient stone walls. A low-hanging archway led to an intimate space with five two-person tables. An elderly lady with weathered skin was feasting on what looked to Jon like a version of Italian cannelloni. Her moans suggested he may need to come back and get his own.

A young woman with thick black curly hair stood behind a small counter, sizing him up from head to toe. "American?"

Jon laughed. "Yup."

The woman grabbed two English menus from the counter, looked over his shoulder. "Are you with someone?" Her accent was strong, but her English good.

"No, I'm alone. I'm not here to eat. I'm looking for Marcus."

The woman's eyes narrowed. "Why?"

Nosy, Jon thought. "He's a friend."

The woman furrowed her brow, gave him another once over, then shook her head. "Not possible."

Perturbed, Jon asked, "Why not?"

"Marcus has no American friends."

"Okaay . . . can I speak to him, anyway?"

She put down the menus. "He's not here. It is his days off."

"Days?"

"We work five-day shifts. He will be back in two days."

"I won't be here in two days. Can I have his address?"

A couple entered the café, squeezing in the tight space behind Jon. The woman greeted them in Catalan and led them to a table in the back. When she came back, she asked, "What is this about?"

"A personal matter."

Jon's evasiveness seemed to stoke the woman. "Hmm. He lives an hour away. You have a car?"

"I'll get one, if necessary."

"You must want to see him badly. Who are you really?"

"Not very trusting, are you?"

"I can smell BS a mile away."

Jon couldn't help but laugh. He was the same. *What the hell?* "I work for the American government."

She raised a brow. "Is Marcus in trouble?"

"No, not at all. I'm hoping he can help me find someone."

The woman stared at him, stayed quiet for a few seconds, nodding as if coming to a decision. "I believe you. I will call him."

"Please don't. To be honest, he won't be happy I'm here.

I don't want to give him a reason to avoid me."

"You swear on your mother's life you are not here to bring him trouble?"

Jon's mother had been gone for many years, but he still took the request to heart. "I swear."

"All right." She found a napkin and jotted something down. "Here's the address. Don't tell him I gave it to you or he'll be angry with me."

Jon pocketed the napkin. "Thanks." As he left the café, Jon realized he was really liking the Spanish way of thinking.

***

Calafell, Spain

The seaside village made Jon think of his time in Israel months before. Like Tel Aviv, Calafell was on the Mediterranean, boasting mild winters, and a vibrant pedestrian promenade lined with swaying palm trees. The salty air of the sea reached him before he ever laid eyes on it.

Jon glanced at his watch. He was in no particular rush. There was time for a quick look around the picturesque village. Charming shops tucked into the cobblestone streets, several displaying colorful pottery. He purchased a hand-painted candy dish for Granny, then turned left on the Avenida Sant Joan de Déu, taking in the magnificent sea view. A couple passed by walking a small dog, their two young children skipping ahead. African street vendors peddled t-shirts, having set up shop on the promenade fronting the beach.

Ashleigh would have loved it here, Jon thought.

He felt the tug of bittersweet memories and imagined his fiancée walking with him hand-in-hand. He was in college when Ashleigh died. And yet there were days it seemed like just yesterday. He recognized the tension building in his chest, as if a hand was clutching his insides daring him to explode from the pain. Sweat sprouted on his brow, his pulse quickening. He patted his jacket pocket, feeling for his pill bottle, its presence yielding a mix of reassurance and unease. He flashed back to a time not long ago when he woke up on a Florida beach, hung over after one of his more severe anxiety attacks.

He'd been diagnosed with PTSD, but the label meant nothing to him. All he cared about was preventing the paralyzing episodes. And he was determined to do it without pills. Unless he had no choice. Leaving the bottle in his pocket, Jon took a seat on a wooden bench overlooking the water, focusing on the steadily rolling waves until they turned hypnotic. He remained there for ten minutes, willing his symptoms to subside. Only then did he rise and keep on going. It was time to meet Marcus Burnett.

**

New York City

Doug was back home, the West Side apartment quiet as a morgue. The redeye flight hadn't really affected him. He was exhausted all the time anyway. What were another five hours of having sleep elude him? He tossed his travel bag on the bed but had no energy to start unpacking. He left the room, went to the kitchen and grabbed a Heineken from the fridge.

Who cares if it's eight in the morning? No one's here to scold me.

He searched through all the drawers looking for the bottle opener. After five minutes, he let out a primal scream. He threw the bottle against the wall, knocking a framed photo to the floor, the golden liquid cascading down the floral wallpaper. He watched as shards of glass scattered, as if running away from their abuser, one sliding under the sofa. He let out a string of curses. He knew he needed to get a broom but didn't care anymore.

Until he realized the fallen photo was the one of him and Erica on their wedding day.

He rushed to pick it up, nearly slipping on the wet floor, and using his sleeve, wiped the beer splatter from the frame. Careful not to cut himself on the broken glass, he took the photo to the sofa, staring at it. What an incredible day. They were married in Asheville, North Carolina. It was a washout. The skies had opened just as Erica began reciting her vows. Not a sprinkle, but a deluge. Everyone went running indoors. Except for Erica, Doug, and the priest. They had huddled close under the gazebo, laughing, crying—the wind-blown rain soaking them—and finished their vows. To his credit, the priest never broke stride. By the end of the ceremony, he was their only witness. Doug and Erica had laughed every time they reminisced, wholeheartedly agreeing they wouldn't have changed a thing.

Doug took the damp picture with him to the bedroom, lay down and clutching it to his chest, finally fell into a peaceful slumber.

**

Calafell, Spain

"Qui ets?" Marcus Burnett asked, studying Jon standing in his driveway. He spoke with an American accent but was otherwise an unremarkable guy. Dark wavy hair flecked with a few white strands, jeans, Caltech sweatshirt, Adidas. A failed attempt at trendy was made with black-rimmed retro glasses. When Jon didn't immediately reply, he translated, "Who are you?"

Jon held out his ID. "Agent Steadman from the New York FBI."

Marcus looked at him quizzically. "Aren't you a little far from home? I thought you guys only did domestic stuff."

"Usually. But the case I'm working on led me to you. So here I am."

"Did I miss a tax payment back in the nineties?" he

chuckled. "Not that there was much income. I was still in college when I left the States."

Jon smiled. "We're not after you." He made a show of zipping his jacket. "Can I come in?"

Marcus appeared wary but stepped aside. The hallway led to a living room with a view of a dining table. No fancy computers or science books around. A girl no more than six years old was sitting on a sofa watching what sounded like cartoons. Marcus said something to her in Catalan and she left, a pout on her face.

"Cute kid." The little girl reminded Jon of Randy. He made a mental note to spend another afternoon with him when he was back in town.

"Thanks." Then, "Tea?"

"Sure."

When they were seated on the sofa, Marcus asked, "So what's this about?"

Jon pulled out a printout of the article he and Luanne had found and passed it to Marcus.

Marcus looked dismayed. He barely glanced at it, then folded it neatly and handed it back. "How'd you find me?"

"We have good resources."

"Why are you here after all this time?"

Jon said, "The man who caused the accident is being blackmailed by a hacker stealing personal info."

"And you think I'm somehow involved?"

"I don't know. He made a list of people who may have it out for him."

Eyebrows raised, Marcus said, "Are you saying my name was on it?"

Jon shook his head.

Marcus firmly set his teacup on the coffee table, its contents nearly spilling over. "Would you stop with the bullshit? Why are you here?"

"Because your name *wasn't* on it. And that's fishy. The man who changed the course of his life? He never even mentioned you."

Marcus's face reddened. "If anything, he should be on my hit list! He turned to see his daughter standing in the hallway, holding back tears. "It's okay, honey." This time, Marcus spoke in English. "Daddy got upset. You can go back to your room. I'll come in to read *Good Night Moon* in a few minutes." When she closed her door, Marcus said, his voice calmer, "Maybe Davis accomplished what I can't."

"What's that?"

"Putting the trauma behind him. That day was the worst of my life. It took years just to get past the nightmares. I dropped out of college. Finally had to move. My girlfriend was working as an exchange nanny in LA. When she left, I followed her here. Been in Calafell ever since."

Jon understood the man's psyche better than most. He hoped to get past his own nightmares one day, find peace. "If it's any consolation, I know what it's like to accidentally kill someone. It lingers."

Marcus looked at him, his face a mask of confusion. "That must have been awful. Thank God that wasn't me."

Jon furrowed his brow. "What do you mean? The boy died after you broadsided his father's car."

Marcus shook his head. "No, he didn't. He was severely hurt. They had to amputate both his legs. But he survived."

The shock on Jon's face was apparent. He unfolded the article. "But it says here . . ."

"Does it say he died in the accident?"

Jon read quickly. "Says the driver was arrested for drunk driving. A child was found dead at the scene . . ." Jon cursed under his breath. "How did I miss that?" Davis had never mentioned a son. He and Luanne had interpreted it to mean it was Theo's child who had been killed. "It was someone else's child."

Marcus nodded solemnly.

Jon jumped to his feet. "I need to go. Thanks for the help."

Marcus escorted Jon to the door. "Take it easy on the kid.

He's been through a hell of a lot. The sins of the father and all that."

Jon thanked him again and walked out. Standing on the street, he read the article again. He needed to find the son, no longer a kid. He would be now in his late twenties, around his own age. Jon understood what Davis was not prepared to see. The number one suspect was Theodore Davis's own son.

Franklin Oakley.

CHAPTER 39

Franklin Delano Oakley was a double amputee. While he had no memory of the accident, he could vividly recall the day in family court. His father's drawn features, beseeching eyes attempting to hold his young son's gaze. Even then, Franklin's anger was a growing cancer inside him, having turned malignant with the man's refusal to demand shared custody of his son. Franklin was old enough to understand the hearing was just for show, his father never intending to care for the child he'd crippled.

By the time Franklin graduated college, he was friendless, his resentment a living, breathing thing. Later, when he'd been fired by ItsRelative, they claimed it had nothing to do with his disability but with his attitude. What a crock! If they were stuck in a wheelchair their whole lives, wouldn't they have an attitude? Who were they to judge him?

At first, he'd planned to sue the company if for no other reason than to make them sweat, but he didn't have the money for a retainer. His mother had plowed through his earnings, said she needed it for his care, but he knew it was for her alcohol supply.

At his lowest, he'd contemplated suicide, but he couldn't do it. He just didn't have what it took. When Wang explained the app he'd created, Franklin finally saw a glimmer of opportunity and learned to redirect. He'd maintained access to ItsRelative's confidential database, keeping abreast of new firewalls and breaking through them. When Wang got on board with salvaging DNA samples before they were dis-carded, Franklin's access allowed him to match the samples to their hosts, learning the identity of each submitter. It was his chance to right the wrongs. Make society pay for its failings. If he had to suffer for a visible disability, why not those who had unseen genetic ones? In time, Franklin realized he could exact his revenge *and* build a thriving business. Off people's tainted DNA.

He knew he'd hit the motherlode when he found two high-profile submissions—a soon-to-be royal carrying a genetic mutation and a politician highly predisposed to Alz-heimer's. They had used ItsRelative for genetic testing, un-aware of his prying eyes. Yet, the lucrative part of his venture came from selling the data to benefit struggling businesses. As he'd expected, the bottom line had the power to quiet one's conscience. Peter Cromwell of OBooks was the rare exception, defaulting on their agreement. Franklin would have found a way to quietly end their contract, but when Cromwell brought in the Feds, he was left with no other option than cutting their ties in the most permanent fashion.

***

Squaw Valley

Theodore saw Bernie's number pop up on his cell. The PI was pissed.

"Why didn't you tell me you had another child? For God's sake, Davis."

"I didn't see how it was relevant."

"Seriously? You make a list of people who may have it in for you and leave off the adult child you abandoned?" He had done his homework before calling.

"I didn't abandon him! He was just seven at the time. His mother prevented me from seeing him, then moved away. He knows nothing about Abigail."

"But now he's what? Twenty-seven? He could be harboring a lot of animosity."

"Listen to me Bernie, you're barking up the wrong tree."

"If you want me to do my job effectively you need to tell me everything. Leaving out a disabled adult child is not everything."

"Mea culpa. But I don't want my son dragged into this mess. He's been through enough."

Bernie didn't respond to that. "I'll stay another couple of days, see what I can find here and keep you posted. But you'd better answer this first—are you prepared for me to follow the lead wherever it takes me?"

Theodore hesitated a moment and then said, "Yes." He hung up never once thinking he hadn't mentioned where he was speaking from.

***

Salt Lake City

Franklin was dying to know Nicole Davis's reaction to the letter he'd sent her. Was she wondering who her husband was pushing on the swing in the park all those years ago? Or did she have a sneaking suspicion that her husband was a low-life, two-timing shmuck? Franklin could only imagine the look on Theodore's face when his wife confronted him and told him to move out. He needed to find a way of confirming it all went as planned.

Franklin's thoughts turned to the strange cars. Because of Wang's carelessness, two unfamiliar vehicles had been stationed on the street. One had since left and not returned. If it was the police, he couldn't figure out why they needed two cars to begin with. Still, the fact that no one had come to the door to question him led Franklin to believe they didn't have enough to go on. They were watching and waiting. Let them.

He'd repeatedly told Wang never to come to the house.

The unfortunate episode created a situation beyond his control, and he'd had to eliminate his only friend. Just like in the video games, the better player won. Still, Franklin would miss him. It wasn't an intentional betrayal, but it was a betrayal nonetheless, and *that* was something Franklin would never tolerate again. He hoped the suicide note he'd written was believable but knew his work connections to Wang would raise flags. Unfortunately, the lingering police presence had prevented him from taking action.

Franklin looked at the front door camera, relieved to find the second car was gone as well. He'd been waiting for it to leave. Maybe the watcher needed a potty break. He picked up his phone and called a car service, getting goosebumps as he thought about his upcoming trip. He was excited and scared. But one emotion soon washed away the others. It would get him to his destination unfettered.

Hate.

***

Salt Lake City

It amazed Bernie how much information was put into an insurance statement. He knew mail tampering was illegal but it was one of the quickest data troves he had access to and he was not above crossing that line.

The insurance was through Medicaid, confirming his suspicion that the mother was not earning much. The letter was a notice that past denials of services had been reviewed and overturned. The biweekly physical therapy could continue. He decided at that moment to stay until the next appointment. If Oakley was going twice a week, the likelihood was he'd emerge from his house again in the next day or two. Bernie knew the notice was surely sent by email as well, so he didn't even try to re-close the envelope. He took a photo of the letter and crumpled it up for later disposal. Then, he called his hacker friend. "I need you to check out a Franklin Oakley." He gave the name of the insurance company and ID number he took off the co-opted letter.

"How much do you want to know?" the hacker asked.

"Start with the basics . . . finances, prior residences. But throw in medical history."

"That'll be extra."

Bernie held his tongue. Then, "Just bill me."

"How about criminal records?"

"Not yet."

"Okay, I'll have the other stuff for you next week."

"Make it today."

"That'll be extra."

Bernie let out a loud sigh. "Yeah, I know."

CHAPTER 40

Haifa, Israel

T erry took the elevator down from her parents' thirteenth floor apartment. The last few weeks had been trying. She'd been pulled from the Mossad mission. Yosef explained they would try other methods to identify the White Knight. No longer needed, she was being kept out of the loop.

When she returned to her lab, she quickly found the work had piled up while she'd been away. She kept long hours, fully aware of how vulnerable her research was to being stolen. On top of it all, she missed Gabe terribly. She understood he needed to get back to his own job and see his family. With everything seeming so dismal, she'd decided to put her work on hold for a few hours and spend time with her parents. It proved to be a wise decision. Her mother, Hannah, had put things in perspective, reminding her of her good fortune while feeding her homemade baklava.

By the time she got to her car, she felt a lot better. Tonight she'd call Gabe and talk about fun things. Like their upcoming wedding.

***

At one a.m., Terry sat up in her bed. She'd set the alarm to wake her up when Gabe's workday would be over, but she hadn't yet fallen asleep. It was hard without Gabe lying next to her. She let out a breath of relief when he picked up, his voice cheerful. "Hi, sweetheart. Isn't it really late there?"

"I can't sleep without you," she said.

"I know just how you feel. How about some good news?"

"That would be great."

"Since it didn't work out for us to go to my parents' vacation home last time, they're suggesting we try again. Any chance you can squeeze in a trip to South Carolina?"

Terry was about to give him a list of reasons why she couldn't do it, and then stopped herself. Hadn't her parents just reminded her of what was most important? "Yes! Let's do it. It may take me a week or so till I can get there. Is that okay?"

"Sure. But the sooner the better. I don't like being away from you."

Terry felt her eyelids drooping. "I love your voice, motek. Can you stay on the phone till I fall asleep?"

Gabe spoke sweet nothings to her.

The phone was still in Terry's hand when she woke up the next morning.

***

MountainCare Rehabilitation Center
Salt Lake City

Jon and Bernie stood outside the rehab facility. The car's thermostat had registered a brisk outdoor temperature of thirty-four degrees, but Jon was quickly learning in the Rockies, when the sun shone bright, it felt like a spring day. The trip from Barcelona to Salt Lake City was long, yet he'd magically slept most of the way and was more refreshed than he'd felt in a long time. He'd touched base twice with Luanne, keeping her in the loop as best he could. Her day job was keeping her busy. Jon missed sleeping beside her.

Bernie had contacted him once he learned that Oakley

had worked at and was fired from ItsRelative. Ironically, early in his tenure, Oakley had subjected himself to company-wide employee DNA testing. It was fair to assume Oakley knew of his connection to Abigail—that they were half-siblings. If losing his legs provided motive, finding Theo's love child offered opportunity. Theo's son had become their prime suspect.

Now, Jon could connect Oakley to Wang, the alleged man behind the DNA theft. But the cord tying Oakley to Peter Cromwell, Caroline Atwood, and Congressman Taylor remained thready. Was Oakley simply a client of Wang's, hiring him to mess with his father? Or were the two men working as a team? The connection between the men proved enough to subpoena Oakley's insurance company. Which led them here, to the rehab center.

Jon agreed to meet Bernie and check out the only other place he was known to frequent, get as much on Oakley as possible before bringing him in for questioning. The optics of arresting a down-on-his-luck paraplegic were not optimal, and Matthews had cautioned him to be damn sure before making an arrest. Loomins was on standby, dividing his time between the inquiry into Wang's suicide and keeping an eye on the Oakley house. If Jon determined there was enough for an arrest, Loomins would make a move.

Bernie dropped his cigarette on the ground, crushing it with his shoe. "How do you want to play this?"

Jon said, "Make it like I'm Oakley's friend. I'll take it as it comes."

"I like your style, Steadman."

"Wait here. Shouldn't take long."

Jon walked inside the white stucco building and found the directory that led him to a rehab common room. He was dressed casually in fitted jeans and V-neck forest-green sweater, his hair just past the collar. He looked around. No sign of Oakley. Six patients were positioned around the space each with a dedicated physical therapist. Some walking, climbing steps, or engaged in table exercises. Two were amputees.

It brought back repressed memories from when Jon had spent months rehabbing his leg. Despite this, he was thankful to be mobile, but still had a noticeable limp and periodic pain.

A blond pony-tailed woman around his age—mid-to-late twenties—was finishing a session with a middle-aged man. Jon had timed his entry well, assuming if he showed up on the hour he would catch someone available to talk between patients.

Jon raised a hand in greeting. "Hey, I'm looking for my buddy, Franklin Oakley."

She eyed him. "Who are you?"

"Name's Jon. I made up to meet him here. We're gonna grab some lunch."

She looked skeptical.

He smiled, the one he'd been told was flirty. "There a problem?"

Slowly, her smile grew in return. Shook her head. "I didn't think Franklin had a lot of friends. Certainly not like you."

"Like me?"

"Uh, nothing."

"No, say it."

"It's not nice. About Franklin." She giggled.

"I swear I won't tell."

"Well, let's just say, you look pretty cool. With-it, you know?"

He laughed. "Thanks, I guess."

"And you know Franklin . . ."

Jon was distracted by one of the nearby seated patients. His pants were rolled up, and he was unlatching a prosthetic leg. "Ah . . . gotcha. Well, we know each other since we were kids. Grew up on the same block. No one was cool back then."

"In LA?"

"Huh?"

"Where you grew up."

"Yeah, that's right . . . so where is he?"

"On vacation. He didn't come in today. It's weird he told you to meet him knowing he'd be out of town."

Out of town? Seeing the woman's concern, he quickly regained his bearings. "Wait a sec." Jon made a show of looking at his phone. "Damn! I messed up the day. I hate these phones. It's next month. We made these plans a while ago. Sorry to bother you." Jon moved toward the door. Then turned, "Do you happen to know where he went? If it's back to LA, I could catch up with him. I'll be there in a few days."

The woman shook her head. "Not sure, but I know he was real excited to finally use the new legs."

Jon felt a rising sense of dread. "Are Franklin's legs like those?" He pointed to the prosthetic leg now resting on the therapy bed.

The therapist turned to look. "Similar, but his are better tech. You'd never know his legs were artificial. He's come a long way. You should be proud of your friend."

"I am. I better give him a call. I really screwed up." He plastered on a sparkling smile. "Nice meeting you."

"You, too." She moved closer to him, enough for him to pick up the scent of her perfume. "Here's my card," she said, a sultry tone seeping in. "You know, in case you need it for anything."

Jon accepted the card, gave it a kiss, making the woman laugh. "I'll treasure it . . ." He read her name off the card, "Jordana." He put it in the back pocket of his jeans, sensing that's where her eyes lingered as he walked out of the room.

Five minutes later, Jon was back in the car, ending a call with Loomins. Bernie was chewing gum. He said, "What's that look on your face?"

"What did you find out?"

"Oakley's gone."

"What? How?"

"Loomins says must've been when he took a short break."

Bernie let out a stream of profanities.

Jon waited him out. Then said, "I got one really good piece of intel."

Bernie spit the gum out the window, turned on the ignition. "What?"

Jon said, "We're no longer looking for a wheelchair."

***

Salt Lake City International Airport

The last time Franklin had been on an airplane was years earlier when he'd moved with his mother to Salt Lake City from Los Angeles. They'd come when his mother remarried, following his stepfather to his hometown. Though his mother was no longer with the husband, they'd stayed for the lower cost of living. Franklin barely had any memory of LA and was fine with it. He had enough crappy memories without adding those to the heap. Now, he was standing, waiting for his flight to board. Standing!

His new prosthetics were incredible. It was the one thing he'd splurged on with his recent financial windfall. He could move like everyone around him. No one could tell they weren't his real legs. When the metal detector buzzed, he told the TSA agent it was an army wound, the result of an IED. The man actually saluted him. He felt empowered. With his new and improved legs, he could do anything.

CHAPTER 41

Lake Tahoe, California

T he cab ride from Reno had taken a little under an hour.
When they got into town, Franklin noted the expansive lake. It looked like blue glass, the snowy peaks of
the Sierra Nevada mountains reflecting on its placid surface.
The more beautiful the scenery became, the angrier he got. His
father should be home in Los Angeles, terrified of having his
infidelities exposed, not enjoying a ski vacation.

The driver pulled over in front of a well-maintained
complex of buildings. A banner above the entrance read, "Welcome, U.S. Ski Team!" Franklin got out, allowing the driver to
retrieve his bags from the trunk. The place was a series of vacation condos, each with its own hot tub and magnificent view
of the lake. Franklin was sick of the snow and cold. "Couldn't
Dad have vacationed somewhere warm?" he muttered under
his breath as he walked inside the hotel lobby.

Today was the longest he'd ever worn the prostheses
and he was feeling drained. He walked slowly to the check-in
desk and offered his mother's credit card. He'd been using it
on and off for years She was so disorganized and had no recol-
lection that it was still active. Anyway, he always paid for the
purchases.

The desk clerk handed him a room key and information
about the facility. Maybe he should have requested a disabled
room so he could easily access the shower after taking off

his legs, but he didn't want to draw attention to himself. He pocketed the key, wondering if they gave him a condo next door to his dad.

Once in the room, he took a look at the shower, and changed his mind. He called the front desk and asked to be moved to a wheelchair accessible room, explaining that his disabled mother may visit and want to shower. The woman cheerfully accommodated him and within twenty minutes he was in a new room. Franklin removed his prostheses and expelled a long-held breath of relief.

***

FBI Field Office
Salt Lake City

Jon sat at one of the office's unused desks and sent an update to Matthews, letting him know he'd hit a dead end with no lead on Franklin's whereabouts. Agent Loomins was appropriately upset, but to his credit he didn't blame losing Franklin on the lack of backup. He accepted responsibility and the anticipated reprimands. Jon didn't know if he'd have handled things differently. They'd caught a break when calls to local cab companies yielded a pickup at the Oakley residence, taking one occupant—a young man—to the airport. Not surprisingly, no one by the name of Franklin Oakley had boarded a flight in the last twenty-four hours. A man with his computer skills could smoothly slip into another identity.

A billion-dollar tax fraud scheme was tying up local FBI field agents. The SLCPD agreed to loan two detectives to pick up surveillance of the Oakley house, recommending to observe rather than approach at this point. See if Francine led them to her son. A mother wouldn't be inclined to actively assist in her child's apprehension. But Francine was sticking to her routine, no sign of distress. As if she hadn't a clue what her son was up to.

Jon's phone rang. Matthews's voice sounded hoarse. "Let's go through it. Talk it out."

Jon reviewed recent events. "To quote you sir, the easiest explanation is usually the right one. Oakley needs a way to pay for travel . . . hacking someone's credit card is too risky. He wouldn't risk being flagged and not have the payments go through."

"Correct." Matthews paused.

Jon understood his boss was waiting for him to make a deduction. "Maybe Franklin asked someone to use their card and pay them back. But his only friend is dead, and he wouldn't dare use a dead man's account, especially given all the attention on Wang's death."

"Where would Oakley gain easy access to a credit card with the smallest chance of being caught?"

The penny dropped. "He's skimming off his mother."

"Sounds like it's time to meet the former Mrs. Davis."

**

The next morning, Jon pulled up in front of the old house. It was scarcely larger than a double-wide. On closer inspection, it *was* a double-wide. The exterior's drab brown paint was chipped, revealing the white stucco beneath. Dead flowers, neglected remnants of a season long gone, littered the window boxes. As Jon got out of the car, a cold wind blew a 7-Eleven Big Gulp across the postage-stamp lawn, the plastic cup coming to a rest at Jon's boot. He picked it up, tossed it in the can by the curb, and walked up to the front door, avoiding the ramp. He hesitated a moment then rang the bell.

"Yeah?" he heard from within.

"Mrs. Oakley?"

"Yeah?" the raspy voice repeated.

"My name is Jon Steadman," he said, loud enough to be heard through the door. "I work for the FBI. We're investigating credit card fraud. We believe yours has been compromised."

The door opened a crack, a chain lock crossing in front of a bloodshot, mascara-smudged eye, imparting a look of skepticism. "My card company would have called. You making house calls now?"

"Something like that."

"Let me see some ID."

Jon held it up to the gap. "May I come in?"

"I'm in the middle of something."

Given the punch of her breath, Jon guessed that *something* was fueling herself with hundred-proof vodka. "I'll only take a few minutes of your time."

The woman hesitated, then stepped back, allowing him inside.

***

Francine Oakley looked worn down. By life. They were sitting at her Formica kitchen table, similar to the one Jon's grandmother used to have in Boston. The walls were decorated with various travel posters of the Bahamas, hung askew, the paper curling out from under their narrow plastic frames.

Interpreting Jon's perusal as interest, Mrs. Oakley said, "It's on my son's bucket list. He's been wanting to get there since he's a kid. Pig Beach."

"*Pig* Beach?"

"Yeah, like real pigs. There's some kind of uninhabited island down there where they swim. Sounds idiotic to me. Dunno what he'd even do there being as he can't swim."

Jon needed to get on topic. "Can you tell me if you've seen unauthorized charges on your credit card?"

"I use only one card. I had another one, but I haven't touched it in ages. Was too hard to keep track of the different bills. Forgot all about it."

"Do you have a computer?"

She dug a laptop out from under a pile of *People* magazines. "Many. My son is obsessed with them."

Hmm. "Log in to your old credit card's website and update your password. That should do it."

It took Mrs. Oakley ten profanity-filled minutes to complete the task. Jon sat awkwardly scrolling through his email.

Finally, she said, "Okay, here it is." Then, "Damnit! You're right. Someone's using my card!"

Jon moved his chair closer, scanning the statement.

Squinting at the screen, Francine said, "Wait, why would someone steal my card and then pay the bill? It makes no sense."

"That's a good question. We're just starting the investigation. This will help us get some answers."

"What will this do to my credit rating?"

Jon said, "Don't worry. Looks like the thief paid on time. In any case, now that it's an open investigation, none of the victims will be liable."

She spent a moment rummaging through her bag, found a pack of Virginia Slims "Can you catch this jerk?"

"That's why I'm here. Let me get a better look at the charges . . . May I?"

She nodded, lit up.

Jon clicked on the account history tab. The past year had only a few small transactions, all paid for. Then an increase in the last twenty-four hours.

The card had been charged the day before. In Lake Tahoe, California.

CHAPTER 42

Truckee, California

J on and Bernie agreed to meet at the Carlyle Café, a fifteen-minute drive to Lake Tahoe. The ride from the airport took Jon across Donner Pass. Tucked high in the Sierra Nevada mountains, the pass—named for the ill-fated party of settlers, many of whom resorted to cannibalism to survive—offered an awe-inspiring, though dizzying vista of the valley below. Jon was astounded by what humans were capable of when they felt threatened.

As a light snow began to fall, Jon struggled to exercise self-control and keep his eyes focused solely on the road. He quickly understood why the car rental agency required snow chains on the tires. Driving the narrow road at an elevation of seven thousand feet required a great deal of concentration. At the peak, Jon pulled over to take in the sight of snow-flakes slowly making their way down to the crystalline waters of Donner Lake far below. Fatigue hit hard and Jon closed his eyes. When he woke twenty minutes later, feeling refreshed, he sent a text message to Bernie giving his ETA, and another to Luanne.

It was eight-thirty in the morning when Jon arrived at the café. Upscale, the earth-toned design contributed to a re-laxed atmosphere, light years from the hectic pace of New York City. Ten minutes passed before Bernie rushed in, wearing a lightweight jacket as if it were a mild spring day instead of late

November, his casual attire in direct contrast to the intense look on his face. Jon stood up and shook the PI's hand. It was chafed and unmanicured. They both sat.

A waitress wearing a stained white apron around her near-anorexic waist approached. Jon ordered a hot cocoa. Bernie declined.

When the waitress stepped away, Bernie said, "I've tried calling Davis several times, but it transfers to voicemail. My gut's telling me he's in danger. All arrows point to his son. He's coming for his father. He has two other siblings, living better lives than his. One being doted on by the same father who maimed *and* abandoned him. With his new legs, he can exact his revenge. Can't picture him attacking an able-bodied man with any success. Still, Oakley could be the common thread between Wang's murder and the insurance scams, DNA theft and the Davis blackmail. We get him, both of our cases will be closed."

Jon listened to the PI's stream of consciousness with interest. Seeing the man wasn't finished, he remained quiet. Bernie went on. "Even if Oakley has no intention of harming his father, my job is to keep the kid from letting Theo's skeleton out of the closet, namely his love child in Santa Fe. That's what I'm being paid for."

The waitress came with Jon's drink. He held the hot mug, waiting for it to cool. The aroma conjured up images of a down-filled comforter and hours of deep sleep. "I agree."

Bernie didn't seem put off by Jon's short reply. "Why are we here? You get some info?"

Jon took a tentative sip, the chocolatey liquid sliding down his throat, then drank some more. "Franklin's been using his mother's credit card. One she thought was no longer active. There was a recent charge at the Squaw Valley condos just outside Tahoe. I wouldn't be surprised if his father is staying there as well."

Bernie said, "Two points for the Feds. I guess that's why you said to bring ski clothes."

Jon nodded.

"What's the game plan?"

Jon said, "We find Oakley. I'll ask him some questions, see where they lead. Make sure his father is safe. With any luck we can put the whole thing to bed. Get an arrest."

"*We?* Where's the cavalry?"

"He's a cripple. We don't need the cavalry."

"I'm pretty sure that word's not PC."

Jon shrugged. "It's how I think of myself. If Oakley was behind the attacks on Ed, Luanne and Wang, he hired out. Besides, I couldn't ask for backup when we have no evidence Oakley's behind the DNA theft."

"Fair. I want to confirm Franklin is behind the blackmail before I tell Theo his own son is the culprit. My reputation is on the line. Mistakenly blaming his kid will get him really pissed, and rightfully so."

Jon looked over Bernie's shoulder as the door to the café opened and Luanne walked in wearing a The Cure sweatshirt and ripped jeans. She was carrying a black duffle. Her hair was shorter, spiky, no lingering maroon tones. Her eye makeup was thick and black. Jon waved her over.

Bernie turned to look and while she was still out of earshot, he asked. "What's the reporter doing here?"

"You recognize her?"

"Sure. She looks just like her byline photo."

Huh?

"She's been investigating this from day one. She's earned the story. Nothing will be leaked until the case is closed."

When Luanne sat down, she kissed Jon full on the mouth. He felt his cheeks redden. He introduced her to Bernie.

The PI pursed his lips. "Ah, got it. Listen Ms. Parker," his tone turning firm. "I'm a private eye, with the emphasis on the private. You're gonna have to keep my client and his family out of the papers. Capisce?"

Jon suppressed his instinct to defend Luanne. She said,

her voice calm, "You have nothing to worry about. I'm looking at the DNA theft, not infidelity. Your client's name will never come out. At least not from me. You have my word."

Bernie looked at Jon who nodded at him. Bernie leaned back, seemingly satisfied.

Eyeing Jon's half-drunk mug, Luanne said, "So, what did I miss?"

Jon repeated what he'd shared with Bernie.

"What's with the ski gear I had to bring?"

"We're going to pay Oakley a visit. I want to be prepared."

Luanne said, "Strong arm a cripple?"

Jon threw a smirk at Bernie, who rolled his eyes.

Not long ago Jon would have said he'd play it by ear, but that method had got him into deep trouble in the past. "Nah, I'll be the consummate professional. Get a feel for the guy, keep it cordial."

Luanne stood, her chair scraping the floor as she did so. "Ready?"

The men got up and in unison said, "Let's go."

***

Squaw Valley Ski Resort, California

"Yes, a Mr. Theodore Davis checked in two days ago," the cheerful desk clerk said, never asking to see Jon's credentials. He was glad about that, preferring to acquire info without them. FBI creds often had the opposite than intended effect. People clammed up.

The clerk said, "You say he was your high school teacher?"

"Yeah. We're having a reunion." Jon gestured to the computer. "How about a Franklin Oakley?"

The woman checked the computer. "Nope."

"That's weird. I thought he RSVP'd. Can someone check

in with a name other than what's on their credit card?"

"Yes, though we're supposed to ask for proof. Usually their driver's license."

"What if they don't have one?"

She seemed confused by the suggestion. "Who doesn't have a license?"

"Some people with disabilities."

She nodded slowly, enlightened. "Oh, right. Well, only one wheelchair accessible room was booked, and Martin was legit. He was so considerate. He switched from a standard room since his elderly mother may come for a visit. I thought that was nice, even if it's funny since he looks too young to have such an old mother, ya know?"

Jon felt a spark of excitement. As casually as he could, he said, "Martin?"

"Yup, Martin Van Buren. He left earlier. Headed to the slopes for the day."

Bingo! Jon asked, "Don't you think it's funny he has the same name as a president?"

The woman looked at him blankly. "President of what?"

Jon shook his head. "Forget it." *What's become of our education system?*

Jon stepped outside where Bernie and Luanne were waiting. "Oakley's staying here, but for some reason he went to the slopes. Why on Earth would someone who's been in a wheelchair his entire life decide to go skiing?"

Luanne said, "Probably *because* he's been in a wheelchair his entire life. He finally has freedom to move around like the rest of us."

Rather than debate the issue, Jon said, "I'm not convinced that's where he actually went." Jon took a moment to organize his thoughts. "Here's the game plan. Luanne, you go to the slopes, see if you spot him there. If you do, call me immediately. Do not approach him."

Luanne asked, "Where are you going to be?"

"I'll look for him in the village. Bernie, you stick around

here. You'll see him if he returns. From wherever he went."

"Are you still sure no cops is the way to go?" Luanne said.

Jon pulled a wool cap from his pocket and donned it. "I'm sure." He walked away, heading toward the village center.

***

Theo came to a hockey stop at the bottom of the slope. He loved to ski, especially early in the season. Since Lizzy was born they'd had few opportunities, but today they'd enrolled her in ski camp. He could see her on the bunny hill, a look of concentration on her face. She was a natural and would soon be ready to hit the green slopes. He considered going over to praise her progress but decided against it. Lizzy was approaching that age of being embarrassed by too much parental attention. Nic was getting a hot stone massage. They'd planned to ski together later, but for now he was glad to have the mental alone time out on the mountain, the air a perfect forty degrees. Not too hot or too cold.

Tomorrow he'd start early. Maybe try a black diamond after all this time.

After tackling a blue run, Theo skied up to the chalet, careful to avoid a clumsy looking man clearly new to the sport. Back at his condo, Theo removed his skis, boots, hat and gloves, placing them in his foyer locker. He would shower, but first needed to check if there were any work emergencies that needed to be addressed.

Ten minutes later, Theo was at his hotel room desk, his laptop open before him. There, in his inbox, sent only minutes earlier, was an email from William Sherman. Trembling more with anger than fear, he opened the email.

Mr. Davis,
I'm disappointed that you haven't shown any signs of re-pentance. I have no choice but to take matters to another level . . .

***

Franklin was still shaken from being in such close proximity to his father. Earlier when he'd spotted Theo, Nicole and their daughter leaving their condo wearing ski gear, he'd decided to follow. It was exhilarating knowing he had the power to physically stalk his prey. He'd nearly bumped into his father. But the man didn't even recognize his own son. Franklin put his phone back in his pocket, hoping his email would remind his father who was in charge.

CHAPTER 43

Squaw Valley

T he best way to describe the village of Squaw Valley was "cozy." Anchored by the luxury condo complex, the hamlet was surrounded by snow-draped pines and junipers that blurred into a carpet of green and white as far as the eye could see. Specialty shops sold fleece blankets, alpaca wool sweaters, and colorful wind chimes. Bespoke galleries showcased art highlighting the majestic local scenery, and intimate eateries served crafted hot beverages and pricey comfort food. The air was invigorating, suffused with an energy Jon knew to be exclusive to the American West. There was a heightened sense of being at the edge of nature's rawness, near enough to absorb the beauty, but any closer and one would quickly find himself in the remote, dangerous wild. If his life had played out differently he'd have lived out here. In a heartbeat.

Walking toward the village center, Jon did his best to implement what he'd learned in FBI training. Observe, notice the little things. File them away. He was confident if Oakley would pass by, he would recognize him, even though his sole frame of reference was a series of photos.

Jon would track down the elusive Oakley. Rather than embark on a wild goose chase on the slopes, he felt confident the plan was sound. Bernie was back at the hotel, watching the entrance for any sign of Franklin, while Luanne scouted the slopes. Still, Jon couldn't shake the feeling he was going about this the wrong way. He considered calling Doug again for guidance but decided against it. The guy had enough on his plate right now. And Jon's pride was getting in the way. He didn't want to come across as a rookie. Jon was determined to apprehend Franklin by the end of the day.

Jon's thoughts turned to his hotel accommodations. He and Luanne would be sharing a room. His feelings for her were complicated, but it wasn't something he could devote his mental energies to at the moment. They were both enjoying the time together and he would leave it at that . . . until there was no choice but to face the dynamic between them. Now wasn't that time.

A wave of exhaustion hit Jon. Since meeting Bernie and Luanne at the café in Truckee, the jetlag had reached a crescendo. He found a bench and sat.

A man wearing a cowboy hat stood in the village center playing an achingly beautiful melody on his violin, a light snow falling lazily around him. Jon closed his eyes, absorbing each note. And there, in that space, he envisioned Ashleigh, her face aglow, smiling, joyous. Content. The image was so vivid, he could see the pores on her face. Reveling in the moment, the music washed over him. As the song died down, Jon mentally grasped at the wisps of his dead fiancée. A deep sense of longing filled him. He opened his eyes, momentarily disoriented.

The cowboy put down his fiddle, gave Jon a knowing nod and walked away. Jon suddenly felt very cold. He tightened his scarf and before he could stop himself, he reached into his pocket. Without another thought, he took two pills from the bottle and swallowed them dry.

***

Bernie was pacing the lobby when his phone rang. Noting who was calling, he picked up on the first ring. "Where the hell have you been, Davis?"

"The blackmailer knows where I am." Davis sounded breathless, desperate. "Somehow he's tracking me and my family. I need protection."

"Listen, Theo, I don't know what you were thinking going off like that without a word."

"I thought it would be a good idea to get away with my family. I was hoping you'd find this guy in the meantime so I could go back to my normal life when we return home."

"Poor decision. Anyhow, it's not that simple. We're here, in Tahoe."

A pause. "Huh? How'd you know where I am . . . and who's *we*?"

"This case is bigger than you can imagine. It's overlapping with a federal case of fraud, extortion, and hacking."

"What in heaven's name is going on?"

Bernie said, "I'm now working with the FBI. We're pretty sure who's behind this. We need to talk."

"So, you're saying I'm just one of several targets?"

"Sort of."

"Stop speaking in tongues and tell me who the hell is terrorizing me!"

Bernie hesitated. "I haven't confirmed it beyond a reasonable doubt . . ."

"I don't care. Tell me *now* or you're fired!"

Bernie had had enough of the pompous jerk. He'd tried to be empathetic, but the guy was asking for it. "It's your son, dammit. Franklin is the one terrorizing you!"

***

The phone slipped from Theo's hand and crashed to the floor. A tsunami of memories nearly caused him to fall beside it in despair. Theo's life had taken a long and winding road. As a student, he'd worked hard to achieve success. His family had no money and he wanted to get out of the rut, make something of himself. At twenty-one, shortly after graduation, he'd met Francine. She was a spitfire back then. And a burgeoning alcoholic. She introduced him to the lure of spirits. Bourbon, whiskey, gin. Drunken weekend binges. Somehow, he'd managed to clean up long enough to take and pass his LSAT, then three years later, the bar. They married at twenty-four and had a child. A beautiful perfect boy. Theo allowed his mind to wander back in time. Something he had stopped doing long ago. He remembered pushing his son on the swings as he squealed in delight, carrying him against his shoulder as he slept, a thumb held firmly in his mouth, his curly brown locks falling delicately across his angelic face.

All gone in a flash. The day that turned his life around was seared into his memory.

It was a rare smog-free LA morning. Francine wasn't feeling well and she'd asked him to take their son to his friend's house on the way to a deposition he'd scheduled downtown. It was teacher training day and the kids had a day off.

The minivan slammed his Toyota on the back right passenger side, sending them into a dizzying spin, the car eventually landing on its side, resulting in a devastating fatality. Since that day, he hadn't touched a drink.

Theo served three years in prison on a manslaughter charge, participating in AA meetings, soon discovering he no longer loved his wife and filed for divorce—something they should have done long before. All they had in common was the drink. She never fought the divorce, never seemed to care enough—or wasn't sober enough—to bother. He worried for his son but knew that was the one area in which he would never prevail. She was a functional alcoholic and more out of revenge than devotion to her child, she would never let him have their boy. They'd gone to court once when she refused visitation. His son was there in his wheelchair, staring at him with an expression Theo didn't recognize. Was it resignation? Disdain? He was an invalid. Would be for the rest of his life and it was Theo's fault. What had Francine told the boy? That after maiming him, his father had abandoned his own son? Theo's hands were tied. Embittered, Francine threatened to press domestic abuse charges. He knew the judge would believe her. For years he'd agonized if he should have fought harder. He certainly had the money. But he came to believe his son was better off without him and seeing the boy in that condition would be a constant reminder of his past destructive ways. His only option was to walk away.

Mercifully, he'd had his law license reinstated. When he met Nicole, he had already opened his own law firm. Slip and fall. He worked hard, putting in long hours and hiring only Ivy grads, paying off his loans in three years. The business did well from the get-go. He moved the family to a sprawling cliffside home in Laurel Canyon down the road from the Zappas. Nicole was supportive of the child support payments he made to Francine, never questioned them. But Abigail would be a different story entirely. A love child. Mixed race. Yes, that was an entirely different story indeed.

"You still there, Davis?" He heard the PI's voice from the floor.

His hand trembling, Theo bent down, picked up his phone. "Yeah." Reeling from Bernie's accusation, he opened the minibar, and poured himself a glass of vodka, taking the first drink he'd had in twenty years. He drank greedily while listening to Bernie's theory. It was preposterous. His son, an innocent child, was a victim of circumstance.

The thought was swiftly pushed aside by the image of his AA sponsor shaking his head, popping into his mind. *Take responsibility,* he would say. *Remember step nine—make amends to people you've harmed.* He'd worked hard on the twelve steps of Alcoholics Anonymous, spending years reaching out to people affected by his drinking. But he'd missed the most important person.

Franklin wasn't a victim of circumstance. He was a victim of his father. *Of me,* Theo thought. For too long he avoided facing what he'd done to his only son, knowing it would take him to a dark place from where he may never escape.

Bernie said, "We believe Franklin has been harboring a deep-seated anger and jealousy."

"Impossible. He was only seven when I left."

"For heaven's sake, Davis, look at the photos he sent you. Swings, smiles . . ."

"I wanted a relationship with him, but his mother wouldn't allow it." He knew he sounded pathetic. Maybe he should have tried harder, gone to see his boy regardless of Francine's threats.

"Did it ever occur to you that maybe he doesn't know that? Think about it from his perspective. His father—the person charged with keeping him safe—maimed *and* abandoned him. Then to add fuel to the fire, you had not one but two other kids—that you support. Kids whose lives he thinks of as charmed. He wants revenge."

Theo refused to accept that his sweet boy had turned into a vengeful criminal. "You're barking up the wrong tree, Bernie. He doesn't have the physical abilities to do anything. And likely not the intellectual capacity either. Hacking into servers, stealing DNA samples, come on."

"You really have been out of touch. Franklin graduated cum laude from Brigham Young on a need-based scholarship. Whatever warped idea you have in your mind of your kid, you'd better readjust it if you want to come out of this unscathed."

Theo was stunned. Had his son actually gone to college? He digested this tidbit of his boy's life. He was proud. And ashamed of his own surprise. He cleared his throat. "This is all just a theory because you can't find the real culprit. I don't believe my own child would seek to destroy me."

"Broken people are capable of awful things, sometimes beyond imagination."

"What are you suggesting?"

Theo heard the PI take a deep breath, then let it out. "If you want the mailings to stop and no longer live in fear of discovery, we need to be sure."

Theo took a moment, he thought of Nic, the true love of his life . . . and felt a crack in his resolve. He stared at the bottom of the now-empty glass, as if the answers could be found there, and whispered, "How?"

***

"I've been skiing since I could stand," Luanne said to Jon. She was seated on a bench, leaning over, locking her ski boots. Bernie was getting fitted for skis. "I may not look it, but I grew up pretty normal. My parents got season lift tickets at Heavenly every winter. I know the Tahoe area slopes quite well." She eyed him, still in his jeans and Timberlands. "Can you ski?"

Jon said, "It's been years. Since before my injury." He patted the side of his leg in emphasis. "Not sure I should get back out there."

Bernie walked over. "It's like riding a bike."

Jon wasn't too sure he agreed, but Theo consented to act as bait, so he'd do his part.

Bernie deserved credit for coaxing Theo into it. If Franklin was in Tahoe, Theo would draw him out. "You two go ahead. I'll gear up, but I'll need a few runs on the bunny slopes to find my ski legs. If Franklin's out here, that's where he's likely to be anyway."

Bernie said, "I'll go with you. I'll meet you outside." He left, not waiting for a reply.

"Me too," Luanne said. She zipped her black ski bib and jacket, donned her matching fleece beanie, placing goggles atop, then attached her lift ticket to a zipper. She had to be the only goth skier this side of the Continental Divide.

Jon pointed out the window to the chair lift, "Theo is over there. You've got the skills to stay close to him. Remember to call me if you see Franklin and I'll take care of it from there."

"Roger that." She left, stomping out like an astronaut, her skis slung over her right shoulder.

Twenty minutes later, Jon stepped out into the bright sunshine. The snow had let up, though not before leaving another couple of inches behind. In this light, the mountain appeared diamond-studded. Now clad in proper attire, Jon dropped his skis to the ground in front of him and clicked in his boots. Luanne came to a hockey stop a few feet away from him, the snow dancing in her wake. "Woohoo! That was awesome!" Then, "No sign of Franklin."

Jon looked up at the mountain from where she'd come and felt a pang of apprehension. It had been years since he'd hit the slopes. He wasn't sure his leg was up to the task. He patted his jacket pocket, annoyed with himself that he'd become accustomed to having his pills with him, and finding their presence a relief.

"Can you hang out here a bit and keep an eye out for Oakley?"

"On it."

Slowly, Jon made his way over to the nearby bunny hill. He spotted Bernie talking to a woman donning a ski school jacket. Jon raised a pole drawing Bernie's attention and waited while the PI reached him. Bernie lifted his goggles to his forehead. "You're looking good. Staying vertical. The beginner's level instructor is starting her shift now. I gave her my number to call if she sees anyone who fits Oakley's description. The previous instructor already left."

"Hopefully we didn't miss him. Just in case, Luanne will keep close to Theo and let me know if she spots Franklin. Why don't you do the same?"

Bernie considered it, readjusting his goggles. "Fine. If you find him first, call me pronto."

Jon agreed and watched Bernie and Luanne ski toward the nearest lift. Jon made his way to a T-bar that pulled him to the top of the bunny hill. To his left were several young children listening intently to an instructor, the sun casting shadows of their small, bundled bodies tilted over V-shaped skis. Jon hoped he wasn't about to make a fool of himself. He'd prefer not to be the butt of six-year-olds' jokes.

He pushed off. By the time he reached the bottom, he

was relieved to know that Bernie was right. It was already coming back to him . . . *Make the 's' all the way down, body forward. Be prepared to fall if necessary.* He allowed himself a mental pat on the back. If he managed to stay on his feet for the next few tries, and Oakley didn't show, he'd move on to the greens.

***

Franklin still couldn't believe he was standing up . . . on skis, no less! The private lesson had done him well, better than if he'd joined the group class. He'd learned basic maneuvers. The prosthetics's technology was incredible, allowing him to move as though they were his own legs.

He was keeping an eye out for his quarry when he spotted a man around his age speaking to a woman wearing a black ski bib, her spiky hair distinctive. Something about her was familiar. Franklin lifted his neck muffler to cover his nose and mouth and watched as the guy headed for the bunny hill, approaching an older man standing near a ski instructor.

Then it hit him. *The woman.* She bore a striking resemblance to the reporter working on what the papers were calling the OBooks insurance scam. Luanne Parker. The reporter he'd put a contract out on! The sight of her caught Franklin off guard, and he nearly tripped over his own skis.

Regaining his balance, he turned to face the other direction, gliding slowly toward the lodge to avoid drawing attention. Panic filled him and it took all his restraint to remain on his feet. Franklin had never seen the younger man before, but the older one could easily pass for the driver who'd been scouting out his house back in Utah. If he was here in California, he must be a federal officer, the younger man his partner.

Franklin waited for the panic to subside bolstered by the realization that they hadn't noticed him. If he acted fast, he should have enough time to get his things from the condo and leave before they caught up with him. He would need to stalk his prey later.

For now, his next step was obvious. Eliminate the clear and present danger.

CHAPTER 44

Squaw Valley Ski Resort

Franklin entered the lobby of the resort's main building. He was wiped out. If he never got back on a pair of skis again, he'd be fine. He needed to gather his belongings and find other lodging.

He was making a beeline to the corridor when the annoyingly cheerful desk clerk looked up, smiling broadly. "Did your friends catch up with you?"

Franklin looked over his shoulder. There was no one standing behind him. The penny dropped. *No!* "Friends?"

The phone rang. She answered the call. "Squaw Valley Condos. Julie speaking. How can I help you?"

Franklin interrupted her. "Are you sure you have the right guy?"

Into the phone she said, "Please hold a moment." She nodded. "From the reunion."

"Oh, right. Which of my friends was looking for me?"

"I didn't get his name, but he was about your age, the other was older."

The Feds. "Did you give him my room number?"

"Sorry, we're not allowed to do that. I'm sure you'll see them later at the event."

She seemed oblivious to the fact that she was a sieve of information. She picked the phone back up and quickly got into a conversation. Franklin was momentarily frozen to the spot, unsure where to go. It was pure luck that he'd evaded the Feds until now. One thing was clear. He needed to move fast, find another hotel in spitting distance to his father. It would be hard with many people coming to town for the upcoming ski competition. Franklin needed help, desperately. The guy who took care of Wang was on standby and could be here in a couple of hours if need be. Franklin made the decision. As soon as he got to safety, he'd contact his hired hand, a man called Gerard.

***

"Where the hell did he go?" Bernie and Jon were standing outside Franklin's room. Jon had asked the chambermaid which rooms were wheelchair accessible. Following a short process of elimination, they identified Oakely's. When no one had answered the knock, Jon took the liberty of letting himself in, using the skills he'd polished up on since Carrie's death.

Members of the U.S. ski team were staying at the facility, and he'd needed to time his entry to avoid them passing in the hallway. Still, it beat sparking an unnecessary red-tape mess if he'd asked for a key from the front desk. Getting a warrant would take too long. Didn't matter, anyway. They were too late. Oakley's stuff was gone. He must have been alerted to their presence and bolted. It seemed like they were always one small step behind him.

Jon leaned against the hallway wall, pocketing his lock pick set. It was identical to the one his former partner—and Randy's mother, Carrie—had used to become an expert. "He won't go far. If he's looking for revenge, he'll stick around. He'll try to find a way to get to Theo."

"You're probably right . . . do you really think he'll hurt his father?"

"No idea, but in either case our best bet remains to stick to Theo like glue."

Bernie shook his head. "Forget it, he'll never agree to that. His wife's planning on skiing with him today. She'll want to know why three people are tailing them."

"Davis doesn't get a vote. My job is to find Franklin Oakley and bring him in for questioning. Determine if he's responsible for the murder and extortion. One lowly philanderer is not going to keep me from nabbing the guy. If Theo's outed, that's too damn bad."

***

Alpine Meadows, California

It took Franklin a couple of hours on his iPad's personal hotspot, while loitering in the Walmart's baby section to find an available room with an accessible shower. It was eleven miles from Squaw Valley, which was the best he could get. When he tried to pay, the credit card was denied. Could anything else go wrong? He decided to risk it and call his mother.

"Hey, Mom."

"Frankie, where the hell are you?" Her voice was gruff, the result of years of smoke inhalation.

"I took a vacation. I'm fine."

"Sure you're okay. You're partying with my credit card!"

"What?"

"You think I'm stupid or something? After all I've done for you! If you need a vacation so bad, use your damn disability money. Like I ever take a vacation. I've canceled the card, if that's why you're calling. Good thing that nice guy stopped by. Or you'd have sucked me dry!"

"I always pay the balance, Mom . . . wait, what guy?"

"The cop. Or whatever he was. He was official and all that."

That's how they found me. My own mother! "What did he look like?"

"What difference does that make? You trying to change the subject? You can forget it. He helped me see you're a petty thief. Just like your useless father." Her words were slurred.

"Mom, for heaven's sake, answer my question! Was the guy tall with a limp?"

"Yeah. That's him. How'd you know that? What sorta trouble are you in, boy?" Her voice was filled with suspicion.

He hated when she called him that. And she knew it. "And you let him in the house!"

"What else should I have done? Like I said, he was official. Don't worry. I never let him near your sanctuary of a room."

At least she did something right.

Franklin calmed himself. "Listen Mom, sorry about the card. I'll find another way to pay for my vacation. If anyone else shows up, don't talk to them. Got it?"

He heard the familiar sound of the microwave dinging. Her dinner was ready. "Yeah. Gotta go now." She hung up.

"Nice talking to you too, Mom," he said to himself. She was as loving as always. *If ever there was someone with the most sullied gene pool, it's surely me.*

***

Gerard stood perched at the top of the Enchanted Forest ski run. He was a skilled skier. One of few bonuses of having grown up in rural Vermont. The snow was different here, but the method was the same. Lean and just shy of six feet, he was built like a runner. He wore the red jacket of a ski patrol medic. Not exactly the typical thug. Which of course he wasn't. He'd been educated at Cambridge University, majoring in Greek philosophy. Turned out there wasn't much of a living to be eked out of the high-brow degree. Plato, Aristotle, Socrates... Morons!

Gerard laughed at the Princess Bride quote. The movie was a classic. Growing up, he'd learned so much from what he deemed iconic films of the last century. During that same phase, he'd realized a particular ability to take care of unpleasant business without the weight of conscience. This skill, as he thought of it, proved significantly more profitable than a teaching position. It's why rather than posturing in front of a classroom, he was now standing on a mountain slope, observing a young girl attempting her first green run.

The kid had finished her class and went straight for the ski lift. She was alone, seemingly intent on trying it by herself. It made things much easier. Her parents were currently on the way up the gondola to a black diamond. He knew this because he'd had his eye on the Davis kid for several hours, keeping watch for her parents. They would be busy for at least another thirty minutes.

Gerard gauged the girl's speed, and pushed off, keeping his distance. As the kid approached the narrowest section of the run, he came up from behind. For the benefit of any nearby skiers, he said, "Sweetheart, you're doing great." He knew the kid wouldn't turn around.

In a swift, smooth motion, he brought his pole down hard behind the kid's legs. The girl cried out, tumbling, skis twisting, one dislodging from her boot. She let out a lungful of air, stunned.

A woman skiing by saw them, came to a stop twenty feet ahead. "She okay?"

"She'll be fine. I got her."

The woman went past.

"You all right?" Gerard asked Lizzy.

The girl's left leg was twisted, its ski lying beside her, the ski on her right leg awkwardly pointing skyward. "Someone hit me," she whimpered.

"Looked like you tripped over your skis."

She appeared confused. He extended a hand. The kid took it, crying in pain. "My leg hurts."

"It might be broken. I'll take you back to the lodge. We can get someone to look at it there."

"I-I don't know. I'll call my parents." Lizzy struggled to maneuver her body, reaching for her jacket pocket.

"You won't get a signal out here," he lied. As she pulled

the phone from her pocket, Gerard bent down toward her. "Let me help."

Swiftly, he pulled a kerchief from his pocket, placing it over her mouth and nose. It was a myth that Chloroform, the go-to knock-out drug of his favorite 70's movies, actually worked. The better, quick-acting drug was Ketamine. In sufficient amounts, it served a dual purpose. Rendering one's prey unconscious and numbing the pain of bodily damage.

The girl was out in seconds. Gerard took the phone from her pocket and powered it off. He would need to move her quickly before they drew any more attention. His uniform would only help so much.

Gerard removed the girl's remaining ski and the poles dangling from her wrists, leaving them temporarily in the snow. He then lifted the unconscious child into his arms. She was lighter than expected. Carrying her, he skied twenty feet to the tree line where he'd left a red Polaris snowmobile emblazoned with a white cross partially hidden from view. He placed the girl on the attached rescue toboggan, then retrieved the remaining equipment, and using a bungee-like cord, strapped down everything alongside the girl. He removed his own skis, clicking them into the rack at the side of the vehicle and waved at several rubberneckers curious to see what was happening, but not interested enough to get involved. He'd learned long ago that human apathy worked in his favor.

The entire episode took no more than five minutes. Gerard covered the unconscious child with a red and white blanket and sped away.

***

"Where's my daughter?" Theo asked the teenage ski instructor who was popping a piece of gum in her mouth. "She was waiting for you. Maybe she decided to try her skills on the slopes."

"You left her alone?" Theo felt his rising anger aware it deserved to be directed at Bernie Patton. The PI had actually convinced him that Franklin was behind the threats. But they never found him. *Even when using me as bait.* Because it *wasn't* Franklin. They were after the wrong man. Theo silently kicked himself for buying into the absurd theory in the first place. Before hanging up on Bernie, Theo said he didn't want to hear from him until he found the right guy. He came to Tahoe to be with his Nicole and Lizzy and that's what he was going to do.

"Excuse me . . . sir." the teen instructor said, as if remembering the proper way to address her students' parents. "When ski camp is over, it's not my job to babysit the kids. You were told the pick-up time. You're a half hour late."

Theo turned to Nic who was shivering, her arms crossed over her chest. The temperature had plummeted in the last few hours, not typical for Tahoe. "Don't worry, I'm sure she's fine."

Nicole said, "We never should have tried to squeeze in another run."

"There was no way to know that stupid gondola would get stuck."

"I'm freezing. Let's find her and get back to the condo."

Theo got out his phone and called his daughter's cell. It immediately went to voicemail. "She didn't answer. She's skiing. She won't hear the phone." He didn't say it seemed to be turned off.

Nicole frowned. "I can't believe she'd go off on her own like that."

"She'll be ten soon. We can't hover over her like we used to. I'm sure she's fine."

Nicole bit her lip. "I suppose." She asked the teen, "When did she leave?" The girl shrugged, popped her gum.

Nicole faced Theo and rolled her eyes. "If she just left she could still be a while. Do you mind waiting here for her while I return my skis and warm up?"

"Sure. We'll catch up with you soon. Try to relax." Theo watched his wife ski toward the lodge, then faced the mountain, and waited.

***

The cabin was sufficient for Gerard's needs. Secluded in the eastern edge of the Tahoe Forest, surrounded by towering Jeffrey pines, the closest cabins were nearly a half mile away. A tiny kitchen, twin beds, bath. He threw one of the mattresses on the floor, brought the kid in and placed her on it. She'd be out for a while. Quickly, he cleaned his gun, loaded it and headed back out to the slopes.

CHAPTER 45

Squaw Valley Ski Resort

Neither Jon nor Bernie had been able to keep up with Theodore and Nicole, both of whom were skilled enough to ski the black diamond trails. Jon would kill himself if he'd tried and Bernie wasn't sufficiently motivated, adamant that his only job was to find out who was behind the letters to his client. And to get his final payment. The retainer Theo had given him was nearly exhausted with all the necessary travel and background checks.

Jon and Bernie lingered at the bottom of the slopes, the younger man bristling. "It's like Theo's going out of his way to thwart our efforts. He agreed to lure Franklin out in the open, but takes the hardest trails, knowing full well his son can't follow him there. What gives?"

"Obviously, he's conflicted. When I told him we hadn't found Franklin, he lost it. Said we were looking for the wrong guy. He's not doing the bait thing anymore. Guy's living in denial. No matter what his kid's involved in, he's still Theo's kid."

"You have kids?"

Jon shook his head. "Nah, I've got a while till then. But I'm real close to my friend's son, Randy. He's turning five soon."

"Like a big brother sorta thing?"

"Hard to define," Jon said, though it felt more like a surrogate father sort of thing.

Bernie looked around. "At least we can keep an eye on

Theo from here. Not sure it'll help in any case. Franklin cleared out of his room, so maybe he got spooked and isn't around anymore."

"We have to assume he's on the mountain. We have no other leads."

Several skiers came racing down the slope. Dressed in yellow and white ski suits, with numbers on them. Slalom skiing. They skimmed the red-flagged gates, schussing down the mountain at breakneck speeds. The two men edged out of the way.

"Know what's going on?" Jon asked.

Bernie pointed to two men hanging a banner announcing a championship beginning that day. "This is a finish line. Looks like there's some sort of pre-competition practice."

Jon said, "If this guy's smart, he'll be dressed like all the other competitors. We'll never find him like this."

"I don't get it, I thought he wears fake legs."

"They're called prostheses. They work just like our legs."

Bernie said, "That's just great. Now what? We need a smarter way to smoke him out."

"He's never been on skis before. That means if he's out here he'll be on the easiest slopes. He'll want to blend in so he'll avoid the bunny slopes. His best bet is to head for the green runs. They're an extension of the black diamonds, so he'll mix in with the competitors coming from the top."

"So, what's the game plan?"

"We check those runs and look for the one guy dressed like an athlete who looks unsteady."

"That could take all day."

"You have a better idea?"

"We could wait at the lodge or the hotel. If he's after Theo, that's where he'll go eventually. Be a helluva lot easier."

"He's too smart. He's not going back there, Bernie. Like you said, something spooked him."

The PI blew a raspberry in exasperation. "Whatever,

Theo's paying me by the hour. Let's just do this."

The two men waited in line for the ski lift. When it arrived they leaned back, poles in hand, and settled into their seats, their skis dangling below them. The safety bar slowly came down and soon they were climbing at a steady pace, their breath creating frosty clouds. Jon adjusted his fleece neck gaiter over his nose, his breath warming his face. The resort was picture perfect, the granite peaks surrounding the clear blue lake, the ski chalet at its banks. Snowflakes fluttered lazily downward as if someone had hit a slow speed button. It felt as if they were in a snow globe.

Halfway up the trail, Jon felt something whiz by him. Instinctively, he ducked down in his seat. Panicked, he let go of his poles and they fell to the ground below.

Bernie said, "Whoa! Stop shaking this thing."

"Someone's shooting at us!"

"Don't be crazy. There's no one—"

Before Bernie could finish his sentence another bullet flew by. "What the–! We're sitting ducks. Help!" The drop was at least thirty feet. There was nowhere to go.

"Try to stay calm."

They were hovering over an off-trail stretch of narrow snow-laden paths snaking between the pines. Jon looked around. The chair lifts in front and behind them were unoccupied. He saw no one. Another shot rang out. Jon made himself as small a target as possible, shielding his bowed head with his arms.

"We need to get off this thing," Jon said, though he had no idea how. "The shooter must be using a sniper rifle, probably up in one of the surrounding trees." Bundled as he was, he awkwardly turned to his seatmate, glad he was calmer. "Bernie?"

Bernie eyes were closed, a dime-sized, blackened hole visible just above his belt clasp, the bib slowly turning red. His body slackened, listing to one side, then toppled forward, the weight of his skis, the only thing keeping him from falling over the safety bar to the rocky, white ground below. Jon did what he could to maneuver in the limited space. He pulled on Bernie's jacket collar, leaning him backward against the seat, his head resting at an odd angle.

Bernie moaned.

"Bernie, Bernie, wake up!" Another shot. This one ricocheting off the steel cables above them.

Bernie whispered. "I'm hit."

Jon forced calm into his voice. "You're going to be okay, just stay with me. We're almost at the top. We'll get help." Jon could see other skiers now congregating near the lift hut, praying the sniper wouldn't dare shoot into the crowd.

Bernie's eyes fluttered. He mumbled something.

Jon struggled to hear "What did you say?"

"The kid . . ." Bernie's eyes closed.

"Come on, wake up!" Jon patted the PI's face with his thick gloves.

Bernie seemed to get a burst of energy. "Franklin. He's not after his father. He's after the kid."

Of course!

How had he missed that? What better way for Oakley to punish his father than by harming his favored child? The one who got everything he never did—a two-parent family, a comfortable home. A loving father.

The lift was moving at an infuriatingly slow pace. Bernie coughed softly, closing his eyes once again.

***

Placer County Sheriff's Office

Sheriff Kyle Harding was an easygoing sort. Relaxed and amiable, many found him an unlikely choice to head a one-hundred-and-twenty-person department. After a couple of years exploring the world he'd entered the academy, deciding to follow in his father's footsteps—a man who had made a career in law enforcement. His dad was a good provider, offering Kyle and his brother a stable childhood. Ample pay and terrific benefits outweighed the few close calls resulting from aggressive casino patrons mixing lifelong frustrations with copious amounts of alcohol. Kyle had come to love his job and the citizens of Tahoe, grateful to work in one of the most beautiful enclaves in the country.

Harding was walking past the front desk when the radio squawked to life, the staccato sounds of a Squaw Mountain security reporting a shooting.

"Anyone on the scene yet?" he asked the muscular female deputy manning the system.

"We've got a car five minutes away, sir."

"Put out an APB. I want the roads in and out of the mountain shut down."

"Yessir." The deputy got on the radio.

Harding grabbed his hat and raced out the door.

***

Squaw Valley Resort

Nic and Theo were in the security office, an officer donning a black uniform was trying to take their statement. Nic was crying in stops and starts. Theo did the talking. "Why are we just standing around here?"

The officer spoke firmly. "Sir, I know this is difficult. We're trying to help you. We've sent out a search party to all the runs, along with a medic. As soon as they find your daughter they'll call in."

Theo grabbed his coat. "Tell me where to go, I'll look too."

"They're professionals, Mr. Davis. You'll only get in the way." The man softened his tone. "Stay here with your wife. We'll keep you posted."

Theo was ready to argue further when he felt Nic's hand

on his arm. He looked up, searched her swollen eyes.

She said, "I know you want to help. I do also. But he's right, Theo. Let them do their job."

Instantly, the fight was out of him. For now—if only temporarily—he knew his place. It was right beside his wife.

By nightfall, it was clear their daughter was officially missing. Two more officers were now in the room, snow dripping from their boots. One of the officers stood in the corner speaking into a handheld radio. Lizzy's phone was still transferring to voicemail. Either it was turned off or the battery was dead. Theo sat beside Nic, silently praying for Lizzy to walk through the door telling some crazy story they'd all laugh about one day, once the horror of the moment wore off.

The officer said, "The sheriff stationed several officers along the main road."

Theo asked, "Why? What for?"

The officer pursed his lips. "Well, how can I put this? We haven't found your daughter's . . ."

Theo felt the blood drain from his face.

"You understand, that's a good thing. We've searched the lodge and combed the entire mountain. She's not here. Means she left."

"How could she possibly leave? She's nine! She doesn't drive. No money to pay for an Uber. She left . . . that's your theory?"

"Under the current circumstances, there are only two viable explanations. He held out his thumb. "One, she was unhappy and decided to run away, or—"

Theo stopped him in his tracks. "She's a happy kid. No issues. She didn't run away."

The officer continued, lifting his pointer finger. "Or, two."

When he didn't immediately continue Theo closed his eyes. He didn't want to face the other option. Though, for the past couple of hours he knew that it was the most likely one.

He forced himself to say it aloud, though softly. "Someone took her."

Though Nic was sitting on the opposite side of the room, she'd somehow heard him. There was a second of silence before she let out a heart-wrenching wail.

***

Jon ran toward the security office, the sound of a woman's cries a familiar, terrifying clarion call. Stepping inside, he looked around the space, relieved to see no one was physically hurt. *No one else, anyway.*

He'd escorted Bernie to the local hospital with a bullet lodged in his stomach. By the time Jon left the ER, the PI was being prepped for emergency surgery. Jon got back to the mountain as quickly as possible, calling Luanne from the road, telling her to stay put in the hotel room. When he saw the melee, he was glad he did so. Cops were everywhere, ushering people off the slopes. There was no mention of an active shooter, yet among the coaxed masses, fear and confusion surpassed irritation. Luanne would be safe in the room.

The parents sat in the corner, appearing shellshocked. Their daughter wasn't there. Bernie had been right. Nicole Davis had her eyes closed, leaning against her husband who was grasping a paper cup, a tea bag tag drooping off the rim. Jon had but one focus. He needed to find the Davis kid.

In the office, stood a tall, broad-shouldered man with a sheriff's medallion pinned on his chest pocket. A deputy blocked Jon's path, his hand raised. "This is a private room, sir. You need to leave."

Jon took out his credentials, handed them over.

"FBI?"

The sheriff approached. "Sheriff Kyle Harding. What does the FBI have to do with this?"

Jon gestured to the sheriff to follow him, the deputy

stepping back. In the hallway, he said, "The kid missing?"

The sheriff nodded.

Jon explained what he could about his involvement. "The Davises are part of a larger investigation."

Harding lowered his voice. "Looks like a grab."

"Agreed." Jon pursed his lips. "I need to speak with Mr. Davis. Alone."

"You think he's involved?"

"No, sir. But at this point, he's the only one who will help us find his daughter alive."

***

"What did you do?" Franklin shouted into the phone. "The mountain is crawling with cops!"

"What did you think would happen? You wanted me to scare off the two guys. I guess my sharpshooting skills are even better than I thought. Moving target, a couple of hundred feet away. He sounded gleeful."

"What about the kid?"

"Change in plans, boss. I have her." Gerard used a mocking tone.

"What are you talking about? I paid you to disable her, break her legs, knock her out. Leave her there for her parents to find. Not kidnap her!"

"What's with all the outrage? Your objective is achieved. From what I understand, you've had no reservations about more . . . significant . . . results in the past."

"This one's different."

"Interesting."

Franklin noted a demented tone. Made him think of Hannibal Lecter from Silence of the Lambs. "Where's the girl?"

"Well, here's the thing. I researched your dear old dad, and it occurred to me he would pay a kingly ransom for the safe return of his kid. The guy's loaded. You never mentioned that juicy bit of info."

Noting the man hadn't answered his question, Franklin was losing his cool, but he had a good sense of whom he was speaking with. A cold-stone killer. "What are you going to do?"

"Now, calm down, boss. You got what you wanted. You're putting the fear of God in the parents. The kid's leg is broken. May never heal right. What difference does it make now?"

"I have a well-designed plan!"

Gerard laughed. "Here's your opportunity to go with the flow. See ya around, boss."

Before Franklin could respond, the man hung up.

CHAPTER 46

Squaw Valley

The entire operation relocated to the Davis's condo, a more comfortable environment than the facility's security office. For Nicole, the constant flurry of activity was a welcome distraction. Theo had agreed to speak alone to Agent Steadman. After twenty minutes, she began to worry. When he returned to the room, Nicole took one look at her husband's slack-jawed, defeated expression and rushed to him. "What's wrong? What did the agent say?"

When Theo didn't immediately reply, she said, "Did they find Lizzy?"

Theo shook his head. "No." He collapsed on the sofa. "Nic, I know this is the worst possible time, but I need to tell you something. Something awful that I did."

Nic's face filled with confusion, then fear. "Will telling me help find Lizzy?"

He rubbed a hand over his face. "It might."

"Then whatever it is, tell me."

He began. "Two years into our marriage, I represented a client named Tyrone . . ."

Nicole listened as the truth tore from her husband's lips, like a thousand tiny knives stabbing her in the heart. By the time he finished, her husband's eyes were wet. "I'm so terribly sorry."

Nic began to shake, her body unable to absorb the shock. Feeling caught up in an alternate universe, she stood, her voice unsteady. "Fix this, Theo. I don't care what you have to do. Find my baby." She strode out of the room, brushing past Agent Jon Steadman standing in the hallway.

***

Jon watched Lizzy's distraught mother rush by. His heart went out to the woman for all she'd endured in recent hours. Her husband had cheated on her, producing a love child she'd known nothing about. Still, even that was overshadowed by the prospect of *losing* a child. Nothing was worse. Jon prayed it would never come to that.

Randy's sweet face popped into his head. He checked the time on his phone. It was nearing the boy's bedtime. He took a chance and called.

"Hi, Abuela."

"Jon, how are you?"

"Hanging in there. I'm out of town, but I've been missing Randy. Is he still awake?"

"Hold on, mi amor. I'll get him for you."

A minute later, he heard the phone being jostled. "Jonny! Can you come over to play tomorrow?"

Jon laughed, reveling in the child's exuberance. The boy's innocence was a panacea. "Sorry, buddy. Not this time. I'm away for work."

"Can you read me a bedtime story?"

"Well, I don't have any of your books here, but I can make something up."

"Yeah!"

Jon spent the next few minutes conjuring up a tale about a young prince who drove cool cars instead of horses and ate peanut butter and jelly sandwiches with his pet tiger. Randy loved it. When Jon finished, he wished Randy a good night.

"Love you, Jonny."

The words pierced Jon's heart. "Love you too, little man."

When the call ended, Jon was more determined than ever to find Lizzy and bring her safely home.

***

Alpine Meadows

Franklin needed to get out of town fast. His plan was disintegrating. The Feds were onto him. The kid—his half-sister—was now in the hands of a psychopath. Until now Franklin had successfully managed to maintain a respectable distance from any necessary unpleasantries. All that had been required to make a problem go away was a hefty payment and the proverbial nod. Admittedly, it was an intoxicating power. This time, it felt too close. Too real. Almost like he was holding a gun in his hand.

Regardless, the unexpected turn of events yielded what he so desperately wanted. Vengeance.

Then why didn't it feel as gratifying as he'd dreamed?

Franklin was a planner, and while he hadn't intended to implement the next phase for several more months, with the advent of Wang's death, things were accelerating quicker than expected. Still, he was ready. He'd spent many hours working laboriously on Wang's spyware, the updated version was locked securely in Franklin's private server, one he accessed remotely.

Dealings with the secretive White Knight had been a challenge, the broker a savvy negotiator. Ultimately several buyers expressed ardent interest, leading to a healthy bidding war. While the parties were sworn enemies of the United States, Franklin didn't think of it as his problem. It was free enterprise. Wasn't that what America was built on after all?

Franklin took comfort in knowing Wang would have never successfully negotiated such a lucrative deal. The rewards were truly his own. He did an outstanding job and would be amply rewarded. While his mother's credit card was preferable—he believed it less likely to attract attention—it was no longer an option. He'd switched to plan B, withdrawing cash from an account he'd maintained in a dead man's name, an identity he assumed early in his hacking career. The balance never exceeded ten grand. It wouldn't draw any attention.

Since changing hotels, he hadn't unpacked his things and could be ready to leave town on a moment's notice. Using his computer, he booked his flight. His funds would be awaiting him at his destination. Once there, he would regroup, initiate the next phase of his plan—setting up shop. A more permanent and professional one. He had a thriving business to attend to.

He rubbed lotion onto his stumps and put on his new prosthetic legs, realizing he didn't miss the old, familiar ones he'd used for years. The sizeable investment in bionics was his first big purchase and worth every penny. Excitement rushed through him. His new life was finally beginning. The trade was on schedule. In a matter of days, Franklin will have unleashed the boldest cyberattack in world history.

***

Tahoe National Forest

The kid had woken twice, listless and groggy. She seemed more confused than scared, oblivious to the condition of her poorly bandaged leg. That was the Ketamine. Gerard sat her up, made her drink some bottled water and swallow several spoonfuls of yogurt, then had her hobble to use the bathroom.

Gerard never liked kids. He could scarcely remember being one himself. Maybe because he was forced to grow up fast, escape the toxic environment of his father's house. When his mother had abandoned him when he was an infant, his father—a car mechanic—wasn't equipped to care for a child.

He was a 'latchkey' kid—no one home when he returned from school, no dinner waiting for him. He learned how to take care of himself. As lousy a parent as his father was, he'd done one thing right—encouraged his son's education. Not pay. He couldn't afford it. Gerard applied for scholarships, eventually getting a full ride, thanks to a mix of merit and need-based grants oddly similar to Oakley.

Despite being stuck with this kid for the next few hours, he didn't regret the decision to alter Oakley's plan. Simultaneously brilliant and stupid, the fact that Oakley hadn't seen a bigger, terrifically lucrative opportunity, was more than a blind spot. *He's an idiot savant. Nothing more.* Either way, what Oakley had said on the phone was accurate. They would both get what they wanted.

Gerard looked at the time on his phone. He'd call the kid's parents in an hour. Let them stew. It would further motivate them. Once he made his demands, he'd wait the agreed upon time and not a minute longer.

The girl was mumbling something he couldn't understand. Once again, he sprayed the cloth with Ketamine and put her back to sleep. The sooner he got the kid off his hands, the better.

One way or another.

CHAPTER 47

Squaw Valley

Sheriff Harding ended the call with Agent Steadman. With the shooting occurring on his turf, the Feds agreed to have him take the lead on the manhunt. It was his responsibility to keep his citizens safe. In cooperation, he left the Feds to deal with the kidnapping. Sure, they were looking for the same perps—the shooting and abduction were connected —but they had yet to fit all the puzzle pieces together. The strategy for now was divide and conquer, then share all intel.

Two people had come forward with reports of witnessing a hurt child being whisked away by a medic on a snowmobile. It meant the abductor had never taken the roads, explaining why with nearly all evacuees passing through the roadblock, the shooter was still on the lam. As long as he had snow under him, he could elude the authorities. Sure enough, one ski patrol snowmobile was missing from the lot. It would have been an easy take. Keys were always left in the ignitions to accelerate emergency call responses. Attentions had been redirected to canvassing the area while maintaining a roadblock.

The way things were lining up, Franklin Oakley was behind his half sister's abduction. It was unlikely, even with advanced prosthetics, that a man who'd never before been on skis had grabbed Lizzy Davis off the slopes. Or shot Bernie Patton. Oakley had hired a pro—someone capable of kidnapping a child *and* shooting a moving human target within a short period of time. They would either need to find Franklin or his accomplice. Fast.

***

Squaw Valley Resort

Jon entered the Davis's condo from the hallway, having left a message for Matthews asking him to call. A palpable toxicity radiated between Theo and Nic, the tension thick as they willed the phone to ring.

A hostage negotiator now sat beside Nicole and Luanne, who'd insisted on keeping Nicole company. Matthews had had the foresight to call one in as soon as it became clear Lizzy Davis had been abducted. A stern-faced woman in her fifties, she'd flown in from San Francisco.

Theo stood, began pacing. "Why isn't anyone calling asking for a ransom? What does that mean?"

Jon knew it wasn't a good sign. But they needed to treat this like a search and rescue, while the sheriff was leading a full-on manhunt for the perp. "We can't speculate. It's still too early. Franklin may just want you to sweat it out. That's what he's been going for all along."

"Stop saying it's Franklin! We don't know that yet. You said yourself that he isn't physically capable of carrying out this kidnapping."

Jon understood Theo was deep in the denial phase, but he'd better move on from it soon. Nicole sat quietly on the opposite sofa, Luanne holding her hand. Jon could only imagine the myriad of thoughts running through Nicole's mind. She appeared on overload.

When she finally spoke, everyone looked up. "Why is he doing this?"

Theo shook his head, remaining silent.

Jon spoke up. "He wants revenge. In Franklin's view, his father moved on, leaving his first born behind. He's had a rough childhood, lost his job. He's angry at the world."

Theo spoke softly. "But me most of all."

The phone rang. Theo lunged for it.

The negotiator said, "Remember what we discussed."

"This is Theodore Davis."

They watched as Theo listened, his hand grasping the phone in a vise grip. The negotiator's eyes were on her tablet's screen. It was opened to the app that was recording the call. Jon knew the FBI would run it through their voice ID system, see if the man could be identified.

Theo hung up the phone, his face deathly pale. "They're demanding two million. He's calling back in two hours to say where to make the swap." He paused, spoke just above a whisper. "He said if I don't have the money in time, he'll . . . he'll hurt her."

Jon suspected the kidnapper's words were more dire, but Theo was protecting Nicole. "You did great, just like we practiced," the negotiator said to Theo. "Did the caller identify himself in any way?"

"If that's your way of asking if it was Franklin, it wasn't."

Jon asked, "How do you know? You've never heard him with an adult voice."

"I just know." His voice didn't falter.

Jon was about to say something when Luanne put a hand on his arm. He took the hint and kept quiet.

Nicole hurried to a laptop sitting open on the room's desk. "I'll check our investment accounts."

The negotiator said, "Mr. and Mrs. Davis, it's important we agree on a strategy."

Nicole turned to the woman, her face beet red, contorted in pain. She was a powder keg ready to blow. Jon braced himself, saw Luanne react similarly.

"Strategy?" Nicole shouted. "There is no strategy! That lunatic has my baby. MY BABY! I'll give him whatever he wants."

The room fell still. Theo approached his wife, his hands up protectively. "Sweetheart..."

"Don't!" she said and he backed away.

The negotiator spoke softly. "We can't risk that he'll walk off with the money and not release your daughter. Don't you agree?"

Nicole's face lost all its color. "Why would he do that if he gets what he wants?"

"A variety of reasons. But those aren't important now. What we need to do is stall him, give the authorities a chance to find him and your daughter. In the meantime, we negotiate a simultaneous swap—he gets his money when you get Lizzy, not before. He's fixated on the cash now, so he has incentive to work with us."

Jon sat on the room's sole club chair. Theo was on the left-hand loveseat, and Nicole and Luanne on the opposite one. It felt like a mediation. Addressing Theo, Jon asked, "What can you tell me about Franklin?"

Theo looked like he was struggling to keep his frustration in check. "Why are you going after him? He doesn't have Lizzy. We need to find the guy from the slopes!"

Jon said, "We're trying. There's an APB out on him. It's likely the same guy who shot Bernie. But we need to go at this from every angle. If we find Franklin, we'll find the kidnapper. Now, think, where would Franklin hide?"

"You're the FBI. Why don't you track him?"

"Because he's a first-rate hacker, Mr. Davis. He can use anybody's name and bank account to get anywhere. I know he's your kid, but if you interfere or withhold information, there will be repercussions."

Theo looked helpless, shook his head. "I haven't seen him in over twenty years. His mother can help you better than I can."

"I tried. She's currently being detained, and not in any condition to help."

"You mean she's intoxicated."

Jon's silence told them Davis was correct.

The three sat quietly for a moment. Then, Theo said, "He likes video games."

Jon leaned forward. "Okay, that's good."

Luanne who had been quietly listening, interjected. "Listen, Mr. Davis, I know this is beyond difficult, but we need you to focus. I understand you haven't been in contact, but can you think of anything that he was passionate about? Something that could help lead us to Lizzy."

Theo closed his eyes, drawing his lips in concentration. "Computers, anything electronic really. And swimming, I guess. We used to have a pool. He loved it. Had this inflatable dolphin he'd hold on to and kick, splashing everyone around. He can't swim anymore." Theo put his head in his hands, a deep sob emerging.

Jon noticed Nicole begin to stand, wondering if she would sit beside her husband, but instead, she sat down again, her eyes focused downward.

He said, "Francine told me she didn't know why if Franklin couldn't swim he'd want so badly to go to a beach."

Luanne perked up. "Which beach?"

Jon thought back. He'd seen the posters on the wall. "Something about pigs. A beach with pigs."

Theo furrowed his brow. "I don't know anything about that."

Luanne was already on her phone, tapping furiously. "Got it! There's a place called Pig Beach. In the Bahamas." Luanne stood, energized. "Bingo. That's where we start."

Jon said, "I'll contact Sheriff Harding, have him alert the regional airports, give them a heads up." He pulled out his phone, making the call. Harding answered on the first ring. Jon brought him up to speed. "Get local law enforcement to keep an eye on regional airports. Tell airport personnel that Oakley could be armed. And that he may or may not have an uncooperative or injured child with him.

Nicole gasped, her tears seemingly dried up. In a halting

voice, she said, "You think he's going off with her."

"Actually, no I don't. He or his accomplice needs to stick around to get the cash. I have no idea why they aren't asking for an electronic money transfer but having an in-person swap is in our favor. It means they have to be around with your daughter in hand. All that said, we need to be prepared for anything."

The kidnapper couldn't have gone far with Lizzy." Jon donned his coat, "I'm going to the Reno airport." To the negotiator, he said, "Let me know the minute the kidnapper calls back with where the money drop will be."

The woman said, "Will do."

"I'm coming with you," Luanne said, sidling up beside Jon as he ran for the exit.

The look on her face told him there was no point or time to argue with the woman. He knew if it were him, he wouldn't take no for an answer either. She wanted the story, and he had no desire to stand in her way.

***

New York City

Matthews received Jon's message and phoned him back.

"Sir, hold on, I'm getting in the car. Heading to Reno."

He heard a car door open and shut, then another. Moments later, Jon came back on the line, giving an update. He explained the ransom demand. "Franklin couldn't get to Lizzy himself. He wasn't skilled enough to abduct her off the slopes. Assuming he has only one accomplice, that had to be the sniper who shot Bernie."

"Agreed," Matthews said.

Jon hesitated, then said, "Something's off." If the son wants his father's money, why all the theatrics? Franklin had access to anyone's money. Sure, it may be symbolic, but why risk getting caught for money he doesn't need? My gut's screaming."

During their past cases, Matthews had learned to not disregard Jon's instincts. "What's your thinking?"

"The sniper is working solo now. We got too close to Franklin and he hired someone to scare us off. For whatever reason, Franklin left Lizzy behind with this thug. Either it was part of their agreement or the sniper went rogue. Franklin wanted revenge, not a payout. He got that with Lizzy's abduction, but he doesn't need the money. This is the other guy at work."

Matthews felt an odd sense of pride at his subordinate's logic. "That sounds on target. Either way we need to get the Davis's daughter back and right now it seems your best shot is the lead to Franklin."

"I'm going to try and get him at the airport. Can you get the powers that be to ground departing flights?"

"No judge will agree to that with what we have so far. Your best bet is Reno. I'll contact the area FBI field office and put them on alert. We need to play the odds, and you're right. Reno has the most flight options for him. I just emailed you a photo of Oakley I got from his previous job ID card. It's clearer than what the PI sent us. Use it as needed." Matthews heard a woman's voice. "Parker with you?"

"Yessir. She's checking my phone for the photo right now."

Matthews said, "Keep her out of harm's way. We don't need another civilian in the line of fire, Jon."

"Doing my best, sir. We're going after Oakley, but what do we do about the kidnapper?"

Matthews paused a moment, then said, "Hope that the negotiator is really good at her job."

CHAPTER 48

Reno, Nevada

J on sped along California Highway 28 north to Reno. They were probably a good hour behind Oakley. Hugging the lake on his right, he nearly mowed down a line of spandex-clad bikers peddling hard up the hill. He crossed the border into Nevada, a blur of casino billboards flying by. Luanne was bracing herself against the car's dash with one hand, scrolling on her phone with the other. "There are only two flights remaining for the day that could make sense for Oakley if he wants to make it to the Bahamas without an overnight layover —JFK and Miami."

"Good work."

When they arrived at the airport, Jon brought the car to an abrupt halt in front of the departure terminal and the two raced inside. Without government plates, he didn't expect the vehicle to be there when they returned.

Jon flashed his badge, rushing past the security line as annoyed passengers looked on. His leg was starting to act up. To Luanne, he said, "You take the JFK gate, I'll take Miami." The two split up and went their own ways.

***

Franklin's stumps were killing him. Not phantom pains but real ones thanks to the surviving nerve endings. He'd been meticulous about caring for his residual limbs, gently donning the liners before securing the sockets to his stumps. But he also knew he wasn't supposed to wear the bionics for more than two hours at a time so soon after the fitting. It was now nearly three. He felt the exertion wearing him down. If he could get on the plane, and detach the legs, he'd have time to recover before they landed, before putting them back on. The thought was distressing but he would only request a wheelchair if there was no other choice. The last thing he needed was to draw attention to himself.

***

Reno-Tahoe International Airport

Jon wasn't sure if he was looking for a wheelchair, but that's where he'd start. It was the easiest thing to spot. Two airline employees were pushing chair-bound passengers toward the Miami gate. Neither was Franklin. The gate attendant called for main cabin passengers to board. Several people stood up and got in line. Jon approached the desk, where a young blonde woman in a red vest and matching lipstick was putting down her handheld speaker. He showed her his ID.

The woman studied it. "Do we have an issue with this flight, Agent Steadman?" Her tone was concerned but professional.

"Not sure yet." Jon showed her the photo of Franklin that Matthews had sent him. "I'm looking for this man. Franklin Oakley. He's likely using an assumed name. He may be in a wheelchair, but perhaps not."

The woman looked closely at the photo. "Many of the passengers have already boarded. But I don't recognize him."

"I'll need to take a look. Please stop the boarding for the moment. If you see him, don't approach. Act normally."

She nodded despite the fear in her eyes. Jon stepped past her onto the jet bridge. And boarded the plane.

***

Franklin was relieved to be in his seat. He pressed the release on his prosthetics, loosening the legs.

***

Luanne did a second walk-through, studying every passenger at the gate. She didn't see Oakley. If he spotted her first and realized who she was, he would be sure to try and dodge her. She wasn't sure what Jon expected her to do without Fed credentials. Two passengers were waiting to speak to the gate agent. She got in line and waited her turn.

***

Jon walked down the aircraft's center aisle, then checked the restrooms. Several passengers eyed him with curiosity. Franklin wasn't there. Jon called Luanne. "He's not on this flight."

Luanne said, "I don't see him at the gate. They just closed the boarding door. I asked the rep and he didn't think he saw him."

"Tell the desk attendant to ground the plane."

Jon heard the exchange. It wasn't going smoothly. "Put him on the phone."

Jon explained the situation, but the man seemed unsure. "You'll need to speak with the pilot, sir. It's a busy night. He might not want to miss his slot for takeoff."

Jon was amazed at the attitude. "Has everyone forgotten 9-11? What's your name?"

"Drew, sir."

"Listen real carefully, Drew. If you don't find a way to hold the plane until I get over to your gate, I will hold you personally responsible for allowing a terrorist to get away."

"T-Terrorist?" The man's voice was thin, panicky. "I'll call the pilot now."

Jon hung up and hurried to the JFK gate as fast as his leg would allow.

***

Franklin looked at his watch. They should have taxied by now. A prickle of fear ran up his spine. *Calm down, there's no way they can find you.* He leaned back his head and closed his eyes. Six minutes later he was woken by a commotion at the front of the plane. A male voice came over the PA system. "Franklin Oakley, this is Special Agent Jon Steadman. Press the call button over your seat. We're coming for you."

CHAPTER 49

W hen Jon reached Oakley's seat, his prostheses were not attached, no legs extending beyond the cuffs of his rolled-up pants. Jon told a flight attendant —a thirty-something well-built man—to call security, then asked his help carrying a red-faced, cursing Oakley off the aircraft.

Once escorted onto the jetway, the attendant seated Oakley in a wheelchair and handed Jon a hard silver case. "Here's the carry-on from under his seat."

Jon thanked the flight attendant and wheeled Oakley into the terminal, past a stunned Luanne watching in amazement. If onlookers were disturbed by the spectacle, they said nothing.

He was met by two armed men who appeared past the age of retirement. Their presence seemed to cause Franklin to clam up. Jon showed them his ID and was given access to a small office.

Once inside, Jon flicked on the light and locked the door. He hovered over the wheelchair, hoping his six-foot frame would be sufficiently intimidating.

Franklin's face was flush with ire. "What the hell is going on?" His air of indignation was laced with apprehension.

"We're going to have a little chat."

"You're not allowed to do this. You're supposed to read

me my rights."

"Is that so?"

Franklin jutted his jaw. "How'd you find me?"

Jon leaned against the wall, crossed his arms, as though he had all the time in the world. "I'm the one asking the questions. Where's Lizzy Davis?"

Franklin's face and tone turned flat. "Who?"

"You really going to stoop that low?"

Oakley darted his eyes as if trying to think his way out. Then shrugged.

Jon was hit with a wave of ferocity, a fireball of anger welling up inside him. He'd seen this scene before. Egomaniacs playing with the lives of the innocent for their own sick reasons.

He let it erupt.

Jon pulled his gun, put it against Oakley's temple. "You don't know me, asshole, but I've got my own issues. And one thing I despise is people who mess with little kids."

Franklin's body began to tremble, his face draining of color, sweat sprouting on his forehead. He did his best to keep his voice steady. He failed. "I'm not scared to die."

"Glad to hear it." Jon cocked the weapon.

Oakley tightly shut his eyes. "Okay, okay. Gerard took her."

Jon took his finger off the trigger. "Who's Gerard?"

"Just someone I met on the web. No idea if that's his real name."

"Where did he take Lizzy?"

"I don't know," he mumbled.

Jon pressed the barrel deeper. "Say hello to the devil from me."

"I-I can find him." Then, "I put spyware on his phone."

"Like you did with Peter Cromwell?"

Oakley gave a near-imperceptible nod.

Jon lowered the gun, his mind racing, desperate to connect the dots. *Did Franklin get his hands on Wang's spyware? Is it*

Franklin who's negotiating its sale with the White Knight? "Now we're talking, Frankie. Get me the location. Now."

"The phone's in my pocket."

"Take it out slowly. I wouldn't want to accidentally shoot you."

Franklin did as he was told, then tapped his phone a few times. "Here are the coordinates."

Raising the gun on him with one hand, Jon took the phone with the other. It showed a series of seemingly random numbers. "What the hell am I supposed to do with this? Put it in my GPS?"

"It's more complicated than that. It's in a beta phase."

Jon wasn't going to stand in the tiny office getting a tutorial. By coming to Reno, he'd already created a greater distance between him and this guy, Gerard. He told Franklin to pull up the tracker, pocketed the phone, and wheeled Franklin out of the office. Luanne was sitting nearby, keeping a close eye, but staying out of the way of two waiting police officers. Before Jon could intervene, one cuffed Franklin and read him his rights. The second officer relieved Jon of the wheelchair's handles. Jon said, "He's coming with me"

The officer appeared perplexed. "What do you mean? We got a call from Sheriff Harding in Placer County. We need to book him."

"Not happening. I need him to help me locate an abducted child. I'll bring him in when the op's done."

The officers looked unsure. Jon got Harding on the phone, put him on speaker for the officers to hear. He explained what he needed to do.

"How long?" the sheriff asked.

"Till I find Lizzy Davis."

"What if he takes you on a wild goose chase?"

A fierce stillness came over Jon, such that one of the officers took a step back. "Then I won't be bringing him back."

Jon walked a few feet away, leaving Franklin momentarily with the officers. He called Matthews, quickly giving him an update, filling him in on where he was headed and that he may have a direct lead to the White Knight. It was time to contact the Mossad.

***

Jon speed-wheeled Oakley outside, Luanne jogging beside him. A tow truck was pulling up in front of their car. He pulled out the keys from his pocket and called out to the driver. "Car's mine."

A middle-aged guy with a John Deere cap got out of the truck, smirked at him. "You're parked illegally, man. You can't just leave a car here like it's a parking lot. We're already here, so you'll have to get it from the pound."

Out of sight, Jon handed his pistol to Luanne. "Help Oakley into the car." He turned, rushing to the man who was already approaching Jon's car, holding a chain in his hand. Jon flipped open his badge case, sticking the medallion in the guy's face "Take it up with the FBI."

The man's smirk turned to distaste, but he backed off.

Jon got behind the wheel. Veering away from the curb, the tow truck driver gave him the finger.

Luanne was in the backseat, Oakley riding shotgun. Keeping the pistol gripped in her hand, she leaned forward, whispered in Jon's left ear. "What on Earth happened in that office?"

Hearing her, Oakley said, "He pulled his gun on me. That's what happened!"

Jon took Oakley's phone from his pocket, handing it to Luanne behind him. He spoke as if Oakley wasn't in the car. "There's a tracker in Gerard's phone. If we're lucky, it will lead us straight to Lizzy Davis. Please navigate."

"Looks like we're heading back to the lake. Fifty-five minutes."

Jon floored it.

Luanne grabbed the door handle. "Whoa!"

"We need to get there before the swap time and the guy bolts. He has me to answer to."

"The Pitbull?"

Jon nodded, his voice resolute. "The Pitbull."

***

New York City

Matthews expected Yosef Kahn would take no issue with being woken up in the middle of the night. He was right. His usual enigmatic self, Kahn showed no emotion when Matthews shared what was known about the hacking attacks on Peter Cornwall, Caroline Atwood, and Congressman Taylor. Seemed impassive to the abduction of Lizzy Davis.

"You think those cases are tied to the White Knight?"

"We have identified one person who appears connected to them all."

Yosef asked several follow-up questions and then hung up, never once saying thank you.

CHAPTER 50

Alpine Meadows

L izzy heard more than she saw. Someone was chewing. Sounded like potato chips. Maybe those funny-shaped ones. She liked the sour cream and onion flavor. Her stomach grumbled and her left leg felt numb. She tried opening her eyes, but only got her lids to half-mast. *Weird*, she thought.

"Mom, can I have something to eat?" She wasn't sure if the words actually came out of her. Her brain was slowly waking, but something was off. Her words sounded slurred and her throat felt terribly dry. Struggling to lift her eyelids, she got a glimpse of the mattress beneath her, wooden floors beyond that. And several feet away, a pair of legs. *A man's.*

"Mom?"

The legs shifted, the chewing stopped.

Large brown snow boots, the tips discolored from drying snow, walked toward her. *Dad doesn't have those boots.* When they were just below her face, she knew something was terribly wrong. She forced out her next words, hoping she'd be heard. "Where am I?"

"You're in a fairy tale, kid. And you're the star." The voice was male, refined, sounded like her English teacher.

I must still be dreaming. It was scary, but so were lots of fairy tales. "Which one?" she asked the wet boots.

"Sleeping Beauty, of course."

Lizzy liked that. The prince—Daddy—would come soon to kiss her. True love would revive her. Before she could reply, a snot-smeared handkerchief blocked her vision.

"Let's hope Daddy's as rich as he looks or you won't be waking up ever again."

The cloth made contact with her face and Lizzy Davis was dragged back into a bottomless, dreamless sleep.

***

Reno—Tahoe

Luanne was a nervous wreck. Sure, she wanted the story, was willing to take risks to get it . . . and had. The lethal hike in the Sonoma mountains and the crazy ATV ride in Texas were still very fresh in her mind. The story had the potential to propel her career to all new heights, but proved more dangerous than she would have ever signed up for. Now, Jon was driving like a maniac and a paraplegic hacker responsible for the attacks—and possibly the deaths of innocent people—sat in the seat in front of her.

Jon's phone rang. He answered via the car's Bluetooth. It was the hostage negotiator.

"Any news?"

"The kidnapper called back with the drop point. He wants the whole thing to go down in thirty minutes. It's just enough time for Theo to get there. The guy knows what he's doing."

"Where's the drop?"

The woman told him.

Luanne looked at the GPS. "No way we can make it in thirty minutes."

The negotiator said, "You don't have to. I'm not recommending the Davises follow this plan. I had told Theo that when the kidnapper calls, to stall him, but he lost his nerve. He was scared he'd never hear from the guy again. Big mistake.

313

Now I'm encouraging them to wait till the guy calls back and negotiate a better arrangement."

Jon asked, "Why? He'll be infuriated at that point."

"No choice. He wants the money left in a drop box. Said he'll be watching and that once he's free to count it, he'll give Lizzy's location. It's too risky."

Jon said, "Go ahead with it."

Silence. Then, "I can't in good conscience tell the Davises to do that. The perp can easily take the money and run. He'll have no incentive to divulge where the girl is. Do you understand what that could mean?"

Luanne heard the strain in Jon's voice. She watched as he glanced at Oakley who sat silently beside him, his face a mask of apathy. Jon said, "I do, ma'am. But I have a trick up my sleeve."

Luanne heard the negotiator let out a deep sigh. "You had better be super confident of it, Agent. A nine-year-old's life is on the line. And you've just placed her survival squarely in your hands."

***

Tahoe City Marina

The marina was deserted in the winter months. Making it a perfect spot for the money drop. Gerard lifted the binoculars to his eyes, focusing them on the black Range Rover pulling into the parking lot. Slowly he scanned the surrounding area. No one else around. The Davis guy was following his directions to the letter. Two million. It would afford him a sabbatical of sorts. Time off from the rigors of his regular wet work. Funny, when he'd entered university he would have been thrilled to one day earn a hundred grand a year. Now he was using his God given talents instead of the useless ones he'd learned at school, earning twenty times that. He was glad he thought to ask for cash instead of a money transfer. There were risks, but the one thing Franklin Oakley had taught him was never to trust computers. Anyhow, what could compare to cold hard cash? The impending money drop excited him, reminding him of the old spy films he loved in his youth.

Gerard watched as Davis got out of the car and retrieved a duffle from the backseat. He rapidly walked toward the pier keeping his head forward as instructed, seemingly desperate to find the wooden crate with an attached red ribbon that Gerard had described on the phone. He hoped the guy would find it already. He needed to keep things on schedule. The kid would be rousing soon and he wanted to be long gone by then. He'd given her a small dose of morphine, which was why when she last woke, she hadn't felt her broken leg. It kept her from screaming in pain. Once the Ketamine and drugs wore off, that would change. Without a phone or a literal leg to stand on, she wouldn't get far. Still, despite the remoteness of the cabin, her cries could attract the attention of any wayward hikers, and he didn't need to take any unnecessary chances. He would keep his word and give the parents their daughter's location. Once he was at a safe distance. With his money. He was nothing if not a fair man.

**

Jon, Luanne, and Oakley sat in the car a half mile up the road from the marina. It was fifteen minutes after the scheduled drop. Jon turned the phone to face Oakley. "Where's the kidnapper?"

As Oakley reached out for the device, Jon pulled it back. "No way you're holding it. Tell me what to do."

"You won't be able to do it yourself. The interface doesn't work like a live app."

Jon's eyes narrowed. "Find a simple way or I'll leave you here on one of those dinghies without your legs."

Luanne grimaced, but Oakley started talking.

Jon followed the instructions. "Is he the flashing yellow

dot?"

Oakley nodded.

***

Ring, damnit! His heart in his throat, Theo repeatedly glanced at his phone. He drove past Jon's car unaware his son was only yards away. When his phone rang, he grabbed at it. "Davis."

"You did well, Mr. Davis. Allow me to reiterate. If anyone tries to stop me from getting the bag, you will never learn where your daughter is. She'll die alone wondering why her parents never came to save her."

Theo swallowed the lump in his throat. "No one will stop you. Where's my daughter?"

"I'll call once I've counted the money." He hung up.

Theo wasn't accustomed to others manipulating him. The emails to expose his misdeed had made him bristle, sparking a righteous anger. This time, despite the extortion, he was eager to meet the lunatic's terms. He had to bring Lizzy home. No matter what the price. Even if the cost was his life.

CHAPTER 51

Lake Tahoe

G erard zipped the duffle, placing it in the backseat footwell of the Chevy SUV emblazoned with the U.S. Forest
Service brown and white logo, and got back behind
the wheel. He had always been a fan of hiding in plain sight.
All the money was there. He intended to leave town once he
counted the cash, then contact the Davises with their daughter's location. But cooler heads prevailed. He knew who he was
dealing with. Franklin Oakley was a computer genius. Surely,
among his significant talents was the ability to track peoples'
movements. He kicked himself for not thinking of it sooner.
He knew both SIM cards and the handsets could be traced. It
wouldn't matter if Oakley was tracking him. Oakley was no
threat to him. Unless he was working with the Feds. Though
unlikely, Gerard was a cautious man. He had stayed alive and
out of prison for one reason only. He was paranoid.

Gerard took several turns, frequently looking in the
rearview mirror. It was the moment of truth. He half-expected
to be followed, which was why he was driving *away* from the
kid. Satisfied no one was tailing him, he pulled up to a convenience store and click-locked the SUV. He didn't want to leave
the money unattended, but the task would only take a couple
of minutes, and no one would break into an official vehicle.
Keeping an eye on the car, he entered the store, and purchased
two disposable phones and a SIM card. Back in the car, he

jotted down several phone numbers from his working phone, then pulled on to the road. When he reached Donner Pass, he lowered his window and tossed out the device.

It was time to get the kid. He wanted her off his hands. The sooner the better.

***

"What's my next turn?" Jon, Luanne, and Oakley had left the marina and were following the yellow dot into town.

Luanne checked the app. "Oh, no!"

Jon asked, "What's wrong?"

She tapped frantically at the phone's screen. "It's gone."

Jon's voice bordered on panicked. "What do you mean? Did the battery die?"

"No, the yellow dot. It's gone." She instinctively looked around. They'd reached a small downtown area with ski rental outfits and boutique shops. There were several cars nearby but she knew the one they were following was a fair distance ahead of them. Careful not to be seen, they didn't yet know the make and model.

Jon slowed the car, unsure where to go. "Oakley, what the hell happened?"

Other than his earlier protestations, Oakley had remained quiet on the ride down from the Reno. Including when Luanne peppered him with questions. She understood it was likely he wouldn't talk, but it was worth a shot. She saw it as an opportunity to get solid quotes from the horse's mouth—the most important source of her exposé.

Oakley shrugged, then seemingly considering the consequences, said, "Let me see it."

Luanne hesitated. "Jon?"

"Show it to him but watch his every move."

Luanne scooted over behind Oakley, the gun now in the elastic waistband of her pants. She held up the phone for him to see so he wouldn't need to shift his body. Awkwardly, he tapped at the screen. "I need to hold it."

Luanne saw Jon nod and she handed the device to the hacker.

Oakley typed and swiped. "Gerard's on to you."

Alarmed, Luanne said, "How do you know?"

"There's no signal at all. Best guess is he took out the SIM card."

Jon swerved the car to the curb, putting it in park.

Luanne said, "What do we do now?"

Oakley voice bordered on gleeful. "Gerard's gone. Guess you lost the kid, Steadman."

Jon unbuckled his seatbelt, turning to face the smug hacker. Without a word, he clenched his fist and delivered a backhanded punch making contact with Oakley's face.

Oakley let out a grunt that turned into a deep howl. Luanne heard something snap as blood began spurting from his nose. "Jon! Oh my God!" She was stunned at the sudden violence.

Oakley's hands shook as he gingerly touched his face, his fingertips turning red. "You broke my nose!" His voice was nasal, stuffed with blood. Luanne saw something she hadn't before. Oakley was deathly afraid. Of Jon.

Jon spoke slowly as if he was placing a heavy weight on each word. "I am going to find that little girl. And you're going to help me."

After a moment, Franklin said, "H-How?"

"Use your tech savvy and figure it out. Or I swear, your nose will be the least of your worries."

***

Nicole rushed to the door as soon as she saw her husband. Haggard, his grey stubble well past a five o'clock shadow, he looked like he'd aged ten years in the last twelve hours. He was accompanied by the negotiator who had been outside the room awaiting his return. "What happened?" She looked past him.

"Where's Lizzy?"

"The man said he'll call back after he counts the money."

Fear gripped her. "What if he doesn't?"

The officers in the room looked anywhere but at Nicole. Only Theo met her eye. He seemed desperate to hold her, be held by her. Something in her broke and she went to her husband, his eyes widening in surprise. And anguish. When he opened his arms, it was as though he'd thrown *her* a life preserver. While the stoic negotiator watched uncomfortably, Nicole and Theo cried together.

CHAPTER 52

Lake Tahoe

T he atmosphere in the car was tense. Luanne had given
Oakley all the tissues she had in her bag which were
now stuffed in his nose. The skin around his left eye
was turning purple. Luanne still couldn't believe Jon had hit
the guy. Granted, Oakley was a despicable human being. But
she didn't expect Jon to go that far. She knew if Matthews got
wind of it, Jon would be cited for brutality, probably lose his
job. But one thing was certain. If it came to it, she'd back him
up, lie if necessary. Oakley deserved whatever he got and she
wouldn't be a party to him getting off on a technicality.

With Jon's okay, Luanne handed Oakley the iPad from
his bag. It was easier to manipulate. He swiped and tapped it
several times, then passed it back to her. "Here, I did it."

Jon said, "Did what?"

Ignoring Jon, he addressed Luanne only. "The app stores
the tracking history."

"You mean the phone's past locations?"

He nodded.

"Show me."

Oakley pointed out where Gerard's phone had been over
the previous twenty-four hours. There were only two places
lasting longer than a couple of hours. And only one had coordinates in a remote section of the Tahoe forest.

Twenty minutes had passed since they'd lost Gerard.

Luanne said, "Jon, we're back in business. I think I know where Lizzy is."

Luanne heard Jon whisper, "Thank you," uncertain if he was addressing her or some unseen force.

"You need to call the sheriff," she said.

"If Gerard gets wind of a police presence he might hurt Lizzy."

"You can't handle this alone, Jon."

"I'm not. I have you."

Luanne was about to argue that that wasn't much better. In the short time she'd known Jon, she'd learned there was no point. Once he made up his mind, nothing she—or anyone—would say had the power to sway him. He would stick to the plan he had in mind. No matter what.

To her surprise, Jon made the call, getting the sheriff on the line. "We got a bead on Lizzy Davis. Perp's name is Gerard."

The sheriff's voice boomed through the car's Bluetooth. "How'd you get all this?"

"I'll explain later. Can you get a team together ready to move when I give the word?"

"I'm on it. Give me the location."

Luanne did so.

Jon added, "Sheriff, if you show yourselves too soon, Gerard will panic, act unpredictably. We can't risk that."

"Understood."

"Have an ambulance on standby as well." Jon paused. Then, with a catch in his voice, he added, "We never know what we're going to find."

***

Sheriff Harding agreed with Agent Steadman's assessment. If they came out in force too quickly, the perp would go to ground and the child would be in further peril. On the other hand, organizing a team to arrive on the scene in time required a great deal of logistics and speed. Officers on the move could easily attract attention. He hoped to balance it all successfully. Too much was on the line.

***

Gerard pulled off the road. The kid was in the back footwell covered in a blanket, drugged. He'd never considered leaving her at the cabin knowing his DNA could eventually be found there. He'd taken protective measures. Ten minutes to the drop off point where he'd leave her. Then he'd be on his way and call the Davis guy to pick up his kid. A car flew by him at top speed heading in the direction from where he'd come. Unmarked. No lights or sirens. But Gerard's gut screamed. Someone was on to him.

Oakley.

That sonuvabitch had led the cops to his door. *Turncoat.* The irony wasn't lost on him. It was exactly why the hacker had hired him to get rid of Wang. He tuned into the police radio frequency. Roadblocks had been set up at various points on and off Route 89. There was no way to avoid them. He took a moment allowing his heart rate to normalize. Davis surprised him by allowing the law to get involved. Gerard considered turning around, dumping the kid somewhere, but only for a moment. The Feds had no information about him. He was certain of it. He looked at himself in the rearview mirror, then straightened his hat and adjusted his sunglasses. Perhaps this was a new opportunity. To learn exactly what he was now up against. And plan accordingly.

***

Officer Peterson waved forward the ranger's SUV, a growing line of cars inching up behind it. The spinning lights atop his cruiser created a dizzying array of red flashes reflecting off large puddles in the road.

The cop eyed the driver, a middle-aged man wearing a

banded, beige hat low on his brow. He gestured for the man to lower his window. "You got business out here, ranger?"

"Yessir, that, I do." The hint of a drawl seeped through. "On fire check duty. As you know, we can get 'em even this time o' year."

The officer leaned cross-armed on the window frame, glad to have a couple of moments to shoot the breeze. The roadblock assignment was boring as hell. "Yup. Lost a coupla houses last season. Some kids who thought the ground snow would put out their bonfire."

"I remember that one well. So, what's happenin'? Didn't hear nothin' on the radio."

The officer said, "It's being kept quiet. Child abduction. We're on standby. Need to rule out a hostage situation."

The ranger frowned. "Jeez, that's tough. Crazy people out there. Can I help? I could call someone to take my shift."

"Thanks, but I'm pretty sure they're covered. They have about ten emergency vehicles already." The cop stepped back, peering at the cars piling up, and tapped the side of the vehicle. "You're good to go, Ranger."

Gerard raised the window and drove away.

CHAPTER 53

A narrow, poorly paved road led to the cabin deep in the woods, swirls of smoke floating up from the chimney. Jon's car spat up gravel, making it impossible to approach stealthily. If Gerard was here, he'd surely heard their arrival.

Jon told Luanne to stay in the car with Franklin while he scouted out the cabin.

"Aren't you going to wait for the sheriff?"

"His team's on standby. If Lizzy's in there, every second counts." He didn't wait for her retort.

Gun drawn, Jon checked the periphery. There was only one primary egress—the cabin's sole door. No movement detected, though the silence could mean a variety of things.

He was glad to have kept the sheriff's team at bay. Their onslaught could easily lead to a hostage situation, not to mention significant danger to the child. He guessed Matthews would have played this differently, which is why he hadn't called him with the latest update.

Jon approached the door, slowly turning the doorknob. It wasn't locked. Aware it could be a trap, he swiftly opened the door and dropped to a crouch. In the event Gerard was inside primed to shoot, the bullet would soar above his head.

No bullet came.

Because no one was there. Gerard was gone. And so was Lizzy.

***

Lizzy crinkled her nose against the pungent odor, a mix of manure, hay, and leather.

"Mommy?" she croaked, her eyelids fighting her.

Why am I so tired? Confused, she slowly recalled waking before. *The brown boots guy.*

No answer came. From anybody.

Lizzy's stomach growled. She was famished and her left leg was tingling. As she tried to shake it awake, the movement sparked a piercing pain. She cried out, forcing herself to stay still. Whimpering and groggy, she sensed movement near her and struggled once again to open her eyes. It was easier this time. She was lying on a bed of hay.

As she looked up, her face was met with the giant head of a horse, its teeth bared in a comical smile. Startled, she emitted a strained scream. The horse ignored her, chewing the feed beside her, neighing contentedly. Its saddle and blanket had been tossed aside, the stall door penning them both inside. A rectangular wooden sign hung on the far wall. "Amigo," it read. Lizzy had ridden before, was comfortable around horses and was grateful for the calm animal's company. She put out her hand, gently petting the beast's muzzle, then its thick, brown mane. "Hey, girl. Will you be my friend?"

The answer came with a soft flick from behind, the wispy tip of the horse's tail brushing against her good leg.

She needed to pee,and wanted to cry, but she'd do her best to hold both in. Reaching into her ski bib pocket, she realized her phone was gone. She was all alone with no way to move. She could try to drag herself out, but the dense snowy tree line was visible above the stall door. Leaving could be more dangerous than remaining in the shelter. It was just her and the horse in a stable. Hopefully someone would come for her soon. She hoped it wouldn't be the evil boots man.

***

With the shades drawn, the only light in the cabin came from a low-wattage fluorescent bulb dangling above the kitchen sink. It took a moment for Jon's eyes to adjust. A half-filled bottle of water sat on a nearby table alongside a used plastic spoon and empty yogurt container. Several more were in the trash. A fire in the hearth was slowly dying out, leaving glowing embers in its wake. If not for the app's tracking history they'd never have found this hole in the wall, the location pin hovering above the isolated location tucked into the Tahoe woods.

But now the yellow dot on Oakley's phone had vanished.

"What have I done?" Jon whispered in the empty room. He'd missed the kidnapper. Their sole lead had vanished like the nebulous clouds of smoke rising into the sky.

***

New York City

Matthews had never heard Jon sound this way before. He was contrite and self-flagellating as he explained that he'd lost the Davis kid's trail. He wanted to tell Jon that quick decisions need to be made during active, life-threatening situations. It came with the job.

But Matthews didn't say that. Instead, he told Jon to hold, muted himself, and summoned Craig into his office, telling him what to do. This needed to be a learning opportunity for Jon, as harsh as that was. Jon was quickly becoming accustomed to taking his own counsel, convinced he knew better than everyone else. That attitude came with a price. Even if Matthews would have made the same choices in this case. Sometimes those choices ended in someone's death. Even a child's.

"Jon, I'm back. We need to do damage control."

"Right."

Hearing the deflated tone in Jon's voice, Matthews said, "Focus, dammit! There's no point in looking back now. We can do that some other time. Now's the time to figure out the next move."

"I don't know my next move. I need help . . . please."

It was what Matthews had been waiting for. Willful collaboration. "The local field office will triangulate all active phones in the area. It's a sparsely populated territory, so maybe we'll get lucky. Trust them to do their jobs."

Sounding resigned, Jon said, "Okay. But what do *I* do now?"

"The hardest thing there is, Jon. You wait."

***

Tahoe National Forest

Jon didn't have to wait long. Thirty minutes later, the cabin was filled with law enforcement officers, medics, and a forensics specialist who was prepping to take fingerprint and DNA samples. Out the window, he spotted a forest ranger on horseback, law enforcement officers in their own right. Thankfully, the medical examiner had been sent away.

Nicole and Theo Davis were at the hotel with one of the sheriff's deputies waiting for an update.

Jon stepped outside, his thoughts running wild. *Who would do such a thing to a child? What if this was Randy?* He wanted to find the guy who took her and put a bullet in his head.

***

Gerard watched the busy crowd of emergency personnel. One man appeared to be running the show. Tall, rugged, young. Casually dressed, with long-ish hair, the guy didn't look like a Fed, but had to be. It was a few seconds before Gerard recognized him as one of the men who'd been in his crosshairs on the ski lift. The lucky one. Then he'd been wearing a hat and goggles. As far as he could tell, he'd hit the other guy square in the gut.

He kept an eye on the Fed and placed the call.

***

Jon felt the vibration in his pocket. He took out the phone realizing it was not his, but Oakley's.

Jon answered. "Who's calling?"

A pause on the line. "Bravo, you got your hands on the phone of the world's greatest hacker."

On full alert, Jon asked, "Where's the kid, Gerard?"

The chuckle came over the line. "Not bad. Of course, that's not my real name, but you've come further than most in my illustrious career."

The man was educated, haughty. Jon did his best to sound nonchalant, keeping the hatred—and fear—out of his voice. "I always enjoy a compliment from a murderer and kidnapper. A deal's a deal. You got the money. Give us the kid."

"Come now. Surely you understand the deal's been forfeited. You're involved, ergo, a breach of contract. The rules were no Feds."

Jon could argue the point but agitating the man would achieve nothing good. Instead he said, "Where are you?"

"Let's just say I'm where you'd least expect me to be."

Jon spun around, looking in every direction. There were close to twenty people around, several on the phone. All appeared legit.

Gerard said, "May I have your name?"

"Steadman. Sear it into your head. I'm the last guy you'll see before you go to prison."

"Let's get the posturing out of the way, shall we? I have a new deal. This time, if you or anyone attempt to thwart it, the kid dies. Understand?"

"How do I know she's still alive?"

"You don't."

There was no card to play. Gerard was in the driver's seat. "What do you want?"

"It shouldn't be too much trouble for you. If anything, I'll most certainly be taking care of a pain in your ass."

"What the hell are you talking about?"

Gerard said, "I'll swap one Davis kid for another."

"What?"

"I want Franklin. The girl for the hacker. He's useful to me. Leave him in the car—with his phone—and make everyone else disappear. Comprende?"

He can see me.

"Let me be very clear, Steadman. They'll be no more chances. You blow this and the kid's history."

The guy was an animal. Still, Jon had nothing to consider. It was a no-brainer. "I'll need a few minutes. But you've got yourself a deal."

***

Gerard felt a rare spark of panic, nearly dropping the phone when Steadman answered Oakley's phone and again when he did a three-sixty. The agent was smart. But not smart enough.

Gerard put down his binoculars, kicked the horse's shank and cantered away.

CHAPTER 54

Tahoe National Forest

J on was back on the line with Matthews, this time glad to have the guidance. "Gerard wants Oakley." Matthews listened attentively while he explained the swap.

When he was done, Matthews said, "Honor among thieves?"

"Gerard probably figures they can run a successful hacking racket together. He springs Oakley and in return gets a cut of the lucrative business."

"Hmm, maybe. Either way, you played it right."

The validation brought Jon a rush of relief. "Thanks. Still, I hate to let Oakley go. There's gotta be a way to keep tabs on him."

"Even if there is, he's a computer genius. I don't think you'll outsmart him in that area. Besides, you have no time to figure it out. You need to make the swap and worry about getting both Gerard and Oakley later."

When they finished speaking, Jon approached the sheriff, asking him to begin clearing the area. Then he went to the car. "Lu, can I have a minute?" He reached inside and took Oakley's prostheses case.

Oakley shouted, "Where are you going with that?"

"New development. Lu?"

Luanne got out of the car, shutting the door behind her and walked alongside Jon. "So sorry Lizzy's not here. Her parents will be devastated. What's the next move?"

"That's what I want to tell you. Gerard wants to swap her. For Oakley."

"That's crazy. That means he'll go free. Are you sure we'll get Lizzy back . . . alive?"

Jon shook his head. "Nothing's for sure. It's risky. But I don't see another way. Do you?"

She seemed taken aback by the question. "Um, no. I don't. What can I do to help?"

"Call the Davises, give them the update. They seem to like you. Better to hear what's happening from you than me or the sheriff."

She pulled out her phone. "On it."

Jon was impressed with her reaction. No one would want the job of telling parents their missing child was still not found, but she was doing it, willingly. He squeezed her arm in thanks. "We have to move everyone out of here. And I need to tell Oakley he just won the lottery."

Jon placed the leg case atop the car's trunk and got in the back seat, keeping as much space as possible between him and Oakley. He handed over his phone and shared the news, the words sticking in his craw. As understanding began to sink in, Oakley's expression changed into a broad grin, a nasal chuckle escaping from between his bruised lips.

It took every ounce of Jon's self-control not to kick out the guy's teeth. All he could do was repeat to himself, *Life isn't fair, but karma's a bitch.*

***

Luanne was shaking. The call with Theo Davis was devastating. He and Nicole had been expecting to hear that they'd found Lizzy safe and sound. Instead, she had to tell them the awful truth. They were at a cabin in the woods but hadn't found Lizzy. She did her best to reassure him that all was still being done to locate her. Luanne was only grateful Nicole wasn't on the line. She never would have been able to keep it together hearing the mother's heartbreak.

Luanne wasn't sure she'd done the right thing by sharing her location with Theo. When he'd begged for it, she simply couldn't refuse. But she chose not to inform him about the intended Lizzy-for-Franklin exchange. For a parent, the plan would be unthinkable—swapping one child for another . . . into the hands of a sociopath. Even if it's what Franklin clearly wanted. Luanne decided to leave that for Jon to tell. If she had to guess, Theo wouldn't fight it anyway. His son would soon be free. And hopefully, if their prayers were answered, so would his daughter.

***

It took another twenty minutes to get everyone out of the cabin's vicinity. A rescue team involved a lot of people, vehicles, and equipment. Though weary of the intended arrangement, Sheriff Harding did the best he could to move things along. He'd seen the worst of humanity and held little hope that the swap would result in Lizzy's safe release.

***

Squaw Valley Resort

Theo paced the room, his wife watching him like a spectator at a tennis match.

"Please sit down, you're making me even more anxious." Her voice was hoarse from hours of crying.

Theo sat. "I can't stay here anymore. I need to do *something.*"

"We've been over this before, Mr. Davis. Let the pros—"

"The pros haven't brought back my daughter!" Then, more calmly, "Am I free to go?"

The negotiator frowned. "I can't hold you here against

your will. But if you interfere with an active investigation, you'll end up having one more big issue to deal with. The sheriff could detain you."

Theo looked at his wife, a question in his eyes, and saw his own agony reflected back. Nicole said, "Go."

CHAPTER 55

Tahoe National Forest

Franklin had thought he was cooked. Now, he reveled in the twist of fate as he watched Steadman and the sheriff round everyone up. Somehow Gerard had cut a deal to free him. He would owe the lunatic, maybe cut him into the business. Not a partnership like with Wang, that would be too much. But give him more lucrative work, should the need arise.

The drive from the airport had been fraught with tension, and then the blow to his face. Which was killing him. He was certain the agent had broken his nose. What he wouldn't do for a couple of Tylenol. All the medics around and no one came to check on him. At least he'd managed to keep quiet the entire ride, despite the reporter peppering him with questions.

Steadman tossed his phone into the backseat. "Wait here," was all he said, and without another word, slammed the door shut.

"My legs!" Franklin shouted. He couldn't get out of the car without them. Where were his legs? The jerk. Forcing him to wait for Gerard to come get him. It would certainly be a while before Gerard felt safe enough to come out into the open. Steadman must have left his legs somewhere nearby. Gerard would surely bring them to him. He turned, watching the last of the emergency vehicles take off. The recent hours had taken their toll and he was drained of all energy. He leaned back, allowing a long-held breath to escape.

He closed his eyes. And waited.

***

Sheriff Harding was the last in the line of vehicles leaving the cabin, radioing the call center with an update. Most cops hated the Feds infringing on their territory, but Harding learned, as in life, if you work together and checked your pride at the door, you can get more done. The FBI resources were far superior to any local sheriff's office. That said, the young agent, Jon Steadman, was a cocky kid. While not an unusual character trait for a Fed, Steadman wasn't typical. If it meant getting the job done, he didn't follow the book. And he had made the Davis case personal. Harding wasn't sure whether that was an asset or a detriment to the job. Only time would tell.

He wasn't happy leaving the scene, or Oakley in the car. If it were his decision, he'd place his officers in the area, grab Gerard on his way out, using Oakley as bait. Steadman was convinced Gerard would smell a trap and any chance of getting the child back safely would evaporate. Steadman had been emphatic. Oakley would remain alone in the car at the cabin, no law officers left behind. Harding understood the concern, but allowing violent criminals on the loose should have at least been discussed. Now he had nowhere to go but back to the office. It felt negligent.

Harding looked in his rearview mirror, the road leading to the cabin no longer visible, wondering if he'd just made the biggest mistake of his career.

***

Gerard brought the mare around, allowing the animal to eat from the nearby shrubs. He felt considerably safer at a greater distance as he watched the crowd disperse, each group getting into their respective vehicles. EMS, fire, police. He saw Agent Steadman exit the back seat of a blue Subaru, a stern expression on his face, then take another spin, scrutinizing the surroundings, his eyes squinting in concentration. Before walking away, Steadman lifted a phone, as if showing it to Gerard and threw it into the backseat beside Oakley. The move unnerved Gerard. While he knew it wasn't possible at this distance, it felt as if Steadman was looking directly at him. Something about the guy got under his skin. The agent appeared driven, with a determination suggesting it was personal between them.

Gerard lifted the binoculars to his eyes. The blue Subaru was sitting there idle. On the trunk was a large case. He zoomed in further. The words on the case read, Symbiosis Bionics. Oakley's legs! He laughed aloud. The Fed had taken them! It made this too easy. But he'd need to get closer. He loosened the reins, lightly kicked the horse's flank. "Let's go, girl."

Man and horse slowly made their way down the hill and through a copse of pines. Gerard pulled on the reins, stopping near the edge of the clearing, the thicket offering ample coverage. No movement from anywhere. He moved the strap off his shoulder, bringing the rifle in front of him, its oak stock leaning on his thigh. That's when he heard the distinct sound of a car engine. Someone was pulling into the clearing. Using his binoculars, he was surprised to see it was not a cop or Fed car, but a Beemer. This just became more interesting. Fed or not, with this new interference, Gerard was no longer bound to divulge the kid's whereabouts. He dropped the binoculars to his chest, stroked the mare's mane. And then raised his rifle.

***

Theo pulled his Beemer into the clearing, opposite a blue Subaru sedan. A small cabin was tucked into the edge of the woods. *Lizzy was here.*

Maybe she was being hidden somewhere on the grounds. He didn't want to think about the details, but various horror stories from the papers came to him—of abducted children. He felt nauseous, ready to hurl. *Keep it together. For your little girl*. Only a thin layer of snow was on the ground. Any disturbance would be obvious. Surely the cops had looked for that. But he needed to search for her himself.

Theo stepped out of the car, traversing the clearing, carefully approaching the Subaru. No one in the driver's seat. He assumed it was an unmarked cop car, an officer keeping an eye on the scene, but how did that make sense? Theo was still debating what to do when he heard a sharp crack. His brain caught on before his body did. *Gunfire!*

Theo dropped down to all fours just as another round hit the car, ricocheting off its side door.

***

Franklin woke to the sound of a sharp crack. His eyes shot open, momentarily disoriented by where he was. *Steadman's car.* He leaned over, managing to open the door, careful not to fall out. "Gerard! You can come out now!" he shouted.

He was answered with another crack, this one accompanied by a dime-sized ding in the door. *A bullet!* Someone was trying to kill him. Franklin ducked down, the door remaining open. He was trapped. Then, he remembered his phone on the seat beside him. Before he could make the call, it rang. He yelled into the mouthpiece. "Help! Whoever this is, help!"

"Hey, boss," Gerard's tone casual as if he hadn't a care in the world.

Franklin spat out his words. "Thank goodness. Where are you? The Feds are shooting at me."

"Nah, those guys are long gone."

"I'm outside your cabin. There's another car here. I can't see who's in it. You gotta come get me. Just watch your back."

"That's precisely what I'm doing."

Franklin heard the icy tone. "W-what's going on? I thought you swapped me for the kid." The shooting stopped. He ventured a look out the window.

"I did, but not for the reasons you think."

"We'll go into business together. I'll pay you back for getting me outa this."

"Will you now? Hmm. As of a few hours ago, I'm two mil richer. And from what I can tell, partnering with you could be bad for my health. No, that won't work."

Franklin felt the tightening grip of fear. "Then what do you want? With my computer skills, I can get you anything."

"Tempting. But you—more than most—know the drive for revenge can be more powerful than money. Right, boss?"

"Revenge?"

"You sicced the Feds on me. Same as the Asian guy did to you. If it weren't for my finesse, they'd have me in custody."

"I did no such thing!"

"You put something in my phone. That's how they traced me to the cabin. Took me a bit, but I figured it out. Traitor."

"I-I . . ."

"Save it, Oakley. You've had a good run. Au revoir."

Franklin stared for a moment at the phone in his hand, then another shot rang out. The phone dropped to the floor. He bent low, taking cover. "Help!" he shouted, aware that there was no one other than a stone-cold killer to hear him.

***

Theo was searching for cover. Stupidly, he'd left his phone charging in the car. Whoever was shooting was an awful shot, getting nowhere near him. Maybe he could make it back to his car unscathed.

Then he heard a phone ring. From inside the Subaru. He sensed some movement, saw someone in the back seat open the far side door. Theo ducked down protecting himself.

The shooting stopped and he heard someone shouting, desperate. Why weren't they driving away? Suddenly, another shot hit the gas tank, followed immediately by the distinct smell of gasoline. And then a whoosh of combusting air.

Fire!

Theo shouted, "Get out of the car!"

"Gerard? Get away from me!"

Who's Gerard? "My name's Theodore Davis. Let's go! We can get out of here together."

No answer.

Maybe the guy had been shot. Theo crab-walked to the car and at a kneel, snaked his hand up to the door handle, opened it and peered inside. A man sat there, arms held protectively over his bent head, looking like a trapped animal. He looked up, his face a mask of fear. And hatred.

Realization hit swiftly. Theo gasped aloud, taking in the sight. The man had no legs.

CHAPTER 56

N early two decades had passed since Franklin had been with his father. A wave of emotion washed over him as he heard his father identify himself. And again seconds later when his father's face peeked past the car door. The whole situation was surreal. He'd despised this man for so long. Yet, now with his life at stake, his father materializing in time to help him, the dominant feeling was relief.

It was short-lived.

Dad came to save me quickly shifted to shock and anger when it dawned on him that his father had come for his other child. His resentment flooded back, as if it had never receded at all.

"Franklin?" Theo's eyes were filled with tears, his face drawn in pain, studying his son's swollen and bruised features. "Are-are you hurt? Your face . . ."

Franklin's eyes darted out the window. "Someone's shooting at me," he said, stating the obvious instead of answering the question.

"We need to get out of here."

Franklin shook his head, his expression morphing into one of fear. The fire was building.

"The gas tank's hit. We need to go. Now."

"I'm not going anywhere with you. He'll shoot me the minute I leave this car."

Theo's voice turned calm, almost soothing. "There's no choice." He held out a hand. "Don't worry, I've got you." Seemingly realizing the irony of his words, he beseeched, "Please, son."

Another shot, this one shattering the window of the open car door inches from Franklin's head. He grabbed his father's outstretched hand and let himself be pulled out the other door.

***

Theo grasped his son's hand. It was soft, uncalloused. Pulling him to the edge of the seat was easy enough, his body lighter given the absence of two limbs. The stumps were covered in long elastic liners. "Where are your legs?" The heat intensified, the smell of gasoline reeked. He saw Franklin peer out the back window eyeing a large box on the trunk. It was surrounded by flames.

"They're gone," Franklin said, his tone bitter.

Without asking, Theo lifted Franklin, protectively leaning over his son. "I'm gonna get us to my car. Hold on tight. Ready?" Franklin's arms encircled his father's torso as Theo took off. At that moment a shot rang out. It hit the Subaru. For a millisecond, the atmosphere seemed to hold its breath. And then, as nature demanded, the car exploded into a raging ball of fire.

***

Placer County Sheriff's Office
North Lake Tahoe

"He could see me," Jon whispered to Luanne who stood beside him outside a two-story stone building that housed the sheriff's office. One of the deputies had given them a ride.

Luanne's eyes widened. "You think Gerard was there, at

the cabin?"

"It was the way he spoke. I can't put my finger on it." Then, "The ranger."

"Huh?"

"Did you see the forest ranger on horseback?"

Luanne shook her head. "I was in the car with Oakley. Poor vantage point. You think it was Gerard?"

"Maybe. Several people were on their phones, but they all looked legit. The ranger was too far away to see, but he could have made the call to Oakley's phone. And if it was him, he could make a quick exit unencumbered. Blocking the roads will mean nothing if he has a way to get around while avoiding them."

Luanne said, "Gotcha, but this is all speculation. With today's tech, someone could be watching you from Canada."

"True, but we know he's nearby. He just got his money. Maybe he stuck around."

"Can't imagine why. First thing a criminal does is get as far away as possible from the scene."

Jon held the door open for Luanne and together they entered the building, making a beeline for the sheriff's office. Jon held his creds aloft, ignoring the looks of staff working nearby. Jon knocked on the office door, then opened it a moment before hearing, "Enter."

A large desk dominated the room. On it, thick black binders were piled high beside a multi-line phone system, a slew of loose papers obscuring the rest of the surface. The sheriff stood up behind it.

Jon said, "Thanks for having one of your deputies give us a ride."

"Sure thing."

"I know you're not happy with this plan." It wasn't a question.

Harding said, "Correct." Then, "What can I do for you?" he asked.

"There was a ranger on horseback on the hill behind the

cabin."

The sheriff furrowed his brow, remembering. "Yup, it's not unusual. They're patrolling. On the lookout for unauthorized campsites. Even though we offer designated grounds, there are always some tourists who want to do their own thing. Usually teens leaving behind empty beer cans and pit fires they don't put out properly. The forest is nearly 900,000 acres. Of tinder."

"Did you recognize the ranger?"

The sheriff shook his head.

A red flag waved in Jon's mind.

Harding must have seen the look on Jon's face. "I'll put in a call. See if any rangers were out at the cabin earlier." He pressed a button on his phone console. "Mike, get me someone at the American River Ranger District Office."

"What about the horse?" Luanne asked.

The two men turned to face the reporter.

Jon asked, "What?"

"The horse. Can you describe it?"

Jon paused, thinking back. He closed his eyes, conjuring up what he could. "Black, has a white stripe down its mane. Made me think of the cartoon skunk, Pepé Le Pew."

The office phone rang. The sheriff answered it, gesturing for Jon and Luanne to wait outside. Jon hesitated, but left when Luanne gave him a look.

Ten minutes later a deputy told them the sheriff wanted a word.

Back inside, Harding said, "All the rangers were accounted for. None were anywhere near the cabin over the last several days."

Jon asked, "How on Earth did they all report in over the last few minutes?"

"They didn't. They only had to check the app. The horses have chips."

Luanne said, "Then, it *was* Gerard, dressed as a ranger. Incredible."

Jon was irate. "He's playing games with me! With all of us. Stringing us along while a little girl remains at his mercy." A pause, then, "Is that normal? To have a horse microchipped?"

"Sure is. Like with dogs. Or tagging cattle."

Luanne said, "I wrote an article on this topic last year. The microchip is essentially an electronic device the size of a grain of rice."

Harding nodded. "That's right. It's implanted just below the base of the horse's mane. If a horse gets out, the owner can use GPS technology to locate it easily. It's been a God send. Used to be at least ten dead animals found during these winter months. They'd run astray, too many backwoods, no food."

"What if the horse Gerard was riding is microchipped?"

"I suppose we'd find its owner, though I doubt it's Gerard."

"It would be a start."

Luanne asked, "How do we get the horse's ID number without having the horse to scan?"

The sheriff looked stumped.

Jon said, "That's exactly what I'm going to find out."

CHAPTER 57

New York City

Matthews listened to Steadman speaking at a locomo-
tive pace as if someone was chasing him. He knew
the feeling. The last few days felt like a constant race
to get his act together both personally and professionally. It
had been radio silence with the Mossad director. Who knew
what Kahn was up to?

Jon was talking about Google Earth, inquiring if there
was a way to visually pinpoint an individual if you knew their
specific location and time. Something about the case involving
a child seemed to enflame him . . . more than usual. Jon had
even called him "sir" several times. If nothing else, Jon was an
onion, a series of layers that stung as you peeled each one back.
By the time Matthews hung up, he knew whom to enlist for
assistance.

An hour later, Matthews ended the call with his contact
at the CIA—a man he despised—who sat in an enviable position of power. And who owed him big time. Not long ago, Matthews was asked to submit a report about a case they'd worked
on together in Rome. Jon and a CIA operative had come terri-
fyingly close to dying. And the CIA man was to blame. Rather
than rat him out, Matthews strategically contacted the guy,
and the two adversaries arrived at a mutual understanding.
Getting the spook's help today would only be a small percent of
the payback.

The man had come through.

Matthews opened the secure email and found a vivid satellite image, impressed with how rapidly the technology had evolved in recent years. He studied the photo. A uniformed forest ranger donning a banded hat obscuring half of his face, binoculars hanging on his chest. His mount was a good-looking horse with a white stripe along its mane. Matthews zoomed in on the photo and immediately knew he'd hit the motherlode.

***

Placer County Sheriff's Office

Jon and Luanne were walking out the building when they heard the melee. A radio crackled. *Fire rescue in on the way.* A dispatcher repeated a location. Then called out, "All-points bulletin!"

Sheriff Harding rushed toward Jon and Luanne, heading out of his office. "Explosion outside the cabin."

Hurrying alongside the sheriff, Jon said, "What exploded?"

Jon was a step behind when he heard Harding say, "Your car, Agent Steadman. Your car exploded."

***

Tahoe National Forest

The Subaru was engulfed, the surrounding trees in danger of catching fire. It was a bizarre sight . . . a raging inferno surrounded by warped metal debris littering the now-charred grass fronting the snow-laden cabin. Fire trucks were parked askew, their hoses on full blast.

The sheriff parked at a distance. He and Jon exited the patrol car, Luanne staying behind. Jon stared at the blaze, his mind spinning back in time to his college days. *That* day. He knew the horrors of fire. How it stole lives.

Harding said, "If they don't get this under control soon we could have a much worse situation."

Jon felt the heat on his face, forcing down memories he'd been trying for years to bury. "Won't the snow put it out?"

"Not if the underlying tinder is dry, or if the cabin catches. We could end up with a devastating fire on our hands."

Neither one spoke the obvious. *Where was Oakley?*

Jon and the sheriff checked their weapons and instinctively made for the cabin. Each pulled his weapon. Harding said, "Take the lead? I've got your back."

Jon answered by moving ahead and kicking in the front door. When no shots were fired, he stepped aside, Harding rushing past him into the one-room cabin.

"Clear!" Harding called. The interior was just as they'd left it. No Oakley. No Gerard. No dead bodies.

Keeping their firearms in hand, the two men exited, once again facing the active scene. It took twenty minutes until the fire was under control. By then, the wreckage was complete. If Oakley was inside the car, he'd been incinerated. Maybe taking his legs was a mistake. Jon stopped the train of thought before it took him down a perilous path.

He stepped back to the edge of the clearing, out of the way of the firefighters doing their jobs. As he did so, he sensed movement behind him and swiftly pulled his pistol. An astonishing sight faced him. Theodore Davis, his face burnt and scraped, trudged toward him. In his arms was his son, Franklin Oakley, barely conscious.

Jon holstered his gun, heard a delirious Franklin mumble, "Daddy?"

A lone tear ran down Theo's reddened cheeks. "Right here, son. I'm not going anywhere."

CHAPTER 58

Tahoe National Forest

While Jon, Luanne, and Sheriff Harding waited for the ambulances to arrive, Theo told them all that had happened. Franklin was in and out of consciousness, and by the time the medics put him in the back of the ambulance, he was unresponsive. Theo wanted to escort him to the hospital, but the medics refused, and minutes later, he too was driven away by a second ambulance. Harding arranged for one of his officers to stay at the hospital and inform them when Franklin woke up.

Now, Jon was seated beside Luanne in the backseat of Harding's cruiser. His phone buzzed. It was Matthews.

"Dusty." His boss sounded excited.

"Dusty?" Jon asked.

"The horse. Gerard's horse's name."

Jon couldn't hold back the frustration. "Who cares?"

"If you shut up for a minute, *you* will."

An exasperated sigh. "Fine, I'm listening."

"I got a satellite picture of the horseman. Can't see much of his face, but enough to know he isn't a legit ranger. We're running his partial photo and an NCIC criminal background check. Your instincts were right."

"What about the horse?"

"Kudos to Ms. Parker. The saddle blanket was embroidered with the horse's name, Dusty. We contacted local registries. Dusty has an implanted chip. We tracked its owner."

"You serious? That's great! Who is it?"

"Name's Louise Simmons. She's a bit of a hermit, inherited her father's land, a horse ranch a couple of miles due west of the cabin. He used it to breed horses. When he died, she sold the business, including the horses. All except two. One is Amigo, the other Dusty."

"So, she loaned Gerard one of her horses."

Matthews said, "We haven't been able to reach her. Doesn't look good."

Jon felt his stomach flip. "You think she's—."

"Let's not jump the gun. Local field office personnel will help you check on the Simmons lady and look for Lizzy Davis."

"No. I'm doing this solo."

"No chance."

"Listen, Doug. We've been down this road already. I can't risk a hostage situation." Jon heard himself say "I." "You bring in the troops, and Gerard could freak."

"You'll be walking into a trap."

"I seriously doubt that. Gerard got what he wanted. Two mil and Oakley. He's long gone . . . without ever sharing Lizzy's location. There's no reason for him to stick around anymore. He figures Lizzy will die eventually."

"Always so sure of yourself. What if you're wrong? Have you even considered that possibility?"

Jon heard something in his boss's tone. Worry. "I've been trained for this. *You* trained me for this. I don't know what I'll find at the horse farm, but I'll be ready. If Lizzy's there, I'm going to bring her home."

When Doug didn't reply, Jon understood the old adage, "Silence is acquiescence," was in play, and took advantage of the opening. "Gotta run. I'll call with an update." He hung up before Matthews could say any more.

***

Bald Mountain, California

Jon stood outside the ranch house, a wood-beamed structure in need of repair, nestled at the base of the mountain. After speaking with Matthews, he clued in the sheriff and sent Luanne back to town. Echoing Matthews's stance, the sheriff insisted on coming along this time as Jon's backup and was now standing beside him. Jon's adrenaline spiked, his gun at the ready. *Déjà vu.*

Five full minutes passed in silence before Jon signaled Harding and sidled up beside the open front window. The smell hit him hard. The smell of death emanated from somewhere inside the house. Using his good leg, Jon kicked the door open. No response. He nodded to Harding who came in behind him, systematically clearing the home.

"Over here," Harding shouted from the back of the house. Fear gripped Jon as he reached the open bedroom door.

Sheriff Harding stood aside. Relief was followed by stifling guilt.

Louise Simmons was in bed, a bullet lodged in her temple.

***

"Lizzy!" Jon shouted her name over and over and he went through the house once more. He and Harding checked every closet, under the beds, even the clothes hamper. The house had no basement or attic. The child wasn't there.

Crestfallen, he'd been certain he'd find Lizzy in the house. He was out of leads.

Think, goddammit!

"What led us here?" he said aloud more to himself than to Harding.

The satellite image that found Gerard. And Dusty. The horse's microchip. "The horse!"

Jon raced outside, Harding close at his heels, both desperately scanning the property. A gust of wind blew snow off the trees, the flurries swirling around them. The place was desolate. Jon and Harding rounded the house and suddenly found what they were looking for.

The stables.

The moment Jon entered, the sound he heard filled him with a tsunami of emotion. It was a soft moan. Of a child.

***

Bald Mountain

Jon found Lizzy on the floor of a horse stall fifteen miles west of where her parents were keeping vigil. A young mare hovered above the child seemingly unperturbed by the newcomers. Harding led Amigo into an adjacent stall, the name Dusty written on a plaque affixed to the back wall.

Careful not to move her, Jon smoothed back the girl's hair, cooing "Everything's okay now. Your mom and dad are going to be really happy to see you."

Lizzy's eyes fluttered open, attempting to focus on him. She'd been drugged, her pupils dilated. It looked like shock had settled in. Her left leg was resting at an odd angle, and her lips and skin were scaly, suggesting dehydration. She appeared otherwise unharmed. At least physically. Jon knew first-hand that the child would suffer from another kind of pain. For a very long time.

"I'm calling an ambulance," Harding said, pulling out his radio. "I'll leave it to you to give the parents the good news."

Jon sat on the hay beside Lizzy. He dialed Theodore Davis.

"Davis." The man's voice was strained, terror-filled. He was expecting a call from Gerard.

"It's Agent Steadman."

"Oh my God. What's happened?"

"We got her. Lizzy's alive."
The sound of a dam bursting came through the line.

**

Once again, a small space was overrun with crime scene specialists. Amigo was led to the corral, jittery from the heightened activity.

Nicole and Theo Davis were waiting in one of the many police vehicles, Theo's arms now bandaged. The negotiator had escorted them from the hospital, insisting they stay put until their daughter was brought outside. Jon knew it was to protect them from seeing the conditions their daughter had been kept in. He also knew it could have been a much worse scene.

Jon stepped aside as a medic stabilized Lizzy on a gurney, covered her with a Mylar blanket, and escorted her outside to the ambulance. Theo and Nicole bolted from the car, racing to their daughter's side, both sobbing loudly.

"My baby, my sweet baby," Nicole cried, kissing the child's face, Theo tearfully waiting his turn.

The two men made brief eye contact. Theo mouthed the words, "Thank you."

Jon nodded, the glimmer of a smile on his lips, and went to find the sheriff.

CHAPTER 59

T he next morning, the officer babysitting Franklin at the hospital informed Sheriff Harding that the patient was awake, who in turn called Jon. Franklin had suffered second-degree burns to his face and arms. His father had saved his life.

At the hospital bedside, Jon gave over custody of Franklin to Sheriff Harding, who loosely cuffed Franklin's bandaged arm to the bedrail. Perhaps Harding intended it as symbolic. With Franklin's leg stumps covered with a sheet, he wasn't going anywhere. As Jon left to deal with the pile of paperwork, he heard Harding ramble off Franklin's Miranda rights.

Matthews had contacted the local field office to help with the interrogation. Jon was waiting for them to arrive.

"Franklin?"

Theodore Davis stood in the doorway, his five o'clock shadow and puffy eyes declaring his fatigue. His face appeared sunburnt. "Can I have a moment with my son?"

The officer said, "Not till after the Feds ask him some questions."

"Please." His voice was filled with anguish.

Jon came up beside Theo, "It's all right, officer. A few minutes won't matter."

Theo approached his son. "Frankie," he said softly.

354

Franklin looked up, his face a mask of anger and pain. "Don't."

Theo eyed the shackles, keeping a respectful distance. "I know it's hard to believe, but I wanted desperately to be in your life. It was out of my hands."

"Liar!" Franklin shouted, spittle escaping his lips. The venom in his voice made Theo recoil. "While you were living in a fancy house in LA, Mom and I were in a double-wide, eating fast food for dinner."

Theo said, "I'm so sorry, son."

Franklin shook his head. "Don't call me that. A father is supposed to keep a son safe. That was your job. I'm a cripple because of you! Instead of making things right, you forgot all about me." Franklin's eyes glistened. "You started over again, giving everything that should have been mine to your other kids. Money, education." Then he added in a whisper, "Love."

Theo was crying openly. "I've never stopped loving you."

Clearly irritated by the family drama, the officer said. "Time to go, Mr. Davis."

Theo moved to embrace his son. Simultaneously, Franklin leaned away and the officer held up a hand. "No physical contact."

Theo looked torn but nodded reluctantly.

The officer ushered Theo out of the room. As the door closed behind him, Jon saw Franklin's face grow calmer, a single tear sliding down his cheek.

CHAPTER 60

Los Angeles

The dream started out benign enough. Jon was standing in a field of lavender, a Mediterranean beauty beside him, her jet-black curls blowing wildly around her exotic face. She was speaking too softly to be heard above the sound of the wind. Jon moved closer. Suddenly, the woman's face turned ghostly white. "Get out," she said. The field was now a smoldering sea of lava, grotesque pigs paddling through the blackened ash. "Get out," she repeated.

Jon ran, his feet soon leaving the ground. He flew past the charred remains, above the trees, out toward nothingness.

***

When Jon woke, he was covered in sweat, wisps of the dream lingering, Luanne lying beside him. It was three a.m. The anti-anxiety meds made his dreams more frequent and vivid. He badly wanted to wean himself off them, but decided after months of fighting his inner demons, to trust his shrink. During the waking hours, the pills helped him function like a normal person, but like most things, they came with a price. For now he was willing to pay it. But not if the nightmares persisted. He closed his eyes and fell back asleep.

***

The next time Jon opened his eyes, the sun was streaming through the bedroom window. Luanne stirred, opened a
smudgy, black-lined eye. "Morning. Hungry."

Jon laughed. "I've never met a woman with an appetite
like yours. What can I get you?"

"I should still have a few things left from the last
binge. Go ahead and forage through the fridge. Bring whatever
doesn't have mold on it."

"Lovely."

Jon kissed her, got out of bed, pulling on his pants. His
phone rang.

"Jonny?"

There were only two people in the world who called him
that. Granny and Randy. "Hey, buddy!"

"Can we go to the aquarium?"

He loved how kids had no social graces. Not too different than himself. "What does Abuela say?"

"Abuela!"

In the background he heard Randy's grandmother ask
how he managed to call Jon on his own.

He didn't hear Randy's answer, but sweet laughter came
through the line.

After a minute of the phone being jostled, Randy said,
"She said yes. When can we go?"

"How's about next week?"

"No! That's too long. I want to see the sharks."

Jon chuckled. "That's understandable. Okay. If I get a
flight back home today, we can go tomorrow."

"Yay!" Randy cheered. "Abuela will make sandwiches for
us."

They spoke for another minute and said their goodbyes.
Jon grabbed what he found in the fridge along with some stale
doughnuts and came back to the bedroom, sitting on the edge
of the bed.

Luanne patted the comforter beside her. "Join me?"

"Wish I could but can't this time."

"Something to do with that phone call?"

"In part. Remember that kid I told you about? Randy?"

"Yeah, your old partner's son."

"Right. Well, he wants to go to the Brooklyn aquarium."

"Okaaay. So, you're hopping on a plane for that? If it helps any, I want to go to the aquarium in Marina del Rey. It's only an hour away."

Jon smiled. "It's not only that. I have a job to get back to. You know, my job—the one based in New York." Aware he'd had a bizarrely similar conversation with another woman—Melanie—not all that long ago, he pondered if his priorities were in order. He thought of Randy. Carrie.

They were.

Luanne pursed her lips. It was adorable. The tough goth chick in child mode. She stayed quiet, pensive.

Jon leaned toward her, took her in his arms. "Let's enjoy the day. I can catch the redeye."

"All right. We can check out Venice Beach, then head to Santa Monica Pier."

"Sounds good to me." Jon stood, gathering his things.

"Jon?"

Luanne's tone made Jon turn to face her. "Yeah?"

"I can't do the long distance thing. I'm not an East Coast girl. I'm not even an LA girl. When you get on the plane tonight, that will be it."

Jon felt a jab. That sense again of being untethered. Disconnected from anyone he got too close to.

Luanne said, "You look sad."

"I am. . . . but you're right. I've made that mistake before and it's not fair to anyone. For what it's worth, I'm so glad Ed hired you. You're an outstanding journalist. I never would've met you otherwise."

Luanne perked up. "Change in plans! Grab your jacket." She jumped out of the bed and headed to the bathroom.

"Where are we going?"

"To see Ed. Cheer him up. He's been in the hospital for weeks."

Jon stopped her in her tracks and brought her in for a kiss. "You're a good woman, Luanne Parker."

Luanne took Jon's hand and showed him just how good she was.

***

Cedars-Sinai Medical Center
Los Angeles

When Jon and Luanne arrived at Ed's hospital room, it was empty. Jon felt a twinge of fear. He'd spent more than his fair share of time in hospitals. And Ed was only here because Jon hadn't helped him when he'd been asked.

A nurse in pink scrubs and matching Crocs passed by in the hallway. Luanne and Jon caught up with her.

"Excuse me," Jon said, pointing. "Isn't this Ed Hernandez's room?"

"It sure is," said a familiar voice from behind.

Jon and Luanne turned, their mouths agape. Ed stood beside a young woman whose lanyard badge read, *Melissa K., Physical Therapist*. He was dressed in a hospital gown, its hem skimming his pale, spindly shins. His cheeks were drawn and stubbly, but there was a broad smile on his face.

Luanne rushed over, wrapping her arms around his newly svelte waist. The therapist did not look pleased. Ed grimaced. "Still a bit sore."

"Oh, sorry. I'm just so glad to see you're doing so well."

"It's been a long road. I'm told for a while there it was touch-and-go. My system shut down."

Jon shook the man's hand.

"Jon. What are you doing on this coast?"

"Tracking down the people responsible for you being here. With Luanne's help."

Ed nodded. "I told you she was a find. From the looks of you, I'm guessing you had some close calls yourself."

"I signed up for it, you didn't."

Ed nodded in agreement.

Jon said, "We need you back on the beat. How much longer will you be hobbling around?"

Ed laughed. "Not sure. Missy?"

The physical therapist said, "If you keep at it, you'll be discharged next week, then have out-patient therapy for another month."

Jon asked Ed, "Then, back to work?"

"You bet. Need to be there when my trusty associate gets her name on the byline of the biggest story of the year."

Luanne beamed. "I'm gonna keep trying to get Oakley to speak with me. Give him a chance to tell his side of the story."

Ed said, "I'm duly impressed. I knew you had what it takes."

The therapist put a gentle hand on Ed's back. "Ed's worked real hard in rehab. He needs to rest."

Luanne and Jon took the hint and said their goodbyes, grateful their friend was still among the living.

***

Santa Monica Pier

Luanne held on to the crook of Jon's arm. Her other hand grasped the paper cone of cotton candy, her tongue searching for the pink tendrils clinging to her lips.

"Yum! I haven't had one of these in forever."

"You know it's spun sugar, right?"

"And your point?"

He laughed. The breeze off the ocean carried the distinct smell of piers all over the world...tangy seaweed mixed with tar and wood. People strolled along the wooden-planked wharf, buying souvenirs or waiting for a carnival ride. Jon pointed to the Ferris wheel. It felt so . . . joyful. He could finally tell his shrink he did his homework and was having fun. "Want to go for a spin?"

"Sure." Luanne hurried to the restroom to wash her hands while Jon purchased two tickets. They met back at the wheel. "Sticky, but worth it," she said.

They rode the wheel, gliding upward toward the apex, where they were awarded a spectacular view of the coastline. It seemed to go on forever. The sun was making its gradual descent into the Pacific, golden light spreading across the water. Luanne shielded her eyes from the glare. "It's beautiful, isn't it?" she said.

Luanne's black lipstick had been licked off and he could see what she must have looked like as a teenager. Jon took in the elegant angles of her neck, her jawline. "Sure is."

She smiled, and if Jon hadn't seen it himself, he never would have believed it possible. "You're blushing."

"That's what happens when we humans are embarrassed."

He pulled her close. "I thought you were a tough broad."

She didn't laugh. "Only when I need to be. The rest of the time I'm a cream puff. No . . . a cotton candy."

Jon said, "Let me taste some of that."

She tilted her head upward and they kissed the rest of the way to the ground.

CHAPTER 61

Los Angeles—New York City

J on and Luanne parted as they'd planned. A clean break. Getting on the plane back to New York, his heart was heavy. Without her—or Melanie—in his life, he was single once again.

He made a mental note to get in touch with the permanent members in his life—Granny, Gabe and Terry. He knew those relationships would bolster him, if he made sure to nurture them. His thoughts soon turned to Bernie and Ed. Both the P.I. and the reporter were recuperating from their injuries, each tough in their own way, eager to get back to work. By the time Jon's plane landed, his mood had improved. He was excited to see Randy.

***

FBI Headquarters
New York City

The next day, Jon's first stop was at the office. He had missed Matthews's deadline by three days and was mentally building his defense when Craig gave him the eye.

"What?" Jon asked.

"He just walked in."

Jon turned and saw his boss dressed in a pressed dark

suit, holding a leather briefcase. He looked more put together than he'd even seen him.

Passing Jon's desk, Matthews raised a brow, nodded, and entered his office, closing the door behind him.

"What happened to him?" Jon asked.

Craig said, "His wife's influence, no doubt. At the funeral, he said she hated how sloppy he looked when he got home from work. I suppose he's trying to make her proud now."

Jon had missed that part of the eulogy, probably while he was outside the chapel getting his own head together.

The rest of the morning was spent typing up the endless case reports. Livingston's Farmstand Industries and seven other companies were being charged with a felony violation of the Computer Fraud and Abuse Act. OBooks declared bankruptcy resulting in what Peter Cromwell was desperate to avoid. Hundreds of employees out of a job.

Franklin's phone and computers were confiscated. The geek squad upstairs was working around the clock to determine if Franklin had somehow managed to deliver an updated version of Wang's spyware app ahead of schedule. With only days left till month's end, office tensions ran high. If delivered, the only way to prevent the spyware from landing in North Korean hands would be to intercept the White Knight. Unfortunately, that trail had gone cold. And thanks to Matthews, any intel from the Israelis was inaccessible.

Ten minutes to noon, Matthews's door opened. "Steadman."

Jon stood, ignoring Craig's smirk. He mentally reviewed his defense one more time.

Inside Matthews's office, Jon took a seat on the old sofa across from his boss.

Matthews said, "I've put my place on the market."

At first Jon was confused. He was primed for battle and thrown off by the personal nature of his boss's opening line. Apparently he was being given clemency. He needed to quickly recalibrate. "Oh?"

Eyes downcast, Matthews said, "Too many memories. Every room—the kitchen, bedroom, even the bathroom. It's too much."

"Where will you go?"

Matthews said, "Not sure yet. I need to stay in the city for the job. Maybe I'll move closer to work. Erica had a sizeable life insurance policy. I could use some of it and put a down payment on a loft in Soho."

"That must be some policy."

Matthews nodded. "She was savvy with money."

"You were lucky to have her."

Offering a tentative, somber smile, Matthews said, "That's for damn sure."

***

Isle of Palms, South Carolina

Terry stood at the kitchen sink washing a caked-on dish, then handed it to Gabe to dry.

"The shakshuka was delicious," Gabe said.

Terry had cooked the egg and tomato dish knowing it was one of her fiancé's favorites.

Gabe poured two glasses of Chardonnay, took her hand and led her through the French doors to the second-story rear veranda. The natural beauty of the island was soothing. Gabe stretched out on the cushioned wicker sofa, putting his legs on Terry's lap and drank back his wine. "What do you think about getting married here?"

Terry looked behind her into the home. The place was designed for upscale comfort. Tastefully decorated in pale colors, the focus on the expansive windows looking out on the Atlantic.

"It's beautiful. Serene."

Gabe jumped up, grabbed his phone, nearly knocking

the glass out of Terry's hand. "Great, I'll let my parents know it's a go!"

"Wait, what? I didn't say I want to get married here, Gabe."

His face fell. "So, you *don't* want to get married here?"

Something inside Terry broke. "Everyone is placing demands on me. As if I don't have a say in my life anymore."

Gabe took a step back, his brows furrowed. "Is that how you feel? Like I'm controlling you somehow?"

Terry shook her head in frustration. "I don't know!" She didn't intend to shout.

Gabe fell back into the chair across from the sofa. "I'm sure you're under a great deal of pressure."

"You have no idea. I thought this . . . job . . . would be quick and we could get back to Israel."

"Terry, sweetheart, I needed to come back to the States anyway. My life is here. My parents, my job. My friends."

It felt like a punch to the gut. "Your *life*? I was under the impression we were building a life together."

"That came out wrong—"

"Are you saying you have no intention of going back to Israel with me?"

Gabe shook his head. "That's not what I mean. What I'm saying is we need to discuss it. It's not an open and shut case. We both have lives in different places."

"Gabriel, you know I am responsible for a prestigious genetics lab in Haifa. It's not something I can do from the States."

"I do understand and while my job may not be as impactful as yours, I work for my uncle and love it."

Terry's eyes left Gabe's. "How did we never discuss this before?"

"Would it have mattered?"

"I don't know," Terry whispered.

"Does that mean if we'd discussed this sooner, we wouldn't be together now?"

Terry was torn between tears and shouts. "I don't know. I don't know anything anymore."

"*Anything*? What are you saying?"

"I can't think straight. Maybe we're going too fast. Maybe we need to wait with the wedding." The words just seemed to fly out of her.

Gabe's face registered his devastation. "I can't believe you're saying this. We love each other." He approached her, his arms open wide, his eyes beckoning.

Terry took a step back. "I can't think straight," she repeated. "I need to get out of here."

"Should I join you?"

She shook her head. "I need to be alone. Have time to think."

Before Gabe could respond, Terry walked out, the front door closing quietly behind her.

***

Los Angeles

Theo slept in the basement. Neither he nor Nic was willing to be away from Lizzy. And if either moved out of the house, it would be traumatic for her. What started out as a need to provide stability for Lizzy with family dinners, school updates and birthday parties, in time turned into a slow coming together. When Theo suggested marriage counseling, Nicole simply nodded. He hoped one day he could reunite with Abigail, introduce her to Nicole. For now, they had scheduled their first therapy session.

The relationship with his son was significantly more tenuous. Franklin's sentencing was coming up in a few months. The charges were multiplying with each claim of privacy infringement and wrongful termination. Class action lawsuits were being filed against Oakley's clients, most in the process of declaring bankruptcy.

In the interim, Franklin was convalescing in the medical unit of Vacaville Prison, north of San Francisco. Luanne Parker went ahead with her exclusive story, while the public was still interested. One day, if Oakley decided to talk, she'd run a follow-up piece. The *LA Times* story headlined, *Paraplegic Hacker Plays God,* had taken on a life of its own, getting picked up by various news outlets around the world. Finding an unbiased jury would be near impossible. As yet, no hard evidence was found to prove Oakley was responsible for the contract killings of Jason Wang and Peter Cromwell, or the attacks on Ed Hernandez and Luanne. The added murder and assault charges would allow prosecutors to push for a life sentence. Without them, the lawyerly pundits estimated a ten-to-fifteen-year sentence.

On Nic's coaxing, Theo began writing letters to the prison address. He was humbled by his wife's heart. Emails were not permitted and many of the envelopes were returned unopened for even the most minor infringement—colored stationery or an address label. Theo hoped at least some of the letters had made it into Franklin's hands, and that he was reading them.

Given all that had transpired—their decades-long estrangement and Franklin's abhorrent vengeful acts—Theo didn't know if they would ever truly reconcile. Yet, he took the first steps anyway, knowing that's what a devoted parent does.

***

Nassau, the Bahamas

The hundred-foot yacht was docked beside other vessels of the rich and famous. CEOs and politicians preferred this marina. The water was translucent, schools of fish visible even from the vessel's bridge. Gerard took a sip of his Mai Tai, considering how many jobs he'd need to take on in order to purchase the boat. Davis's two million would only get him so far.

Gerard entered the oak-paneled cabin and lifted the newspaper off the brown leather chair. He preferred the hard copy paper to the online format. His aversion to technology had proven good foresight and he would use it only when necessary. He sat, letting out a satisfied sigh and re-read the article on Oakley.

The spontaneity of the Davis job had been a thrill —changing course midway, throwing everyone off kilter. It had made things more interesting, and in his estimate much harder to get caught. Though to his credit, Steadman came pretty darn close.

The guy got what he deserved. Gerard had followed Oakley's courtroom saga and would be there when he got out. Whenever that would be. He was a patient man.

Gerard flashed back to the Fed's determined face filling his binoculars. Perhaps Steadman was the perfect adversary. As he placed his pen down, Gerard made a decision. He and Special Agent Jon Steadman would meet again.

CHAPTER 62

Isle of Palms, South Carolina

T erry walked along the seashore, staring out at the white-capped waves, her thoughts a tangled mess. *How had things turned around so drastically in the last couple of weeks?* She loved Gabe and he loved her. Yet somehow, they'd allowed a substantial wedge to come between them.

The wind picked up, carrying with it the salty scents of the ocean. Terry sat down in the sand, pulled off her sandals and dug her toes into the cool granules. It was dusk and the lights of the beach homes allowed her a glimpse of strangers' lives. People preparing dinner. Laughing together. Being on the outside looking in was one of the loneliest feelings Terry ever had.

How will we get past this? The issue was not the wedding; it was the bigger picture of what their lives would be. If she was honest with herself, there were things they'd been ignoring all along. Gabe had grown up in the United States with American family and friends. Though Terry had spent some of her childhood in Boston, she was a true sabra. It wasn't fair to ask Gabe, the man she loved, to pick up his life and move across the globe to a land where he didn't speak the language or have a job. Or family.

Terry dropped her head in her hands, allowing the tide of sorrow to wash over her. By the time she looked up, the sky had darkened. In the distance through her tears, she saw a figure silhouetted against the horizon walking in the rolling surf toward her. Perhaps someone else weighed down by life's burdens.

Not wanting her anguish on display, Terry rested her head on her knees listening to the soothing sounds of the sea. She would wait a few minutes till the person passed by, then head back to the house to face the music with Gabe. Whatever that would entail.

"Are you all right?" The words were carried on the breeze.

Terry lifted her head. Slowly, the figure became larger, clearer. A woman.

"You look . . . lost," the woman said.

Terry wiped her face with her hands and stood up. In the dim lighting it was hard to make out the woman's features. Terry stepped closer, squinting in the darkness. Now mere feet away, the moon drifted past its cloud cover. Terry met the eyes of a seventy-something-year-old woman with white, neatly styled hair brightened by the light of the moon.

"Hello again, Doctor Lavi."

Terry's heart skipped a beat. "The White Knight."

A growing smile slowly spread to the woman's intelligent eyes. "Yes, my dear. Since I met you at the conference , I've made a spectacular acquisition. A software you may already be familiar with." She extended her hand in greeting. "Perhaps it's time you and I had a proper chat."

Terry swallowed hard and took the offered hand of Charlotte Colbert.

CHAPTER 63

New York City

"**R**andy, wait up!" Jon watched the five-year-old skip ahead of him, as if he didn't have a care in the world. It made his heart leap. There were times the boy's face turned sad, his eyes somewhere else entirely. Jon understood. He'd been there. Even now, all these years later he was *still* there. But Jon also knew that like himself, Randy had loving grandparents. He would grow up knowing he was someone's pride and joy.

The trip to the toy store was a special birthday treat. Jon told Randy he could pick two things as long as they added up to no more than twenty dollars. He delighted in the boy's intensity as he painstakingly calculated which items he could get, asking for help with the math. In the end, he chose a Tonka truck and an old-fashioned model airplane set after Jon told him he'd help him build it.

The day was glorious. Randy now stood, hands on his hips. He was growing by leaps and bounds. Jon had taken to calling him, "Little Man."

"C'mon, you old or something?" While he still confused some sounds, Randy's speech had taken off, the pendulum swinging to the other end. He was a chatterbox. Carrie would be overjoyed. Her mom—Abuela—credited Jon. The spinning and repetitive hand motions persisted, particularly when Randy was under stress. Jon was hopeful that with continued therapy, those behaviors would diminish over time.

Jon escorted Randy to the fourth-floor apartment, and hugged him. Ten minutes later, Jon left with a sense of tranquility and a care package that would feed him for a week.

***

Jon ran down the stairs. No point in taking the elevator when he was heading out for a jog anyway. It was a perfect Sunday morning, the December temperature hovering near fifty degrees, optimal for his planned two miles. The day began with a high-octane cup of coffee while reading the second of a two-part exposé on the consequences of technology without morality. He took pride seeing Luanne's name in the byline. The dated black-and-white photo showed off her short spiky hair and up-the-ear piercings. He laughed at her guts. She was going to make a dent in the rapidly changing world of journalism.

Jon was glad to finally break in his new running shoes. Despite his bad leg, he'd grown to love jogging as much as he had before his injury. Runner's high was a real thing, and he'd learned exercise had the power to stave off his symptoms. He hadn't needed a pill in days. Maybe next time he'd invite Matthews to join him on a run in Battery Park. The man was a bundle of nerves.

Jon exited his building, the weekend offering a reprieve from the city's ever-present commotion. He placed his earbuds in his ears, turned on his playlist and stretched his legs using the curb's fire hydrant for stability. A woman walked past, stopping at his building. Jon watched as she found the intercom pad beside the locked door, dragged her finger down the list of tenants, stopping midway. She pressed the buzzer. Then again. No one responded. "Damn!" she said.

Jon took out an earbud, said, "Who are you looking for?"

The woman was near thirty, svelte, dressed in a belted black peacoat, well-fitting jeans and expensive sneakers. She lowered her Ray-Bans, meeting Jon's eyes, and pursed her lips. "What's it to you?"

Jon made a face. "No good deed," and turned away.

From behind, he heard her say, "I'm looking for Jon Steadman. You know him?"

Facing her once again, he took a closer look. The woman now had her jaw jutted, as if raring for a fight. *Tell her you never heard of him.* "You're talking to him."

She eyed him up and down. *"You're* Jon Steadman?"

"What's it to you?" he mimicked.

A glimmer of a devious smile. "Touché . . . and sorry. I'm under a lot of stress. It's taken me a while to find you."

"Apology mostly accepted. I've been out of town. Why are you looking for me?"

"It's sort of complicated. Can we go inside and talk?"

"No. First of all I'm about to go on a run. And second of all, maybe you're not from around here, but New Yorkers don't invite strangers into their homes. Either tell me what you want or I'll see ya around."

She appeared to be debating internally, then stopped, took a breath, her eyes momentarily darting around with what Jon thought was . . . trepidation. "Have it your way." Then, "Carrie sent me."

Jon froze, a shot of adrenaline running through him. "Carrie?"

"Carrie Santiago."

"This some sort of joke?"

The woman shook her head solemnly. "Carrie was my best friend growing up. Our dads were in the military together. Same unit. As kids, we moved around from country to country. Sort of shared a weird childhood. I spoke with her shortly before she . . . ." She frowned, seemingly holding back emotion. ". . . before she died. She told me to contact you for help if I got in over my head. As much as I hate to admit it, I am. Way over."

Still reeling from the mention of his dead partner, Jon remained silent, took out his key and unlocked the building door. "Come on. Let's go talk." He held the door open for her.

The woman walked inside, removing her sunglasses. "Why the change of heart?"

"Any friend of Carrie's is a friend of mine."

When they were inside his apartment, Jon gestured to the sofa. The woman sat. He made two mugs of chamomile tea and handed one to her. "Now, tell me what this is about."

The woman lifted the mug, blew the steam off the top, and told him.

The End

***

Want to know what happens next? Find out in Duplicity, Jon's next thrilling adventure.

ACKNOWLEDGEMENT

It takes a village to bring a book to fruition. Vengeance is no exception. Heartfelt thanks go to my alpha and beta readers whose input made this book a cleaner, tighter version of the one I gave them. Kudos to Glenn Bochner, Ken Germain, Wes Higaki, Sossie Brown, Marcia Schwartz, Elana Joffe-Cohen, and the sharp-eyed Karen Sheff.

Much appreciation to the bookshops and libraries supporting my work. A special shoutout to Marx Hot Bagels, where the best sandwiches in the Midwest are served.

I'm humbled by how much my readership has grown since Spree launched last summer. It's been a remarkable and thrilling ride so far, and I'm grateful for each and every one of you.

As always, love and thanks to my dear family and friends for all your encouragement throughout this obsessive journey of mine. It means the world to me.

ABOUT THE AUTHOR

Nellie Neeman

Nellie is an avid traveler, swim-
mer, and hiker who uses her
own adventures as inspiration
for her stories. She currently
resides in Cincinnati and Jerusalem with her husband and
Lexi, the wacky Labradoodle.
Learn more at www.nellienee-
man.com

BOOKS BY THIS AUTHOR

Spree: An Action-Adventure Novel (A Jon Steadman Thriller Book 1)

He barely survived a killing spree. Now he's on a mission to prevent the deadliest attack in U.S. history . . .

Jon Steadman is desperate for closure. After the love of his life dies in a campus bombing, his relentless quest for answers reveals bizarre violent incidents involving other unsuspecting students. When copycat blasts add to the tragic body count, he's certain he's stumbled on a lethal conspiracy.

Teaming up with his best friend and pursuing a theory connecting the genetic dots, Steadman finds every avenue blocked by powerful people ready to kill to protect their secrets. As his hunt takes him across the globe, he exposes a sinister terrorist plot known only as The Event.

Can one ordinary man step up and stop ruthless killers from executing a devastating catastrophe?

SPREE is a story of one man's battle to overcome the wounds of the past and find redemption in fighting for what's right. An action-packed thriller, SPREE takes the reader on a whirlwind ride of unexpected twists and turns until the very last page.

Resurrection: An Action-Adventure Novel (A Jon Steadman Thriller Book 2)

Four powerful men. One terrifying secret. Can FBI rookie Jon Steadman stop them . . . before they bring democracy to a lethal end?

Jon Steadman is back, facing off against a shocking conspiracy of global proportions.

Rookie FBI Agent Jon Steadman is butting heads with his insufferable boss and battling his personal demons, when he is called upon to investigate a radical U.S. congressman. Jon is partnered with Ivy-educated, single mother Agent Carrie Santiago and brilliant Israeli geneticist Dr. Terry Lavi, a woman he prefers to avoid. But, when the FBI, CIA and Mossad combine forces, conflicting allegiances and old resentments begin to flare.

As the mystery unfolds, their pursuit uncovers a decades-old plot, exploiting the far edges of science, aimed at bringing America to its knees. The mission takes them across the globe and face-to-face with an untold evil that will threaten their very survival.

Duplicity: An Action-Adventure Novel (A Jon Steadman Thriller Book 4)

FBI Agent Jon Steadman pursues a deadly conspiracy exploiting mankind's most profound desire, in his most challenging case yet.

Struggling to keep his destructive tendencies in check, Jon is mystified when his dead partner's childhood friend shows up on his doorstep. The hotheaded woman fears she's committed a devastating mistake. Cutting-edge science has made her deepest wish possible, but the technology comes at a heavy price. Scared for her life, Jon agrees to help.

When the investigation takes a lethal turn, Jon soon discovers that unleashing an unchecked genetic power may sabotage mankind's ability to endure.

As Jon's own suppressed yearnings begin to stir, he's forced to contend with a long-buried trauma. Desperate to repair the broken fragments of his damaged relationships, he must choose between the long road to redemption and the depths of despair.

Made in the USA
Monee, IL
19 September 2021